LIBRARIES N
WITHDRAWN FROM STOCK

D0247966

SLEEP TIGHT

Copyright © Rachel Abbott 2014

Rachel Abbott has asserted her right to be identified as the author of this Work in accordance with the Copyright, Designs and Patents Act 1988

All characters and events in this publication are fictitious and any resemblance to real persons, living or dead, is purely coincidental.

All Rights Reserved.

No part of this publication may be reproduced, stored in a retrieval system, or transmitted, in any form or by any means, without the prior permission in writing of the author.

Published by Black Dot Publishing Limited

ISBN 978-0-9576522-3-1

Find out more about the author and her other books at

http://www.rachel-abbott.com

LIBRARIES NI
WITHDRAWN FROM STOCK

Prologue

The girl was smiling as she left the noisy, packed pub, and shouts of laughter were ringing in her ears as she wrestled the heavy door open, letting in an icy blast of cold air. She turned and shouted, 'Night!' to anybody who might be looking her way and a few arms were raised in a farewell salute, but most were otherwise occupied with pint glasses, or were gesticulating wildly to emphasise some part of the latest funny story being shared with anybody who was prepared to listen.

The door slammed shut behind her, cutting out the warm yellow light and the happy sounds of young people enjoying themselves. The dark night settled around her and the sudden silence hit her like a physical blow. For a moment she stood still.

Shivering in the early winter chill, she wrapped her scarf tighter round her neck and folded her arms, hugging herself to keep warm. She really was going to have to find a coat that she liked enough to wear on a night out. She smiled at her own vanity, and reminded herself that it was only a fifteen-minute walk back to their flat, so if she walked quickly she would soon warm up.

The silence was momentarily shattered as the door to the pub swung open again, the light from inside spilling its amber glow across the wet pavements. Above a burst of loud music coming from the warm bar she thought she heard somebody shout her name, but the door swung closed with a bang, and all was silent again.

The few folk who were out on the streets of this part of Manchester were hurrying along, disappearing down side roads that led to their homes. The miserable weather and the early cold bite appeared to have kept people indoors tonight, and who could blame them?

A few yards ahead of her a couple stopped to kiss, the girl wrapping her arms round the boy's neck, standing on tiptoe to press the whole length of her body against his, and the night felt warmer for it. She smiled again as she looked at them, thinking how wonderful it felt to be in love. She and her boyfriend had only recently moved in together, and she had never been so happy.

She reached the junction with the main road, and waited at the crossing. There wasn't much traffic, but being one of the main roads into and out of Manchester, it was never completely quiet.

She hurried across when the road was clear and made her way to the quieter streets on the other side, away from the halls of residence and the modern housing. She had been thrilled when they had found a flat in an old Victorian house – the whole of the ground floor was theirs and, although it was still a bit scruffy, they were working on it. Best of all, it was on a lovely peaceful tree-lined road, which gave each house a sense of privacy.

She turned into the first road. The small park on her right was usually full of children playing, but at this time of the night it was deserted, the only movement coming from a single swing that was swaying gently, silently.

Her flat shoes made little sound on the pavement, and she had a strange feeling of being cut off from the rest of the world. She glanced towards the windows of the houses as she passed, but most were protected from view by high hedges and those she could see were black, with just the lifeless reflection of the street lights making the rooms beyond seem eerily deserted.

The feeling that she wasn't alone sneaked up on her. There wasn't a single moment – the scuffing of a shoe, the glimpse of a dark shadow – that persuaded her. It was something else entirely. It was the feeling that somebody's eyes were boring into her back. She just knew.

Her body grew rigid, and every nerve ending tingled. Should she run? Or would that be a signal to him to chase and catch her? Should she turn into somebody's drive? But he could be on her before she reached the door.

Was it better if he knew that she was aware of him? If she turned round to look, would that precipitate a reaction? She didn't know.

But he was there. She just didn't know how close he was.

Without thinking, she turned her head quickly. The street was empty. Wasn't he behind her? He was *somewhere*, she was certain. She glanced across at the park and thought about the swaying swing. He could be walking alongside her now, hidden behind the shrubs that lined the dark, unlit pathway.

A flash of recollection from earlier in the night pierced her mind. Amongst all the laughter and fun in the pub, there had been just a moment when she had felt uncomfortable. She had quickly spun around on her bar stool, almost expecting to find the invasive presence of an unknown man standing inches from her back. But nobody was there; nobody was even looking. She had brushed the feeling aside, allowing the pleasure of the evening to envelope the frisson of discomfort and squeeze the life out of it. But it was the same. It was exactly the way she felt now.

Just ahead was an entrance to the park. If he was in there and he was coming to get her, this is where he would do it. She had seconds to make a plan. She was going to act as if there was nothing to worry about, and then the moment she drew level with the gate, she would run. And if she had to, she would scream.

Two steps, and she would be there. She unfolded her arms and dropped them to her sides. She could see the corner of her road just ahead, but it was even darker down there, the thick trunks of the trees she loved so much casting deep shadows on the narrow pavement, their stark black branches blending into the night sky.

One, two – and *run*.

She didn't risk a glance at the park's open gateway, and couldn't hear if anybody was following her over the thump of her feet and the gasping of breath.

She was ten metres from the corner when it happened. She was almost there, almost home, almost safe.

A dark figure emerged from behind the last of the black trees, and stood still, legs spread wide, waiting to catch her.

PART ONE

Olivia

1

The shrill peal of the doorbell shatters the sombre silence of the house, and I stop pacing. I feel an irrational burst of hope. Could this be Robert? Has he forgotten his keys? But I know it isn't. I know exactly who it is.

It's the police, and they are here because I called them.

I should have known what might happen. I should have understood better what Robert had been telling me in everything but words. It's now three hours since he left with my babies, and every bone and muscle in my body is aching with their loss.

Where are my children?

Has there been in an accident? *Please, no.*

The thought hits me like a physical blow and vivid images appear on the blackness of my closed eyelids. I open my eyes, but I can still picture them in the back of Robert's car in a ditch down a dark lane, driven off the road by some maniac driver, lying there waiting to be discovered. I see blood on their foreheads and in my mind I listen for their cries, just to know they are alive. But I hear nothing except the sound of birdsong coming through the open car window. I can't see Robert in this vision.

Terrifying and awful as those images are, I don't really believe they've had an accident. In my heart I know it might be something else. Something far more sinister.

When I answer the door, a wide-shouldered young PC is standing there looking sturdy and competent in his stab vest and short-sleeved shirt. I know what he is going to ask me; I know the drill. It's just like last time.

I wonder if he knows who I am. Does he know that the Olivia Brookes who called tonight is the same person as the Liv Hunt who called seven years ago because her boyfriend was missing? Will it make a difference?

Even after all these years I still have nightmares about that terrible night, and I wake each time drenched in icy cold sweat. My boyfriend had called to say he was leaving the university lab and he would see me soon.

It wasn't a long walk home, but two hours later he still hadn't arrived. I was distraught. I remember clinging to my baby girl, whispering to her, 'Daddy will be home soon, sweetheart.' Not that Jasmine would have understood. She was just two months old at the time. It was a lie, anyway. Dan never came home, and I never saw him again.

I thought there could be nothing worse than the fear I felt that night, the hours of waiting, wondering what could possibly have happened to my darling Dan.

But I was wrong, because this time it's far worse. This time the terror is like a hard ball, bouncing painfully around my chest, my head, my gut.

The policeman wants details, of course. He wants to understand why I'm so concerned. The children are with their father, so surely there should be nothing to worry about? Have I tried his mobile? I don't think I need to answer that.

Robert left at six o'clock. He said he would like to take the children out for a pizza. I would have gone with them, but he was adamant that he wanted to spend more time alone with them. God, I hate to admit this, but I was *pleased*. Given how I feel about him, I thought this would be good practice for when we are no longer together. So I let them go.

It was okay for the first hour. I didn't expect them back, and I found things to do to keep myself occupied. I knew Robert wouldn't eat any pizza; he would want dinner alone with me after the children were in bed. So I'd started a chilli – one of his favourites – as a thank you for taking them out.

When I had done everything I could think of, I returned to the living room but it felt so empty. I am never without at least one child by my side except when they are in bed. Jasmine is at school, of course, but Freddie's only two so he's with me all day, and Billy is at nursery, but only in the mornings.

The house felt hollow, as if the air had been sucked out of it, leaving a cold, silent void. Looking at the living room with fresh eyes – the eyes of the new, disaffected me – I realised what a sterile space we've created. We've taken the idea of a neutral palette to a whole new level and there isn't a splash of colour to be seen or a single personal item to be found; not a photograph of a child or a random knickknack bought on a whim. Each painting has been chosen not because of the emotion it evokes, but because its sheer neutrality blends seamlessly with its innocuous surroundings. Every ornament has been selected for its size, to create the perfect balance. And, of course, Robert doesn't like toys in this room.

Who lives here?

It could be anybody. Maybe, for Robert, the decor was an inevitable outcome of living in my flat for too long, where orange walls and emerald green throws appeared to live happily side by side. But those colours radiated joy. What does this room tell you?

Nothing.

I have answered all the questions the policeman has asked. We have already determined that Robert wouldn't have taken the children to visit family or friends after their meal. Neither Robert nor I have any family. My parents died years ago, when Jaz was a baby, and Robert never knew his father. His mother died when he was a child, and we have no siblings either. These are cold, hard facts, not choices.

But how could I explain that I can't think of a single friend he might have gone to see with the children? How had we become so isolated? So alone?

I know why, though. Robert wants me to himself. I am not to be shared.

I should have known something was wrong when he wanted to take the children out without me. That was something he never did. If only I had listened, *really* listened, to what he was saying, I might have been able to stop it all before it was too late.

'Olivia,' he'd said, 'there's nothing strange about a father taking his children out for a pizza, is there? After all, some dads only *ever* get to see their children on their own.'

Was Robert trying to tell me something? Has he guessed how I'm feeling? If this were anybody other than Robert, I would think that maybe – just maybe – he has accepted that I might leave him and he's trying to prove he could cope on his own. But this isn't somebody else. This is Robert, and nothing is straightforward.

In my head I have gone through every possible scenario to explain where they might be, and each of them fills me with dread. I don't know which is worse: the image of my babies lying hurt somewhere, or my other fear. The one I daren't put into words.

2

It's gone eleven now. Five hours since I have held Freddie's warm body in my arms and inhaled his sweet smell. I can't bear the thought of him being confused. And Billy. He needs his sleep. He gets grumpy when he's tired. And my lovely Jasmine will want to be home with her mummy by now; she never likes me to be far away and thinks far too much for a seven-year-old.

If Robert just brings them back safely, I'll forget all my stupid ideas of leaving. I'll learn to live with the constant scrutiny, as long as my children are unharmed.

Bring them home, Robert.

The police have been searching the house just like the last time when I lost Dan, as if I might be hiding my children somewhere. They're out knocking on doors and waking up the neighbours. What have they seen? What do they know?

More police are arriving now. Detectives this time.

'Mrs Brookes?' My thoughts are interrupted by a voice. I look up into the kind eyes of a woman who doesn't look much older than me, but she must be because everybody calls her ma'am.

'Do you mind if I call you Olivia? My name's Philippa. I'm afraid we've now called all the local pizza places, and nobody remembers seeing your husband and children.'

'Maybe they changed their minds and went for a burger instead. They could have done that, couldn't they?' I'm clutching at straws, and we all know it.

'Why didn't you go with them, Olivia?'

How can I answer that? I don't *know*. He's never done this before. I feel I have to make something up, although I don't know why.

'Robert thought I looked tired, and could do with a bit of a rest. He was trying to help.'

'Do you have a stressful job? Is that why you were tired? Or have the children been playing you up a bit?'

Does she think I've hurt my children?

'They're good kids – I promise you they are. And I don't work. There's enough to do looking after the children and Robert.'

I've never really worked, other than for a few months before I had Jasmine. By the time my maternity leave was over, Robert had asked me to marry him and he didn't want me to work at all. He wanted me at home, looking after him, and it suited me just fine. But now I don't know why I was content with that decision. Content with being nobody in my own right.

The questions keep coming, but all I want to do is scream at them all. *Stop asking inane questions. Find my children.*

'I'm sorry to have to ask you, Olivia – but would you mind going upstairs with one of my officers? We'd like you to check if anything of the children's is missing. Clothes, favourite toys, books. You know the sort of thing.'

What? I stare at her wordlessly for a moment. *Why would anything be missing?*

I push myself up from the sofa, feeling like a woman three times my age as tense limbs struggle to take my weight. I don't know what they are thinking, but this is ridiculous. *Why would anything be missing?* The thought revolves in my head like a ticker tape.

One of the detectives follows me upstairs and I recognise him but I can't think why. Not that it matters. I decide to start with Jasmine's room, which I know will be tidy so it will be easy to see if everything is where it should be.

I walk over to the bed and lift the cover, expecting to see Lottie – Jaz's rag doll – lying on the pillow. She's not there. I whip back the duvet. *Where's Lottie?* Even at seven, Jaz loves to have Lottie in her bed, but there is no sign of her. I look at the policeman in my anguish, but he just watches me and says nothing.

I walk slowly over to the wardrobe. I almost don't want to open it. But he's still watching me. I gently pull on the handle, as if doing it slowly will change the outcome. Jasmine's pink backpack is not on the shelf. Suddenly I'm like a wild thing, pushing coat hangers backwards and forwards, pulling open drawers.

'Nooo!' I am wailing, dragging out the one syllable into twenty. *Where are my daughter's clothes?*

I hear a thundering up the stairs, and Philippa appears at the door. She comes over to me and holds my arm. She doesn't have to ask questions – she can tell from my face what has happened. I've been trying not to admit it to myself, but now I have to face the truth.

He's taken my children.

3

Tom Douglas stood up wearily from his desk and stretched his arms above his head. Since his boss, Detective Chief Superintendent James Sinclair, had taken early retirement for health reasons, working at the Met hadn't been the same. The new guy was good, but he was too much of a numbers man for Tom's liking. And it wasn't just that he controlled the budget with a rod of iron. That was his job. To Tom, the new DCS seemed to want to solve crime by numbers too, as if a magic formula could be applied according to a predefined set of criteria.

Tom had originally taken a job with the Metropolitan Police to be close to his daughter, Lucy. His ex-wife, Kate, had upped sticks and moved to London after their divorce, and he had followed. In many ways this had been his dream job, but there wasn't much about his London life that appealed any more. Kate had taken Lucy back to the North-west after her new relationship fell apart, so there was nothing keeping Tom here now and once again, he was missing Lucy.

He grabbed his leather jacket from the back of the chair and picked up his keys. There were few signs of life at this late hour and, although the lure of his soulless apartment wasn't exactly appealing, he did need some sleep. And some food; at least he could still enjoy cooking. He started to think about what he might prepare for a late supper.

As Tom switched his desk lamp off, his phone began to ring. He glared at the handset for an indecisive moment, but he knew he'd have to answer it – he'd never been able to resist a ringing phone.

'DCI Douglas.'

'Tom, I'm glad I caught you. It's Philippa Stanley. I could do with a bit of info, if you've got a minute.'

As soon as she mentioned her name, Tom knew he was in for a long conversation, so he pulled out his chair and sat down, dumping his jacket and keys back on the desk. Philippa had been an inspector on his team just before he left Manchester, and she had already jumped up the ladder to match his rank of Detective Chief Inspector. There was no stopping her. She was definitely heading for the top.

'Hi Philippa. Good to hear from you. What can I do for you?' he asked.

'I need to pick your brains about an old case – seven years old, in fact. Apparently you were getting a lift home from PC Ryan Tippetts and he got diverted to go and deal with a woman called Olivia Hunt, who had reported her boyfriend missing.'

Tom knew there would be no friendly catch up with Philippa – she was all business. He could picture her clearly. She would be wearing the same version of her 'uniform' as always: a white blouse with an open neck, not showing too much cleavage, a straight navy-blue skirt and elegant but sensible shoes – what his mother would have called court shoes. Her short dark hair would be shiny bright and tucked behind her ears, with no make-up other than a subtle lipstick. She'd always looked perfectly neat and feminine, but any sex appeal she might have had had been beaten into submission by her imperious attitude.

'Strangely enough I *do* remember, yes. I'd forgotten the name, but if it's the one I'm thinking of, she had a small baby that wouldn't stop crying, and she was adamant that something had happened to her boyfriend. When Ryan learned that the missing guy was a Muslim, he acted as if that answered everything. In his view we were bound to find the guy beaten up in some alley – which, of course, we never did. I gave him a right bollocking for his attitude, and apologised to the girl. What do you need to know?'

'I'd like your impression of her – the girl.' Philippa answered.

'Why? What's up?' Tom asked. This was a long time ago and the records would contain all the details, but Philippa wouldn't be asking without reason.

'I'll get to that – I don't want to cloud your judgement. Tell me what you remember, and then I'll explain why I want to know. I've tried speaking to Ryan about this by the way. He's a DC now, although God knows who made that astonishing decision. He has an over-inflated opinion of his unacknowledged brilliance, and yet he's still as bloody useless as he's always been. I thought I might be more likely to get some sense out of you.'

Tom wasn't sure if this was Philippa damning him with faint praise or not, but he decided to ignore it because this wasn't a case Tom would forget in a hurry. Not because of that night specifically – but because of what happened later.

'As I said, the first time I met her she called because her boyfriend – an Iranian lad, I think – hadn't come home. It wasn't that late, though, so we did think that maybe he'd just buggered off to the pub and would turn up in the early hours looking sheepish and apologetic. But the boyfriend was quite strict about his religion's anti-drinking rules, apparently, so the girl knew this couldn't be right. We registered him as missing, but after a bit of digging we found there had been some activity on his credit card. He'd bought a train ticket from Manchester to London, and then later that night he'd booked a flight to Australia. He sent her a text message too, I think, saying he was sorry. It was transmitted from somewhere around Heathrow. You'll be able to check that. I seem to remember he didn't catch the flight he'd booked – but he'd bought a flexible ticket so he could have gone at any time, and once Olivia had heard from him there wasn't any reason to follow it up.'

'It all ties in with what we have in the records. That's some memory, Tom.'

'Well,' Tom answered with a laugh, 'I don't think I would have remembered it quite so clearly if she hadn't become my case again a couple of months later. You know what happened next, I presume?'

'I've read the file, but you tell me.'

Tom paused. He could see Olivia Hunt now – a look of such desolation on her tear-streaked face that the whole idea of investigating her seemed ridiculous, but also inevitable.

'She'd sold her flat and was about to go and live with her parents – out of necessity, I think, rather than desire. Anyway, the day she was due to move, she drove round to her parents' house to find out why her dad was late with the van they'd hired to move her stuff. She found her mum and dad dead in their bed. Carbon monoxide poisoning from a faulty boiler and a blocked air inlet, it turned out. We investigated it, and we looked at Olivia very closely. To lose her boyfriend and then her parents in the space of a couple of months seemed more than odd – especially as the boyfriend had paid a significant deposit on the flat and put it in her name, *and* she was the only beneficiary of her parents' will. The Foreign Office tried to track down the boyfriend's family – I think his name was Dan?'

'Danush Jahander,' Philippa interjected.

'Yes, that's it. They wanted to find out if his family had heard from him. It wasn't easy with the relationship between Britain and Iran being what it was, so I don't think they found anything either one way or the other. Olivia was already in a state of shock because her boyfriend had dumped her and left her with a tiny baby, but she completely fell apart when her parents died. She said her father was paranoid about safety, and an accident like this didn't make sense.'

'But nothing was proven – either against her or anybody else.'

'That's right,' Tom said. 'It seemed to be just a tragic accident. Olivia was utterly distraught. She'd completed the sale of her flat that very morning, and she couldn't stay at her parents' house – nor did she want to. She had the baby to worry about too, but I seem to remember that the guy who bought the flat from her offered to let her stay on. He had somewhere else to live so I think he let her move back in. But I can't remember anything much about him.'

'His name was Robert Brookes. He ended up marrying her.'

'Well, something good came out of it then,' Tom said with a smile. 'But all this information is in the files. What can I help with?'

'I need to know what you thought. Not what the evidence suggested, but what you thought of Olivia – how much credence you gave to her, and how good you think she might have been at acting.'

'Okay, but you're going to have to tell me why,' Tom responded.

'Because I'm with her now. This time it's her husband – Robert Brookes – who's missing, and so are her three children.'

4

They want to know about Robert, to understand our relationship. How can I explain it to them when I can't even figure it out for myself? All I know is that Robert rescued me from everything at a terrible time in my life. First I'd lost Dan, and then just two months later, I lost my parents. Dead. Both of them.

I don't know what I would have done if Robert hadn't come into my life at that moment. He was a virtual stranger to me then. He was just the man who had bought my flat, but somehow he seemed to understand what I needed and had steered me through the worst time of my life.

Since Dan had gone I'd been sleepwalking through the days. The only thing that penetrated the fog of my confusion was the realisation that I had to sell the flat that Dan and I had lived in together. I couldn't afford it on my own, and every corner of the place reminded me of him: the furniture we had bought from junk shops and car boot sales, the hideous pale pink paint we had used in the kitchen because it was free. Every nook and cranny held a memory. But I was out of options. Jaz and I were going to have to go back home to Mum and Dad's and, much as I loved them, I didn't know how I would cope.

When Robert arrived to move into the flat on a freezing cold day I was still there, standing in the hall with Jaz in a buggy, my boxes around us, waiting for Dad to arrive. My dad who, it turns out, I was never going to see again.

Robert was the only person who seemed to know what to do afterwards. He let me stay in the flat and he kept his old place on for a couple of months. He wouldn't hear of me trying to find somewhere else to live, and when he finally had to move in, he let us have the spare room. He even dealt with the funeral and the sale of my parents' bungalow for me.

I know I should be grateful, and I am. I don't know how I would have coped without him then, but his constant silent demands for praise and recognition for all he does for us have become exhausting.

And he is always watching, looking at me. Even when the children are being funny and making me laugh, he doesn't watch them. His eyes are on me, and he smiles when I smile. If I walk out of a room, he watches me as I go. I can feel him staring. And when I return, he is still looking at the door as if his eyes have never left it.

It's why we don't have friends. On the few occasions that I have tried to mix with other couples, Robert's gaze never leaves me. If I talk to a woman, he is wondering what I'm saying and I have to suffer an inquisition on the way home until I have recounted every word. If I talk to a man, he's by my side in seconds.

For the first time in years, I long for Sophie. Sophie was the closest thing I ever had to a sister, and a vivid memory of her eyes, brimming with laughter, flashes into my mind like a bright, white light – there and gone in a second.

When I met Sophie, she drew me into her world and everything became more fun; life was our adventure. I had seriously believed we would be friends forever, but all Sophie had ever wanted was to join the army, and within weeks of leaving university, she was off to Sandhurst to begin her training. Suddenly she was no longer part of my everyday life, and nobody has ever filled her place.

So here I am, alone, with just one thought.

Where are my children?

I can sense that the police are getting increasingly concerned. It's mid-morning, and nothing seems to have advanced at all since last night. I can't stop shaking. My hands are clammy and clumsy and each time somebody tries to tempt me with coffee or tea I have to say no because I don't think I could hold the cup. There's a change in the atmosphere. It's much more urgent, and I know they are seriously worried about my children.

Philippa has already told me they are checking the cameras on the main A roads. I know how crucial the first twenty-four hours are, though she's kind enough not to remind me.

When they discovered some of the children's clothes were missing, they started asking me about passports. I'm sure they think he's abducted them and taken them out of the country as part of some ridiculous custody battle. But they don't have passports, and neither do I. We don't go on exotic holidays. We like Anglesey, an island off the coast of North Wales. It's only a couple of hours' drive, and we know our way around.

Philippa has come to sit down next to me again. I worry when she does this. I always expect it to be bad news.

'Olivia, I think the time has come to notify the press about your children. I know they're with their father, but we haven't managed to track him down. You gave us a picture of the three of them last night, but can you find some more photos for us, please? It might be useful to have some individual shots as well as group ones.'

I stand up, hoping my legs will hold me, go to the sideboard and pull out the box of photos. I'm not sure that I can bear to look at them, because all I see when I picture my children is pain. Surely if there had been an accident, somebody would have found them by now? Maybe my children are in a hospital somewhere, crying for me and wondering why I'm not there. But why am I even thinking that? I know this is no accident.

I carry the box to the dining table, but somebody has left a coat scrunched up on the floor, and in my clumsy, inattentive state I trip over it. I'm caught just in time, but the photos fly everywhere.

I recognise the man who catches my arm now. I couldn't work it out earlier, but he was one of the policemen who came when Dan didn't come home that night. The one I didn't like; the one who searched under the beds and in the wardrobes as if Dan might be hiding there. I suppose it's all part of their procedure. I hadn't remembered his name until I heard Philippa say, 'Is that your coat, DC Tippetts?'

Tippetts. It fits. There's something mean sounding about the name, and he has a rat-like face with a pointy nose and beady eyes. I can't help feeling glad he is not in charge.

I look away from his face and down at the mess all over the floor. Trivial as it is, it's nearly enough to make me collapse and I grab the back of the sofa for support. Pictures of my children are smiling up at me from amongst the debris.

On the top is a picture of Danush. I've tried not to look at his picture for so long, and I stifle a gasp as I devour every feature. Curly black hair down to just below his collar, brushed back from his face, his dark brown eyes are sparkling with laughter and his generous mouth is smiling down at a lovely young girl with long blonde hair and bright blue eyes, wearing a cream baker boy hat with a shiny buckle on the side.

Philippa looks at me, and then back at the photo.

'That's you, isn't it?' she says, barely able to keep the disbelief from her voice. Yes, that was me.

I had a bit of an obsession with hats at the time, and I used to try to persuade Sophie to wear them too – I even offered to lend her my favourite black fedora, but she said the only hat she would ever wear, and even then only under duress, would be her army officer's cap.

It suddenly hit me that not only has Robert has never met Sophie, he's never met Liv either – he's only met Olivia – the sensible, vanilla version of me.

I look at Dan's picture. What would he think of the person standing before him now? My hair is still long, although the striking blonde has faded into a pleasant light brown. My old obsession with choosing the brightest, most vibrant shades has disappeared, along with my love of danger and excitement. Sophie and I did some wild things together, usually with Dan cheering on the sidelines – everything from skydiving for charity to bungee jumping from a bridge. But now I realise that I've settled for mediocrity. How had I let it happen? How did I lose myself?

At the back of my mind there's a little voice, telling me that if my children come back – no, *when* they come back – I must revert to being that person. I have to find a way to rediscover myself. Perhaps Robert isn't the uninspired one after all.

I push the photo of Danush into the pocket of my jeans. I don't think it's a picture that Robert will want to see when he gets home. Because he *will* come home – he has to.

I can't believe I've slept. I refused to go to my bedroom to lie down, even though the living room was full of people talking. But I think exhaustion must have taken over – or perhaps my body just couldn't take any more stress.

I wake to sounds of instructions being fired at everybody in the room. Suddenly, instead of the slow, plodding, subdued tones of concern there is a heightened sense of excitement.

'Cancel the press briefing. Don't tell them anything; we'll fill them in later.'

I don't think they have realised I'm awake, but the sense of urgency is driving me to shake off the last vestiges of sleep. The empty void inside me starts to fill with a strange sensation that I can only believe is hope, and I struggle to sit up. Philippa notices, and casts a silencing glance around the room. They take her cue and leave as she sits down next to me.

'Olivia, we've got some good news. Your husband's car was picked up by cameras in North Wales, and the children appear to be in the car with him. That was a few hours ago, and we've not seen him since, but we've got the local police looking out for him.'

My first thought is relief. They're alive. Thank God. Then I suddenly feel dizzy. *Oh no – not that, Robert.*

'Where was he? Where in North Wales? Are you sure it was him?' I know Philippa can hear the panic in my voice, but she remains calm.

'He was crossing the Menai Bridge into Anglesey. And it was definitely his car. Do you have some idea where he might be going? He hasn't been picked up on any cameras since, and that's unusual.'

She's looking at me with concern.

'He'd take the side roads,' I tell her. 'He always says it's a mistake to stick to the A roads when the others are so much more interesting.' I have to ask. I can't help myself. 'Do you think he could have got as far as Holyhead without being picked up again?'

'I know what you're thinking. You're thinking of the ferry port, aren't you?' Philippa leans over and reaches for my hand. 'Don't worry. We've got people checking the details of all the boats. He wouldn't need a passport to get to Ireland, but he would need some form of identification. Nobody's booked anything in his name yet.'

She turns her body through forty-five degrees so she is partially facing me, and I focus on looking at her, thinking only of what I can see in front of me and not what is trying to send piercing warning bells through my brain.

'What are you not telling me, Olivia?' she asks. 'Do you know where he might have gone?'

It was safer when I could block out the thoughts, but now I must face my recollection of the first time we went to Anglesey. Robert took us all to South Stack Lighthouse, to the west of Holyhead. We stood looking out to sea, a cold wind whipping my hair back from my face. I loved it. It made me feel alive. I was gazing at the magnificent breakers, listening to them crash on to the rocks below, my thoughts a million miles away, when Robert told me that earlier in the year a man had jumped to his death off these very same cliffs.

'This is the perfect place to die,' he'd said.

I remember it clearly. I'd turned to look at him with a puzzled expression on my face, but he was staring down at the turbulent water far below.

'If I lost you from my life, this is where I would come,' he'd said. 'This would be a beautiful place to remember you. You do know that I couldn't bear life without you, don't you?' he'd said.

But I'm still *here*. Has he guessed I've been thinking of leaving him? He can't have – at least, I don't see how. I close my eyes and try to stem the panic.

A sob bursts from my throat, and I curl up in a ball on the sofa, trying my best to nurse the pain and drive the memory from my mind.

5

The waiting – the uncertainty and the frustration of being unable to do anything – is unbearable. I begged Philippa to let me go to Anglesey, even if she wasn't prepared to take me, but she insisted that the local police are best placed to make enquiries. They know the area. Nothing I can say or do seems likely to change her opinion and angry, defeated tears continue to pour down my cheeks. Clutching a sodden handkerchief to my eyes, I shut out the sounds in the room and focus on the faces of my children, willing them to come back to me, whispering words of comfort and reassurance that they can't hear.

Vaguely, through the gulping sounds of my sobbing, I hear a change in the voices again. This time it is different. No staccato instructions or sense of purpose. It almost feels as if the breath has gone out of the room on a large sigh. I don't know if it is a sigh of sorrow and distress, or something else completely.

I feel the other end of the sofa compress. Somebody is sitting there, stroking my damp hair away from my face. I can hear a voice, but the words don't penetrate.

'We've found them, Olivia. They're safe. Your husband and children are all safe, and they're on their way home. They're okay.'

I can hear the smile in Philippa's voice, and I'm glad something has pleased her, but it takes a moment or two for her words to sink in.

'What?' I ask shakily. 'Where were they? Are you sure they're all right?'

Philippa reaches out and takes my hand, giving it a reassuring squeeze.

'They were found at a bed and breakfast in Anglesey – one you often stayed at, according to your husband.' Philippa looks at me closely. 'And they're absolutely fine. You've nothing to worry about.'

Before I have a chance to fully absorb any detail other than the fact that my children are unhurt and on their way back to me, I notice that DC Tippetts is packing up his bag. The others seem to have gone already, and only Philippa and Tippetts are still here.

Are they going? I don't think I could bear to be on my own when Robert gets back. I look around in panic. It seems Philippa has read my mind.

'Don't worry, Olivia. DC Tippetts will stay here with you until your husband gets home.'

I stare at her in alarm. I don't feel any sense of empathy from this man, and I don't want him here.

'Can't you stay?' I ask, rather helplessly.

She looks from me to DC Tippetts. I can see she's puzzled and I get the sense that this should be a job for a lowly constable, but at this moment I feel as if Philippa is the closest thing I have to a friend. She gives a small, barely perceptible sigh.

'Well, I was only going home to my cat and a few hours' sleep. Go on Ryan. You get off.' She turns to me. 'Okay, Olivia. I'm not going anywhere. I'll stay with you.'

I look at her, and I know my eyes must look wild. I'm confused, lost, but so overwhelmingly relieved that they are safe.

'Why don't you go upstairs and give your face a quick rinse so the children don't see you so upset,' she suggests gently.

God, I must look dreadful. My hair feels like knotted straw.

My legs are still wobbly, and Philippa helps me to my feet and guides me to the bottom of the stairs.

'Will you be okay?' she asks. But I *have* to be okay. I need to get my strength back before the children come home.

I drag myself upstairs and into the bathroom and catch a glimpse of my face in the mirror. Red eyes, black mascara smudged around them, and blotchy cheeks.

The crying hasn't finished. I sit down on the toilet seat and sob with relief. *Thank God.*

What was he doing? What was he *thinking*?

Gradually, the tears subside and I get up and try to repair the damage. I clean my teeth, brush my hair and slap on some rarely used foundation to cover the worst of the blotches. Nothing will cure the red eyes, but perhaps the children won't notice.

I spend the next hour sitting on the edge of the sofa, my knees tightly together and my hands clasped, twisted, rubbed. I can't keep them still.

Then we hear it. The sound of a car on the drive, the headlights sweeping a path of pale light across the wall as the car turns.

I am out of my chair so fast, flinging the door open.

Robert is running up the drive towards me with arms outstretched, and I vaguely hear him shout to me. But I dodge around him. I have no time for him now.

I just want to get to my babies.

6

I don't want to leave the children. I want them all in one room, with me lying on the floor across the door so nobody can get near to them.

I take a final look at my two boys and drop a gentle kiss on each of their warm foreheads, in awe of their innocent beauty as they sleep. I make my way quietly to Jasmine's room. She knows something is wrong, because as hard as I tried I couldn't stop the tears as I raced to the car and hugged my children's little bodies tightly to me. But thankfully I can see she is close to sleep, Lottie clutched to her cheek.

I kneel down by the side of Jasmine's bed and tenderly stroke her hair back from her face. 'Sleep tight, my darling,' I whisper.

I don't hear a sound, but I know I am being watched. I turn my head, and I can see Robert's silhouette, backlit by the landing light. His face is in shadow, but I know he's smiling. He turns and I hear him making his way back downstairs to where Philippa is still waiting. I don't want to, but I know I have to follow.

Kind as Philippa has been, she is still asking searching questions – and most of them seem to be directed at me.

'Olivia, your husband says that you knew he was taking the children away for the weekend. Could you have forgotten?'

Robert is wearing his anxious face, as if he is concerned for my wellbeing. He tries to sit next to me on the sofa, but I stand up and move away. I can't bear to look at him.

He gives Philippa what can only be described as an apologetic expression, as if he needs to excuse my appalling behaviour.

'I didn't forget. He said he was taking them for a pizza.' I enunciate every syllable through gritted teeth.

'Darling,' Robert says, moving across to sit on the arm of my chair and stroking my hair with his hand. I want to slap it away, but I'm scared this will make me look even more demented. 'You packed their bags. Don't you remember? How would I know what a two-year-old needs?'

I can't push Robert off, but I jump up again and go to stand in front of the fake fire that we never use. My earlier fear and panic have transformed into a ball of rage. I spin round and glare at him, waving my hand towards his face and making a stabbing motion with my index finger to punctuate every word.

'I thought you were all *dead*.' My voice cracks, and comes out much weaker than I want it to. 'How *could* you, Robert? How *could* you?'

Robert turns to Philippa and gives her the benefit of the full shrug action – hands out, palms facing upwards, as if to say, 'Do you see what I have to put up with?'

It's not long after this demonstration of my volatility that Philippa decides to leave. While Robert goes to get her coat, she speaks to me quietly, squeezing my hand.

'If you're worried about anything, Olivia, this is where you can contact me. Call me if you need to.' She passes me a business card, and I quickly push it into my pocket as my husband comes back into the room. If he sees it, I know he will take it from me.

Robert shows Philippa out, and when he comes back into the living room he's smiling, looking pleased with himself.

I always thought I was clever, but clearly I'm not clever enough. Robert is the master, and my brief burst of anger is seeping away, to be replaced by fear. I am frightened of my own husband – of what he might do.

'Why did you do that, Robert?' I ask, although I have already guessed the answer. I can hear the quiver in my voice, and Robert will know that the adrenaline of panic has gone – and with it, my fury.

I'm scared, and I can see the satisfaction in his eyes.

'Do what? I just took our children away for a couple of days. I don't know how you could have forgotten.' He attempts a puzzled look, but he knows I'm not fooled.

I turn away from him. I can't bear to look at him. When I speak, my words come out at little more than a whisper.

'You *know* I didn't forget. That's not what you were going to do *at all*. You were going for a bloody *pizza*.'

I watch him in the mirror and see the corners of his mouth lift ever so slightly. Violence doesn't come naturally to me, but if I had a weapon, I swear I would kill him right now.

He reaches out his hands to my shoulders, and I only just prevent myself from flinching at his touch. He turns me round and looks into my eyes, as if that will make me believe his lies.

'I wasn't *ever* just going for a pizza. You know that.' Robert puts his head on one side and just looks at me. 'I wonder if that's how it feels to be a divorced woman. Each time her children go away with their father, she has no idea what they're doing or where they're going. They could be anywhere. Just imagine.'

Like a child, I lift my hands to cover my ears. I don't want to hear what he is saying. I want to get out of the room, but he is between me and the door, and he's still talking. Still telling me how I am the only thing that matters in his life.

He comes towards me, and reaches out to grab my arms and pull them down to my hips. I don't try to resist. He stands very close – so close that I can see the individual pores of his skin.

He leans forwards to whisper in my ear and I feel his breath, hot on my cheek. 'If you leave me, Olivia…'

PART TWO

Two Years Later

7

Friday

There was a buzz in the air as Tom Douglas walked into the pub where members of his team were celebrating their latest success. It was impossible to identify individual voices through the hubbub, but somehow noise had a different feel to it when it was celebratory. Voices were pitched higher, people spoke more quickly, odd bursts of laughter penetrated the general commotion. This, however, was one hell of a night for a celebration.

Tom had been back in Manchester for several months now after a brief sabbatical in Cheshire following his resignation from the Met, and he was loving his new job. He'd inherited a good team, with one or two notable exceptions that he knew he needed to deal with. He couldn't put it off for much longer, but it would have been a mistake to cause any disruption when they were so close to cracking a major case. And today it had all paid off. Two years of hard slog – most of it before he joined the team – had finally resulted in getting the irrefutable evidence they needed to arrest a serial rapist.

Pushing his way through to the bar, Tom lifted his hand in greeting to various members of his team and tipped his open fist back and forth in the air in the universally understood gesture for 'Do you want a drink?'. Several pint glasses were raised, with index fingers pointing, suggesting a refill would be good. Tom turned to the barman.

'Can I give you my credit card, so you can keep them coming?' he asked.

It was no secret that Tom had money, although most people had no idea he had inherited it all from his brother. His team deserved their drinks and Tom was delighted that he could afford to buy a few rounds. They'd worked hard, and the bastard who had been grabbing these girls at knife point and then waving two fingers at the police because they couldn't find a single scrap of evidence was going down for a very long time. He liked to think Manchester was now a safer place. And so it was – but he wasn't daft enough to think that in the overall scheme of things this was going to make a huge difference. So many crimes, and always so much more to do.

He decided to stay for an hour, and then leave them to it. Most of his team were reasonably relaxed around him, but the younger ones and the lower ranks – with the possible exception of the cocky Ryan – were intimidated by him, and they'd have a much better time when he was gone.

Anyway, he was debating whether to call round and see Leo. It had been a while and neither of them seemed quite ready to break the apparent deadlock in their relationship – if that's what you would call it. It looked like it would be down to him, and not for the first time.

Leonora Harris. The joy and the pain in his life. It was nearly a year since he'd met her, and he had hoped they would become close. When he had first bought the cottage in Cheshire next to Leo's sister, he'd had no thoughts at all about starting a new relationship. In fact it was probably bottom of his list of priorities. But Leo was so different from other women. Straight as an arrow and honest to the point of painfulness, she had suffered a difficult childhood and had been scarred by the indifference of her father. She had made it clear that she kept all men at arm's length, but Tom was hoping to be the exception to that rule.

There was something special about Leo. She had a unique style, carrying her tall, slim body with a careless elegance. She tried so hard to hide her vulnerability beneath a slightly acerbic manner, but Tom had never been fooled.

He had known it wasn't going to be easy to get close to her, but had hoped that by always treating her with honesty and respect he would be able to break down the barriers against men that she had been building all her life. She was hard work, though. It was a case of two steps forwards and one back – although sometimes he felt it was the other way round and that he was constantly in retreat. She seemed to want to see him and be with him, but then suddenly the barriers would come up and she would push him away, making herself unavailable for sometimes weeks on end. He didn't know if she was testing him, but he suspected so. How long was this going to go on?

Leo had been very clear from the start that she 'didn't do relationships'. Sex was one thing – but he mustn't assume that would make them a couple. And he mustn't assume that if it happened once, it would happen again.

Tom exhaled a deep breath. He couldn't live like that, not knowing whether he was in a relationship or not, and always living by her rules. She wasn't having it all her own way, but he knew that once they had made love he would be lost. He was just holding on to the very edges of sanity where Leo was concerned, and being that close to her would tip him over the edge.

'Sir!' There was a yell from behind that jolted him out of his reverie. He turned round, and saw his team raise their glasses to him in a toast. He grabbed his pint off the bar and saluted them back. 'Cheers,' they all yelled in unison. That felt good. He would put Leo out of his mind, and maybe not go round to see her tonight. He didn't want to play games – it wasn't his style. But if he called to say he was out celebrating, she would be fine. 'You didn't have to call. If you hadn't turned up, I would have assumed you were busy,' she'd say, just to let him know there were no obligations on either side. Bloody woman.

He felt his phone vibrate in his pocket. Speaking of bloody women, here was another one – his boss, Detective Superintendent Philippa Stanley. She'd become even more serious, bordering on officious, in the intervening years since she had worked for him, and she had received one promotion after another. He'd like to think she was ringing now to congratulate the team for a job well done, but it was unlikely. She would do that formally, but she would never call him in the pub for that purpose.

Lifting the phone to his ear, he knew he wouldn't be able to hear a word she said.

'Hang on, Philippa, I'm going to go outside. It's a bit rowdy in here.'

Tom put his pint back down on the bar. He wasn't much of a pint drinker so it was no great loss, but he didn't think it would do his credibility much good to order a glass of red wine. Forcing his way back through the group pushing towards the bar for their free drinks, Tom finally made it outside on to the pavement.

'Sorry, Philippa. There's a bit of a celebration going on and I couldn't hear a word.'

'Can you hear me now?' she said, completely ignoring all mention of the festivities.

'Yes – loud and clear. What can I do for you?'

'I thought you should know that we've been called out on a missing-from-home case. We sent somebody out to do a risk assessment, but one of the advantages of having a duty sergeant who looks as if he should be stuffed and stood in the corner is that he has a memory as long as my arm. So he flagged this one with me even before it got into the system.' Philippa paused and Tom waited, knowing she hadn't finished. 'Do you remember that I called you in London a couple of years ago about a girl from way back – the one whose Iranian boyfriend disappeared, and then her parents died?'

'I do, yes. The husband had taken their kids out somewhere and hadn't come home. Is that right? I seem to remember you sent me an email to say they'd all turned up safe and well. What's happened now?' Tom asked, knowing she wouldn't have called him out of the blue about an old case.

'This time the husband has come home from a business trip and claims that *she's* disappeared. The wife, Olivia. And so have the children.'

Bloody hell. What was it with this family? Tom lifted his hand and ran it through his short hair.

'And is it for real this time or another waste of resources, because in the past nobody actually *did* disappear, did they? We all ran round like silly buggers only to find that there was a perfectly valid explanation all along.' Tom said. 'It might seem as if Olivia's life has been nothing but a sequence of disappearances, but it feels more like a series of communication problems to me. What's your thinking this time? I presume you don't believe it's just another stupid game or you wouldn't be calling. You sound concerned.'

He could hear a sigh from the other end of the phone. At this point in the investigation, it wasn't something that would normally bother a Detective Superintendent, but he could tell she was worried.

'Philippa?' he said, pushing her for a response.

'According to the PC who went to check it out, it's a very odd situation. Her car is in the garage, her handbag's in the kitchen. If she's just upped and left, she hasn't taken a purse, clothes, or any of the children's things. Nobody leaves with nothing, so I'm not sure what to think. Our guy – PC Mitchell, I believe – is still at the scene, of course. Done a basic search, but we need to get somebody more senior out there to assess it.'

'How long has she been missing?'

'The husband doesn't know. He claims he knows for sure she was there earlier today, but when he came home this afternoon, they were gone. It's ten o'clock now, and he called it in at about eight. The youngest boy is still only four years old, so he can't believe she'd have kept him out this late. But she wasn't expecting her husband home until tomorrow, so it may be absolutely nothing.'

'But you don't think so.' This wasn't a question. Tom could hear it in her voice.

'It's something she said when he – her husband – didn't come home with the children the last time. I got involved because of the history, and I spoke to her personally. She kept repeating the same phrase over and over: "He wouldn't do it. Tell me he wouldn't do it."'

'Wouldn't do what?' Tom asked.

'I don't know. She wouldn't tell me. But whatever it was, it was scaring her senseless. I'll be honest with you, Tom, the look of terror on her face when she said it has haunted me ever since.'

8

Tom pushed his way back into the packed pub, his eyes searching for Becky Robinson. It had made his day when he discovered a few weeks ago that she had applied for a promotion to Detective Inspector for the Greater Manchester force, but he had been less happy when he had seen her. She was too thin, and her eyes seemed to have sunk into her face. He wondered whether he would get an opportunity today to find out what had happened to her, because whatever it was it had certainly knocked her for six.

He had enjoyed working with Becky in London when she was his sergeant, and had found her smart and perceptive – just the kind of person he needed on this case. But he had to be sure she was up to it.

Becky was standing with the rest of the team clutching a glass of what looked like orange juice, but although she was smiling, her eyes looked blank and glassy. Tom lifted his hand, and Becky plus several others turned to look at him. He beckoned Becky towards him, and she turned as if with relief to put her glass down on the nearest table. Nobody looked disappointed that he hadn't signalled them.

'Sir?' she said, turning her dark eyes towards him.

'We've got a job, Becky. Woman and three children missing from home. I'll just pay for the drinks, and I'll fill you in on the way. Is that okay with you?'

'No problem. Would you like me to drive?' Becky asked, as Tom signalled the barman, making signing gestures with his hand.

'A kind offer, but no thanks,' Tom answered, remembering some of the white-knuckle rides he had had with Becky at the wheel in London. 'Come in my car, and we'll get somebody to give you a lift back when we're finished.'

They walked in silence across the road to the car park. Tom flicked the car's remote and waited until they were both strapped in with the engine running before speaking. He glanced sideways at her but she was staring straight ahead, clearly trying to avoid eye contact. This was so out of character.

'Becky, you know I was delighted you'd applied to come and work in Manchester, and even more delighted when you got the job. There was stiff opposition, and these days it's not always easy to get transferred, as we both know. But what's it really about? You're not yourself, and you look as if somebody's kicked you in the gut, if you don't mind me saying so.'

'Thanks a bunch,' Becky said, but at least there was a glimmer of a smile, and Tom could feel some of the tension in her spine ease a little. 'I'm okay though. Glad to be away from London, and I really don't want to talk about it. Not even to you. If it affects my job, just tell me please, sir, but otherwise can we just not mention this again. Nobody else knows me from before, so they probably think I'm always a miserable sod. I'd rather it stayed that way.'

Tom nodded his head slowly, pulling the car out of the car park, and pointing it in the direction of the Brookes' home. He knew the feeling, and if she didn't want to tell him, he'd leave it at that.

'Well, I hope you realise you can talk to me any time you want to. You know I'd never repeat a word. And by the way, when we're on our own, Tom's still fine. You don't need to go all formal on me.'

'Okay, got it. Are you going to tell me about the case now, or what?' she asked, a flicker of her old, slightly cheeky self coming to the surface.

While he was driving, Tom filled her in on everything Philippa had told him about Robert Brookes' disappearance two years ago, and then took her through all he could remember of his first meeting with Olivia Brookes almost nine years previously.

'I know at the time my radar was telling me there was something more to it, but I can't remember exactly what. I was with Ryan and he just ran through the queries as if by rote, not even trying to dig deeper when the occasion arose.'

'When you say "Ryan", do you mean *our* Ryan – as in Ryan Tippetts?'

Tom gave a single nod of the head.

'Oh, bloody hell. Poor girl.'

It clearly hadn't taken Becky long to get Ryan's measure.

'So what do you think happened to the boyfriend then?' Becky asked.

'I've no idea. Last we heard there was evidence of him booking a flight, so we can only presume he left the country.'

They were both quiet for a few moments. Saying that Olivia had been distraught at her boyfriend's disappearance wouldn't adequately convey the shock and fear that the girl had appeared to be experiencing. Any woman whose boyfriend abandoned her, leaving her with a new baby, might be expected to be distressed, but it had seemed more than that to Tom.

'That was only the start of it,' he continued. 'Two months later, both her parents were dead, and she was the one who discovered them.'

Tom had a vision of a hysterical Olivia as she screamed over and over again that this could not have been an accident. But try as they might, they couldn't find evidence of any crime. They'd even suspected the missing boyfriend. He was studying for a PhD in engineering, and maybe – just maybe – it was all a clever ploy to get the insurance money.

'So, if I've got this right, boyfriend one does a runner. Parents are found dead. Future husband comes to the rescue. Seven years later he buggers off with the kids. She says he lied about where they were going – so what did she think? That he was *abducting* them?'

'I don't know. Philippa thinks there was something odd about it.'

'So if his abduction scheme failed two years ago, is this his second attempt, only with slightly more finesse?'

Tom glanced at Becky with raised eyebrows. 'Go on,' he said.

'Well, if he really wanted the kids so much two years ago, he could have seen off the wife for good this time, and abducted the kids again – have them in hiding somewhere. He's had two years to plan it.'

Tom's phone interrupted them at the perfect moment, before speculation took over, and he pressed the screen on his dashboard to answer. A voice filled the car through the Bluetooth speakers.

'DCI Douglas?' It was the gruff voice of the duty sergeant.

'Speaking,' Tom answered.

'Just had a call from PC Mitchell, who's at the Brookes' house with the father, Robert Brookes. I gather you're heading over there now?'

'That's right. We'll be there in about ten minutes. Problem?'

'Well, there might be. It's odd, anyway. PC Mitchell has been filling in the missing-from-home form, and he asked the father for some photos of the kids. The usual stuff. He says Mr Brookes went to the sideboard to get some, and the photo box was empty. He thought his wife might have shifted them, but to make life easier he said he'd print one off his computer. There are none there, and no trace that any have ever been there – none in the trash. Nothing. Same with his phone. Same with his wife's phone, which is still in her handbag, by the way. According to Mr Brookes, there isn't a single image of his wife or any of his children in the house.'

9

Becky was delighted that Tom had asked her to go with him tonight. It wasn't that she was naturally anti-social, but she was struggling to be normal around anybody at the moment, and at least Tom knew her 'from before', as she thought of it. Nowadays, she always imagined people were looking at her and pointing, sniggering behind their hands like schoolchildren.

She had no evidence at all of this behaviour since arriving in Manchester, but life had been like that for weeks before she left the Met, and any time she entered a room she assumed that people stopped talking, or changed the subject because they were gossiping about her.

Arrogant cow, she couldn't help thinking. *Why would anybody be interested in me?* But she knew why.

As they pulled up outside the Brookes' home, Becky couldn't see much detail of the house. Although it was close to the longest day of the year the sun had set about an hour earlier, but there was still just enough light for her to be able to make out that it was quite a substantial property on an attractive tree-lined road. When she first joined the police she had been shocked to learn that troubles came to people who lived in houses like these. As a girl from a rough part of London, she had lived under the misapprehension that it was only impoverished people who had problems. How wrong had she been? It had taken her a while to realise that the only difference was that those with more money had a tendency to hide their problems out of a misplaced sense of shame.

When children were missing, though, shame didn't come into the equation at all. Becky knew that all policemen hated any case involving the potential for harm to children, and she was no exception. She had never been religious, but in her mind she kept repeating a cross between a prayer and a promise. *Wherever you are, kids – we're going to find you.* She only hoped it would be true.

Tom interrupted her thoughts.

'Okay, Becky. We've done enough interviews together to know the score. I'll make the introductions, and then I'll back off and observe. You can take over the questioning. Unlikely as it seems at the moment, this may just be a guy whose wife has taken the kids to stay with friends, but given their history I want to make sure we don't miss anything.'

Becky nodded and opened the car door, closing it quietly so as not to draw too much attention to their arrival on this peaceful road. The police car parked up the drive wasn't on view to anybody except the neighbours opposite, but Becky didn't want to have to deal with well-meaning callers at this point. 'Well meaning' was a bit of a euphemism anyway; the ones who came knocking to see if they could 'help' were invariably just there to find out what was going on.

As they walked towards the front door a bright security light came on but failed to pick them up in its beam. Becky turned to Tom and shrugged, glad not to have been blinded by the light but wondering at its effectiveness.

Tom pressed the doorbell, and they heard its piercing single tone resonate around the house. A PC whom Becky didn't recognise opened the door, and she saw a flash of relief on his young face, no doubt glad to see senior officers who could take the weight off his inexperienced shoulders. He had the look of a skinny young colt – all long gangly limbs that didn't quite know where to put themselves.

They were shown into a living room, and a man stood up from the sofa and just looked at them without speaking. He seemed to be focusing on Tom's face, and his eyes narrowed slightly.

'Mr Brookes? I'm Detective Chief Inspector Tom Douglas, and this is my colleague, Detective Inspector Becky Robinson. You probably don't remember, but we have met before, sir, when your wife's parents died. I was an inspector then.'

Becky noticed a slight jolt as Robert Brookes' eyes opened wider. He held out his hand, and Tom shook it. He turned to Becky and gave her a brief nod, without bothering with a handshake. Clearly she wasn't sufficiently important to warrant such a common courtesy.

Brookes seemed small and insignificant next to Tom. He was a few inches shorter than her boss, with much narrower shoulders. His hooded eyes sat below heavy brows, and as his glance darted from her to Tom and back again, the whites picked up the soft glow of the table lamps dotted around the room, turning them into yellow beams in a shadowed face. She felt as if she were being scrutinised by a night owl, waiting to pounce on its prey.

'Thank you for coming.' Brookes said. He seemed lost, as if he needed somebody to tell him what to do next.

'Can we sit down, sir?' Tom indicated the sofa, and Robert flopped back on to the cushions as if he feared his legs weren't going to hold him up for much longer. Becky took a seat on the facing sofa, and Tom sat down on an upright chair slightly to the side.

'I know you will have already told PC Mitchell most of this,' Tom said, nodding at the young PC who had melted into the background somewhere behind Brookes, 'but if it's okay with you, DI Robinson and I would like to go through things with you again, just so we understand your concerns.'

Robert Brookes nodded his head without speaking, and Tom glanced at Becky.

'Are you absolutely sure that your wife hasn't taken the children away for a few days, as she wasn't expecting you home until tomorrow?' she asked, seamlessly taking over the questioning.

'She wouldn't have done that without telling me, and I spoke to her every single day, at least once and usually twice. She was here. I spoke to her this morning.'

'Where were you, exactly, and how long had you been away, sir?'

'I've been at a conference in Newcastle for a fortnight. Olivia took the children on holiday for the first week, but she's been home since last Saturday. I wasn't due back until tomorrow, but I thought I'd come home a day early to surprise her. I even stopped in town to buy flowers and wine. I just expected her to be here.'

Becky could see Tom watching Robert Brookes from the side, and wondered if he was picking up anything. She certainly wasn't. Brookes never met her eyes, and his glance seemed to constantly flick around the room.

'So she didn't know you were due home today? It must have occurred to you that she might have gone to stay with a friend, as you were away. I presume you've checked with everybody you know?' Becky couldn't fail to notice the flash of irritation on Robert Brookes' face.

'We don't do that. We never go and stay at other people's houses. We don't have that kind of friend. And she would have called me by now. It's past our scheduled call time. Nine o'clock every night. Seven o'clock most mornings, before she gets the children up. Just to say hello.'

'How do you know she was here, sir? Did you call on the house phone or on her mobile.'

'Neither. We used FaceTime on our Macs. It's a bit like Skype. We both have laptops, and it's so much better to talk face to face than just to listen to a voice. She always calls from our bedroom – so I can see her propped up against the pillows and picture her in our bed. It reminds me of home. She's never missed a call when I've been away in two years.'

Becky spotted Brookes glancing over at Tom. He must have realised his expressions were being watched, and it was making him uncomfortable. She always felt a bit bad about this. The guy could be going out of his mind with worry. On the other hand…

'Is that your laptop, sir?' she asked, pointing to a thin leather case on the sofa next to him.

'Yes. I brought it in here in case she called. I've tried her repeatedly. But she won't call now.'

Tom Douglas interrupted the flow of questioning.

'What makes you so sure she's not going to call you, Mr Brookes?'

Robert Brookes put his head back and closed his eyes briefly. 'Because her laptop's here. I found it upstairs in the bottom of the wardrobe.'

'And what have you done with it, sir?' Becky asked.

'I've put it on to charge. The battery was flat. I just did it automatically. I often had to remind her to do simple things like that.' His gaze rested just above Becky's head, but she could tell he was looking far beyond that, at an image nobody else could see. She would have dearly loved to know what it was.

'Okay, let's move on. As we understand it, your wife and children are gone, but nothing at all of theirs is missing. No favourite toys, no secret stash of money, no spare mobile, a rarely used credit card – nothing at all?'

'*Jesus Christ*,' Robert exploded. 'How many times am I going to have to repeat this? You should be out looking for her, not asking me to go over all this stuff again. There is absolutely nothing missing. She had no secret stash of money – she didn't earn anything, and I know where every single penny goes. The kids' stuff is all here and her one and only mobile is in her fucking handbag. *Nothing* is missing. *Nothing.*'

Except, of course, a woman and three children. But Becky didn't say that.

'I'm sorry if this is irritating you, Mr Brookes, but I need to check every detail. In your mind, then, your wife went missing sometime between your conversation with her this morning and four o'clock this afternoon?'

'*Yes.*' Robert's teeth were so clenched together that the sound could barely escape.

'Has your wife reported anything strange happening to her recently? Has she felt threatened by anybody? Or have the children mentioned anything unusual – have they been followed or have they spoken to anybody they didn't know?'

Robert looked from Becky to Tom and back to Becky again.

'She hasn't said anything to me, but there might have been something. She may have decided not to tell me, because she knew I would worry when I was away.'

'What do you mean, sir?' Becky asked.

'There's nothing concrete, but she hasn't seemed quite herself recently. She's been a bit jumpy, nervy. And I've heard her whispering to Jasmine a couple of times. I don't allow whispering in the house. I think it's divisive. I had to have a word with her about that.'

Bloody hell, thought Becky. It sounded as if he'd reprimanded his wife. And how would he have done that? Would he have punished her? Had he snapped?

'So you think she had a secret?'

'No, of course it wasn't a secret. Stop twisting things. I think maybe she was concerned about something, and maybe Jasmine was too. She wouldn't want me to know if I was going away, because she knew how important this conference was, and she knew for a fact that I wouldn't go if I was worried about her. But before you ask the inevitable next question, I have no idea what she was concerned about.'

To Becky's irritation, her phone began to vibrate at that moment, and she stood up and excused herself.

10

Tom hadn't decided what to make of this situation yet. Olivia hadn't been expecting her husband home until tomorrow, and given their history it seemed more than likely that she had simply taken the children somewhere and not told Robert. Maybe a friend had picked her up, and although her belongings were in the house Tom couldn't believe there wasn't a logical explanation. Trouble seemed to follow this couple around, though, and in his experience that was rarely a coincidence.

If Olivia had been abducted, according to the original feedback from PC Mitchell she must have let her abductor into the house because there was no sign of a break-in, and no evidence of a struggle either.

'Okay Mr Brookes, if you don't have any idea who or what was bothering your wife, let's backtrack a little. Let's go back to everything that's happened since the last time you spoke to her. Just talk me through it, please. PC Mitchell can take notes.'

Robert Brookes leaned his head back on the cushion of the sofa and stared at one of the lifeless paintings on the wall opposite, as if seeking inspiration. Tom saw him give a slight shake of the head and then he sat upright, leaning forwards slightly to rest his forearms on his thighs.

'I spoke to my wife this morning, as usual. I didn't even give her a hint that I was coming home early to surprise her. I left Newcastle at about one o'clock and drove straight home. I stopped for petrol, if you really want to know that level of detail, and then I called at the flower shop in the high street and a couple of other shops to pick up a few treats – a bottle of wine, some comics for the kids.'

Robert ran the fingers of his right hand through his hair, leaving it standing up in furry peaks.

'I got back here at just after four – and you can ask the nosey old bag across the road if you don't believe me, because she saw me arrive. She was, as always, looking out of her window. Mrs Preston, she's called.

Never misses a trick.'

Tom couldn't help noticing Robert's lip curl as he spoke about his neighbour. She was definitely somebody they would need to talk to.

'Go on. What did you find when you got in the house?'

Robert gave him a puzzled look. 'What do you mean?'

'Well, I presume your wife wasn't here. What did you do? Did you call anybody? Did you check anything? Just walk me through it, please.'

Robert's face had a mottled red look about it. 'For Christ's sake – I've told all this to your mate here.' He signalled dismissively over his shoulder with his thumb. 'Why do I need to repeat it? Why aren't you out looking for her?'

'We would be out looking, sir, if we had the first idea where to start. That's why I just need you to run through things again for me, if you don't mind.'

Robert closed his eyes and clamped his lips together for a few seconds before he continued talking.

'I came in. I shouted and got no reply. Obviously,' he said with slightly greater emphasis than was entirely necessary. He paused, but as Tom had failed to react to his irritation, he continued. 'Olivia's handbag was on the table. I emptied it, and everything was still there. Her wallet, her debit card, her phone – even her bloody house keys were there. I checked the garage. Her car is there. She loves that car, and I can't imagine her even *thinking* of going anywhere without it. And then, when I finally remembered to get my suitcase out of the car and took it upstairs, I found her laptop. That's all I know. She was here this morning, and now she's gone.'

And not once have you mentioned the children, Tom thought.

'What would she normally be doing on a Friday afternoon? Was there a pattern? Would she have walked to the shops, had friends round for coffee? What about the children?'

'The children were at school. They finish at three thirty and Olivia would have either driven or walked to pick them up. She wouldn't have had anybody round.'

As Robert Brookes finished speaking, the door from the hall opened. It seemed that Becky had caught his last few comments. She glanced at Tom and he gave her a slight nod.

'Mr Brookes, when children go missing one of the first things we do is contact the school. We didn't think this would wait until Monday, so we tracked down the head teacher and had a word with her. Your children weren't at school today, were they, Mr Brookes?'

Tom was watching Robert closely. He didn't know for sure where this was going, but Brookes' face was a picture. A muscle twitched in his cheek, and he put a hand up to rub it, but the twitching wouldn't stop.

'According to Mrs Stokes, the head teacher, you and your wife decided to take the children out of formal education a couple of weeks ago. You decided they were going to be home schooled from now on. Their last day at school was the Friday before the half term holiday – exactly two weeks ago. And nobody has seen or heard from them since.'

After Becky's revelation, Robert Brookes had looked from one of them to the other, stood up and left the room without saying a word.

Tom watched him go, but decided to give him a moment. He needed to talk to Becky.

'What do you reckon then?' Tom asked.

Becky shook her head. 'It's all a bit weird. According to Mrs Stokes, Olivia Brookes was very close to tears when she pulled the kids out of school, and she – Mrs Stokes, that is –tried hard to persuade her to change her mind. But Olivia said her husband was adamant, and all the papers had been signed.'

'Did she say anything about the children: their behaviour, any signs of abuse, anything at all that we can pursue?'

'No, she said they're good kids. Jasmine is a bit quiet, but the two boys are like any boys of their age – full of energy, can't sit still, clumsy – I think the word she used was rumbustious.'

'And the parents? What did she make of them?'

'That's a different story, I'm afraid. Apparently Olivia Brookes had been struggling a bit lately. On a few occasions she'd forgotten to pick the children up from school. Each time it happened they tried to call her, but there was never an answer, so then they had to call Robert. He always left work and rushed to pick the children up, and Mrs Stokes said he made all sorts of excuses for his wife, but none of them rang true.'

'And what was Olivia's excuse?'

'She didn't have one. Just said that she had been confused and thought her husband was picking them up. But since that was something he never did because he had a full-time job, it seemed a bit strange.'

Tom didn't like the sound of this one little bit. Why would Robert Brookes want the children taken out of school? Could it be so they wouldn't be missed? And did Olivia have some stability issues?

'Okay, Becky, we need to get him back in here.'

'Fine – but before we do that, Mrs Stokes told me a couple of other things. During the week, she brought round a box with some of the children's notebooks so Olivia could see where they were up to in their learning. There was nobody home, which wound her up. "Home schooling means home schooling, not gallivanting around all day," – or something like that,' Becky said in a high-pitched voice which Tom assumed was a vague imitation of the head teacher. 'Anyway she left the box of books with the neighbour across the road.'

'Interesting, but Olivia could have gone shopping, or even taken the kids for an educational trip to a museum for all we know.'

'True, but the lady she left the books with told Mrs Stokes she hadn't seen anybody here for days. Anyway, the other thing I asked her about was photos. I thought she might give me details of the school photographer so we could get some pictures as they are conspicuous by their absence here.'

'Good thinking,' Tom said. He was glad to see that Becky's eyes had regained some of their usual sparkle.

'Well, it might have been a good idea – but to no purpose. Apparently, Olivia Brookes had requested for the last two years that the children didn't have a school photo taken at all. No explanation given. She just didn't want any. So we still don't have any pictures.'

Becky had asked PC Mitchell to go off and find Robert Brookes, and the young policeman had reported back that Robert was lying on his bed.

'He said he'd be down in a minute, ma'am, but he was muttering about school – says he knew nothing about them being taken out and home schooled.'

'Did you believe him?' Becky asked.

'I don't know. He never looks you in the eye, does he? I can't get a handle on him. Sorry, ma'am.'

'That's you and me both, I'm afraid.'

They heard a door slam upstairs and guessed Robert was on his way back down, so they took their seats and waited. He entered the room and moved back towards the sofa, his face pale but with a red flush staining his cheekbones like an angry rash.

'Sorry, but I just needed to take a moment. I don't know what to say in response to the news from the school. I...'

'That's okay, Mr Brookes. We'll come back to it, I'm sure. But for now we need to think about how we can find your wife and children. Are you certain you have no photos at all?'

Becky was watching Robert Brookes closely. He was shaking his head as if he was totally bewildered. She couldn't decide if it was real or if he was acting a part.

'I've never liked photos around the house. I prefer a few tasteful pieces of art.' Robert indicated the paintings that adorned the walls, although Becky couldn't quite reconcile the word 'tasteful' with what she was looking at. Not that she would have the first idea, as she had to admit to herself.

'I used to take photos of Olivia, but she didn't like it. She hated pictures of herself, although I don't know why. My wife was very beautiful.'

Becky was silent but she risked a glance at Tom. Had he picked up on the same interesting use of tense? They both waited for Robert to continue.

'I thought we had pictures on our phones and on the computer. There was a box of photos in the drawer too, but I can't find any. I'm sorry, but I don't know what's happened to them all. Olivia must have had a sort out.'

Much as he wanted to labour the point of the photos, Tom could see that he wasn't going to get any more sense out of Robert on that subject, so he decided to change tack.

'You said your wife had been on holiday recently, Mr Brookes – for the first week that you were away at this conference in Newcastle.'

'That's right. We went several times a year, always to the same place in Anglesey. Well, that's not entirely true. We had always *been* to the same place, but when Olivia tried to book for October last year, it was closed, so she found somewhere else. I checked out the new place online obviously, and it looked okay from what I could see. I had a word with the landlady, to make sure she sounded a responsible type of person. Given what happened to Olivia's parents, we're doubly cautious when it comes to staying in other people's houses, so I wanted to be clear about security, alarms, that sort of thing. I didn't have time to go myself, but we were due to go again in July, as soon as school broke up.'

'Can you give me the details and dates, so we can get somebody on the phone to the landlady to check that your wife was there?'

Robert pursed his lips in obvious irritation. 'Of course she was bloody there. I spoke to her. She turned the computer round in the room so I could see what it looked like. She even showed me the beach out of the fucking window. There's no doubt *at all* that she was there.'

Tom looked completely unperturbed by his outburst and Becky remembered him telling her that by far the best way to take the sting out of minor tantrums was to ignore them.

'I'm sure you're right, Mr Brookes, but just give me the details anyway, please. PC Mitchell will write them down, and we'll get on to the landlady to check a few things out.'

Robert Brookes grudgingly passed on the information and, closing his notebook, PC Mitchell made his way into the kitchen.

Tom leaned forwards. 'Mr Brookes, when DI Robinson spoke to Mrs Stokes, she mentioned there had been some problems with your wife from time to time, forgetting to pick the children up from school being an example. And you say you didn't know she was taking them out of school. I'm sorry to have to ask this – but in the light of everything we've heard tonight, I need to know whether your wife has any mental health issues. Please be honest with us. It may be important.'

Robert put his head in his hands, but not before Becky had noticed his eyes cast down and his shoulders slump in a classic pose of shame.

11

Tom couldn't ignore the warning bells ringing loudly in his head. He was sure Robert wouldn't admit to there being anything wrong with his marriage to Olivia – whether or not that was the case – but Tom had to try to understand her state of mind, to assess whether she had left voluntarily or whether she had been the victim of a crime.

Robert had finally recovered himself and answered the question about Olivia's mental health by saying that he'd had a few concerns, but she was just a bit forgetful sometimes. He said they'd managed to create strategies to make it easier for her to remember what she should be doing. Did that mean she could have taken the children somewhere and literally be lost, or have forgotten where she was going? Tom knew that the Manchester and Cheshire police were on the lookout and the hospitals were all being checked, so hopefully if that were the case, they would all be found quickly.

Tom could see that Becky's gentle probing was falling on deaf ears as Robert's eyes had glazed over, his mind apparently somewhere else entirely.

One other thing was bugging Tom. The house was very orderly. Given that there were three children living here, it was more or less immaculate. Everything seemed to be defined by the word 'tasteful', and yet there was something clinical about its perfection. So why then, if Olivia had been here until this morning, was there a fine layer of dust over every piece of furniture?

The lack of photos was a serious concern. If they had been a family that just didn't take photographs at all, it might make sense. But the fact that there had been some and now they were missing was difficult to explain. Tom needed somebody to look at the two laptops, and as soon as PC Mitchell had finished talking to the landlady, he could get on to organising that.

No sooner had this thought crossed Tom's mind than the door opened and the PC beckoned him into the kitchen. He seemed a little nervous, and Tom guessed he hadn't long been allowed out on his own. Poor lad. Not the most straightforward of cases.

'Sir, I've spoken to the landlady in Wales. She's confirmed that Mrs Brookes and her three children were there for a week, and left last Saturday. She said they all seemed fine, and were looking forward to their next holiday in the summer.'

'Okay, thanks,' Tom responded, his attention diverted by a large cork noticeboard on the wall. A couple of metres long, it was completely empty, apart from a few drawing pins.

PC Mitchell was talking again, and Tom turned to him.

'Sorry, what were you saying?'

'I was saying that, according to the landlady, Mr Brookes paid his wife a visit while she was staying there. She said,' he consulted his notebook, 'I was sorry not to meet Mr Brookes when he visited this week. We've spoken on the phone, of course, but I was disappointed he didn't give me a knock to say hello. He was gone by the time I got up in the morning.'

Tom looked at the policeman. 'Are you sure that's what she said?' He immediately felt guilty, because the young constable looked alarmed and stood up a little straighter, his long lanky arms ramrod stiff at his sides.

'Yes sir, I'm sure. I wrote the whole thing down.'

'So what the hell is going on?' Tom asked, a rhetorical question aimed at nobody but himself. 'Right, we need to get the local police in Anglesey to pay the landlady a visit – tomorrow morning will be fine – but first thing – and we need them to question her. Tell them to jog her memory and extract as many details as possible, no matter how trivial. I'm going back in there to talk to Mr Brookes; find out why he lied to us. We need to canvass the neighbours starting early tomorrow morning, before they all bugger off to do whatever they're doing over the weekend. You know the procedure?'

PC Mitchell nodded slowly.

'Good lad, but if you get stuck just ask us. Okay? We've all been new, you know. And it's better to ask than to cock it up.'

Tom walked across to the noticeboard and peered at it intently. He turned his head.

'Come and look at this, and tell me what you see,' he said.

PC Mitchell looked puzzled for a second, then he pointed to the top left corner of the board.

'One of the drawing pins has a scrap of paper attached. It looks as if something's been ripped off.'

'Well done.' Tom looked down and pointed. 'There's a drawing pin on the floor too. Something was here. So what would you do next?'

'Check the bins?' PC Mitchell suggested.

Tom nodded.

'Get some gloves on, and see what you can find. I'm interested in the bins anyway. If Olivia Brookes and the children have been here all week until this morning at least, I'd like to know what you find.'

Tom gave the policeman a reassuring nod, turned on his heel and pushed open the door from the kitchen to the living room.

Becky was still asking questions, but she was running out of steam. Tom took over. He wasn't going to ask Robert about his trip to Anglesey yet. He had a feeling that Robert would clam up completely once he was aware of how much they knew.

'Mr Brookes, we'd really like to take your wife's computer to check it out. Would that be okay with you? We might be able to find something on it that gives us a clue about where she might be. We'd like yours too, so we can check your FaceTime records.'

'What for? It will only show you when I called her. I don't record the conversations.'

'We can check where she was speaking to you from.'

Robert was shaking his head in frustration.

'She was *here*. Don't you think I recognise my own bedroom when I see it on a screen?'

'Well, that will help us to set a time frame. According to your neighbour who spoke to the school head teacher, Olivia hasn't been seen all week. When you had your calls with her, what exactly did you see in the shot – just a pillow behind her head, or more?'

Robert lifted his hands and put them on his head. It seemed to Tom that he was literally trying to hold back steam from escaping.

'I don't know how many times I need to repeat this. She was *here*, speaking from *our* bedroom with *our* cushions propping her up. Here. In this house.' Robert said each word slowly and distinctly, punctuating them with a stab of his finger. 'And not just today, but every fucking day this week. Just because the nosey old bat across the road didn't see her doesn't mean she wasn't *here*. That woman might spend a fair proportion of each day by the window, but she's not there twenty-four seven.'

'Okay. Can you tell me if there are any other computers that Olivia had access to? A home computer, perhaps? Or did the children have anything with an Internet connection?'

Robert shook his head. 'It's the only computer she used, and we didn't agree with children accessing the Internet at all. They weren't allowed near our computers.'

Tom bit back a response about school and homework. This was none of his business, but his daughter Lucy, who was only a little older than the Brookes' eldest girl, used the computer all the time. He hoped that he and his ex-wife had instilled an awareness of all the right safety measures into their daughter, but to forbid her to use it would surely have put her behind her classmates at school.

'So there are no more computers in the house, then?' Tom asked.

'Only the one in my study, but she wouldn't have used that. It's password protected.'

'Can you show me, please?' Tom asked.

Robert sighed as he pushed himself up from the sofa. He bent down to pick up a bunch of keys from the coffee table and led the way from the room. As he inserted a key into the lock, Tom glanced at Becky, whose brow was furrowed in a puzzled frown.

'Why do you keep this door locked, Mr Brookes?' Becky asked.

Robert tutted, as if the answer were obvious.

'Because I work in here. I don't want the children getting in, and I don't want them touching the computer. I opened the door for your constable, but it's a habit to always lock the door behind me.'

'Does your wife have a key to this room?' Tom asked, suspecting he knew the answer before he even posed the question.

'No, she doesn't need one. She cleans in here when I'm at home, not when I'm away.'

Tom nodded his head, as if this were a perfectly normal state of affairs.

'Just one last question, Mr Brookes. You say you were in Newcastle for the whole of the last two weeks – is that correct?'

'Yes, of course it's correct. I already told you.'

'Well then, can you explain how – according to the landlady of the guest house in Anglesey – you visited your wife in the middle of last week?'

Robert Brookes spun round on his heels.

'What did you say?'

'I asked you whether you did, in fact, visit your wife in Anglesey during her holiday with the children last week.'

'No. I've told you. I never left the hotel in Newcastle during the whole two weeks. I was snowed under with work, and there was no way I could leave. Ask anybody.'

'We will, Mr Brookes. Thank you.'

❖

It seemed to Becky that they had learned a lot, and they had learned nothing at all. They had questioned Robert Brookes for another half an hour about everything from the conference venue to his conversation with Olivia that morning, and had nothing more to show for it than a list of people who could apparently verify that Robert was in Newcastle.

She looked across at Tom, who was exchanging contact details with Robert Brookes, and she couldn't help comparing the two men again. Tom's calm and relaxed demeanour somehow accentuated Robert's nervy behaviour. His fidgeting and constant flicking of the eyes from one person to another without ever making eye contact was disconcerting to put it mildly.

PC Mitchell poked his head around the door and, not wanting to disturb Tom, Becky went to see what he had found.

'DCI Douglas asked me to check the bins,' he explained. 'The waste bin in the kitchen was empty, and appeared to have been cleaned and disinfected, judging by the smell. So I had a look in the dustbin. That was empty too, except for two things. A John Lewis carrier bag, which had nothing in it, and this.'

PC Mitchell unrolled a large sheet of paper and spread it on the kitchen table.

'I think it used to be on the wall, because the tear in the corner matches the scrap that's attached to the drawing pin.'

Becky looked at the chart and took out her phone, thinking a few photos might be a good idea.

'It looks like a schedule of some sort,' PC Mitchell said.

A schedule of some sort was the understatement. Covering about two metres wide by one high, it was a half-hourly breakdown of each day for the past month, and a blank one for the month ahead.

Becky bent over and peered at it closely. The level of detail was staggering. '3.20 pm – going to pick children up from school. 3.40 pm – back from school with the children.' This was the last entry, and for that very day. Each element of Olivia's day was mapped on here. Not the children's timetable – she had noticed there was a separate small blackboard for that, with reminders clipped neatly to the bottom. But this sheet of paper detailed every time Olivia left the house and every time she came back in again. It also listed any phone calls she'd received, however trivial. 'Phone call at 10.13 am. Wrong number.' What was *that* all about?

When questioned about his wife's mental health issues, Robert had implied that they had set up solutions to help Olivia, which would suggest there was a forwards-looking plan she had to follow. This schedule appeared to be written in retrospect – either what she was about to do or what she'd actually *done*, rather than what she *planned* to do. Sometimes there were remarks like 'Returning to Sainsbury's – forgot the eggs. Back in 20 minutes' as if it was a message to somebody. And she'd written on the board today – or yesterday, as it was now well past midnight – that she had returned from school with the children. But the children hadn't even *been* to school.

She looked more closely at the chart. Most of the entries used pencil, red pen, blue pen – even children's crayons. But the entries for the last few days were all in the same pen, and she couldn't be absolutely sure they were the same handwriting as the previous ones. She needed to get somebody else to look at this. Not that it meant anything. Olivia could have written those entries days ago. As could Robert, for that matter.

12

Saturday

Robert waited fifteen minutes after the house was emptied of bodies with their relentless questioning and the beeping of their mobile phones. He grabbed a bottle of water, his car keys and his wallet, and made his way out of the front door. The security light came on, but the beam wasn't shining on their drive, as it should have been. It was shining straight across the road into Mrs Preston's window. It must have been knocked out of alignment somehow, and he could see a shadow standing back from the bedroom window opposite. He knew the light would have alerted his neighbour and she would be watching with interest. Well, no doubt she would get the opportunity to have her say, because he was fairly certain the whole street would be questioned as soon as they were up and about.

He'd planned to leave as quietly as possible, but as the nosey old bat was watching anyway, he revved the car and was about to speed off down the road with a squeal of tyres, just to wind up the silly bitch, when he noticed a car parked further down the road. Not a car that was normally on this street. It didn't take him long to work out what it was. *Bastard police.* He eased his foot off the accelerator and, with his car emitting the gentle hum of an expensive engine, he slowly and almost silently made his way off the drive. If he was followed, he would just have to have another think.

Much to his amazement, when he reached the long straight road towards the M56 there was nobody behind him. His suspicions must have been wrong. The roads were empty at one o'clock on a Saturday morning, and he would have easily spotted a car tailing him.

He had a couple of hours' driving ahead of him, but in spite of his exhaustion he felt totally awake. It was an effort, but he forced himself to stay within the speed limit. He wanted no undue attention tonight. He didn't know how all the systems of the police worked together, but if his name was down on some list of 'persons of interest' he didn't want to be flagged up. It was a rough night, though. Following such a sunny day, a fierce wind had blown up from nowhere, and the trees were swaying violently from side to side.

An hour and fifty minutes later, courtesy of the total absence of traffic at this ungodly hour, Robert arrived at his destination. At just before three o'clock in the morning it would be entirely inappropriate to ring the doorbell – at least if he wanted to get the right result. This had to be handled well, and he was going to have to bide his time and keep his temper in check. He imagined that people who ran B&Bs had to be up at a reasonable hour to start preparing the guests' breakfasts, so he would just have to wait. It might have been an impulsive decision to come here in the middle of the night, but he needed to be sure he was the first person to speak to the landlady today.

At this hour of the morning the guest house was in darkness. A wide drive led to the front door of the property, and a single outside lamp created a halo of light around the main entrance. Robert could just make out a number of tall chimney pots silhouetted against the starlit sky, and the white painted window frames standing out from the traditional grey limestone of the building.

He pushed the soft leather seat of his Jaguar XJR into recline and leaned back, closing his eyes. He couldn't sleep, though. All he could see were vivid images of Olivia – from the moment he met her up until the last time he saw her.

Checking his watch every few minutes, time dragged and he tried to close his mind to all thoughts of his wife. But it was impossible. By five o'clock, his limbs were twitching with inactivity and his emotions had run the gamut from rage to fear. He had to get out of the car.

As he pushed the door open he was hit by the tang of sea air, and he could hear the waves gently lapping on the sand. He turned and looked at the beach, bathed in the early dawn sunlight of a June morning. And he looked again. Something was wrong here, but he didn't know what it was. He gave himself a mental shake, and set off on his walk, away from the small harbour. He strolled to the far end of the bay and sat on a smooth rock looking out to sea, his thoughts coming in waves to match the ebb and flow of the tide. He had hoped the cool morning breeze would have blown away the cobwebs and allowed him to think rationally about his next move, but he was wrong.

By five thirty he thought he should return to his vigil, and he made his way slowly back to the car as an orange sun began to melt away the shadows.

Finally he saw a chink of light through some closed bedroom curtains. Somebody was awake. Time dragged, and it was a full twenty minutes before he saw the curtains pulled back and the light switched off. He left it a further five minutes before he felt it might be safe to approach the house. He pushed open the car door and closed it quietly behind him.

He walked towards the back of the house where he hoped the kitchen would be. A window was open, and he could hear a radio playing quietly. The presenter announced the next song. Michael Bublé. He almost smiled. Olivia hated Michael Bublé. She said his music was anodyne. How appropriate for today.

There was a smell of frying bacon – and Robert realised that he had eaten nothing for nearly twenty-four hours. He hadn't even stopped for lunch on the way home the day before. The idea of food made him feel slightly nauseous, and he swallowed the saliva that threatened to choke him.

He gave three sharp raps on the back door and heard a voice call quietly, 'Coming,' with that hint of a warm Welsh accent, and a clatter of pans as if she were moving the frying pan off the hob.

Robert realised that he probably looked like a tramp, with his crumpled shirt and the dark shadow of his unshaven face. Maybe that was a good thing.

The lady who opened the door was exactly as he would have expected. Probably in her early sixties and looking all of her age, she nevertheless had a relaxed expression that said all was well with her world. Her grey hair was cut short in a practical, no-nonsense style, and she wore a too-pink lipstick. She smiled pleasantly, but beneath the smile he could sense a hint of wariness.

'Good morning,' she said, maintaining the welcoming air. 'What can I do for you, dear?'

Robert returned the smile and held out his hand.

'Mrs Evans, my name is Robert Brookes. Do you think I could come in for a moment? I'd like to talk to you about my wife.'

13

'*What?*' Tom Douglas was not given to yelling at people down the phone, but then he'd rarely had people on his team as daft as Ryan Tippetts. 'Ryan, we waited until you said you were in place before we left. We've no idea what's happened to Olivia Brookes and her children. They could all be dead, or he could be holding them somewhere. We don't know, so I wanted you to keep eyes on the house in case she came home or he went out. What part of that did you fail to comprehend?'

Tom listened impatiently to Ryan's explanation, and didn't believe a word of it. Some rumpus at the end of the road that he had felt obliged to investigate? Not a chance. He was probably asleep. And how come he'd realised only now – hours later – that the Jag was missing from the drive?

'Yes, I do accept that he could have put the car in the garage, but did it not occur to you to check as soon as you realised it wasn't visible? We can't justify formal surveillance on Robert Brookes at this stage, but it's common sense to let us know if he leaves, isn't it?'

He listened to more excuses for about ten seconds and then noticed Becky was signalling him from outside the door of his office, clearly with something that she urgently needed to tell him. He'd had enough of DC Tippetts for now.

'Ryan, watch that house like a hawk – understand? And let me know the minute he gets back, if indeed he *ever* gets back.' Tom put the phone down carefully. Early in his career he had learned that slamming the phone down did no good to anybody, and the person at the other end heard nothing more than a click, the same as if the phone had been replaced normally. So it was his first step to restoring calm after a frustrating call. He took a deep breath and beckoned Becky to come in.

'We've just heard from the police in Anglesey,' she said. 'They got to the guest house, B&B – whatever – at about eight o'clock. They thought it would be early enough, but they were wrong. The landlady had already had a visitor. Robert Brookes was there just after six this morning.'

Shit. This was all they needed: a suspect in what may or may not be a crime going on the rampage and trampling over potential evidence. He'd crucify Ryan when he got hold of him.

Becky was still hovering just inside the doorway, so Tom signalled her to sit down, glad to see she was looking slightly better today. Perhaps the excitement of a new case had driven out some of her demons, whatever they were.

Becky gave an exasperated shrug. 'Bloody witnesses. Sometimes I could string them up. The police said that Mrs Evans seemed really uncomfortable talking to them, but she apologised. She said she'd been completely wrong. Robert Brookes hadn't visited his wife last week. In fact, she'd never met him until this morning.'

'So why did she tell us he was there, then?'

'Well, she now says she was probably a bit confused. There had been a visitor one night, and she'd been sure it was Mr Brookes. But perhaps it was one of her other guests who had somebody to stay over for the night. She says she has so many that sometimes she gets muddled.'

Tom thought for a moment. 'Did the local guys believe her?'

'I'm not sure they did. They said she seemed flustered and keen to move on. They tried to push her, to find out why she'd changed her story, but she just got upset. She was adamant that she's never seen Robert Brookes before, though, and that bit they *did* believe.'

'All a bit too convenient, if you ask me. What did Brookes say to her? Anything significant?'.

'Not really. He asked if he could see the room Olivia had slept in, but when she showed him he just stared at the bed, then walked over to the window and looked out at the beach. She said he was muttering about the colour of the sand, but she didn't know what he was talking about, because it's just, well, *sand* coloured. And that was it. Oh, and he kept looking at his watch. He probably realised the local police would be coming round any time soon, because we told him that last night. We don't know where he is now, though. Very possibly on his way home, or at least, we can hope so. I've got somebody checking the cameras, see if we can pick him up on the A55 or the M56, but if we don't spot him soon we'll need to widen the net.'

'Keep me updated on that. I want to talk to Robert Brookes the minute he's back.' Tom pushed his frustration to the back of his mind, and leaned back in his chair. 'What do you make of it all, Becky? Give me your gut reaction.'

Becky shrugged. 'I think Brookes is as guilty as sin.'

'Of what, though?'

'I'm not sure. I keep going back to the fact that he took the children once, so has he done something with them and killed Olivia? There was the whole bit about the kids being taken out of school, which he claims he knew nothing about, and then the schedule we found in the bin. He had no real explanation for that, did he? But he seems to have kept tabs on every move Olivia made.'

Becky was right. They had quizzed Robert about the need for such a detailed timetable, but he was adamant it was designed to help Olivia, although Tom couldn't see how. It also suggested that Olivia was there until just before Robert got home, but the timings for picking the kids up from school were nonsense.

'It's the whole idea of the thing that creeps me out,' Becky said, pulling a face as if she were eating something unpleasant. 'If it was just a diary of events, in case of forgetting things, that would be one thing. But it's got everything on it. I'm surprised it didn't say when she'd been to the toilet, to be honest. Then there was the locked study door. We need to get a better look at that computer. He wasn't at all keen on us looking too closely last night. My every instinct is screaming that there was a complete lack of trust between the two of them.'

'And the missing sheet?' Tom added. When the house had been searched, PC Mitchell had noticed there was no bottom sheet on the bed in the master bedroom, so he checked in the laundry bin on the landing and there was nothing in there either. A utility room housed the washing machine and tumble dryer, but they were both empty. Of course, the sheet could have been washed and put back in the airing cupboard, but the rest of the bed was made, so it had seemed a little odd.

Becky shook her head. 'No idea what that's about, but we've flagged it, of course.'

'No joy from hospitals, I gather, and nothing on any local CCTV?'

'No sign of a woman and three children on foot, and as she wasn't in her own car there's not much else we can check there. We've looked at the recent calls on her mobile as well. Nothing – she doesn't seem to use it.'

Tom put his clasped hands behind his head.

'Robert Brookes says he spoke to his wife every day, and she was at home. But I don't think anybody's been in that house for days. There was the dust, which could be down to bad housekeeping. But who disinfects their bins, and doesn't dust? More to the point, the dustbin was empty of any household waste. The bin men come on a Tuesday – three days before they went missing.'

'I know, and I checked the fridge,' Becky said. 'There was nothing out of date, and there was no milk – the one thing guaranteed not to last. And not a single vegetable to be found anywhere.'

'In other words, we have a schedule full of lies, and we have Robert Brookes swearing she was in the house until Friday. But nothing, absolutely nothing, is missing from the house.' Tom leaned forwards again. 'Apart from a woman and three children, of course. What's the plan you've drawn up?'

Becky pulled a sheet of paper from the pile she was clutching and handed it to Tom.

'An incident room is being set up. We're going to interview the neighbours to see if anybody has seen Olivia Brookes in the past two weeks. Somebody's going to talk some more to the head teacher, just to try to get a better understanding of the whole "home-schooling" malarkey. And we're going to take a look at those computers – all three of them. For now we've just got the laptops. We've alerted the press, although the absence of photos is a bit of a nightmare. We'll issue an urgent plea for Olivia to get in touch with us, if she's still alive and kicking – promises of confidentiality and all that, of course. We'll try to see if anybody at all has recent photos of the children from kids' parties, school trips and so on. We were going to look into CCTV from the hotel where Brookes was staying – the garage in particular – to see if he was lying about visiting his wife in Anglesey. But that seems irrelevant now. What do you think?'

'I want it checked anyway. I don't trust Robert Brookes, Becky. There's something not right about him. He's hiding something, but I don't know what.'

'If my theory's right and he's killed her, what about the flowers, and the other presents? They suggest he was expecting them to be in the house when he got back, don't you think?'

'Not necessarily.' Tom was about to put forward an alternative, infinitely more sinister theory when his mobile vibrated on the desk. He was at a loss to know why this was ever called 'silent mode' as to him it was even more distracting than a subtle beep. He saw it was his boss.

'Philippa, what can I do for you?' he asked, groaning inwardly because he was sure that given her interest in this case, Ryan's spectacular performance last night would by now have come to light.

But he was wrong.

'When Robert Brookes took the children off for that holiday or whatever it really was a couple of years ago, naturally I wrote my report based on the facts, but at the time I thought there was something odd about it all and I decided to attach a note of my own impressions of the family – a nice trick that I seem to remember you taught me, Tom.'

This was rare praise indeed from Philippa, but Tom decided to say nothing and let her continue.

'I wrote down a couple of things that may be relevant now. One was the fact that I felt Brookes somehow seemed rather pleased with himself, although outwardly his response to his wife's obvious distress and confusion was sympathetic, and the other was the fact that we learned from the school that Jasmine had retained her real father's name and talked about him as if she knew him. She always spoke of him in the present tense. We didn't think much about it then and I don't know if it's still the case, but before we become obsessed with the notion that all four of them are buried in the back garden, I think you should see if you can track down Danush Jahander.'

14

'I shagged the boss.'

Tom Douglas was about to take a sip of espresso from a dinky little cardboard cup as Becky made her pronouncement. Coming as it did, as a complete non sequitur, Tom could only think that she had been slowly plucking up the courage to reveal the source of her obvious melancholy.

He took a mouthful of his coffee and waited.

'That's why I'm so miserable. I shagged the sodding boss,' Becky repeated, a slight tremor in her voice. Tom glanced at her, and she looked away – out of the side window.

They were parked down the road from the Brookes' house, waiting for Robert to return home. He'd been clocked on the M56 heading in this direction so they were fairly sure he was on his way back, and they'd decided to be ready for him. In theory, while they waited and drank a much needed cup of coffee purchased en route, they were trying out a few different ideas on what could have happened to Olivia Brookes, although Becky had made her opinion very clear.

Tom turned in the driver's seat so that his whole body was angled slightly towards her. He wanted her to know he was listening. He gave her a moment. He saw her shoulders rise and fall, as if she had taken a deep breath, and she turned back to face the front, staring straight ahead through the windscreen. Tom looked at her worried face, her lips clamped tightly together.

'I thought it must be something like that,' he said, keeping his voice neutral.

Becky spun round towards him. 'What? Had you heard something? Did somebody tell you?'

'Don't worry – nobody's said a thing to me. Do you want to tell me what happened? Like which boss for example?'

Becky turned back to face the window.

'Peter Hunter.'

A Detective Chief Superintendent, no less. That really was the boss. Tom had never been a big fan of Peter Hunter since he'd taken over from James Sinclair while Tom was still working for the Met in London. He was a good copper, no doubt about it. But as well as his obsession with treating crimes as items on a spreadsheet, he was the sort of guy who thought he was still young and hip despite being in his mid fifties. He always pretended to be up to date with the latest music, not quite getting the fact that he just wasn't. And he liked to use what he believed to be trendy words, which just made him sound ridiculous in Tom's view. He had an impressive career behind him, but instead of winning respect within his team for his undoubted ability, recently he seemed to be losing it as they quietly scoffed at his posing. An affair with a junior officer won't have helped either, and it was a sure thing that it wouldn't be a secret.

Tom said none of this to Becky.

'I thought I loved him,' she continued. 'He was so attentive, so thoughtful. We could only meet three or four times a month, but he rang me all the time when I was off duty, and he just made me feel great.'

Tom closed his eyes and stifled a groan. He knew Peter Hunter was married. He had met his wife, who seemed pleasant enough, but in spite of that he wasn't one little bit surprised about his extra-marital behaviour. He was more surprised by Becky.

'I know it was stupid. I knew he was married, but I think I was mesmerised by him.'

Becky was quiet for a few moments, and Tom thought maybe it was time for him to speak.

'You're not the first to be dazzled by somebody like him, you know. It's the old wealth, power and fame bit, renowned for being huge aphrodisiacs, and Peter certainly had power. I gather it's over now?'

Becky gave a bark of unamused laughter.

'*And how*. His wife came to see me.'

Tom didn't know whom he had the most sympathy for – except it definitely wasn't Hunter.

'She told me her husband was unfortunately addicted to adoration, and that I wasn't the first and wouldn't be the last. I said that I loved him, and she laughed at me. She said I was confusing infatuation with love, and it was time to grow up; that I have an idealised concept of what love is, and it's not all about passionate nights, and flowers. That was the general gist, anyway.'

Mrs Hunter had a point. It was all so easy when romance ruled the day. Tom's mind flipped to Leo – terrified of letting him get too close in case being together was the very thing that would drive them apart. He couldn't force her to drop her guard, though, so he could either wait it out or move on. He dragged his thoughts back to Becky, who clearly wanted to get it all off her chest.

'I asked her why she put up with it, if this wasn't the first time. Do you know what she said? She told me that she despised him for his weakness. He was less of a man in her eyes, and he'd hurt her very badly. But love was about so many things, and she had long ago decided that perfection was unattainable. What do you make of that?'

'She could be right – I've certainly never experienced perfection. Have you? Even those we've loved all our lives are highly unlikely to be perfect.'

Becky was quiet for a moment, so Tom continued.

'I'm sure that what you had with Peter felt great. Secrecy itself can be intoxicating. But in the short times you had together, it would have been all about giving each other your undivided attention. At home he might be the person who expects to be waited on hand and foot, or speaks with his mouth full, or picks the hard skin on his feet when he's watching the television, or farts in bed.'

That, at least, raised the hint of a smile from Becky.

'Some people can live with these things,' he continued, 'and some can't. I once knew somebody who divorced his wife because she wouldn't let him put his football trophies on the mantelpiece. Peter and his wife may have rubbed along just fine together, and she may prefer to live with somebody who she thinks less of for his infidelities than to be with somebody who on a daily basis irritates the hell out of her for his thoughtlessness and lack of consideration. We don't know. We're not in their marriage.'

Becky dropped her head. He gave her a moment.

'What was the outcome?'

'Basically, she told me to "get out of Dodge". Either I looked for another position or she would have words with her uncle – who naturally just happens to be the Deputy Commissioner – and she would see to it that my career was stifled. I'm not sure she could do that, but it was all irrelevant because he never spoke to me again, other than to refer to me as Sergeant Robinson when, and only when, he had to.'

Tom could see how difficult it was for Becky to admit this.

'I read a saying once,' he said. 'I'm not sure where it's from but it goes something like this: "If a man tries to steal your wife, the best form of revenge is to let him have her." Switch genders, and that's how it might have ended for you and Peter. Imagine she'd chucked him out and he'd ended up on your doorstep. How long do you think it would have lasted?'

Tom watched Becky's face as she weighed up what that would have been like. Poor kid still looked like death warmed over. 'Thanks for telling me, Becky. It must have been hard on you and you must miss him.'

Becky turned to him with her eyes wide open. 'You think I'm like this because I'm *missing* him?' She gave a harsh laugh. 'You're wrong. I feel wretched for so many reasons, but mainly I feel so guilty. I don't know who I am any more. That's what's been eating away at me. I've always thought of myself as a kind, thoughtful person, but I'm sure Ruth Hunter sees me as a callous, manipulative bitch. So which one of us is right?' Becky paused. 'And then there's my total stupidity, which obviously needs no further explanation.'

This time her smile was more genuine, and it seemed to Tom that this might be an appropriate moment to change the subject. He didn't want Becky to think he was dismissing her confession lightly, but there was little he could say. She was going to have to come to terms with it herself.

He watched her as she took a huge gulp of coffee, and he could almost see her dragging her mind away from the dark place that was still haunting her.

'Speaking of dodgy marriages,' she said, 'there was one thing I noticed last night when we were talking to Brookes. It seems he always chooses to call his wife when the children are out of the way. Either before they get up, or after they've gone to bed. And then, on top of all of that, he kept going on about finding his wife. He's barely mentioned his kids. Have you noticed that?'

'I certainly have.'

'It seems odd, seeing as how last time it was the children he appeared to care about. Unless he knows exactly where the children are, of course, which brings us neatly back to my theory.'

Becky turned to Tom with a trace of a cheeky smile, but before he could respond Tom glimpsed some movement out of the corner of his eye. He turned to look through the windscreen just as Robert's Jag swung through his gates.

'Hang on, Becky, here he is, and unless I'm mistaken, that's our very own DC Tippetts chasing him up the drive. Come on,' Tom said, scrunching his now empty coffee cup and thrusting it into a paper bag. 'We can't wait for bloody Ryan to put his foot in his mouth again.'

15

The drive back from Anglesey had seemed much quicker than the journey there. Why was it always the case that when you want to get to a place it seems to take forever, but when you don't the trip flashes by? He hadn't been in a rush to get home because he knew he was going to have to face some backlash from the police. They hadn't asked him to stay at home, but they wouldn't be pleased that he had questioned Mrs Evans.

At least he was reasonably confident that the landlady wouldn't say anything she shouldn't to the police now. He was sure she had understood the implications of repeating everything she had told him.

He patted the breast pocket of his suit jacket and felt the resistance of the photo that was nestling there. What luck that he had happened to notice this picture on Mrs Evans' noticeboard, crammed in amongst so many others. There was no way he was leaving it there for the police.

Robert pulled into the drive and glanced in his rear-view mirror. A man was jogging behind the car, speaking urgently into his mobile as he ran. Not one of the police who had been there the night before, but he was sure he was a policeman nevertheless. What now?

As Robert opened the car door and started to get out, his ears were assaulted by a racket coming from his neighbour's garden.

'Sir, I'm glad you're back. Can we go in the house, please?' the policeman shouted. 'I need to talk to you, and I'd rather talk inside, if it's okay with you. It's a bit noisy out here.'

Robert tutted with frustration. Typical that his neighbour had chosen this weekend to hire a digger and demolish his front drive ready for some fancy new cobbles.

He walked into the porch, retrieved a bunch of keys from his pocket and hunted through them, taking his time to find the right one. He needed to get his thoughts together and be ready to explain himself. Finally he inserted the key in the lock and opened the door.

As he turned back to the porch to invite the policeman inside, he noticed a small box with Olivia's name on the top.

'What's this? Do you know anything about it?' he asked the policeman.

'Yes – your neighbour across the road has been keeping hold of it for your wife. The head teacher from the school called round earlier in the week with it. She's stuck an envelope on the front, with a note in it.'

Robert bent down to pick the box up. What the hell did he need with school stuff now? He carried it inside and dumped it in the hall, ripping the envelope off and shoving it in his pocket. He turned back towards the policeman.

'What?' he said, planting his legs firmly apart and folding his arms. The policeman could make what he liked of his stance, but he was damned if he would apologise for what he had done.

'Could we ask you, Mr Brookes, not to leave the house without letting us know where you're going in future? We were concerned last night when we discovered that you'd gone.'

'Am I under arrest?' Robert was struggling to keep his temper at bay. He had enough to worry about without this ape telling him what to do.

'You managed to get me a right bollocking for not noticing you'd gone out and I didn't know where you were. Don't do it again – okay?'

Robert was tempted to smile, because the policeman had failed to realise that in the few minutes they'd been standing on the doorstep the two detectives from the previous evening had walked up the drive, their footsteps masked by the sound of shattering tarmac, and had witnessed this comment.

It was the woman who leaned forwards and spoke as quietly as she could. 'Thank you, DC Tippetts. We'll take it from here.'

Robert saw the man's eyes close as if in disbelief that he'd been overheard. Dropping his head, he turned and walked out of the house without raising his eyes to either of his senior officers.

'Sorry about that, sir,' the inspector said, with a smile that didn't go further than the corners of her mouth. 'DC Tippetts is correct, though, Mr Brookes. We would prefer to know where you are. We may have news; we may need your help. There are any number of reasons why we might need to speak to you – and not only did we not know where you were, but you had your phone switched off.'

'So why were you watching me then? Surveillance, is it?'

The senior policeman spoke for the first time.

'It's not surveillance of you, sir. It's the house. We want to know if and when your wife returns.'

Robert shook his head.

'Well, as you can see, she hasn't. Okay?'

Tom Douglas was looking at him carefully, and Robert could tell he was weighing him up.

'Really, sir? And how do you know she hasn't returned? We can only see the hall – she could be in the kitchen, the living room, the bedroom. I didn't hear you call out. Did you, DI Robinson?'

Robert felt a sudden rush of blood to his head. *Crap. He should have thought of that.*

Tom was watching Robert very carefully, and could see how uncomfortable the man was. He was absolutely certain that Robert knew his wife and children would not be here. How could he know that?

Robert was quickly trying to cover his mistake by talking; shifting the emphasis away from the fact that Olivia wasn't here.

'Well, no doubt you've heard the news from Anglesey that I'm not a liar. Mrs Evans got it wrong, as I'm sure she's told the local police. Perhaps you believe me now? Perhaps when I say I haven't seen my wife since I left here two weeks ago you might give some credence to my story?'

Tom stayed quiet, knowing Becky would step in.

'I'm sure you appreciate that in a case like this we have to check everything. We have to suspect everybody. Mrs Evans has confirmed that she has never seen you before, so I'm sorry for the mix up, sir.' Tom knew Becky was softening Robert up by apologising.

'Well, believe it or not I *knew* I hadn't been there, so I wasn't mixed up in the slightest.' His brief smile indicated a sense of victory.

'So why did you go to Anglesey, Mr Brookes?' Tom asked. 'We're investigating a missing woman and three children, and to have somebody – no matter who it is – interviewing potential witnesses is at best unhelpful, and at worst detrimental to the investigation. Do you *want* us to find your family?'

Robert looked shaken. *Good,* thought Tom. And so he should be.

'I'm sorry – but I wanted to know why the landlady had lied. I couldn't see any harm in it.'

'If you want to know anything, you ask DI Robinson, or you ask me.'

Tom gave Robert a moment to absorb what he'd said. 'Now, before we jump to the conclusion that something has happened to your wife, one thing we need to do is look into your financial situation. We need to know if she had enough money to disappear and leave everything behind her.'

Robert's face relaxed. He looked almost as if he thought that was funny. Somehow, Tom wasn't surprised. Given the locked study door and the schedule on the wall, he was beginning to realise that Robert Brookes very much liked to be in control.

'You'd better come in then, I suppose,' he said, with little grace. 'Look, you know I've been up all night – so I'm going to need some coffee to keep me going. Sit down, check the house, do what you like. I'll be back in a few minutes.'

Robert disappeared into the kitchen, leaving Tom and Becky standing in the hall. Becky just looked at Tom and he frowned.

'For somebody who wants us to find his family, he's not being exactly co-operative, is he?' Becky said.

'No, but there could be lots of reasons for that. If he thinks she's just upped and left him, he could be feeling any emotion from shame to despair. If he thinks they've been abducted he could be scared, or feel guilty that he didn't protect them better.'

Becky nodded. 'And if he offed the lot of them, or even just the wife, he could be feeling scared, guilty *and* in despair.'

Before Tom had a chance to respond, the door from the kitchen opened, and Robert ushered them into the living room. Nobody sat down.

'Right. What do you want to know?'

'We'd like to know what money your wife has access to: credit cards, bank accounts, etcetera. Obviously we can check this, but it would be better if you could talk us through how the money is managed in the home.'

'That's easy. My salary is paid into an account in my name, and I use that to deal with all the household expenses – mortgage, utilities and so on – plus any other major expenditure. Olivia collects the bills and we have what I'm sure you can imagine is an exciting bill-paying day each month. There's a separate household account that I put money into for food, and odds and ends for the children. Olivia has a debit card on that account, and when we do the bills we check what's been spent and what's left. If there's any money in the account, it's rolled over into next month, or if she needs more, we top it up.'

'Have you checked the account recently, Mr Brookes?' Becky asked.

Robert's top lip curled slightly as if it were a thoroughly stupid question.

'Of course I have. I checked it yesterday. There's nothing unusual. A cash withdrawal in Anglesey, probably for ice creams and stuff, and then this week a Sainsbury's shop. Exactly as I would have expected. Nothing else at all, apart from filling up with petrol once.'

'What day was the shopping done?'

'Monday. And she spent £78.03, if you want to know.'

'If the account was for food, what did your wife use if she wanted to buy herself something – a new dress, for example – just on impulse?' Becky asked.

Robert laughed.

'Olivia is the least impulsive person you could ever wish to meet, Inspector. She buys stuff online. She does a bit of research and chooses a few things, then we complete the transaction on my credit card when I get home. Same for me and the children, except for their shoes. She likes to get them properly fitted. Olivia loves Internet shopping. Everything can be sent back, so she can try things on and show me, and if she doesn't like something, back it can go. You don't understand what she's like. She hates responsibility. I like looking after her, and she looks after me.'

This just sounded like more evidence of control to Tom, but he knew he shouldn't judge. If Olivia Brookes had issues, maybe this was the way they managed their lives.

'Look, go and check her wardrobe if you've concluded that I'm a tight-arse.' Robert extended his arm sharply upwards and stabbed with his index finger towards the bedroom. 'It's full of clothes. Good clothes. Designer, some of them. Check her make-up bag – all Chanel or Dior. Not that she ever wears much. She doesn't need it. There's nothing Olivia can't have. She has everything she's ever wanted.'

For just a second, Tom saw a faraway look in Robert's eyes as if he had left the room and was visiting another place or another time. His eyelids dropped slightly, but not before Tom had glimpsed something that looked like regret in Robert's eyes.

16

As he entered the incident room, Tom sensed a quiet buzz of energy from the ten or so people hunched over their desks, speaking softly on phones or sharing information with colleagues. Becky would have briefed the team by now, but his presence would indicate that she had his full support. The day-to-day running of the investigation was down to her, but with Philippa Stanley breathing down Tom's neck given the history of this family, he also needed to keep up to speed.

Tom felt as if he had been up for hours, but it was still only eleven o'clock in the morning. He had a strange feeling that this day was going to get worse before it got better. Walking over to Becky's desk, he nodded a polite 'Good Morning' to those he passed, and pulled out a chair.

'Update?' he asked as he sat down.

'The press have been informed, and it made most of the morning news bulletins, although it was too late for the papers. But it's a Saturday, and I suspect fewer people pay attention to the morning news on TV. It might jog somebody's memory, but without photos it's a bit of a non-starter. The house-to-house is under way, and the techies are looking at the laptops. They're going to give us a preliminary update in about...' Becky looked at her watch, 'five minutes, with any luck. We need to commandeer Mr Brookes' desk-top computer too, despite the fact that his wife was kept out of his study by a locked door.'

Tom could hear the indignant undertones at the thought of Olivia being barred from entering a room in her own house.

'Any joy in tracking down Danush Jahander?'

'Ah – well not specifically. When he went missing originally there was a note in the file about his brother, a...' Becky scrolled down the screen on her computer, 'Samir Jahander. He was much easier to locate because he's a doctor and lives and works most of each year in Dubai. But it seems he occasionally spends weeks working voluntarily in Iran, and that's where he is now.'

'So a dead end?'

'We've left a message asking him to call us, but in the meantime we spoke to his wife. As far as she knows, Samir hasn't seen his brother since he visited him in England about a year before Danush disappeared. His name was mud in the family, and Samir came over to try to persuade him to leave Olivia and return to Iran. There was an almighty row, and in the end Samir left without accomplishing his mission.'

'And since then?' Tom prompted.

'Samir told his wife he'd heard from Danush once, she thinks it was about two years after he disappeared. He was only calling to let his family know he was alive, but apparently he also said that thanks to Samir's intervention in his relationship with Olivia, he had been forced into making the worst decision of his life and he would never forgive his brother. According to the wife, Samir and Danush had a major argument, and her husband has never mentioned him since.'

Tom pulled a face. 'Did you manage to get any photos we could use?'

Becky rooted through the piles of papers on her desk, which Tom knew would be much more organised than they appeared to be.

'The only ones we have are from when he was with Olivia – so they must be at least nine years old. They're the ones she provided at the time.' He could see Becky's eyes lingering on the smiling face of Danush Jahander, his full lips turned up in a beaming smile displaying perfect white teeth, and his curly dark hair brushed back from a smooth, broad forehead. A bit different from Becky's fifty-odd-year-old ex-lover, he couldn't help thinking – and a damn sight better looking.

Becky's phone was ringing, so he left her to it while he stared at Danush Jahander's photo. He looked like a decent guy, with what appeared to be a genuine smile that definitely reached his deep brown eyes, but Tom wasn't naive enough to believe that looks counted for much. He could have been a right bastard for all they knew.

He was momentarily distracted by Becky's conversation.

'Are you sure about this, Gil?' she asked. There was a pause. 'Okay, well could you please surface from below decks and explain it to DCI Douglas, who's sitting opposite me right now. I think we need to understand a bit more about this. Right – we'll see you in a few minutes then.' Becky hung up.

Tom gave her a quizzical look, and waited.

'Gil's going to explain how FaceTime works, and what's been going on with the two laptops. A bit technical for me, I'm afraid. I might understand it, but not well enough to repeat it and have it make sense. Are you okay to hang on, or do you want me to give you a call when he gets here?'

Tom agreed to wait and took out his mobile to make a few quick calls – one of which was to Leo. He had been planning on suggesting they got together tonight, but he had no idea what time he would be finished here. Maybe he should offer to cook them a late supper, if she could buy the ingredients. They had to eat, after all. But there was no reply, and he didn't have time to leave a message. He looked up as he heard footsteps approaching the desk.

'Gil, pull up a chair,' Becky said.

Tom smiled and nodded at Gil Tennant. As unlike a stereotypical technology geek as you could imagine, he was almost dapper in appearance. Short and slender as a teenage girl, today he was wearing mustard-coloured jeans and a black polo shirt, with immaculate black suede trainers to match. Tom had noticed on a few occasions that Gil was a man who liked to co-ordinate his shoes: a strange, but harmless fetish. His wiry hair was gelled into submission, and he looked permanently surprised – a look that Tom sometimes suspected was down to a bit of surreptitious eyebrow plucking.

'Okaaaay,' Gil said, drawing out the word dramatically. 'A few interesting facts here. What do you know about FaceTime?'

Tom looked at Becky and shrugged. 'I know what it is. I've used it on my Mac at home. But let's assume nothing. That's probably best.'

'FaceTime is used to communicate between any two relatively recent Apple devices: iPhones, iPads, Macs, whatever. It's a video link – just like Skype, really. Okay up to now?'

Tom hid a smile at being spoken to as if he were six years old, and nodded.

'Right. Well the thing is, if FaceTime calls are made between computers rather than mobile phones, as they were in this case... *allegedly*,' Gil stressed the word, paused and gave them both a little smirk, 'the contact is between email addresses, so we can use the computer's IP address to identify the user's location.'

Tom tuned out while Gil explained in unnecessary detail the difference between the various technologies and the intricacies of tracing people. He had been through this before, so he let his mind wander to Olivia Brookes and the first time he had met her, one wild and windy November night almost nine years ago. He shouldn't have been there at all, really, but Ryan

Tippetts was giving Tom a lift home when the call came through. Ryan had been asked to visit Olivia and Tom had gone with him.

His lasting memory was of Olivia rocking back and forth, clasping a crying baby to her chest and repeating over and over again, 'Dan wouldn't leave us. I know he wouldn't leave us. Please find him.' It had been heartbreaking to watch her. Tom's daughter Lucy was only a little older than Olivia's baby, and he knew how Kate would have reacted in the same circumstances. Of course, that was when he and Kate were happy.

Tom realised that Gil had paused again, looking from one to the other and back again to see if they were keeping up with him.

'Now, let's start with Mr Brookes, shall we?' he beamed at them both. 'Am I right in saying that he claims to have contacted her daily?'

'Yes,' Becky added. 'Up to Friday morning.'

Gil made a clicking sound with his tongue and wagged his index finger in the air.

'Not true, Mr Brookes. We've checked his laptop, and he did contact his wife using FaceTime – every night and most mornings. But only until Wednesday. After his Wednesday evening call, there are no more calls from his laptop.'

Gil had finally captured Tom's interest. So Robert had lied about when he'd last spoken to his wife. Why did that not surprise him?

'But we've checked the log on Mrs Brookes' laptop too, and the interesting thing is that the log is showing no calls between her and her husband *at all* in the last two weeks. Which means, if I need to spell it out, that when he called her she definitely wasn't speaking to him from this laptop. She must have been using a different computer, or maybe an iPad.'

That didn't make sense to Tom. If Olivia had been in the bedroom, lying on the bed as Robert said, she would have needed something mobile. But, according to Robert, apart from Olivia's own laptop – which Gil claimed she definitely didn't use – there was no other suitable device in the house.

Gil hadn't finished. His head swivelled from side to side, looking first at one and then the other with a cat-that-got-the-cream expression. 'However... there *are* several calls from Mrs Brookes' computer to a Hotmail account over the last few months, and the IP address appears to be,' he paused for effect, 'in *Iran*.'

Becky had been scribbling notes as Gil spoke, but at this news she stopped and looked up. Tom intercepted her look, and no words were necessary.

'The next thing we would normally do is contact the Internet Service

Provider and do all the paperwork to get them to release details of the precise location where the call was received. But I don't fancy your chances with an Iranian ISP, frankly.'

'You are absolutely certain this IP address is in Iran, are you Gil?' he asked. 'When was the last time contact was made?'

Gil's perfectly sculpted eyebrows nearly shot through the ceiling.

'I'm *absolutely* certain, DCI Douglas. I don't make mistakes like that. The last contact with the Hotmail account was just over two weeks ago.' Gil consulted his notes. 'Two weeks ago yesterday, to be precise.'

Tom picked up a pencil from the desk and rotated it in his fingers. Was it possible that Olivia Brookes had just decided she was off with her Iranian lover, and that was all there was to it? But it didn't feel like that.

Why had Robert lied about when he'd spoken to her? Gil said the last contact was Wednesday – although not on Olivia's laptop. Robert said she was definitely there, in their house, until Friday – but that didn't ring true either. So why was he lying?

'Sorry, Gil. I just need a moment to think,' Tom said. 'There's nothing confusing about your explanation, just about this bloody Brookes family and their mix of truth and lies. Is there more?'

'A bit. As I mentioned, we know Robert Brookes was making calls to his wife's email address until Wednesday. We've tracked where the device that *received* the calls was situated. It appears the calls were received in France.'

Becky looked bemused. 'She hasn't got a passport, so how the hell did she get there?'

'She probably didn't.'

Becky sagged in the chair and pulled a face.

'Huh?' she said.

'We're pretty sure it's a fake IP address. She must have bought it on the Internet – it's easy enough to do. But if you want to find out the *real* IP address, you're going to have to do some more paperwork, I'm afraid.'

'Why not route it round the world to disguise it, and confuse us completely?' Tom asked. His own brother had made a fortune out of this particular technology, and it wasn't the first crime he'd been involved in where locations had been disguised in this way.

'Not much good with FaceTime. The signal wouldn't be strong enough and the video would degrade. We can get the details of her real location from the provider, but her husband wouldn't be able to – which I imagine was her intention. It's going to take time, probably two or three days and, as I said, lots of lovely paperwork.'

Gil was quiet for a moment, looking eagerly from one to the other.

'I know this may be stating the obvious, but can I just draw your attention to the fact that just because Robert Brookes contacted his wife's *email address* on FaceTime, there is absolutely no evidence at all that it was Olivia on the other end of the call. We only have Robert's word for that. Anybody who knows her email address and password could have answered Robert's calls. He could have done it himself, come to that, just to make us believe that she's alive and kicking. So even if we track the location down, there is absolutely no guarantee we will find Olivia at the end of the trail.'

Great. Just great, Tom thought. So all we know is that Robert lied about speaking to Olivia on Friday. We don't really know if he *ever* spoke to her in the last two weeks – it could all have been set up. And that was the only evidence we had that she is actually alive. Maybe Becky had been right all along.

But if Robert had killed her, where the hell were the children?

17

He lay on the bed, his head propped up on four pillows. Having been up all night, Robert needed to sleep but his mind was spinning. He wished he hadn't involved the police now, but it had seemed the right thing to do. If he hadn't reported Olivia missing he would have looked as guilty as sin. But oddly it seemed that filing the report hadn't diminished the suspicions that were already surrounding him. And that was something he needed to deal with.

It was reaching the point where he was going to have to give the police more – more information than he wanted to – but there might be no other choice. They were going to find out anyway, sooner or later, and so maybe if he were the one to show them the evidence rather than leaving them to find it themselves, it would score him a few points.

Olivia, why did this have to happen?

He had always known he was second best and that nobody would ever replace Danush in her eyes, but he had tried so very hard to make her love him. She said she did, but he could sense the void hiding behind the words. She didn't understand how that had made him feel – how his heart raced with the desire to pump some emotion into her and bring back the laughing, carefree girl he'd first seen all those years ago and instantly fallen in love with. To Robert it seemed as if a spotlight shone on Olivia wherever she was, and everybody around her faded into the shadows. She was all he could see. But back then she hadn't even known he existed.

He had known what he'd needed to do. He'd made himself indispensable, an essential part of her life. Without him, she couldn't function. He had proved it to her over and over again. But still she remained contained within herself, and he was never sure whether the armour she protected herself with was to stop him getting in, or to avoid exposing the gaping wounds beneath.

His gaze flicked around their bedroom, resting for a brief moment on the dressing table, picturing Olivia sitting there, brushing her hair. When they'd bought this house, he had made sure that the upstairs could be adapted to provide a whole suite for them – a bedroom big enough to hold a comfortable sofa, a dressing room and a luxury en suite bathroom. He wanted Olivia to feel spoiled. It was decorated predominantly in shades of cream and grey with a few accents of plum. It looked like something photographed for a very expensive magazine – but somehow it had failed to create the feeling of an intimate hideaway that he had striven for. His eyes stung as he remembered his initial hopes for their life together.

Brushing aside all wistful thoughts of what might have been, he focused on his anger and on everything he had discovered in Anglesey. He leaned across the bed to where he had thrown his jacket, pulled the creased photo out of the breast pocket, and held it in both hands. Mrs Evans had seen him looking at it, pinned to her noticeboard with a collection of snapshots.

'When was this taken, Mrs Evans?' he had asked, forcing his voice to remain steady.

'Just last week. Your wife was on her way out of the door as one of our regulars was taking snaps of the house. She always sends me copies. It's a shame Olivia wasn't full face to the camera, because she's such a pretty girl, isn't she? Would you like the photo, Mr Brookes?'

Robert had wanted to rip it from the wall and tear it to shreds, but that wasn't going to help, and he might just need it.

'Thank you, Mrs Evans. I appreciate it. Do you have any others of my wife?'

But she hadn't. This was the only one.

He stared at it, but whichever path his mind travelled down, it came to dead end after dead end.

From where he was sitting against the headboard, he could see the road opposite. He had been watching the police knocking on doors, speaking to all the neighbours and sharing the fact that Olivia was missing. He knew what they would all be thinking.

Finally they had reached the house of Edith Preston directly opposite, and he was certain she'd have plenty to say. Whether it had any substance or not was another thing. He expected her to invite the policeman in, sit him down, and give him chapter and verse on her thoughts about the Brookes family, so it was a surprise when she stepped outside the front door and started to point.

Robert sat up further in the bed. What was she saying? She grabbed the policeman's sleeve and dragged him across to just in front of her sitting room window – probably to indicate where she had been standing, peering through the curtains as always. And then she pointed. First to the road, then to the drive. Then she did a funny twisty action with her finger: point and curl, point and curl. What was that about?

The policeman took out his notebook, and was clearly asking her to repeat everything, because she went through exactly the same hand movements again.

Mrs Preston continued to chat with the policeman for another five minutes without further gestures, until finally he walked down the drive grabbing his radio as he did so.

What the hell had the bitch said?

Robert was sure it would be something incriminating, and a memory nagged at the back of his mind. It was yesterday evening when he had gone back out to the car to get his suitcase. Mrs Preston had come across to say hello. But there was something else; he just hadn't been listening. Was it really only yesterday? What was it she'd said that hadn't made sense?

He couldn't remember clearly. His brain was exhausted – not just through lack of sleep, but through an overload of thoughts and feelings.

Robert swung his legs off the bed. He needed to do something.

He walked over to his wife's chest of drawers and randomly started to pull the drawers out and rummage around, not really expecting to find anything. His patience lasted two minutes. With a howl of torment, the rage that he'd been bottling up for hours got the better of him and he ripped each of the drawers from the chest and hurled them one at a time across the room. He moved to the wardrobe and yanked clothes from their hangers to fall in a heap on the floor. He kicked them as hard as he could, meeting no resistance from the soft fabrics. Robert sank to the floor by the side of the bed and wrapped his arms around his bent legs. Resting his head on his knees, he finally gave in to deep wrenching sobs, trying – but failing – to thrust all feelings of guilt from his mind.

18

The press release had generated a higher number of responses than Becky had been expecting, but most of them were a waste of time with lots of people phoning to say that a woman with three children had turned up in their street or town. Of course, when questioned in any detail, the children were the wrong ages or ethnicity but it was going to be pretty difficult for this particular family grouping to go unnoticed for long, and it might still prove to be a valuable line of enquiry. Eventually.

If only somebody had a photograph of these children. They hadn't had much luck tracking down pictures from children's parties, and until school was back on Monday it was proving to be a bit of a thankless task. The best they had at the moment was Billy doing a handstand against a wall and pulling a silly face.

In spite of all the problems, Becky was delighted to be running this investigation. It felt like a great opportunity for her to win the respect of the team, and she was determined not to fail. Telling Tom about Peter had been difficult, but the right thing to do. She wanted him to hear it from her perspective, and not pick up gossip from any of her ex-colleagues and senior officers at some national meeting or other. The pain of it all was starting to fade, and she was beginning to replace the feeling of desolation and self-loathing with one of relief.

Their affair had felt so wonderful at the time, but when Tom had mentioned the fact that she might have ended up with Peter for life, she had actually felt rather queasy at the thought. He would inevitably have fallen off his pedestal, and then what would she really have thought about him? When he ceased to be the powerful, sexy figure that prowled the corridors of the Met and became the person who left his underpants on the bathroom floor and fell asleep every night watching the news with his mouth open, was there enough in their relationship for it to last?

Glad to have something better to think about, she dragged her mind back to the here and now. The case was her focus.

She heard a subtle cough and looked up to see one of the young PCs standing by her desk. She had no idea how long he'd been there.

'Sorry, Nic. I was miles away. Trying to get inside Olivia Brookes' head. What can I do for you?'

'It's about the passports, ma'am. Mr Brookes said they – that's his wife and children – don't have any, but we decided to check anyway. He was lying. Both Mrs Brookes and Jasmine have passports, both acquired in the last eighteen months. There's nothing for the younger children, though. I thought you'd like to know.'

Becky frowned. Was Robert lying, or did he know nothing about these passports? And if Olivia had gone abroad, what about the other two children? She bit her bottom lip in concentration.

Noticing that Nic was still standing in front of her, she looked up.

'Something else?'

Nic nodded, an enthusiastic smile on his young face. She was beginning to wonder if she had finally reached the age when policemen look as if they should still be in short trousers. This one definitely did.

'We've had some feedback from the house-to-house. Mostly dull and uninteresting, but the lady who lives opposite had plenty to say on the subject. There are two items that might be relevant. First of all, she swears Robert Brookes came home in the early hours of Thursday morning. She says it was at about two o'clock. According to her, something must have knocked the Brookes' security lights askew, because in the last couple of weeks she's been woken a few times by the full beam shining into her bedroom instead of on to their garden. The first time it happened, it was a fox. But on Wednesday night – or rather Thursday morning – it was definitely Robert Brookes' car. The car's fairly distinctive, and she says he left it on the drive and went into the house. She was just going to sleep when the light came on again, but she ignored it that time. When it went off for a third time, though, she got up again to see what on earth was going on – just in time to see Mr Brookes driving his car into the garage. It happened again last night when he went on his little jaunt to Anglesey, but we know about that.'

Becky made a note on her pad. This was very odd. Robert had been adamant that he hadn't left the hotel in Newcastle. Originally they had been interested in his movements during the first week – the week that it was claimed he had visited his wife in Anglesey. But now it was the second week that Nic was talking about, and this put a new spin on things.

They would have to look again. It would be better to check if his car left the car park on Wednesday night before accusing him of anything, though. That CCTV footage had to be a priority.

'Go on, Nic. What else was there?'

'It appears Mrs Preston is a nosey old soul. The week before, when Mrs Brookes was in Anglesey, Mrs Preston had gone round the side of the Brookes' garage. There's a narrow path there that she pointed out to us. She said she was putting the Brookes' dustbin back. It had been by the gate since Friday night; presumably Mrs Brookes had put it there for collection while she was away, and Mrs Preston said it was making the road look shabby. Anyway, there's a small window in the side of the garage, and she looked in. The car – the little Beetle Mrs Brookes has – was there. Mrs Preston had seen no signs of life in the house for the previous few days, so she knocked on the door and nobody answered. She said she checked the garage every day after that, and the car never moved. When she looked on Thursday morning, she expected to see Robert Brookes' car there too – but it had gone.'

Becky steepled her fingers and rested her chin. 'Do you know if the bin was left out for collection this week?'

'No. Mrs Preston says she didn't see it, but it doesn't mean much because she was out all Tuesday morning, so Mrs Brookes could have wheeled it out and back herself.'

'Okay, that's good work. Tell me what you make of it, Nic?' Becky had her own ideas, but she was from the Tom Douglas school of thought: no such thing as a bad idea.

'Well, ma'am, if Mrs Brookes was in Anglesey for the first week, how did she get there without her car?'

19

The annoying sound of his phone vibrating on the desk jolted Tom out of his meandering thoughts. He was struggling to find any direction to follow in this case. But his irritation evaporated when he saw who was calling.

Leo.

'Hi Leo. Did you see I phoned you earlier?'

'I did, but that's not why I'm calling,' she replied, her quiet voice and matter-of-fact tone making it clear this was not the call of a woman to her lover. 'At least, it's not the only reason.'

Of course not. That would make her appear too available. Tom smiled and waited for her to speak.

'I've got some bad news for you, I'm afraid.' Tom leaned forwards and rested his elbows on the desk. If Leo said it was bad news, then it wouldn't be anything trivial.

'It seems somebody broke into your cottage last night,' she continued, her tone softening. 'I'm sorry, Tom. I'm sure you need this like a hole in the head. Anyway, according to Ellie and Max, the alarm didn't go off. They would have heard it for sure, because they always sleep with the windows open. They were going out somewhere about half an hour ago, and as they drove past your place they noticed one of your windows seemed to be open, and there were bits of paper and other debris flying around. So they went to take a look.'

Ellie was Leo's sister and she lived next door to Tom's weekend cottage in Cheshire. She and her husband Max kindly kept an eye on the place while Tom was in Manchester – which seemed to be most of the time these days.

Leo hadn't finished.

'They've called the local police, and your old mate Steve has just arrived. He probably decided to make it his business when he heard whose house it was. Ellie and Max are still there, but they weren't sure if it was okay to call about a personal matter while you're working, so thought they should ask me first. I offered to pass on the news.'

Leo was right. This was all Tom needed. It wasn't that there was anything particularly valuable in the house. There were a couple of paintings that his brother had bought as investments, but as far as he was aware nobody knew he had them and he was sure most people wouldn't know by looking at them that they were worth anything.

'What did they take, Leo. Has Max had a chance to have a look?'

'Well, that's the thing really. He said nothing seems to be missing – at least, from a cursory glance around the place. He would have expected them to take some of the more portable stuff, like your fancy iPod player, or some of your more techie bits and pieces from the study. But although it's clear that they were in there – there are papers strewn everywhere – they've ignored all the obvious things.'

'And the alarm didn't go off?'

'So Ellie and Max said. And they would definitely have heard it. I know you set it when you left, because I was with you. Max told me he hasn't been in since then. He's just done what he calls his external patrol to check there's no sign of any problems.'

'I can't believe the alarm is faulty – it's brand new. And I didn't choose a cowboy firm to fit it, either.'

'Max wondered if you took files about some of your cases home, and perhaps that was what they were after as it seems they were only interested in your papers.'

That didn't make sense to Tom.

'On the odd occasion that I take files home, I always bring them back the next day. I sometimes make my own notes, but nothing that would be any use to anybody else.' He paused to consider what to do. 'Listen, Leo – it's a bit manic here today. Could you do me a favour and phone Max back and just ask if he wouldn't mind securing the house? I'll have a word with Steve about the alarm to see if his guys know why it didn't go off, but I'm not going to be able to get down there until this case is a bit clearer.'

'No problem. Consider it done. Bye for now,' Leo responded.

'Wait a minute, Leo.' Tom could have kicked himself. Why did he always make all the running? 'I called earlier to say it was likely to be a late one tonight, but if you don't mind shopping for some ingredients, I'll happily come round and cook us both a late supper. What do you think?'

'Sounds like a plan,' Leo said in exactly the same tone of voice as she had used to discuss the break-in. Tom would have loved to hear a note of pleasure, but at least she hadn't sounded bored by the idea. 'Send me a list and I'll see you when I see you.'

'Okay, I'll text it to you when I've got a minute. See you later.'

Tom hung up, his mind doing somersaults as it switched between Olivia Brookes, the break-in at his cottage and Leonora Harris.

Although he had more important things to worry about, Tom knew he wouldn't be able to focus until he had spoken to his friend Steve Corby, an inspector in the Cheshire police, to get his take on what had happened at the cottage. They had a brief conversation after he ended the call to Leo, and it seemed the intruders knew what they were doing. They got in by removing a pane of glass from the study window so it didn't trigger the contacts, and they had managed to disable the alarm once they were inside. The only reason papers had been strewn everywhere was because they didn't replace the glass and it had been blowing a bit of a gale in Cheshire the night before.

Thankfully, Max had taken on the task of getting the place secured, and Tom would have to try to get down there as soon as he got a day off. Perhaps he could persuade Leo to go with him. It would at least give her an opportunity to see her sister.

He had no idea what burglars could be looking for in his house. Perversely, he felt more unsettled by that than he would have been if anything of value had been taken. But there was nothing else he could do for the moment, and he was relieved to switch his mind back to somebody else's problems.

He pushed open the door to the incident room and cast his eyes around. Everybody seemed to be occupied, and Becky was busy chatting to one of the young PCs. She was looking serious, so perhaps they had caught a break.

'What's up, Becky? Have we got something?'

She frowned and gave a slight nod, walking towards her desk. Tom kept pace.

'It's probably nothing, but Mrs Evans just called from Anglesey and left a message. The local guys gave her my number. She'd like to speak to somebody in charge, preferably a lady policeperson – her words, apparently.'

'Maybe she's just remembered something. Why the worried look?' Tom asked.

'Nic took the call and he said she sounded as if she was crying. She was really distressed. I'm not worried. I'm just wondering what on earth would make her cry. I guess I'd better find out.'

Becky sat down at her desk and consulted the message that Nic had given her. She picked up her phone and dialled. Tom took the seat opposite and listened to what Becky was saying, but it wasn't very enlightening.

'There's no need to get upset, Mrs Evans. I'm sure you haven't done anything wrong at all. No, really – it's fine. Just tell me what happened and what was said.'

Becky's side of the conversation was peppered with long pauses, but after a couple of minutes she looked up at Tom with wide open eyes.

'You've done really well, Mrs Evans. Thank you for telling us, and don't worry about a thing. Do you have a copy of the photograph?'

Photograph? Could they finally be in luck and have a picture of these children?

'Can you let me have the name of the person who sent it to you, then – and contact details if possible. That would be a huge help. Yes, I've got a pen. And something to write on.' Becky looked at Tom and shook her head with a small smile. 'Yes, I've got that, Mrs Evans. Don't worry. No, you don't need to repeat it. And if I've got any questions, I'll call you back. Thank you, and please don't upset yourself any more. You've done the right thing.'

Becky hung up, and Tom looked at her expectantly.

'Just give me two minutes to brief somebody, and I'll be with you,' Becky said, pushing her seat back. 'I need to pay Mr Brookes another visit. If you're coming, I'll tell you on the way.' Becky walked quickly over to Ryan, who appeared to be the only person not on the phone, passed him the note and gave him some rapid instructions that Tom couldn't hear.

'Ready?' she asked, picking up her bag and keys. Her movements were brisk and purposeful, and there was a determination about her that hadn't been there before.

'Ready,' replied Tom. Whatever Mrs Evans had told Becky, her eyes were glinting with anger.

20

Becky had clearly decided she was driving, and marched towards her car without giving Tom a chance to express an opinion. He couldn't avoid getting in her car forever though, and at least the roads were marginally less chaotic than the London streets in which he had first experienced her rather manic style of driving. As she drove, Becky repeated everything Mrs Evans had told her, punctuating each indignant comment by swerving round another car or slamming her foot hard on the brakes as she realised she was about to have a head-on collision with a vehicle coming the opposite way.

'So, what do you think?' she asked, when she had completed the story, totally unperturbed by the number of near misses.

Hanging on to the grab handle in an effort to maintain his balance, Tom hoped he had managed to absorb the key points.

'Apart from the fact that Brookes is a bastard, I think it sounds highly suspicious. How do you want to play this?'

Becky chewed her bottom lip. 'Well, I'm happy to question him, but actually I think he sees you as more of a threat than me. I've seen the way he looks at you – he doesn't know what you're thinking, but I'm just a dumb woman, unworthy of his concern. If you're up for it, I think you should question him. I'll watch and listen – see if there's anything I can pick up on.'

Tom had been hoping she would say that, but didn't want to bamboozle her. There was no time to discuss it further, though, as he realised with some relief that they had arrived at their destination. The car skidded to a standstill at the bottom of the Brookes' drive.

'I don't think we should muddy the water with the information about the laptops or the passports just yet,' Becky said. 'I want to get a clear reaction from him when we tell him what Mrs Evans said to me.'

Tom nodded his agreement as they walked from the car to the top of the drive. There was a sudden grating sound of metal scraping on something solid.

'Christ – that noise went right through me. What the hell is it?' Becky said, screwing up her face.

'Sounds like the neighbour's not quite got the measure of that digger he's driving,' Tom answered with a smile. No doubt the guy thought he could save money by doing a job himself that would be best left to the experts. A loud expletive came from next door as the sound of machinery came to an abrupt halt. The digger seemed to have cut out.

Robert opened the door within seconds of their knock, as if he'd been watching for somebody to arrive. He looked truly dreadful.

'Do you have any news?' he asked. His eyes looked dull and lifeless, and Tom couldn't read their expression.

'I'm not sure, sir. We haven't found your wife and children, I'm afraid. But there have been some developments.'

Robert opened the door fully, and indicated that they should come in. His face had returned to what Tom now recognised as a fairly habitual scowl with his chin lowered towards his chest. When looking at Tom, he just raised his eyes, and there was something slightly eerie about the expression.

Robert stood in the centre of the hallway, not suggesting that they come in or sit down, only closing the door fully when the digger started up again.

'Well?' he said.

'Earlier this morning, you went to see Mrs Evans at the guest house in Anglesey,' Tom stated.

Robert pushed his hands into his trouser pockets and leaned casually against the wall. 'You already knew that. We've spoken since then.'

'I know, Mr Brookes. But could you tell us what you said to Mrs Evans, please?'

Tom could see a slight stiffening of Robert's body. He must have guessed they knew more than they did earlier.

'I wanted to find out why she'd said I'd visited Olivia ten days ago when I knew for a fact that I hadn't. She confirmed that she'd never seen me before.'

'But she didn't see *who* the visitor was. She was never introduced.'

'She may not have been introduced, Chief Inspector, but she's a seaside landlady. She saw exactly who visited – and she knows it wasn't me.'

'Really. And what else did she tell you?'

'What do you mean?' Robert tried to look confused, but failed.

'Come on, Mr Brookes. Stop playing games. She told you that whoever was *claiming* to be Robert Brookes stayed the night in your wife's room. She told you that, didn't she? It wasn't a visitor for some other guest. It was a visitor for your wife.'

Robert's mouth settled into a hard line, his casual stance replaced with a defiant pose – legs apart, arms folded.

'And did you expect me to repeat it? Did you expect me to admit that another man had apparently slept with my wife?'

'If it's true, then frankly, yes,' Tom answered. 'You claim you want your wife and children found, so don't you think it was quite a vital piece of information?'

Robert didn't answer.

'Not only did you avoid telling us this, but you also asked Mrs Evans not to tell us. In fact, from what she's said to us, you threatened her.'

Robert scoffed. 'Hardly a threat, Chief Inspector. I asked her to say nothing. I wanted to protect Olivia's reputation.'

'You threatened Mrs Evans' livelihood. Physical violence isn't the only form of intimidation, Mr Brookes, and saying you would slam her business on every review website, which is where most of her customers find her, and call it a "house of ill-repute", which I am sure are her words, not yours, was a dirty trick.'

Robert's eyes darted from Tom to Becky and back. But he didn't speak.

'How long have you known your wife was having an affair? And just how mad did it make you?'

'She wasn't having an affair. She wouldn't...' Robert stopped mid sentence.

'Were you about to say, "She wouldn't dare," Mr Brookes?' Tom asked.

Robert lifted his hand and scratched his head. Tom knew he was rattled. He opened the file in his hand and took out a photograph, but held it face side down for the moment.

'You may have got Mrs Evans to tell us that she made a mistake. You may even have managed to convince yourself that she really *did* get it wrong, and the visitor was to another guest room. But there's one thing you *were* right about. She did sneak a look at who was going up her staircase. She told us something she didn't dare tell you – that the man who slept in your wife's room was of a non-white ethnic origin. She wasn't quite sure where he was from – either Middle Eastern or maybe mixed race were her best guesses. Does that mean something to you? Does it suggest to you who it might be?'

Robert shook his head. 'Of course not. I think she's making this up as she goes along.'

Tom turned over the photograph that Becky had provided en route.

'Do you recognise this person, Mr Brookes?' he asked.

Robert looked at the photo, and his lips narrowed into a thin line.

'Yes.'

'Could you please identify who you believe this to be?'

Robert paused, and when he spoke it seemed to be with great difficulty.

'It's Danush Jahander.' He looked at Tom with cold flat eyes. 'Why are you showing me a picture of him?'

'How well did you know Danush Jahander,' Tom asked.

Robert shook his head.

'Never met the guy. I've seen his photo, though. When I first met Olivia, the flat was full of pictures of him. Like a shrine, it was.'

'You bought that flat from your wife – that's right, isn't it?' Tom asked.

'Yes, it's how we met.'

'But it seems that all three of you went to Manchester University – that's certainly where your wife met Mr Jahander. Did you not know them there?'

Robert's mouth curled up at one side in a sneer.

'Do you have any idea how many students there are at Manchester University, Chief Inspector? I was a nerd – obsessed by computers. I didn't really become human until I started work and realised I would actually have to communicate if I wanted to achieve anything in this life. Then I met Olivia, and she turned me into the family man I am now. Why are you asking me about Jahander, anyway? He's long gone.'

'Would you be surprised if I told you that Danush Jahander may have been the man visiting your wife in Anglesey?'

The tension in Robert's face appeared to evaporate and Tom saw something akin to amusement in his eyes.

'Is that funny, sir?'

Robert looked down.

'Not funny at all. No. But he disappeared years ago. He's never been heard of since, as far as I'm aware. He's hardly likely to have turned up in Anglesey of all places, is he?'

'He hadn't disappeared altogether. It seems his brother has had some contact with him.'

Robert's head shot up. This was clearly news he was not expecting at all. His eyes narrowed, but he said nothing.

'There's something else we'd like to discuss with you. Do you think we could sit down?' Tom asked.

Robert shook his head. 'No need. I'm fine standing up. Just tell me.'

'Okay – tell me about your trips to Anglesey. How many times have you been, and where did you stay?'

Robert blew out a long breath through pursed lips, as if he thought the question irrelevant.

'We've been going for years. We used to stay at a guest house in Moelfre. Sometimes I went, and other times Olivia went alone with the children if I was working. It was a safe place for her. The landlady knew us well.'

'Tell me again why you changed to the guest house in Cemaes Bay?'

'I'm sure I've told you all this – when Olivia tried to book last October, after our summer holiday, she got an answerphone message to say that the B&B was closed for the foreseeable future due to illness. She passed me the phone so I could hear it for myself. It was a voice we didn't recognise, so we guessed it was the landlady who was ill. Olivia did some scouting round and found the new place. I checked it out online, and I was due to go with them in the summer.'

'So Olivia has visited there three times without you – October, Easter and last week – and you had never been there until the early hours of Saturday morning? Is that correct?'

'Yes. I've told you all of this.'

'Was Oak Cottage the guest house in Moelfre?' Tom asked.

'I don't remember telling you that, but yes, it was.'

'You didn't tell us, Mr Brookes. We had the local police check out the various options, and they confirmed it.'

'So why are you asking me then?'

'Would it surprise you to hear that the guest house is open for business, and the landlady was disappointed when your wife cancelled the bookings for this year? She hasn't been ill at all, and appears as hearty as ever.'

Robert's brows knitted together.

'Perhaps she changed her mind about taking bookings – it's a possibility, isn't it?'

'Or perhaps your wife needed to change guest houses so she could entertain her lover. If the landlady had met you before, that wouldn't have been possible.'

'That's a ridiculous idea,' Robert scoffed.

'Is it? We also understand from Mrs Evans that she had a picture of your wife, and you took it. You are fully aware that we haven't got any photos of your wife or children, and that we've been very keen to find something we can issue to the press. Why did you keep the photo from us?'

Robert was looking increasingly uncomfortable, and didn't appear to have an answer. He looked down at the floor.

'Could you get the photograph for us now, please. We'd like to take it with us and have copies made. We'll return it to you as soon as possible.'

Tom was shocked by the expression on Robert's face when he looked up. His eyes were narrowed and his mouth had tightened further. Robert's voice was quiet, but harsh.

'I don't have the photograph. I tore it up.'

21

Robert thought the police would never go. He'd kept them standing in the hall, but it hadn't made any difference. The Chief Inspector had found it difficult to contain his anger when Robert told him he had destroyed the photo, and that DI Robinson seemed to be studying him as if he were something on a petri dish.

He grabbed the keys from the kitchen table and went into his study, booting the computer up on his way past and making his way over to the bookcase while he waited for the operating system to spring into life. He didn't think he'd got much time. Shifting a load of books to one side, he prised open the bookcase's false back and retrieved the leather covered document case from where it had been hidden since the day they had moved into this house. He hammered the plywood back into place with the heel of his hand, then put the books back. He stuck the document case into a bag, and picked up the phone.

'Taxi, please. Can you pick me up in twenty minutes from outside St Peter's Church on Broom Road?' He paused. 'The name's Paul Brown. Thank you.'

Looking anxiously at his watch, he clicked on an icon on the lower left side of his screen and a video window opened. He just wanted one more look. There she was: walking around the kitchen, doing normal everyday things, emptying the dishwasher, making a cup of tea. She was so very beautiful. He wasn't sure he could bear to delete this file – and every similar file on his computer – but he knew he'd have to.

Suddenly there was a crackle and the screen went black.

What the…?

He reached over to the desk lamp and pressed the button. Nothing. A fuse must have gone. *Shit.*

Robert walked hurriedly through to the kitchen and wrestled with the door into the garage. He pushed past the bonnet of Olivia's car to get to the fuse box and looked inside. All the switches were up.

'Christ,' he muttered. 'A power cut, in this day and age?'

He'd have to check if the whole street was out, or if it was just their house. This was the last thing he needed, and he could practically feel his blood pressure rising.

Flinging open the front door, he marched down the drive and out into the road. He stood still, arms akimbo, and turned around to see if anybody else was looking bemused. At least next door's digger was quiet for the first time this weekend.

Seeing his neighbour peering into the hole he had dug, with one hand on his hip and the other scratching his head, Robert called out to him.

'Have you lost power just now, or is it only me?'

'Oh, bugger. It's cut you off too, has it? Sorry, mate. My fault, I'm afraid. How are you, anyway? Any news on Olivia? I bet this is the last thing you need. I'm really sorry.'

Feeling the tension in him explode like an overfilled balloon, Robert stomped up his neighbour's path.

'What do you mean it's your fault? What the fuck have you done, you idiot?'

The neighbour looked at him in surprise.

'Calm down, Robert. It seems I've just accidentally sliced through the electricity cable. Donna's calling them now. I'm sure they'll give it priority. Sorry for the inconvenience. Especially now.'

The whole street would inevitably know about Olivia – the policemen going door to door this morning would have seen to that. *Shit.* He'd never had much time for his jerk of a neighbour, but now he just wanted to grab him round the throat and throttle him.

'Do you have any idea how important it is that I get my computer online now – this very second?' he yelled. He couldn't fail to see the shock in his neighbour's face, immediately replaced by an air of belligerence.

'Stop shouting the odds at me. It was an accident, that's all. Yelling's not going to solve anything.'

'Fucking imbecile!' Robert shouted as he turned back towards the house. But his neighbour wanted the last word and took two steps to follow Robert before stopping and shouting.

'Excuse *me*. If it wasn't for your bastard leylandii pushing out roots that have completely destroyed my drive, none of this would have been necessary. But I never said a word. Jesus – I'm not surprised Olivia had issues.'

Robert swivelled back round and was sorely tempted to punch the guy's teeth in, but Donna was watching from the doorway, her mouth open. She'd surely phone the police immediately if he started a fight and, given that one of their number was sitting up the road, watching the show from his car, it wouldn't take them long to get here either. He didn't have time for this. Without another word, he spun on his heel and stomped back into the house.

Taking the stairs two at a time, he dashed up to his bedroom, grabbing another bag from the spare room on the way past and trampling on Olivia's clothes that were strewn around the room. Pulling open drawers he took the minimum that he would need. He wouldn't be able to use his credit card after he left town, so he would have to withdraw the maximum on each of his four cards on the way through. That should keep him going for a while. He'd take a taxi to the office and nick one of the pool cars. Nobody would miss it until Monday, if then. He'd sign it out to somebody who was on holiday.

He picked up the photograph he had taken from Mrs Evans' wall. He didn't need it any more, but he wasn't going to leave it here for the police to find.

Now that he had a plan, he suddenly felt calm. There was just the computer. But when he thought about it, nothing on there was really incriminating. The police wouldn't understand, but that was their problem.

Two minutes later, he was packed and gone – out through the doors to the terrace, down the back garden, over the fence and into the field.

22

Sunday

As far as Tom Douglas was concerned, Sunday was just another day in the week. He'd never really thought about weekends being any different because criminals certainly didn't decide to give it a rest on Saturday and Sunday, so he was back in the incident room by seven thirty in the morning.

He could have done with making a trip to Cheshire to sort out whatever had been going on at his cottage, but Olivia Brookes and her three children were still missing and there was something about this that he just didn't like the smell of at all. He'd gone round to Leo's at the tail end of what had seemed like an interminable day yesterday, and that had left him feeling even more tired and frustrated. On the one hand, she had been sympathy itself with regard to his cottage and had volunteered to go there today and do some sorting out for him. But on the other, all he'd wanted to do was to take her to bed, make love to her and sleep soundly next to her naked body all night. And, for just a moment, he had thought they were making progress.

She'd bought the simple ingredients he needed for chicken in mascarpone and white wine sauce – something he could knock together in minutes, and cooking always relaxed him. He loved Leo's loft apartment: the openness of it, the warmth of the bare brick that made up one wall, and the sturdy beams holding the whole place together. In one of the many old converted warehouses of Manchester, this renovation had been done with real style, and Leo was gradually stamping her own personality on it.

As he'd cooked, he had talked to Leo where she sat curled up on the sofa, the glass of red wine she was holding almost matching the dark stain of her lipstick. Since the first time he had met her, he didn't think he had ever seen Leo wear any colour at all. She always wore black and white, but somehow in the most amazing combinations. The only colour came from her lipstick, or the occasional chunky red necklace, or a deep red nail polish on her toes but never her fingers. Tonight she was wearing figure-hugging white trousers with a sleeveless black-and-white striped top that hung loose but somehow managed to simultaneously mould itself to her figure as she moved. Her long ebony hair was wavy tonight, the way he preferred it, and she had been giving him all her attention as he browned the chicken in olive oil and told her about his day.

'So what's your gut feel, Tom? Forget the evidence for a moment. You're usually so good at seeing past the obvious.' Leo had said.

'There's something intrinsically wrong about Robert Brookes. Well, to be honest, it's not just Robert. It's the whole set up. I met Olivia – the missing woman – almost nine years ago.' Tom described his past encounters with Olivia and her family as he added the white wine and a couple of bay leaves to the pan and started to chop the tarragon. 'The trouble is, I never really bought it that it was an accident that killed her parents. And neither did Olivia.'

'So what did you do about it?' Leo had asked, not unreasonably.

'Nothing.' He'd seen Leo frown and realised that this didn't sound like the Tom Douglas she knew. 'Look, I tried. But nobody had anything to gain from their deaths except Olivia as far as we could tell. And she was devastated. She was the most vocal in saying it couldn't have been an accident. She kept repeating over and over again that her father was obsessed with alarms. And she was right. The burglar alarm was state of the art and they had more smoke alarms than I've ever seen in a house.'

Tom had poured in the chicken stock and given everything a stir.

'The scene-of-crime boys could find nothing at all. The burglar alarm had been switched off, which according to Olivia wasn't unusual when they were in the house. But there was no sign of forced entry. We had to let it go.'

'Was Olivia married by this time?' Leo had asked.

'No. She'd only just met Robert, but he was waiting at her old flat and he called to find out what was keeping her. He got me at the other end of the line. When I told him what had happened, he rushed straight over to see what he could do to help.'

Judging that the sauce had reduced enough, Tom had whisked in the mascarpone and added the tarragon and some black pepper.

'For some reason, I was never satisfied. We did wonder if the Iranian boyfriend had something to do with it, but we couldn't find anything to support that theory, and anyway nobody knew where he was.'

Tom knew Leo was fascinated by everything to do with his work, particularly since she had decided to go back to university. When he met her, Leo was a life coach – and a good one at that – in spite of, or perhaps because of, her natural aloofness and her ability to withdraw and view things without emotion. The fact that this extended to her own life, leaving her appearing cold and distant, was beside the point. But Leo had finally been persuaded to take her sister's offer of some money – just enough to pay her way through a university course – and study psychology. She'd already decided she wanted to be a forensic psychologist, although she had many years of studying ahead before she would achieve that goal. Maybe because of this, she was always keen to listen to Tom and try to understand more of the criminal mind. But dinner was ready, and he'd wanted to relax.

'Enough. No more work – let's eat.'

Leo had jumped up eagerly from the sofa. She might not like to cook, but she certainly liked to eat. Glancing at her plate of food and then up at Tom, a lascivious smile had lit up her face and, as she'd picked up her knife and fork, she'd leaned towards him slightly.

'You're the best, Tom Douglas. So much more than just a pretty face.'

That was one thing he hadn't been called before, but if she was dishing out compliments he was happy to take them.

The conversation over their meal had been light-hearted. Leo had chatted about spending her whole day failing to find the perfect lamp for the corner of the living room and given Tom's look of horror at such a waste of time, she had teased him about his attitude to shopping in general but furniture shopping in particular. Tom never made any bones about the fact that he was clueless when it came to interior design, and had paid a company to sort the house out for him here in Manchester just as he had in Cheshire. Leo thought that was madness, and had selected every piece in her apartment with huge care.

Listening to her soft voice, laughter bubbling just below the surface as the gentle banter continued, Tom had begun to feel the cares of the day drain away. Inevitably they had spoken about the break-in at his home but, with Leo's promise of driving over there in the morning, Tom was able to push it to the back of his mind.

Music had been playing softly in the background. He didn't even notice who was singing, but the voices were gentle and soothing. One track grabbed his attention. He had heard it before, but a long time ago and the voice was haunting.

'Who's this, Leo?'

'Judy Tzuke. It's called "Stay With Me Till Dawn". I know it's really old, but it was my mum's all-time favourite record. She used to sing it when she was washing up.'

The title of the song had taken Tom's breath away, and he would have loved to think it was significant, but somehow he knew how the evening was going to end. Pretty much like every other evening they spent together. The attraction between them sparkled fiercely. Every touch sent ripples of tension through Tom's body and he was sure it was the same for Leo. But she always pulled back at the last moment.

Reluctantly, he had stood up from the sofa, ready to leave. Leo had reached out a hand and grabbed his arm.

'Stay, Tom,' she'd said.

He'd looked down at her and reached out with his other hand to wrap a thick strand of her silky hair around his fingers.

'And tomorrow?' he'd asked.

Leo had just shrugged, and he felt the momentary weakness sucked back into her body, armour back in place. He knew what that meant. He could spend the night loving her, falling deeper into her trap, and tomorrow it would be as if nothing had happened. As if they were back to being friends, with the occasional overnight stay being at Leo's whim. It wasn't the first time she'd asked him to stay but, tempting as it was, he had managed to resist. So far.

He bent down and brushed his lips over her brow, tilted her chin with his hand and gently kissed her on the mouth. He felt, rather than heard, a slight groan and she closed her eyes for just a second. She leaned in towards him and he'd placed his hands under her elbows and lifted her to her feet. She pressed the length of her lean body against his.

'Tomorrow?' he'd asked again, his lips close to her ear.

He felt Leo's back stiffen slightly.

'I don't do tomorrows. You know that.'

There had been no other option but to release her. Something had to happen soon, though. This was fast becoming unbearable. If he gave in, and God knows he wanted to, this would forever be an unbalanced relationship with Leo calling the shots. He had to wait until she was truly ready, or walk away, difficult as that would be.

So now here he was on a sunny Sunday morning, aching with

frustration and knowing that – rightly or wrongly – he was completely smitten with a woman who would never commit to more than a single night.

'Morning, boss. You look a million miles away. Good night, was it?' Tom came back down to earth with a bump. He should have known Becky would be in early too, and as he shook himself back into the here and now he was pleased to see that a little more of Becky's naturally ebullient nature and slightly sassy attitude seemed to be resurfacing.

'A confusing night, if I'm honest. I've been mulling over everything we've learned, and I don't know what to make of Robert Brookes or the whole situation. If he discovered his wife was sleeping with somebody else, perhaps he's the sort of nutter who would do her some serious damage. But if that's the case, where are the children? Can we do a check to see if he owns any other property – because if they're not all dead, he could be hiding them somewhere.'

'Well, you know what I think. I don't know how, when or why, but he's killed her. I just hope the kids are safe.'

The room was slowly filling up as Becky spoke, most people yawning as they walked towards their desks. Until they found these children they all knew they were in for some long days. Computers were being switched on, messages checked. The incident room was slowly coming back to life.

From the corner of his eye, Tom saw Ryan Tippetts punch the air. 'Yay,' he shouted.

Grabbing something off the printer, he smiled and strolled over to Tom, waving the sheet of paper that Tom could see had a photo on it.

'DCI Douglas. As always, good police work has paid off.' His expression radiated self-satisfaction.

Tom merely nodded and waited, doubtful that Ryan had done anything on his own initiative.

'I spent most of yesterday afternoon trying to contact the woman who took the photo of our Olivia in Anglesey.' Ryan was nodding his head slightly and turning from side to side as if playing to the audience.

Tom thought he looked like a skinny-faced version of one of those Churchill dogs in the back of a car window.

'And?' Tom prompted.

'It looks like finally I've hit the jackpot.'

Ryan held out a photo.

Tom and Becky looked at it, and then up at Ryan.

'It's not the best photo in the world, as you can see. Olivia was turning back to avoid the snap – or that's what the woman who took it said – but you get about three quarters of her face. Enough for somebody to recognise her. So, we can use this for the press, can't we?'

With his eyes on Ryan's self-satisfied face, Tom held his hand out for the photo. He looked down, just to confirm what he knew already.

'Ryan, am I right in thinking that you met Olivia Brookes about nine years ago with me, and then again two years ago with Detective Superintendent Stanley?'

'Yeah – seem to always be in the shit don't they, this family?'

'Look at the photo, Ryan. Is this Olivia Brookes?' Tom asked.

'Well, according to the woman who took it, yes. This is the one she sent to the landlady, the one that Robert Brookes snaffled.'

Ryan was beginning to look a little puzzled, his thunder stolen in some way that as yet he didn't appear to have grasped.

'Is this the woman you met two years ago, DC Tippetts? Look again.' Tom was barely keeping his anger in check.

'Well, now you mention it, she does look a bit different – but women always make themselves up to look different, don't they?'

Tom turned away in disgust.

'Grab your keys, Becky. I've no idea who this is, but even after nine years I can tell you without a shadow of a doubt, this is *not* Olivia Brookes.'

23

The incident room was buzzing with theories and Becky had asked Tom to stay and brief the team while she went to see Robert. She needed confirmation that this picture was a copy of the photo Robert had taken from Mrs Evans, and she also needed to ask him if he knew who this woman was, and why she might be impersonating Olivia. More to the point, why the hell hadn't he told them? At least she now understood why Robert hadn't seemed more upset by his wife's apparent infidelity. If Olivia wasn't the one at the guest house, what did it matter who had come to visit?

Robert Brookes had been hiding too much from them, and as soon as they knew what excuses he had concocted for failing to give them all the facts, they were going to make a decision about next steps. It might be time for Mr Brookes to be formally interviewed. They hadn't got enough to arrest him, so he'd be able to leave at any time – and Becky had no doubt that Robert Brookes would choose that option. She was going to get him, though. Whatever he'd done, he wasn't going to get away with it.

Becky felt better than she had done for months. The stupid, ridiculous relationship with Peter Hunter had left her badly shaken, and now that she was able to see things in some sort of perspective, she recognised she was more disturbed by the fact that she had fallen into the age-old trap of the older, powerful man and the young naive girl than she was by the fact that he had dumped her. And she wasn't that young, either. She should have known better, and was ashamed of her gullibility.

Tom had helped yesterday. He was so non-judgemental with people, probably because the sins of ordinary mortals were as nothing next to the iniquities they had to deal with in their job.

As she drove back towards Robert Brookes' house, Becky thought about the Tom she had first met all those years ago when he had been senior investigating officer in the Hugo Fletcher case. He'd seemed sad when he'd joined their team at the Met, and she could only surmise that this was because of his recent divorce. But he was so enthusiastic, and really geed up the team. As time had passed, though, his sadness hadn't diminished but his enthusiasm had. She'd started to notice a slight touch of cynicism in him that hadn't been there before, and she'd never entirely understood it – although perhaps the failure to solve a high-profile case had got to him. The good news was that the old Tom seemed to be back. The former disenchantment seemed to have disappeared, and he was as passionate as ever about the job.

Why couldn't she have fallen for Tom?

Becky snorted quietly. That would have been far too easy. Why fall for a tall, good-looking, single guy, who actually appears to care about other people, when you can have some middle-aged, married philanderer whose only interest seems to be in satisfying his own ego?

She turned the car down the narrow, tree-lined road that led to the Brookes' house. The individual styles of each property and the way they sat within their plots of land at slightly different angles to the narrow, bendy road made this one of the more interesting suburban streets. However blissful the location, though, Becky shivered slightly at the thought of facing Robert Brookes again. She gave herself a mental shake as she pulled her car on to the drive.

Despite being told by several neighbours the day before that both the Brookes' cars were normally kept in their large, attached brick garage, Robert's Jag was still on the drive. She was pleased she couldn't hear that dreadful digger today, although she could see the equipment was still outside the neighbour's house. Perhaps they'd decided to respect the peace of a Sunday morning.

Having radioed ahead and been informed that there had been no sign of Olivia Brookes returning during the night, she opened the car door. It was so *quiet*. All she could hear was the twittering of birds in the trees, and the distant hum of a lawnmower. She looked up and saw the curtains were open in what she knew to be Robert and Olivia's bedroom, so didn't feel too guilty about raising the knocker and giving three solid thumps of metal on metal.

Becky turned her back to the door as she waited, and looked across the road at the one house that had a view past the trees and shrubs and up the drive. The lady who lived there – Mrs Preston, if she remembered correctly – had been a useful source of information yesterday, and Becky could see why. Although she was standing back from the window, the good lady seemed to be unaware that the light coming through from the patio doors at the back of her sitting room was casting a clear profile of her image against the net curtains at the front. Becky smiled to herself and turned back towards the Brookes' front door. She banged again.

No answer.

Bugger, she thought. Perhaps he was in the shower or something. Or maybe he'd decided to ignore her.

There was a narrow path down the side of the garage to the back garden – no doubt the path Mrs Preston had taken to check on the Brookes' cars – and Becky decided to investigate. As she passed the garage she peered in to check that Olivia's car was still in place, and wasn't surprised that it was exactly where she'd last seen it. Tom had made an interesting observation, though. He'd said that for a woman with three children, at least two of whom would have to be in child seats, a two-door Beetle had to be the daftest car to choose. Did that suggest that Olivia was the sort of impetuous woman who didn't always think things through?

Round the back of the garage, Becky could see a door which she knew from a previous visit led into a utility room and then on into the kitchen. She tried the handle, but it was locked. She wandered further round to the rear of the house where huge glass doors allowed the morning sun to flood the large kitchen with light. This was Becky's idea of a dream kitchen – one she could cook in and eat in. There was even a comfy chair she could curl up in to read a book. As a room, it was almost a complete home in itself. But there was a sort of sterility here that she would have had to fix if it were hers. The worktops were devoid of clutter; there were no pictures on the walls – not even paintings by the children stuck on the front of the fridge with bright-coloured magnets. It was very chic, with its shiny cream units and black-granite worktop, but it seemed too bare and lifeless to be part of a home. Even the crockery in the glass-fronted wall cabinets was matching cream and black. She would want to add colour – a bright red free-standing mixer, some mad patterned salad bowls from somewhere Mediterranean, green and blue water glasses – anything to bring some life to the place.

There was nothing to see in the kitchen, though. No Robert Brookes, and no sign that he had eaten breakfast there, although Becky had to admit that if he had, he would no doubt have cleared his plates away and tidied up. It was that kind of kitchen.

She turned to look down the garden. It was enormous. The section closest to the house was laid with lawn, broken up by beautiful curved flower beds. A hedge of yew trees separated this part of the garden from the rest of the extensive plot, and Becky could just make out a climbing frame and a Wendy house beyond. Personally she'd have expected the children's area to be closer to the house so Olivia could keep an eye on them from the kitchen window, but the garden was quite spectacular and it must be heaven in the evenings, sitting on the wide stone-flagged terrace, sipping a glass of cold wine, surrounded by all these sweet-smelling flowers.

She turned back towards the house. Now what?

Not really expecting much, she decided to try the terrace door, just in case.

To her surprise, it slid silently open and she stepped inside the kitchen, closing the door behind her. There was an ominous stillness about the place. The windows cut out all sense of life outside these four walls, and Becky suddenly felt claustrophobic – something she had never experienced before. It was as if the air had settled immobile around her, and she couldn't breathe. She spun round and opened the glass doors as wide as she could and took a gulp of air.

'Get a grip, Becky,' she muttered under her breath. She turned round, half expecting to see the stationary figure of Robert Brookes framed in the doorway to the hall, gazing up at her from beneath his hooded eyelids. But there was nobody there. She breathed out and took a step further into the room.

'Mr Brookes,' she called out. Silence.

She ventured forwards, first into the living room, and then into the hallway. She called again. 'Mr Brookes.'

Nothing.

She had to go upstairs. She couldn't just stand here. For God's sake, she was a Detective *Inspector*. But this house gave her the creeps.

She tried the door to the study, and was staggered to find it unlocked. Unlocked, but empty. The only sign of life was the computer's screen saver flashing its multi-coloured images around the room.

Becky silently made her way up the stairs.

'Mr Brookes,' she called again. She pushed open each of the bedroom doors, and found them empty. Finally she reached the closed door at the front of the house. She knocked gently, and then more firmly, calling out yet again. 'It's Detective Inspector Robinson, Mr Brookes. Are you there?'

Finally, she turned the handle and pushed the door open.

With a gasp, she surveyed the wrecked room. What on earth had happened here? And where the hell was Robert?

24

Shoving supermarket bags randomly into the back of her car, Sophie Duncan realised she had been operating on autopilot. She had no idea whether she'd bought the right things or not, and had the horrible feeling that she would get home and realise she had forgotten something vital and have to come straight back again. She didn't mind shopping for food, though. It was largely a mindless exercise as far as she was concerned – she was no kitchen goddess – and she'd arrived just as the shops had been opening, so she'd managed to escape before the Sunday hordes turned up. Whatever had happened to the day of rest?

As she turned the key in the ignition, the local radio news came on. More about Olivia Brookes and her three children. Sophie felt the now familiar twinge of unease somewhere deep inside, but brushed it away. Olivia would be okay. She had to be.

It was now eighteen months since Olivia Brookes, or Liv Hunt as she would always be to Sophie Duncan, had turned up out of the blue after more than seven years of no communication, and it had to have been one of the best days Sophie could remember for quite a while. There had been a dearth of good days around that time, and she had been struggling to cope with the idea of being out of active service for the foreseeable future. Her body felt like it belonged to a stranger. Somebody feeble, and not at all like her. She was sick of the fact that it no longer obeyed her commands, and seemed to have a mind of its own.

But the day Liv came was a red-letter day, and she had momentarily forgotten her injuries.

When the doorbell had rung, Sophie's mum had started to struggle to her feet, but Sophie waved her hand in a flapping motion.

'Sit down, Mum. I need to move around, or I'll end up being desk-bound for the rest of my career.' Ignoring the predictable, 'And a good job too,' that her mother muttered, Sophie had slowly and steadily made her way to the front door of her mother's 1930s semi.

Opening the door, she had let out a shriek. 'Liv? Liv – is it really you? Oh my God. Oh my God. Let me look at you. I've missed you so much.'

There were tears in Liv's eyes as she had looked Sophie up and down and taken in the extent of her friend's injuries, so Sophie had done her best to lighten the moment by attempting a little twirl, raising her good arm in the air and shouting, 'Ta da!' as she spun round on the better of her two legs, nearly falling over.

'Oh, Soph – what happened? It said on the news that you were rescuing people from an attack on one of the dam projects when the bomb went off. Are you going to be okay?'

'Course I am. Just a bit of damage to various bits, but as long as they can get all the parts lined up and operational again, I'll be right as rain. Come on, Liv. Smile. I could be dead – as some of my mates already are.' For a moment, Sophie had thought she might lose it, but she'd had years of practice at keeping a smile on her face.

'Let's get you sat down, and then we can open a bottle. Any excuse, eh?' She'd dragged Liv into the sitting room, her arm around her friend's waist. 'Look who we've got here, Mum.'

'Ooh, Liv, you're a sight for sore eyes,' Sophie's mum, Margaret, had said. 'We've missed you, you know. Both of us.'

Sophie had seen a flash of guilt cross her friend's face and came to her rescue.

'Yes, well – we're both to blame. If I hadn't buggered off to the other end of the earth to fight somebody else's battles, things might have been different. Liv's been doing the grown-up stuff – getting married and having babies. I've been playing war games.'

It hadn't been anything like that at all, really. When she'd left Manchester – initially for officer training at Sandhurst, and then ultimately on her first deployment – she had done everything she could to keep in touch with Liv, but within weeks of Sophie leaving the country, her friend had stopped writing. She had always assumed it was because she hadn't been there for Liv when Dan went AWOL. She had literally been about to board a flight for Iraq at the time, though, and you can't tell the British Army that your best friend's upset so you're sorry, but you can't get on the plane.

There had been a couple of letters early on, up until the time when Liv's parents died – and then it all went quiet. Sophie had understood that the grief must have been so intense that maybe even writing a letter was too painful, so when she heard from her mother that Liv was marrying a man called Robert she had sent a card with a long note wishing the couple all the happiness in the world. That also had seemed to fall on deaf ears.

Sophie wasn't one to bear a grudge, though; life, as she well knew, was way too short for that, and at least Liv was here now, although the last seven years seemed to have aged her more than Sophie would have expected. The skin looked tight around her friend's eyes and mouth as if she didn't smile enough, and the bright light that used to shine from Liv seemed to have been reduced to a pale glow.

'Let me get the wine, and then we can settle down and have a good long catch up,' Sophie had said, limping towards the door.

'No wine for me, thanks, Sophie. I'm driving and I need to get back for the kids.'

'Ooh – plural now. How many have you got?'

'Three. And I have to leave to pick them up from school in about half an hour.'

'Well, you can have a glass surely?' she had asked, clinging on to the edge of the door for support.

'Not really. If I turn up for the children smelling of alcohol, they'll have social services on me before I can say, "It was just the one glass."'

'It can't be that bad,' Sophie had said. But she'd looked at Liv's face, and somehow knew that it was. 'Okay – cup of tea, then?'

Sophie's mum was struggling to her feet.

'Sit down, Sophie. I can manage to make a cup of tea, and you two have a lot of catching up to do as Liv doesn't appear to have long.' Sophie hoped her friend hadn't picked up the slightly sharp note in her mum's voice. She was obviously thinking: *Why wait so long and then only come for five minutes?* But it was a start.

'So, Liv, tell me about your life, your husband, your kids – I want to know every sodding detail.'

She'd heard her mother mutter, 'Your language, Sophie,' as she went out of the room. The two friends had shared a smile, and it felt good.

'No, Sophie – tell me about what happened to you. I couldn't believe it when I saw your picture come up on the news. We don't watch it very often, but I put it on for five minutes, and there you were. It must have been awful.'

'You don't watch the news? How do you know what's going on in the world? Do you read the papers?'

'Oh, it's just Robert. He wants me to be happy, and he thinks bad news upsets me. He sort of filters it – tells me the good stuff, keeps the bad stuff from me. It's his idea of taking care of me, but I have a quick catch-up every now and then when he's not around. Never mind that. Just tell me.'

So Sophie had told her about Iraq, Afghanistan and her career in the Intelligence Corps. She had kept the emotion out of her voice, but hadn't tried to hide the fact that she loved her job. She had known she was gabbling, but she'd wanted to get her story out of the way before her mother came back in the room. She'd told Liv about the day of the bomb, and the carnage. She was being lauded as a hero, but so many had died and she had only managed to save a few.

When she heard her mother opening the door, she'd quickly changed the subject.

'Do you remember the day we met? You were doing a happy dance in your room, skipping round upended suitcases, kicking clothes, picking them up, throwing them in the air. You were a maniac.'

Liv had turned to Sophie's mum, trying to look indignant. 'Your daughter just barged into my room without knocking, and stood there watching me.'

'You should have seen her, mum. A real slob, she was – and blamed it all on her dad for being obsessively tidy. I had to fold everything up and help her put it all away. Even when we lived together I had to tidy up after her every few weeks.'

'Yes, and you always left me a charming note saying "Lazy Cow" or "Messy Mare" or something equally derogatory, if I remember rightly. But we did have a great time, didn't we?' Liv had laughed, almost looking like the girl Sophie had first met.

'*You* did.' Sophie had said, pointing an accusing finger. 'I felt like your minder. You were so daring - up for absolutely anything. You volunteered for every hare-brained stunt going, and dragged me into it too, if I didn't keep an eye on you. I think every man in Manchester was in love with you. I sometimes felt like your bodyguard, fighting them all off.

Liv had grinned. 'Rubbish. And anyway, once I'd met Dan, I never even looked at anybody else.'

Liv's face had fallen at the mention of Dan.

'Poor you. I know it must have hurt like buggery at the time – sorry, Mum. But look at you now. Happily married and three kids. Did you ever find out what happened to Dan?'

'No. I never heard another word.'

Sophie had nodded and looked down at her clasped hands. She hadn't known whether it was an appropriate time to tell Liv what she had found out, but she'd never been one for keeping quiet.

'I met Danush's brother – Samir,' she'd said in a soft voice.

'*What?*' Sophie had suddenly known she shouldn't have started this. She had thought her friend would be over Dan by now but, judging by the eagerness with which she leaned towards Sophie, her eyes wide with expectation, that was far from the case. 'What did he say? Where did you see him?'

'In Dubai. I caught a nasty bug when I was in one shit hole or another – can't really remember which. Anyway, I was airlifted to Dubai and taken into hospital. When they said I'd be treated by Doctor Jahander, I did wonder. I remembered you telling me that Samir was a doctor, although I'm sure it's a fairly common name. But as soon as I saw him I recognised him. I'd met him before – don't you remember – when he came over to read his brother the riot act for shaming the family by living in sin with an un-chaste white woman, when he should have been marrying his cousin, or something?'

She could tell by Liv's face that she remembered it well. But it was only weeks later that Liv had found out she was pregnant, and so if Danush had had any thoughts of leaving Manchester after his PhD, they were quashed.

'Samir has a job at the hospital in Dubai, which is where he makes his money, and then he spends a few weeks every year working on a voluntary basis in some of the poorer areas of Iran. I liked him.'

In Sophie's opinion, Olivia had the right to know what Samir had said about Danush. So she'd told her. Maybe this would finally put an end to any dreams she was clinging on to.

By the time Sophie had finished, Liv was clearly fighting back the tears and it was only a few minutes later that she'd said she had to go. Sophie hadn't known whether she would ever see her one-time best friend ever again. She hadn't mentioned the fact that Liv had never responded to her letters – that conversation had come much later and with far more tears.

But it was all a long time ago. The months had passed quickly, and so much had happened between then and now.

Sophie shook herself out of her reminiscences. It was time she started to think about the future. She would soon be back on active duty. She had undergone endless operations on her leg, but the final round seemed to have been successful, and she was just waiting for the wound to heal. More importantly, she'd completed a course in Pashto, the language favoured by the Taliban, while she had been recuperating. And she'd been here for her mum, whom she was getting desperately worried about. Her arthritis was getting steadily worse, but at least they'd had the stair lift installed, so she could get up and down to her bedroom.

When she'd first come back from Afghanistan, Sophie had had some savings, and she'd wanted to put money aside to make sure her mum could afford the help she needed. But her mother was having none of it. She was adamant. She wouldn't let Sophie spend a penny of it. It was perhaps just as well now, because in the last twelve months nearly all of those pennies had gone, and she'd have a hell of a job explaining that to her mother.

Sophie pulled her car into the short drive behind her mum's silver Fiesta, a car that hadn't been driven in the last two years but which her mum insisted on keeping for 'when I'm ready to drive again'. Everybody knew that would be never but nobody had the heart to tell her.

Sophie's mind was spinning with all these different worries as she retrieved the first of the shopping bags. Balancing it on her knee as she put her key in the front-door lock, she called out to her mother.

'Only me, Mum.' There was no response. Perhaps she was sleeping.

Sophie went back out to the car and collected the rest of the bags and took them through to the kitchen to start unpacking them. Maybe she should check on her mum first.

She stood at the bottom of the stairs. The stair lift was at the top, so there was no point looking in the sitting room.

'Mum,' she called again softly, not wanting to wake her if she was sleeping. 'Would you like a cup of tea and a biscuit?'

There was a pause.

'That would be lovely, Sophie. Thank you.'

Every hair on her body stood on end, because the voice that answered from the upstairs landing was definitely not her mother's.

25

As soon as Becky reported that Robert Brookes was missing from the house but his car was still there, Tom told her to call the crime scene team. Given the state of the bedroom as described by Becky, it was far from clear whether there had been some major disturbance at the house, or even a break-in. It was the perfect opportunity for getting their guys in, even if it turned out that Robert had simply gone out for a run and left by the back door. Not that Tom believed it for one single moment. He'd gone. Scarpered.

'Bollocks,' Tom muttered under his breath. He really should have seen this coming. But they'd had no basis up to now to carry out anything more than a standard search of the house. It had been too early to start pulling the place apart, and whatever his growing suspicions about Robert Brookes, he had planned on bringing him in for formal questioning before he made any decisions about calling in a full forensic team.

What about the woman impersonating Olivia at the guest house? Could Robert have paid somebody to go in his wife's place in an attempt to conceal the *real* date that she went missing? But this was the third time this 'Olivia Brookes' had stayed there, or so they had been told by Mrs Evans. They needed to find out who the woman was, and quickly. Something about her was niggling at him, but he couldn't for the life of him think what. And then there was the overnight visitor. Was he just another pawn in Robert's game?

Tom knew his driving was erratic as he made his way towards the Brookes' house. His head was all over the place this morning with the whole Leo situation, the burglary in Cheshire and now bloody Robert Brookes, but when he realised he had almost mowed down a cyclist, who admittedly was on the wrong side of the road, he pulled his thoughts back round to the job in hand – driving with due care and attention. That lasted all of about five seconds until his phone rang. He touched the button on his console to answer.

'Tom Douglas.'

'Tom, it's Leo. I'm at the cottage. Are you free to talk for a moment?'

'You must have made an early start, Leo. Thanks for going. I appreciate it.'

'Well, I set off before eight. I didn't sleep too well.' Tom decided not to mention that made two of them. 'Tom, do you think…' Leo paused and Tom waited. He heard her take a deep breath. 'Never mind. It's probably a conversation for another day. Anyway, back to the house. Max and Ellie managed to tidy up most of the mess and get the house secure again, but it does look as if the intruders were interested in your papers. One of the cupboards in the study has been completely torn apart – they've even taken up the floorboards in there. I've no idea why. Nowhere else seems to have been damaged.'

Tom could understand it perfectly. The study was the only part of the house that had floorboards, being a slightly later extension. The rest were flagged floors.

'And they've been in the loft,' Leo continued. 'All the boxes there had been turned upside down. Max and I went up to have a look, but I didn't want to root through your papers or anything, so it was a bit difficult.'

'Feel free to root away, Leo. I don't have any secrets hidden up there, so do whatever you need to or want to. I'm not expecting you to tidy it all up, you know. I'll get there as soon as this case has finished and do all that. But it might give us a clue as to what they were looking for. Seriously, I don't mind you looking at anything at all, love.' Tom bit his bottom lip and screwed up his face. Had he really just called her 'love'? He just hoped she would put it down to his northernness, and not read too much into it. Not that she could read any more than was already there.

In typical Leo fashion, she didn't miss a beat. 'Fine. I'll see if I can work out what was of particular interest to them, and get back to you. Are you busy today?'

'I certainly am. Our mate Robert seems to have done a bunk, so it's all systems go here.'

'Will I see you later?' Leo asked, a slightly tentative note to her voice.

Tom wasn't sure how to respond. It wasn't like Leo to sound unsure of herself. She hated to show any vulnerability.

'It depends how the rest of the day goes.' He wasn't intentionally playing it cool, but he really didn't know if they were going to be here all night or not.

'Okay. You know where I am, but if it's late and you're too tired you don't need to call. I'll see you when I see you. Hope you manage to solve your mystery.' With that Leo hung up, leaving Tom wondering whether she was finally beginning to trust him. She wasn't the only one who was vulnerable, though. The break-up of his marriage had ripped him to shreds, and then a couple of years ago he'd become too close to somebody he could never be with. Of course, Leo knew nothing of that.

He was slightly surprised to find himself turning into the Brookes' road, having very little memory of how he got there, but he was pleased to see Becky had done her stuff. The road was full of vehicles, and he knew a thorough search would be under way. At least now they might actually begin to find out what had been going on with the Brookes family.

26

Although he had already been inside this house more than once and traces of him might be found anywhere, Tom decided to don the requisite outfit to protect the scene from further contamination before stepping into the house. His disposable polypropylene suit and shoe covers crackled as he walked, and he noisily made his way towards the kitchen where he was sure he would find Becky. She was talking to the crime scene manager – a huge black guy with a perpetual grin on his face. As Jumoke Osoba, commonly known as Jumbo, would tell anybody who asked, he'd always loved the sense of the unknown, of a surprise waiting round every corner. A new crime scene to him was the equivalent of a six-year-old delving into their Christmas sack of presents. With each new piece of evidence that he discovered his grin widened, and his enthusiasm was contagious. Naturally, he toned it down if there was a body, but this was the perfect scene for him. No obvious evidence at all, and no bodies to worry about.

Tom couldn't help thinking that the word 'yet' was hanging in the air, but he pushed the thought to the back of his mind. He noticed Becky was drinking from a bottle of water and she looked a little flushed. He'd have a quiet word later to check she was okay, but first he needed to talk to Jumbo.

'Hey, Jumbo – good to see you. We've got the A team today, I see.'

Jumbo let out a bark of laughter.

'Yeah, Tom. Only the best for you, my friend. I am so looking forward to this.' He laughed again, a slightly high-pitched sound that seemed so incongruous coming from a large black man. Tom couldn't help smiling as Jumbo continued, rubbing his enormous gloved hands together in barely suppressed glee. 'There's nothing obvious. We're going to get cracking now, and see what we can dig up for you.' Jumbo's eyes drifted towards the terrace and he turned back to Tom with eyebrows raised in a silent question. Neither saw the necessity to speak, but Tom was sincerely hoping that it wouldn't come to an excavation.

As Jumbo strode purposefully out of the kitchen to brief his troops, Tom made his way over to Becky.

'You okay?' he asked. She looked at him vacantly and then appeared to shake herself.

'Yes, sorry – I'm fine. I'm being unusually fanciful, that's all. When I came into the house, I got this weird feeling, as if I were entering a morgue, for some reason. The quiet was almost deadly, and I genuinely expected to stumble over a corpse at any moment. It was quite a relief when the crime scene boys got here, although Jumbo himself was a bit of a turn up for the books. Where did we find him, then?'

'He's the best there is, just wait and see,' Tom said, walking over to the window and peering out into the garden. 'Do you think Robert's really done a runner, or has he just gone for a long walk?'

Becky shook her head. 'He's gone. I can feel it. We're pretty sure he went out the back way, and it seems a bit extreme to climb over a fence if you're just going for a walk. There's a shoe print in the soft earth, and he dragged one of the kids' plastic chairs from their play area over to the fence too.'

'So why did he do it now? What piece of information have we got that made him so afraid that he had to up sticks and go? Was it that we know Olivia wasn't where he said she was? Was it the photo of the other woman? Are we getting too close? I bloody hope we are – we need to find these kids.'

'He's running scared, Tom. He knows we're on to him,' Becky answered. 'We just don't know what he's done with her – or the kids.'

Tom shook his head. It had made more sense when they'd thought Olivia was having an affair with her dark-skinned visitor at the B&B, but the fact that this other woman had been pretending to be Olivia for the last three holidays suggested duplicity of some considerable magnitude. But on whose part? Had Robert known before this week that Olivia had never been to the new guest house in Anglesey?

Becky held up her empty bottle of water. 'I'm just going to dump this, and check where we're up to. There's a hell of a mess upstairs. It looks like there was a fight in the bedroom, but when I showed Jumbo round he didn't think so.'

As Becky walked off towards the front of the house, Tom heard the unmistakeable sound of Gil Tennant's voice, obviously here to do some investigating into Robert Brookes' computer before it was carted away.

'DCI Douglas, good morning,' he said as he walked into the kitchen. Tom was pleased to see that Gil hadn't disappointed on the shoe front once again. Despite the overshoes, Tom could just make out the edge of some dark red trainers, and was certain that once the coverall was removed these would be a perfect match to either his shirt or trousers.

'Morning, Gil. Sorry you've been dragged out on a Sunday. Did you catch Becky on your way in?'

'I most certainly did. She told me Mr Brookes normally keeps his study door locked, so I'm looking forward to finding out what secrets are lurking in there.' Gil rubbed his hands together.

'Brookes told us his computer was password protected. Is that likely to be a problem?' Tom asked.

Gil simply raised his chin and looked smug, which Tom guessed was all he was going to get for an answer.

'At least the power's back on. I gather the plonker next door cut through the electricity cable yesterday afternoon, so let's hope he restricts his digger activity today,' Gil said.

'Tom? You got a minute?' Jumbo's voice penetrated the general hubbub of the house. Everybody instantly fell silent – certain that something significant had been found. Tom dodged around Gil and took the stairs two at a time with Becky in hot pursuit. The voice led them to the master bedroom.

'That was quick, Jumbo, even by your standards. What have you found?'

Jumbo clearly had something in his hands, but for a moment Tom was stunned by the total chaos in the room.

'Christ, was there a tsunami and I missed it?' he asked.

'Ah, yes. That's the first thing. Becky – okay if I call you Becky, DI Robinson?' Jumbo didn't pause for permission, but carried on. 'Becky wondered if there had been a fight in here, but I think this has all been created by one person. I would guess he stood here,' Jumbo took a massive step to his left, 'and pulled out drawers, flinging them round the room. There doesn't seem to be much evidence of anything being thrown back. There's one imprint of somebody sitting on the bed, and only the women's clothes have been ripped off their hangers. I would say that this is our Mr Brookes having a bit of a paddy.'

A paddy was the understatement of the year, if the condition of this room was anything to go by.

'Do you think he was looking for something?' Tom asked.

'I doubt it, because he certainly wasn't methodical. However...' Jumbo paused and flashed his trademark grin around the room, 'if he had been looking, he did a rubbish job. As you can see, some of the drawers he pulled out ended up upside down, but some were just flung and righted themselves. And just lookie here at what we found taped to the bottom of one of these drawers.'

Jumbo passed two plastic evidence bags to Tom, and in each one was a passport. He looked up at Jumbo, his expression framing his question.

'One British passport in the name of Olivia Brookes. One in the name of Jasmine Jahander. And I don't know if it's relevant, but there are Iranian visas in both of them dated last October.'

As they both had cars at the scene, Becky and Tom had to travel back separately to the incident room – a fact that frustrated Tom because he really could have done with using Becky as a sounding board. They already knew Olivia and Jasmine had passports, in spite of the fact that Robert had specifically said they didn't, but Olivia had obviously hidden them from him. If they had both travelled to Iran last October, though, who had looked after the boys?

Tom hadn't detected any hint of a lie when Robert had said that Olivia didn't need a passport, and neither did the children. So Olivia would have had to hide them because he was certain Robert would know nothing about the Iranian visas. And Jumbo had found them in about five minutes, so goodness knows what else he was going to unearth in that house. Tom didn't have long to wait to find out. His phone beeped and his screen flashed up with the word 'Jumbo'.

'Hey Jumbo, don't tell me you've solved the whole crime inside an hour?' Tom said, not entirely joking.

'Ha – you would be surprised at all the little slimy bits we're finding hidden under stones here. Just wait until you speak to Gil. He's been jumping up and down in excitement, and had my guys climbing ladders all morning.'

'Ladders?' Tom said in amazement. 'What the hell have ladders got to do with his computer?'

'I'll leave that to Gil. I won't steal his thunder. But seriously for a moment, Tom – I don't like the feel of this. I don't know why yet, but I just get the sense that we're going to peel back layer after grimy layer until we get to the bottom of what's been going on in this house.' Jumbo paused, and Tom heard him take a deep breath, as if to clear his mind of distracting speculation. 'Anyway, back to facts rather than conjecture. Have we managed to get credit card and bank records yet?'

'No. We've only just requested them. Why?'

'I'm particularly interested in purchases made from John Lewis recently. We found an empty John Lewis carrier bag in the dustbin – just about the only item in there, which I know you had already picked up on. There are a couple of things upstairs that are still in their packaging with John Lewis labels on – in the boys' room there's a duvet cover with a train on it and some pink pyjamas, which I presume were for the daughter.'

'And these are suspicious items?' Tom said, not quite able to keep the puzzled note out of his voice.

Jumbo's booming laughter came down the phone.

'Ha – you must think I'm losing it, Tom. No, but they may have been bought at the same time as something else. One of my girls was checking out the kitchen, and she noticed that all the knives in the knife block were present and correct. However, being an eagle-eyed, obsessive sort of girl – just the kind I like – she took them all out individually to fingerprint them. She noticed that the knives are Sabatier knives – you know, they usually have three circular steel rivets on the handle? Well, all bar one of them are Sabatier Diamant knives. The extra one looks almost identical, but is actually a John Lewis knife.'

Tom was impressed. The girl must have been very observant, not that it was necessarily significant.

'I can hear your brain whirring, Tom,' Jumbo yelled down the phone over the sound of what appeared to be drilling in the background. 'But the most interesting thing was that all the knives had Olivia's prints on, and nobody else's. With the exception of this one, which only had Robert's prints on it. And only one set of prints. It had either been very thoroughly washed and he was the only person to touch it afterwards, or it's brand new.'

Tom knew what was coming before he spoke.

'There's not a trace of blood on it, or on any of the other knives. We've checked. But I think this is a replacement, and a very recent one. Which is why I want to check if Robert bought it and, if so, when. Once we've done everything else, I think I'm going to be getting the luminol out in this house. I don't think we've got much choice, do you?' Jumbo wasn't smiling any more. Tom could tell from his voice.

'You think you're going to find blood?' he asked quietly.

'Don't know, if I'm honest. But that knife has got me wondering. Where is the original from the set? Then there's the fact that nobody has seen or heard from Olivia Brookes in over two weeks – with the possible exception of her husband, whose word I don't think we can exactly trust.'

'I couldn't agree more,' Tom responded.

I'll keep you informed.' Jumbo rang off just as Tom pulled into the car park.

Christ, he thought. Don't let him have killed them all, if I've let the bastard get away.

27

Becky stormed into the incident room on a blast of nervous energy. She couldn't believe how pathetic she had been at the house that morning. She'd been known to take down two men at a time when she'd needed to, and yet she was spooked by an empty house. How the hell did personal emotional turmoil manage to sap a person of all their strength and determination? Well, bugger that. She was going to get it back. She wasn't going to wimp around like some feeble eighteenth-century noblewoman, swooning at anything that made her jump. *Bugger* that.

She strode over to her desk, her mouth set in a grim line of decisiveness and saw Tom glance at her, and nod his head slightly. He'd be pleased she was getting her confidence back. Everybody here had seen the sorry-looking wreck who had turned up a few weeks ago, but now they were going to see the real Becky Robinson.

'I want to get everybody together and run through where we're up to, given what's happened this morning. Is that okay with you, Tom?'

Before Tom had time to answer, Becky's phone signalled an incoming message and she heard Tom's vibrate at the same time.

Jumbo.

'You both need to see this – found in a notebook in Jasmine's bedroom,' the message said. There was an image attached. Becky opened it and stared at the screen. She glanced up and her eyes met Tom's.

'Shit,' Becky muttered. She sent the image to her computer and bent over her desk, blowing the picture up to a sensible size. It didn't look any less disturbing, and she quickly printed a few copies and passed one to Tom.

'What's he done to them, Tom?' she asked, knowing that he had no more idea that she did. Without waiting for a reply, she walked over to the evidence board and pinned a copy of the picture on it.

The room fell quiet. Every head turned towards Becky as they sensed something had happened.

The image taken from Jasmine's notebook had done nothing to diminish Becky's determination, but she felt a heavy weight in her chest now as the suspicion that she had failed these children shattered her new-found confidence.

Without a word, members of the team walked up to the board, and Becky handed out a few copies of the picture. Tom pushed his chair back and moved closer, perching himself on the edge of a desk.

Becky stood and looked at the image once more before speaking. They had already been told that Jasmine was a child who was meticulous in her school work, and if this picture was anything to go by her drawing skills were probably slightly above average for her age, as each element of her composition had been painstakingly detailed.

The picture showed a tiny room. They could see the two back corners, and three walls that Jasmine had shaded a dark grey colour. There were no windows, and nothing in the room apart from a red box. Nothing, that is, except three children, huddled in the corner. They appeared to be sitting on the ground with knees bent. In the centre was a girl with long dark hair, and on each side of her was a little boy, both of whom had yellow hair that Becky interpreted as blond. The girl had an arm around each of them. There were tiny black oval shapes on the face of the youngest child, which could be tears. On one of the walls there was an open door, but it was high off the ground.

Underneath Jasmine had written: 'Hiding from the enemy'.

There was silence as the team absorbed the implications of the image. Becky gave them a few moments.

'Okay, we weren't expecting this, but let's have your ideas,' she said to the hushed room.

'Is there a cellar in their home?' Ryan asked.

'No, and not even a large enough cupboard for this to be somewhere else in the house. We need to get Jumbo to shift Olivia Brookes' car to make sure there is nothing in the garage floor, but I doubt it.'

'Does he own any other property – a lock-up or anything?' Nic added.

'Not that we've found. But maybe we need to dig a bit deeper. The thing is, Jasmine drew this *before* they went missing, or it wouldn't have been in the house. So this is somewhere they have been before, unless it's all in her head. Does anybody believe that?'

The silence said it all.

'We're assuming the enemy they're hiding from is Robert – but is that too much of an assumption? Could this be something to do with their mother? Ryan, you were there when Robert took the children for the supposed weekend away without Olivia's knowledge. Did she strike you as somebody who would hurt her children, or lock them up somewhere?'

For once, Ryan was looking anything but cocky. It was the most serious Becky had ever seen him.

'I might be wrong, but I'd say she was absolutely terrified of what Robert had done to the children. I honestly can't see her hurting them, but it might be worth asking Superintendent Stanley for her view.'

Becky looked at Tom and he nodded his silent agreement to speak to Philippa, although Becky was fairly sure that the answer was a given.

'Could it be somebody else? Has any other name come up that nobody has thought to mention?'

Once more there was silence, and Becky wasn't surprised. Robert had hinted that there might be something Olivia and Jasmine were worried about, but this was major – not a slight concern that somebody might be making a nuisance of themselves.

'Okay. Nobody needs telling that we have to find this place. It has to be our number one priority. Whatever has happened to Olivia, there is a possibility that these children have gone to this hiding place – they might be safe and desperate to be rescued, or they might be locked in and unable to escape. Any hint, any suggestion, we need to know. What about neighbours? We need to check them again – but not just for information. Look for sheds, cellars, attics. Has one of them taken in the children? Nic, can I leave that to you to organise, please?'

Nic nodded and turned back to his desk.

'Right – let's talk about *this* woman.' Becky banged her finger three times on the blown-up photo on the board of the woman who had been posing as Olivia Brookes at the guest house. 'We don't know who she is and, although we know Robert has seen her picture, he omitted to mention to us that somebody has been impersonating his wife. *Why did he do that?*'

A hand shot up from the back of the room.

'Is it possible that Robert put this woman in the guest house and has harmed Olivia and the children? Could she be working for Robert to help cover his tracks? Looking at the daughter's picture, it does seem as if she was afraid of somebody.'

Becky nodded her head slowly. 'Sounds plausible. Does anybody else have a view?'

Tom stood up.

'We found passports for Olivia and Jasmine at the house this morning. Both of them had Iranian visas, which were dated for the half-term week in October last year when Olivia was supposed to be in Anglesey. It looks like she might have lied to Brookes about her whereabouts before, so isn't it possible that she's just left him? The woman at the guest house could be helping Olivia, not Robert.'

'But was she *actually* in Iran with Jasmine, and – maybe – Danush Jahander? If she was, where were the boys? Or was she locked away somewhere? Had Robert discovered she was about to run off with Jahander and was that the start of it all? It must be obvious to everybody that it's a priority to find out who this woman is,' Becky stabbed her finger at the photo on the board again. 'Why was she impersonating Olivia, and who the hell asked her to do it? I think we need to consider a television appeal.'

Everybody was quiet for a moment. Becky couldn't help thinking she was missing something, but she couldn't put her finger on it. They needed to move on.

'What else have we got? Yes, Erica,' Becky said, pointing to a slightly harried-looking woman at the back of the room. She knew Erica had four children, so guessed that – not for the first time – she'd had a nightmare with childcare this morning.

'We've got Mrs Preston saying that Robert came home in the middle of Wednesday night or actually Thursday morning, and was gone again by the time she got up. This was supported by another neighbour who walks his dog at five fifteen every morning before he leaves for work at six. He said Robert's car shot off the drive and nearly knocked him over.'

'So do we think he came back to check up on them, wherever they are – or were? And if he did, he might have come back on other nights too. Any joy on the CCTV from the Newcastle hotel?' Becky asked.

'Nothing in the lobby area, no. But the manager said there are other ways out, and not everywhere is necessarily covered. He could have gone out through the kitchens for example, if he didn't want to be spotted.'

'What about the car park?' Tom asked.

'We requested the footage immediately, but we've only just got it because it comes from a different company – not the hotel. We're going to start on that as soon as we've finished here.'

'Start with Wednesday night,' Becky said, 'but I want the whole time he was in Newcastle covered. I want to know about every second his car was out of that car park.'

In the brief lull while the team assimilated all they had learned, the door to the incident room was flung open with some force, and a serious, slightly breathless Gil almost sprinted up the room in his red shoes.

'You are *so* going to want to see this,' he said.

Much as Becky didn't want to be interrupted, Gil's intensity suggested this was important. He plonked down his laptop and stabbed his finger on a few buttons until it connected wirelessly to the whiteboard. Despite the writing on the board, the image was clear for all to see.

On the screen there was a video, and to Becky it was obvious this was the inside of the Brookes' kitchen. The door opened, and Robert Brookes walked in, carrying a large bunch of white flowers and a carrier bag that appeared to contain bottles. Under his arm were what looked like children's comics. He dumped the lot on the table. Although there was no sound, it was clear that Brookes was shouting, 'Olivia!' and turning to look around. He walked out of the kitchen, and was picked up next in their bedroom, his glance flicking around the room, seemingly confused. Finally Gil clicked something on the screen, which changed back to the kitchen. Robert flung open the door – and, even without the sound, everybody cringed as it crashed into the cupboard. He grabbed his wife's bag and upended it on the table, checking the contents.

Gil clicked off.

'Friday afternoon – at just the time Robert said he was home.'

Becky looked at the puzzled faces around her.

'So where's the video from?'

'Watch this next bit, and I'll tell you,' was all Gil would say. He clicked another icon on the screen.

Into shot came a woman. The video was being taken from somewhere above her and she was walking with her head slightly bowed so they weren't able to see a clear image of her face, but Becky was sure this was Olivia Brookes. She looked at Tom for confirmation, and he gave her a sharp nod without moving his eyes from the screen. There was still no sound, but it did seem that the woman was talking to somebody over her shoulder as she made herself a cup of coffee. A small child came into view, but this time only the very top of a blond head was visible. From his size, the child looked to be about four years old. Both walked out of shot, and the screen blanked for a second before opening up again – this time in the living room. Olivia was walking towards the sofa where she sat down, picked up a magazine and took a sip from the cup of coffee that she had brought with her from the kitchen.

The incident room was totally silent. Stunned by what they were seeing, no doubt. Gil switched off his laptop and turned to his audience.

'Not a very inspiring bit of video, I hear you cry,' he said theatrically. 'But that, my friends, is the tip of the iceberg. The hard disc on Robert's computer is absolutely full of videos of the Brookes family going about their business. Totally chocker. There are cameras hidden in every room of the house except the children's bedrooms and the bathrooms. Glad to know that Robert Brookes did have a modicum of decency in him.'

Becky glanced at Tom and noted that the only change to his expression was a slight narrowing of the eyes. She knew he didn't like Robert, but the idea that the man filmed his wife's every action was so horrible that it made Becky shudder. Did Olivia know about this? She couldn't have done. Nobody would tolerate that level of surveillance. Or was it voyeurism? Did Robert get off on watching pictures of his wife? Would they ever know the answer?

Gil hadn't finished.

'The cameras were very cleverly concealed, high up on top of cupboards. But I think we've found them all now. They're motion activated, and set to respond to movement above a certain height. It's pretty clear he was only interested in capturing video of his wife, so each time she walked into a room the cameras started to film and record. Obviously the kids are in some of the shots with her, but they are all too small to activate the cameras themselves. The bad news is that the cameras are looking down on to the tops of their heads, so we've still got no photos we can use. And I can only assume that when Robert came home from work each night, he deactivated the cameras from his computer, because with the exception of the most recent one, there are no shots of him at all.'

Gil turned around and smiled at everybody, although the smile never quite reached his bleak, tired eyes.

'The time stamps show that the last video of Olivia was shot on Friday – approximately one hour before Robert Brookes got back. Until that point, it would appear that she and the children were all fit and well, and at home.'

❖

The incident room was humming. Everybody had a theory, but to Tom, none seemed to be quite right.

'It seems clear from this that Robert was telling the truth when he said he was expecting his wife to be home when he got there,' Ryan said.

'Does everybody agree with that?' Becky asked.

Nic put up a slightly tentative hand.

'If we assume Robert Brookes put those cameras in place and he usually switched them off when he came home, he'd know he was being filmed, wouldn't he? He was facing the camera when he shouted her name, and he could have bought the presents just for show. I don't think it proves anything, personally.'

Good lad, thought Tom. Exactly what he was thinking. But on the other hand, Olivia had been there until an hour before and it would be pretty easy to check if Robert had been in his car on the way back from Newcastle in the only missing hour – the hour between Olivia being there and Robert's arrival home.

A sudden thought struck him.

'Becky – in that clip Olivia was making herself some coffee, wasn't she? And she was adding milk. Didn't you say there was no milk in the fridge, and there was no empty bottle in the dustbin?'

Becky looked at him and nodded silently.

What the hell was going on?

28

This was the sort of crime that Jumbo loved, chiefly because at the moment, nobody knew whether a crime had been committed or not, and it was his job to find out. He was delighted with the catch on the kitchen knife – his bright spark newbie had done a great job there, and the passports intrigued him too.

When you threw Gil's discovery of the videos on the computer into the mix, and all those dreadful cameras that he'd had people climbing up and down ladders to retrieve, it was adding up to a true mystery. And there was nothing he liked better.

Now that Gil was gone, Jumbo decided to turn his attention to the study. Tom had told him that the door was usually kept locked, and he understood why. Clearly Robert Brookes had no intention of letting his wife discover that her every move was being recorded. But Jumbo had looked at the video too, and there was something that didn't quite add up. He was sure Olivia was acting normally when she made her way around the various rooms, and there was no real sign that she was playing to the camera. In his experience, if people knew there was a camera there, they gave off signals. They behaved differently somehow, as if they were acting on a stage. There was no evidence of that with Olivia, but there were two things. She rarely showed her face – her head always seemed to be down as she walked towards the camera, but up as she walked away. And she never, ever got dressed or undressed in the bedroom. She always went into the bathroom. On one occasion, she'd clearly forgotten something and came back into the room from the bathroom to get some underwear from her drawer. But she was wearing a bathrobe. Who walks from an en suite bathroom into their own bedroom for a pair of knickers and puts a bathrobe on to do it?

He was damned sure that never happened in his house. His wife was a bit like him – big in every direction. But big of heart too, with a booming laugh that rivalled his own. Getting her to put her clothes *on* was more of an issue as she pranced around the bedroom doing her semi-naked Tina Turner impression, which she swore she practised when he wasn't there. He smiled as he thought of her and couldn't help comparing her, throwing back her head for a good laugh, with this Olivia Brookes woman, whose face he had yet to see in any detail and whose laughter he had yet to hear.

He looked around the study and called one of his guys in.

'Let's go through the books, Adam. You know the drill. This guy strikes me as a sneaky little shit, so it would be good to know if anything's odd about his reading, or if there's anything stuck between the pages of his books. Let's see how we go. Get Phil in to help. I'm going to make a start on the luminol in the rooms we've already finished looking at. You okay with that?'

Looking through a bookcase full of paperbacks wasn't a highlight in anybody's day, but it had to be done. He thumped Adam on the shoulder. 'Good lad – it shouldn't take you too long.'

Where to begin with the luminol? That was the question. It didn't help that it was June, so not great in terms of making a room dark enough. But the kids' rooms had blackout blinds, so they were as good a place to start as any, and the en suite didn't have any windows at all so that would be another.

'Let's get this show on the road,' he boomed, to nobody in particular.

It was about an hour later that he heard a shout from downstairs.

'Jumbo, you need to see this.' It was Phil, the technician helping Adam.

'Two minutes and I'll be with you, Phil,' he shouted through the open door.

The luminol hadn't revealed a trace of anything. All the bedrooms were now done; even the master bedroom, which fortunately had some very heavy curtains to block out the afternoon sunlight.

He thudded down the stairs, his heavy tread making them creak probably for the first time in their history, and stood in the doorway of the study.

'What've you got, lads?' he asked. Anybody under forty was a lad to Jumbo.

Adam pointed to the back of the bookcase.

'This looks like just a normal plywood backing, but when we took the books out, we noticed one corner seemed loose so we gave it a bit of a tug. There's a small space behind that's been lined with wood to make a concealed area. It's about thirty by forty centimetres and maybe eight centimetres deep. Unfortunately it's empty, but nevertheless, a hidey hole. It looks as if the books in front have been moved recently too. There are faint dust marks where the books have been dragged to one side.' Adam pointed to the marks. 'Very recent, I'd say.'

'Well done – all photographed and documented, I presume?' he asked, already knowing the answer. 'What the hell was he hiding in there, then? Pity he didn't have his cameras going when he emptied it – that might have helped a bit. Anything of interest in the books?'

Adam shook his head.

'Sorry, Jumbo. The only thing Phil and I noticed is that he seems to have a bit of a thing about Myra Hindley and Ian Brady. He's got quite a lot of books about them, but not on any other serial killers. Strange to be only interested in the one, don't you think?'

'I presume you weren't born and brought up in Manchester, lad. The moors murders isn't a story that's ever been allowed to die around here – if you'll excuse the poor choice of words. With one kid never found, every person for miles around knows the whole gruesome tale. So, I'd like to say it was odd, but I don't particularly think it is.'

He looked around, and could see that everything else seemed to be finished in this room. All the papers had been boxed up to be taken away, and Gil had already moved the computer.

'How's about we try to get this room dark, and let's have a lookie with the luminol, shall we?' he said.

The study had both Venetian blinds and curtains. It seemed that Robert didn't want anybody to be able to look through the downstairs window into this room even in daylight.

While the guys were getting the room ready, Jumbo stepped back into the hallway and saw a couple of people walking downstairs, laden with boxes.

'What have we got here, lads?' he asked.

'Stuff from the loft,' one of them answered, definitely not a lad, but very difficult to tell in their coveralls. 'There's some clothes and other bits and pieces, but we thought this box might be interesting. It's got loads of old papers and documents – seem to be scientific – and then there are all sorts of odds and ends too. A scarf, a picture frame, a pair of gloves, an old programme from a Manchester United match. But the box has "Dan" scrawled on it, and the name on the documents is Danush Jahander, so as he appears to be a person of interest I thought we should go through it properly.'

'Good job.' Jumbo beamed. 'We're going to check out the study for blood now; there's nothing upstairs. Then we'll move into the rest of the downstairs rooms. Catch you in a few minutes.'

Jumbo returned to the darkened room and prepared himself, pulling his mask into place. He looked around him through the shadows cast by a thin beam of light that was getting in through the partially opened door. That was okay – he needed to choose his spot, then he would close the door. He thought for a moment, and then kicked the door shut behind him, pointing his spray at the carpet in the corner of the room. Nothing. He tried another couple of likely spots. Again, no result.

He turned to face the door: six panelled and painted in white gloss. He sprayed, stopped, then sprayed some more. He could feel his heart begin to hammer under his ribs.

'Shit. We've got a hit.' In the dark of the room, Jumbo pulled down his mask and stared at the door and wall, glowing blue from a height of close to six feet down to the ground.

Tom looked around the incident room and he could practically feel the adrenaline pumping through the bodies of this team. They had found blood – and a lot of it. According to Jumbo, the blood had been thoroughly cleaned up with bleach, but before cleaning it had soaked into the wall on either side of the door sufficiently to show a kind of spatter pattern, enough to suggest that this was an adult who had been attacked, not a child. It was too high and, from the shape of the drops, they could tell the blood was falling as it hit the wall, not rising. Jumbo said he would put money on it being arterial blood, and in his opinion there was too much for one person to lose and still be alive.

The clean-up job had been good, and bleach would have destroyed any and all DNA in the scrubbed areas. But in Jumbo's experience, blood spatter like this spread droplets that were not easy to see with the naked eye, and he was confident that they would find a trace somewhere. Nobody ever managed to eradicate every single drop.

So much new information, but no idea where it was all heading. And still nobody had a clue where Robert had gone, or what he was doing for transport. And his mobile wasn't giving them any clues either. He had used his credit cards before they had realised he was missing, and there had been no activity since. An all-ports warning had been issued, but nothing had come through yet. They were organising a press release, now, because Robert Brookes had to be tracked down.

Finding the blood had definitely had an impact on the team. In some cases, sadly it had raised their level of excitement. But for him it was with a sense of sorrow that he had to accept the fact that something terrible had happened in that room.

Becky was sitting with the heels of her hands propping up her forehead, her fingers gripping her thoroughly tangled fringe.

'I know it's what I thought all along, Tom, but it doesn't always feel that great to be right.'

'You're pretty certain about this, aren't you?'

Becky leaned across the desk towards him, eager to make him see her point. 'We know Robert tried to take the kids a couple of years ago, whatever nonsense he spouted about his wife knowing all about it. We know that he's been watching her, waiting for his moment. She's been hiding passports. All sorts of stuff has been going on. I reckon he's gone to pick up the kids from wherever he's got them stashed. He'll be off to start his new life.'

Tom wasn't convinced. Would he really have killed his wife to get the children? Maybe he'd killed them too, or were they locked away somewhere?

Resting his chin on his fist, he looked at Becky and debated whether to comment. She had said all along that Olivia was dead, and she could well be right.

'The blood could be Robert's, you know,' he said, knowing what the reaction would be.

'*What*?' Where did *that* theory come from?'

Tom had to admit that it wasn't really a theory, but maybe Robert hadn't gone missing on Saturday night. Maybe *he* had been killed and his body disposed of? It was a possibility. He hated to say this, but it looked as if that terrace was going to have to come up after all.

Nothing was making sense. Olivia had been there in the house until an hour before Robert had returned home. Had he really had time to kill her, dispose of the body and do God knows what with the children before he called the police a few hours later?

Becky was looking at him as if he'd grown horns, and he was waiting for the next onslaught. Fortunately her phone interrupted the increasingly tense moment.

'Bugger,' Becky muttered.

Tom couldn't resist a brief grin as she picked up the phone.

'DI Robinson,' she answered, clearly trying to sound chirpier than she felt. 'Yes, Gil. What can I do for you?'

Tom could hear no more of the conversation, but Becky started to click on her keyboard.

'Okay, got it. Now what?' she asked. Even from where Tom was sitting he could hear a little whoop of glee from the other end of the phone, and Becky hung up.

'Gil's ecstatic about his latest brilliance. He's mailed me a video segment to look at. And then when we don't understand it, he's going to come up and show us what he means.'

Tom rolled his eyes. 'Why can't the little prima donna just tell us, for Christ's sake? This isn't a TV quiz show – it's a bloody murder enquiry.'

Tom saw Becky's head whip up. It was the first time anybody had actually uttered those words, although it was what they had all been thinking. And now he'd endorsed their thoughts. Well, it was probably time to formally acknowledge it, even without a body.

Without another word, he made his way round to Becky's side of the desk and leaned over her shoulder.

'What are we looking at?' he asked.

'It's the video from the house. Robert's secret pictures,' Becky said, scorn and disgust dripping from her tongue. 'They don't look any different to me than they did this morning.'

'What's the other file he's sent you?' Tom asked.

'More of the same, I think. The time stamp is two months ago, though.'

Becky clicked to open the other video.

'Fast forward it, Becky,' Tom asked. Something was flickering at the edge of his consciousness.

'Open the other one too. Can you run them side by side?' he asked.

'On this computer?' Becky scoffed. 'You have to be joking. Only if you want frame by frame with a two-second gap between. Why?'

'Just take me to the kitchen scenes, then.'

At that moment, the double doors were both thrust open by a grinning Gil, making an entrance.

'Have you got it?' he asked.

'Just about,' Tom answered. 'You didn't give us much time, though.'

'Couldn't wait to show you. What do you think, DI Robinson?' he asked.

'I've been too busy buggering about with my computer, trying to get it to function normally. I haven't even had a chance to look at the screen yet. Just bloody tell me, Gil.'

Looking a little taken aback by Becky's vehemence, he nudged her out of the way and took control of the mouse.

'April 13th – nearly two months ago. Footage from the Brookes' kitchen. Notice the jug of daffodils on the kitchen table. These are the clues. Now, let's look at the footage for the last week, after Olivia is *supposed* to have returned from holiday. I've chosen last Tuesday as an example. Perfectly good footage of the family throughout the day, although mainly Olivia, of course. Now, check out the kitchen. A jug of daffodils on the kitchen table. Now you may not be able to get these two babies to play in sync, but I can. Look and learn.'

Tom and Becky watched two ten-second segments, running side by side on the screen. Olivia walked into the kitchen with her head down. She was wearing a dark grey jumper. She picked up a mug from the table next to a jug of daffodils, and turned round and walked out again.

The two sequences were absolutely identical.

Tom looked at Gil. He knew there was more.

'I have, of course, checked all the videos from the period we're interested in. As you would expect, there was no video for the first week – the week that Olivia was supposed to be in Anglesey. As for the rest – the videos from last week when she was supposed to be at home – they are all fakes. Every single one of them.'

Gil's eyes blazed with satisfaction as he leaned forwards and pointed to the screen with his pen.

'They have been very professionally edited together, because they're not just copies of a whole day from an earlier time. That would have been too easy for us to spot. The sequences either side of the one we were looking at – last Tuesday's video – are not from April 13th.'

Becky was looking puzzled. 'Sorry, Gil. I don't know what you mean.'

Gil tapped his pen on the monitor.

'Okay, I'll show you. Let's look at the video clip immediately before she comes into the kitchen. On April 13th – the original shot – she was dusting the living room. Last Tuesday – the day with the duplicate shot of Olivia in the kitchen with the daffodils – she was vacuuming their bedroom. The bedroom segment is copied from another day entirely, March 29th, I think. It's a masterful and quite brilliant job. Whoever has done this has selected extracts from other days when she is wearing the same clothes. Every detail of her clothes on these days is identical. When she wears this grey jumper, it is always with black jeans and white flip-flops. They had to choose clips with identical clothes, of course, because why would her outfit change as she moved from the kitchen into the living room?'

Gil looked hard at Becky, as if to be sure she understood what he was saying.

'The illusion that these videos have created is that Olivia Brookes came home from her holiday in Anglesey and was indeed in the house all last week, along with her children. In fact, she wasn't there at all. There's no genuine footage since the day she left – theoretically to go to Anglesey. We're meant to believe she was alive and kicking right up until Friday afternoon, but it's not true. I'm afraid Mr Brookes has been playing us.'

Tom watched Becky's face as the penny dropped. His last argument was in the wind. Robert hadn't had a few short hours to dispose of Olivia and the children. He'd had two whole weeks.

29

Sophie Duncan lay on the floor where she had fallen. She cursed loudly, screaming out a torrent of fury and vitriol.

'Bastard. Fucking *bastard*,' she muttered venomously, when all her screaming was done. How the fuck did he know where she lived anyway? Stupid bloody question. He knew absolutely everything about Liv. Every last sodding detail. And she was Liv's best friend, so *of course* he knew where she lived.

And now here she was, tied to a chair and totally helpless. She wasn't worried about herself; it was her mum she was anxious about. She needed to get to a place where she could talk to her – put her mind at rest. But she was shut in this room, about ten feet from a closed door. These 1930s houses were too well built, with solid brick internal walls. If only they had lived in a modern semi, she could just have hollered and the whole street would have heard. But she wasn't getting anywhere.

Her mum would be freaking out, and Sophie hoped to God she didn't try to get downstairs. Robert swore he hadn't hurt her – and he'd better not have done. She would *have* him if he had harmed her mum. He didn't know who he was messing with here. He said he'd brought the stair lift to the bottom of the stairs, disconnected the phone and taken the key to the window lock. The windows were double-glazed and there was no way her mum would be able to break one. Anyway, her bedroom was at the back of the house, and typically the neighbours had gone on holiday, so that was a non-starter.

Sophie couldn't believe she'd let herself get in this mess. When she'd heard Robert's voice from upstairs, she had panicked. How sodding pathetic was that? She was a soldier, and yet she did the absolute daftest thing she could possibly have done. She'd raced upstairs, taking them two at a time, to find him at the top with the serrated blade of a Swiss army knife to her mother's throat.

Of all the dumb things to do. If she'd just stopped and thought there were a hundred other options she could have chosen, because a threat wasn't any use if you didn't know it was being applied, and he wouldn't have hurt her mother. He just needed her as leverage. *He was a fucking nutter.*

He'd made her poor mum tie Sophie's hands behind her back. A clever tactic, because even Robert must have realised that the minute he'd moved the knife away from her mum's throat, Sophie would have taken him down – bad leg, or no bad leg. Then he'd marched Sophie downstairs, making it clear that one false move and he'd be back upstairs in a flash to finish the job with her mother. He'd shoved her in here, in the back room, closed the curtains and then done a much better job of tying her hands and feet to a dining chair.

The questioning had begun.

'What were you doing in Anglesey?'

'Why were you pretending to be Olivia?'

'Who was the man who came to visit you?'

'What do you know about me and Olivia?'

She'd started by saying nothing, but she could see the dark fury in his eyes. His thin lips were clamped tightly together, and he had two red spots high up on his cheekbones. Sophie knew enough about people to know this was anger, and it was all being directed at her. His eyes were black, like wet flint stones, the light shining out of them hard and white. Finally, she had spat the answers out with as much venom as she could muster. She wasn't scared of this nasty little man, but she was scared of what he would do to her mum if she didn't comply.

'Why were you in Anglesey?' Robert repeated, slapping Sophie hard with the back of his hand. She glared at him.

'I'm not some wimpy little woman, creep. I've been beaten up by better men than you. I was shortlisted for the SAS – so I promise you, you've not got a fucking clue. What sort of a pathetic little shit are you, to threaten a pensioner with a knife?' That had earned her another slap. But then the threats had come.

'I won't kill your mother,' he'd said, a mean toothless smile causing his eyes to glint even more brightly. 'I just need to be creative. Have you ever heard your mother scream, Sophie?'

Sophie spat out every expletive she could think of. He could do what he liked to her, but not to her mum.

'I went to Anglesey so that Liv could go where she wanted. Somewhere away from *you*. Somewhere that was her secret, and a place where she didn't have to think about *you*. A place where she felt safe. Safe from *you*.' She spat the last word at him.

'Liar,' he shouted. The glint had gone now, to be replaced with a flat stare. She could see she'd hit a nerve.

'You haven't got any children, Sophie. So whose children did you have with you? Did you take *my* children?'

Sophie laughed at him, and he liked that even less. He lashed out at her leg with his foot. Pure luck guided him to her wound, and she couldn't quite suppress a yelp. It was only a few weeks since her last operation, and it still wasn't totally healed. Her spontaneous cry made him smile.

'Of course I didn't take your children. Do you think Liv would let them out of her sight for a moment, knowing what a fucking psycho you are?' He knew her weak spot now, and it seemed he was determined to exploit it with further brutality as he lifted his foot and brought his heel down hard. Sophie felt the recent stitches burst apart, but she was better prepared this time. She gritted her teeth and waited for the pain to subside.

He wasn't going to win. She had no intention of telling him that the two boys she'd had with her in Anglesey were her sister's children, and the girl was her cousin's. God knows what he might do to them. Her cousin and sister were both single mums and getting child care for the holidays was always a nightmare, so it was a huge relief when Auntie Sophie offered to take them on holiday. But there was no way Robert was finding this out.

'Who came to visit you?'

'None of your sodding business. I'm not your wife, so I can screw whoever I like. And, as it happens, so can she.' She didn't know why she felt compelled to add that, but she wanted to hurt this man, and as deeply as she could. The punishment was swift.

'My wife has screwed nobody but me – and you know it,' he growled, his voice dropping ominously low.

'Do you think?' she asked innocently. 'What would you say if I told you she never got over Danush – she'll always love him, and nothing you can do will ever change that?'

The bastard laughed. With genuine mirth. Poor Olivia. Robert was everything she'd ever said he was.

'What do you know about Olivia and me, Sophie? What's she told you?'

'She's told me everything, you sicko. I know it all. I know who you are, I know what you are. You're a shit – a psychotic fucking shit.' Sophie spat the last word as he plunged the serrated knife into the now open wound in her leg.

As she passed out, she heard him ask the one question she couldn't answer – and she was glad. Glad that he'd never know whether she could have answered it or not.

30

As he got into his car and put the key in the ignition, Tom had to admit he was feeling weary. It had been a day of revelations, but still nobody had any idea how they all slotted together. Somebody had died in that house – but who?

Since Gil had exposed the sham of the video footage, a review of the CCTV had confirmed that Robert's car had left the garage of the Newcastle hotel at 11.39 pm on Wednesday evening, and arrived back there at 8.32 am the next morning. Something else he had lied about. And his credit card statement confirmed that he had made some purchases from John Lewis in Newcastle on Thursday at lunchtime, although they wouldn't be able to find out exactly what he had bought until the following day.

Finally, Jumbo had called through to say that, as expected, they had found a minute trace of blood that hadn't been cleaned by the bleach. It was tiny, but enough to extract DNA from. He had taken Olivia's hairbrush from the bedroom, and had asked for a super-speed rush job. He knew how important this was.

Tom was driving on autopilot, but fortunately the roads were quiet. His mind was spinning. They had so much to go on, but still hadn't a clue what had happened, and now the whole family was missing, including Robert.

It was the video that was puzzling Tom, though. There was something contrived about Olivia's clothing. Were they somehow *both* involved? But in what?

The FaceTime trail had temporarily gone cold, but they would get the court order tomorrow to demand the correct IP address for Olivia Brookes, or at least the IP address of whoever was using Olivia's email address.

Tom had promised to go round to see Leo to find out what she'd discovered about his break-in, if he could get away at a reasonable time. It was good of her to sort this for him. He knew from experience how devastating it could be to walk into a home that had been turned upside down, and he was just glad he hadn't had to see his place that way. It was another thing he should be dealing with but was ignoring. He needed to make sure it was secure, though, because Lucy was coming to stay for a fortnight at the start of her summer holiday, and if her mother got wind of any of this she might just decide it wasn't safe for their daughter to spend the night there. He could do without dealing with Kate if she decided to be difficult.

For once, he didn't feel remotely like cooking, and anyway it was getting late. Maybe they could just go to a local restaurant. He would see what Leo thought – let her make the decision, because just now he felt it would be beyond him.

Three missing kids, and nothing that he seemed able to do about it. He had spoken to Becky about getting an artist to go to the school, or somebody to produce an e-fit. They might not have photos, but the combined efforts of the teaching staff should produce some reasonable results.

Tom pulled his car into one of the two reserved spaces for Leo's apartment, grabbed his briefcase off the passenger seat, and made his way to the lift. He rang the bell and waited. Leo opened the door with a sympathetic smile. One thing he could say for her was that she was always very conscious of his mood. She reached towards him and pulled him close for a hug and a kiss on the cheek.

'Come and sit down. I've got a glass of wine waiting for you,' she whispered softly against his ear.

'What about food?' Tom asked. He knew Leo wouldn't have cooked. He was never sure whether his prowess in the kitchen had made her wary of ever making a meal for the two of them. But he had to eat, and he was certain that if he sat down before a decision was made, he would never get up again.

'I'll sort it,' Leo answered. Tom just looked at her, and she laughed. 'I thought you might be tired, so I had a word with the Japanese restaurant down the road. They're going to do us some tempura, and then steak and salmon teriyaki. I just have to call them about twenty minutes before we're ready – is that okay with you?'

Tom felt overcome with relief. Not his decision, not his job. *Fantastic.*

'Whatever you've decided will be just terrific,' he murmured with a grateful smile as he sank down on to the sofa.

'Crap day?' Leo asked.

'Confused day, and too much has happened,' Tom replied, blowing out a long breath of air through pursed lips as he picked up the waiting glass of wine. 'As I told you on the phone, the bloody husband has done a runner. We hadn't put him under formal surveillance because up until now he appeared to be co-operating, albeit grudgingly and with a few lies thrown in.'

Leo said nothing. Unlike any woman he'd ever met, she rarely expressed an opinion unless he asked for it.

'Anyway, enough about me. How did you get on at the cottage?'

Leo picked up her drink and took a sip. She looked puzzled.

'I don't know what to make of it,' she said, frowning slightly. 'They seem to have rifled through your drawers – but then never having looked, I don't know if your drawers are normally tidy or not. Stuff was jumbled, that's all I can say really. But they completely ignored anything of value in the house. You've got that lovely little abstract painting – a Spanish artist if I remember rightly. Paco somebody? That would have been so easy to take, but it's still there.'

Tom shrugged. 'I guess most people wouldn't know its value. My brother Jack was a collector, and most of his paintings were sold or given to art galleries. I particularly liked this one, so I kept it. But even I don't know what it's worth.'

'Well, whatever it is, it's strange they didn't just whip it off the wall,' Leo said. 'So as far as I can tell, they took absolutely nothing. They upended several boxes of papers, and they were spread all over the floor. But they were Jack's boxes, not yours. What happened to Jack, Tom? You told me he died, but you've never seemed keen to talk about him.'

Tom was silent for a moment. *Jack*. The wild one of the pair of them. The one who had hated school and locked himself in his bedroom building computers, listening to Whitesnake and Black Sabbath at full volume when Tom was trying to study. Putting the essence of Jack into words was impossible, because life with him had been full of colour with never a dull moment.

'You know he made a killing in the whole Internet security field and sold his company for a phenomenal sum of money, don't you?' Leo nodded. 'Well, he went out and bought a mega-fast speed boat and killed himself, the stupid, irresponsible bugger,' Tom muttered the last bit, his throat tightening, and took a long swig of his wine.

'So how did the accident happen?'

'Nobody knows. When he didn't return, a search party went looking for him. They found the boat upside down in the water, but they never found his body. Washed away, according to the coast guard. The manufacturers said they couldn't find anything wrong with the boat, so the assumption was that it was some kind of freak accident. Hitting a wave at the wrong angle when he was going too fast, or something like that.'

Leo stood up and went to get the wine bottle from the table to refill Tom's glass. He couldn't help thinking how great she looked, in a tunic top that was mainly white with a huge black rectangle on one side, and tight black jeans. They should have gone out really, so he could have shown her off to the world.

After she had poured more wine, Leo sat down next to him and curled her feet underneath. She held his hand for just a moment or two.

'Tell you what,' she said. 'I'll order the food now and go to pick it up in about fifteen minutes. You relax.'

Relaxing sounded good, but he knew it wouldn't be possible. He opened his briefcase and pulled out the folder he'd brought home with him. He flipped the file open just as Leo leaned across to give him a soft kiss below his right ear. Tom moved his head slightly towards her and closed his eyes for a moment.

'What do you want with a picture of our local war hero, then?' she asked, with a puzzled tone in her voice.

'What?' Tom said, jolted from the moment. 'What do you mean, war hero?'

'It's Sophie Duncan, isn't it? Is that her name? Don't you remember? There was a programme about her – well, it was actually about heroines of the war in Afghanistan and she was featured. It wasn't a big segment, but because she was from Manchester I remembered her. She saved a load of people from some random bomb or other, didn't she?'

Tom held up the photo – the one that had been taken at the guest house in Anglesey; the one of the woman that Mrs Evans believed to be Olivia Brookes. Finally, and belatedly, Tom remembered where he'd seen her before. He and Leo had watched the programme together on some obscure satellite channel, but he'd been engrossed in something else at the time and had only glanced intermittently at the screen. She was right.

Sophie Duncan.

He needed to speak to Becky. Now.

31

With a weary groan Becky pushed the keyboard away from her and stretched her arms above her head. It was time to go home. It had been a frustrating day, but try as she might she couldn't find a connection between the multiple threads of information that had been revealed over the last fourteen hours, and maybe a good night's sleep was what she needed.

She shuffled the papers on her desk together into a pile and grabbed her bag from the bottom drawer. And then her mobile rang.

'*Bugger*,' she muttered. 'Is there no peace for the wicked?'

She grabbed the phone and turned it round to check who was calling. Unless it was somebody important they could sod off. It was Tom.

As Becky listened to what he was saying, she felt the heavy weight of her tiredness dissolve. Tom had identified the woman at the guest house. Was this the breakthrough they had been waiting for? *Please, please,* she prayed to a God she didn't really believe in.

Sophie Duncan.

Becky had never heard of her personally, but finding out where she lived should be a doddle as she was an army officer.

Nic was still hanging around making himself useful – unlike some others on the team. But then, he was career hungry rather than career disillusioned, so as soon as she had tracked down Sophie's address she called him over, keen to share her excitement at the latest development with somebody.

'This woman might just be able to answer all our questions. DCI Douglas said he'd meet us there, but I don't think we need him at the moment. We'll see what Captain Duncan has to say about why she was pretending to be Olivia Brookes, and then decide if we need to call the boss. Okay with you?'

Nic looked overjoyed. Poor bugger couldn't have much else to do on a

Sunday evening – a bit like Becky herself. As she grabbed her keys and walked out of the airless incident room, she realised that since leaving London she hadn't been on a single night out, with the exception of the celebration after their success with the rapist case earlier in the week. Was that really only a couple of days ago? Anyway, that was something else she was going to sort out. She was going to move on and get herself a social life.

'Ready?' she shouted to Nic, who was gathering together his stuff.

As they drove across Manchester, Becky ran through everything she thought they should ask Sophie Duncan.

'Primarily, we want to know why she was pretending to be Olivia Brookes. But we also need to know if she has any idea where Olivia really is, and who the hell came visiting during the week. That could be totally irrelevant – it could just be Sophie's boyfriend or something. But I want to know. I'd like you to take notes, Nic, but don't ask any questions. If you think I've missed something, have a quiet word and tell me. I may well have done it on purpose, so don't go blundering in there, okay?'

Nic nodded his head in short sharp movements, about twenty times more than was absolutely necessary. 'Yes, Ma'am,' he said. Boy, this lad was eager.

When they finally pulled up outside the house, they were disappointed to see that it was in darkness. The night hadn't quite closed in yet so there was still a bit of light, but Becky would have expected to see some lamps on by now. Perhaps they lived at the back of the house. There were two cars in the drive, so that was a positive sign.

Becky parked on the road, blocking the gate. She had no reason to believe Sophie was going to try to make a run for it, but they had already lost Robert and she wasn't about to lose anybody else.

She pulled out her warrant card so she had it at the ready, and made her way up the drive, Nic striding out behind her, glancing around him as if it were the first time he'd ever been on a suburban street.

Three sharp raps on the door knocker had no result whatsoever. She tried the bell, and heard it ringing inside. Still nothing.

Becky pushed up the flap on the letterbox, and had a good view into the hall. There was nobody there, but she could see a stair lift at the bottom of the stairs. That would suggest that whoever used it – and she didn't know if Sophie's injuries were sufficiently bad to warrant a stair lift – must be downstairs.

'Nic, see if you can get a response round the back, would you? Don't make them jump, though. Be discreet.'

Nic disappeared into the darkness, and Becky waited, continuing to hammer on the door.

The stillness of the night was interrupted by the sound of running feet, coming fast towards her.

'We need to get in there, Ma'am – now,' Nic said, and without waiting for her to comment he put his size-twelve foot out and booted the front door with all his strength.

The door flew inwards, busting the housing for the Yale lock completely out of the frame. Nic started to run towards the back of the house and Becky chased after him. He kicked open the door to a sitting room, and fell to his knees next to the body of a young woman on the floor.

Tied to a chair by her arms and legs, she had obviously tried to move and tipped the seat on its side, narrowly missing a metal hearth fender with her head. Blood was clotted on the outside of her trousers, and Becky thought she might be dead. But as Nic reached out to feel for a pulse, her dark eyes shot open.

'About fucking time. Get these sodding ties off me, will you? Is my mum okay?'

Becky glanced around, but there was nobody else there.

'Upstairs – she can't get down. If that bastard has hurt her…'

But Becky didn't hang about to hear what Sophie Duncan was going to do to her attacker. She ran to the bottom of the stairs and glanced upwards to where she could see a crumpled form. She raced up the stairs and fell to her knees on the top step, reaching out her hand to touch the neck of the elderly lady lying on the carpet.

As her hands made contact, the woman flinched. 'Get off me, you monster,' she said through dry, cracked lips. Becky dragged her phone from her back pocket and spoke to the lady as she dialled.

'It's okay, love. My name's Becky. I'm a police officer. You're all right now. I'm just going to get you an ambulance.' Becky spoke quietly into the phone as she summoned assistance.

As she hung up, she stroked the woman's cheek gently with the backs of her bent fingers. She didn't want to move her in case she was hurt, and she didn't seem to be cold. Nevertheless, there was a coat hanging over the balustrade and with the utmost care she laid it over the woman's shoulders.

'Can you tell me your name, love?' Becky asked.

'Where's Sophie? What did that pig do to my Sophie?'

Just at that moment there was a yell from downstairs.

'Mum? Are you okay, Mum?' Becky turned at the sound of running feet, or rather stumbling feet. Sophie was hobbling towards the stairs, limping, falling, getting up and dragging herself. Nic was trying to support her.

'Bastard ropes, they cut off the circulation. Christ, that hurts. Mum – are you okay?'

'She's okay, Sophie,' Becky answered. 'I've called an ambulance. Nic, can you get some water for both of them please?'

'Sophie, come here darling,' the weak voice beside Becky murmured.

Becky shuffled over so that Sophie could drag herself upstairs and sit next to her mum. Becky could see how much blood had congealed on the outside of Sophie's trousers, and was amazed she had managed to move at all.

'Oh, Sophie – did he hurt you?' her mother mumbled.

'Take more than that psycho to hurt me, Mum. You know that,' Sophie spat out the words. 'But what about you? Why didn't you stay in bed?'

'I wanted to get to you. I was going to try to slide downstairs on my bottom, but when I tried to get down on the floor, I fell over. I was so worried about you, but I couldn't get up. I'm sorry, love.'

Becky could see Sophie was struggling to speak.

'Whoever's fault this is, Mum, it's definitely not yours.' She stroked her mother's face gently.

'Can you tell me who did this to you, Sophie?' Becky asked. 'And why?'

'Oh, I'll tell you who, all right. It was that crazy freak Robert Brookes. He is *so* going to pay for this. Hurting me is one thing. Hurting Liv is another. But hurting my mother is one thing he is not going to get away with. And don't give me that look. What would you do if it was your mother and your best friend?'

When Tom arrived at the hospital he found Becky sitting on a hard blue plastic chair with her head tilted back against the wall. She looked totally knackered, but the night was far from over. Before disturbing her, he decided to grab a couple of cans of coke from the vending machine. Not his drink of choice, but they needed the caffeine, and he was certain the coffee would be vile and would come in plastic cups that were too hot to hold.

He put Becky's can down on the seat beside her and sat down on the other side, opening the can with a pop. Becky sat upright, and turned towards Tom.

'There's one for you there,' he said, pointing with his can.

'Thanks. Let's hope it wakes me up.' She paused. 'You didn't need to come, you know. I can handle this.'

Tom shook his head slowly. 'I'm not here because I don't think you're up to it. I'm here because three kids are missing, and two heads might be better than one. Okay?'

'Okay,' she answered quietly.

'How are we doing with Sophie Duncan, then?'

'Not great at the moment. She refuses to leave her mother until she's been checked over, and then the doctor wants to look at her leg. It seems Robert has done quite a bit of damage to it. As far as I can gather, the original injury from when she was caught in the bomb blast hadn't knitted together properly, so she's had to have more surgery on her leg and the wound was still a bit raw. Our friend Brookes exploited that, although I bet she didn't let on how much he was hurting her. She's one hell of a tough cookie, if you ask me.'

'Did you manage to get anything at all from her?'

'Nope – other than the fact that this was all done by Robert Brookes, who has understandably been called the full range of expletives. I was going to ask her what the hell it was all about, but I got shooed out by the doctor. This was really vicious, Tom. He wasn't playing games. I told you he was a murdering bastard.'

Tom sat back and rubbed his hands over his face. *What a mess.* They should have taken Robert in, and it was his fault they hadn't. But they hadn't had anything to go on, and Robert's solicitor would have got him out in no time. Still, Tom couldn't help thinking that he might have been able to prevent this.

He looked at his watch. He felt they were wasting time just sitting here. There must be other things to be done, but he needed to speak to Sophie Duncan. And now would be good.

'How long is she going to be, do you think?' he asked.

'Not too long. The doctor came out just before you arrived to tell me she was just going to be stitched up.'

Out of the corner of his eye, Tom sensed some movement – the first he'd seen in what appeared to be a fairly dead emergency room. A doctor was walking towards them. He stopped and faced Becky.

'DI Robinson, you can go and talk to Captain Duncan now. She's ready to go home, but we've let her stay until you've spoken to her and her mum's been settled for the night. We're keeping Mrs Duncan in because her blood pressure is through the roof, and we're concerned that the fear of going back into the house might just tip her over the edge. I was given permission to explain that to you. Captain Duncan is in the cubicle at the end. She's a strong-willed woman, that's for sure.' The doctor smiled with what looked like awed respect. 'I wouldn't want to be in the shoes of the man who did this to her.'

Becky and Tom stood up and made their way to the cubicle that had been pointed out to them, pulling the curtain to one side to enter.

'Sophie, this is Detective Chief Inspector Douglas. He's been involved in the case concerning Olivia Brookes from the start.'

Sophie pulled herself slightly more upright on the bed and winced with pain from some part of her body.

'Are you okay?' Tom asked.

'Hunky-dory. What do you want to know?'

'Tell us what happened, from when Robert Brookes arrived at your house.' Tom suspected that Becky knew some of this, but it would be better to hear it from scratch.

'I wasn't there when he arrived. The bastard got in through the front door. It was only on the Yale, so I bet he used a credit card or something. He went upstairs and threatened my mum with a blade on a Swiss army knife. Terrified her to death, or close enough. But it was me he wanted.'

Sophie was quiet, but her lips were set in a narrow line and, from the set of her jaw, Tom could tell she was clenching her teeth. Her fists were gripping the edge of the blue waffle blanket that covered the bed and he could practically hear the sizzling of her anger.

'Look,' she spoke through lips that were barely open, 'I'm feeling pretty crap – can we just get this over with as quickly as possible, please?'

'Okay, Sophie,' Tom said. 'Just answer a couple of questions now and we'll be on our way. We'll catch up with you again tomorrow. Is that all right?'

Sophie nodded, and settled back slightly against the pillows.

'The most crucial thing is that you tell us where Olivia Brookes and the children are.'

'Oh, shit. I knew you were going to ask me that – and I don't know. I honestly don't have any idea where they are. I'm worried sick about them all.'

Tom looked into her anxious eyes, and he knew she was telling the truth.

'After Robert attacked you, he disappeared. We know he's been lying about when he last spoke to Olivia. Do you think he might have hurt her or the children?'

Sophie looked down at her leg and grasped the top of her thigh in both hands.

'You've seen what he's capable of. I don't even know why you're asking me that question.'

She turned her head slightly towards Tom.

'There is one person who might have more of an idea than me where she is. If you can track Dan down, you could ask him if he knows anything,' she suggested. 'I've been trying to get hold of him, but he's not answering his mobile.'

'Dan?' Tom asked, in no doubt whatsoever who she was talking about.

'Danush Jahander – the guy who ran away from Liv all those years ago. Well, he's back, and he wants *her* back. But she was bloody terrified of what Robert would do if he found out.'

Tom looked at Becky. Despite Sophie's obvious discomfort they weren't going to be able to leave this until tomorrow. He thought back to Robert's smug, almost amused expression when Jahander was mentioned. *He knew,* Tom thought. And if he did, what would that have meant for Olivia?

His thoughts were rudely interrupted by the buzz of his telephone. He glanced at the screen as he accepted the call.

'Excuse me, Sophie – this could be important.' He stepped outside the cubicle. 'Yes, Jumbo. Tell me you've got more news?'

Jumbo's deep voice rumbled down the phone. 'I have – and not news you'll be expecting, my friend. The blood at the scene? Well, as it's for you I managed to pull in a few favours. I know a rush job is usually forty-eight hours, but I also know you're worried about Olivia Brookes and the children. So we've done the analysis on the blood and it turned up an unexpected result.'

Tom waited.

'Given the height of the blood spatter, we are fairly sure this is blood from an adult, although of course we'll check that. I know we were all expecting this to be Olivia Brookes' blood, but we were wrong. It's not female blood at all. The blood is from a man, as yet unidentified.'

Tom felt a cold run of fingers down his spine. It was a feeling he'd had many times, but he never quite got used to it.

PART THREE

Olivia

32

Monday

Some people believe that freedom is every person's right, but I have had to fight for mine. And it's been a long and difficult battle.

It began when Robert took my children. That day, he sent me to a darker place than I had ever imagined. I thought I had experienced the worst that life could throw at a person, visited every dark dungeon of despair, but nothing compared to the fear that I had lost my children. And that is exactly what Robert wanted; it was a warning, a taste of what might be if I didn't stay within his control. From that day forwards, I knew I would never again feel we could sleep safely in our beds, and the threat of all Robert was capable of hung over me like a black cloud.

My only option was to leave him, but how could I do that? I had no money of my own any more, and no means of getting any. I couldn't leave a trail; if he finds us, the consequences are too dire to contemplate.

The years since Dan haven't all been bad, but in the brief time I had with him I felt as if my spirit was alive – as if bubbles were effervescing inside me. I sparkled. With Robert there were never bubbles, but I was content to settle for stillness. After Dan and then what happened with my parents, serenity and calm seemed to be just what I needed, but as the years passed I started to realise that it wasn't enough. And that was before I understood it all – before I knew the reason I had lost Dan.

I'd begun to feel as if there was a creeping deadness inside me, encroaching on the calm and replacing it with a black void, a vacuum where emotion should be. And the deadness was growing and penetrating every corner of my soul, reaching out its dark tentacles to smother all natural reactions.

When Robert took my children, two things happened. I realised I had to banish the deadness and bring myself back to life. Not for my sake, but for my children. And somehow I had to use my stagnant brain to work out a solution to the terrible life in which I had found myself. I didn't know how, though. Every idea I came up with was flawed.

I couldn't just leave. I knew what Robert would do if I did, and anyway he had been so clever. He had managed to bring my sanity into question. The whole of our tiny, shrinking world believed that I couldn't cope with life without Robert's help. To an outsider, he appeared to take care of me and provide everything I ever could have wanted.

What I wanted was freedom.

The schedule on the kitchen wall was supposed to be there to help me. So why did I have to write down every action that required contact with other people? Robert said that if he came home unexpectedly and I wasn't there, he needed to know where I was.

Why?

I felt as if I was in a cage, being controlled, being observed. And I knew he was watching me. He couldn't bear me to be out of his sight, and the thought of me having a friend – even just another mother of a child at school – brought out the worst in Robert. His campaign to undermine me would be stepped up a notch.

It wasn't me I was worried about, though. It was my children. Robert's obsession was focused on one thing. Me. To him, the children were just another weapon in his armoury.

From the day Robert took my children, I spent six months trying to find a way to escape – but I had no money and no ability to get us all to a safe place. That was when I found Sophie again, and from that moment I began to hope.

It's been hard to maintain the outward image of the old me for Robert's sake while simultaneously starting to feel alive again. But I did it, and I just pray he never finds us. Nobody knows where we are. Not even Sophie. Especially not Sophie, because she is the only link. She knows so much, but I had to make sure our location is a secret even from her, because I know Robert.

I'm getting worried about Sophie. She was supposed to call me last night, and I've heard nothing. That's not like her. She has been amazing since the word go and I couldn't have made it through the last eighteen months without her. And she gave me a precious gift. That day I went to see her for the first time since I married Robert, she gave Danush back to me.

'Dan loved you, Liv,' she'd said. 'Whatever happened, there is absolutely no doubt in my mind about that, and Samir feels so guilty about what he did. But he thought he was doing the best thing for his brother, and it's all so long ago. Anyway, now you have your husband and three children to think about. Tell me all about them.'

But I hadn't been able to. Not that day. Not after hearing about Dan. More than anything it had made me realise how much I'd missed Sophie, how much I loved the company of other women – and yet somehow I had lost touch with reality and shut myself away. I promised Sophie I would come back to see her again. She suggested visiting our house and meeting the children, but I couldn't let that happen. Robert wouldn't like it. He'd never met Sophie, but he would hate her for no reason other than the fact that I love her.

I waited a couple of weeks, and found a time when I felt reasonably certain that Robert wouldn't check up on me. He had been moaning about a presentation he had to give, and I knew when it was happening. It gave me about an hour and twenty minutes of free time – a rare commodity in my life – and for those few meagre minutes, I felt able to breathe.

I chose some photos to show Sophie, and drove quickly to her house. When I calculated the time there and back, it was going to allow us forty minutes together, which for me was bliss. I couldn't let her know I was coming – her number would have shown on the phone records. Robert received copies of my mobile account too, so I just prayed she would be in. She was.

Sophie hadn't seen Jaz since she was two months old, and when she saw the pictures I knew she would be amazed at how beautiful my daughter had become as a seven-year-old. Jaz is nearly nine now, and she's getting prettier by the day. Sophie had never seen the boys, of course. Both with bright blond hair to offset their sister's dark, silky tresses – as a family we really stood out. Which is why Billy's hair is now dyed a darker brown, and Freddie's has been cut so short he almost looks bald.

Sophie wanted to know all about us. Where Robert and I had met, where we lived. I remember playing the happy wife, talking about everything we have and how close knit we are. I don't think she was fooled, though. She knew something was wrong, because *I* was wrong. I wasn't me any more, and she could see that. I wasn't *Liv*.

When her penetrating glance became too much, I fished in my bag for the photos.

'God, she's adorable,' Sophie had shrieked as she looked at a picture of Jasmine. 'She looks exotic, but then it's not surprising based on her parentage. I don't often say this about men, but Danush was bloody beautiful, wasn't he?' I said nothing, and just sorted through the photos yet again. First Billy, then Freddie. She eulogised about them for the requisite two minutes, but it was obvious she was more interested to see who I had ended up with after Dan.

'Let's see him then. Come on, don't hold back on your knight in shining armour.' By then she knew the story of how we had met.

I extracted a rare photo of Robert and me, taken by Jasmine when I let her use my camera on our last holiday. Sophie looked at the picture, smiling broadly. Then, although her face didn't change, I realised her smile had become forced.

'Tell me again how you met Robert,' she asked without raising her eyes to mine.

So I told her the story one more time, even though I'd already explained how Robert had been the man who had bought my flat, and how he had rescued me when my whole life had fallen down around my ears. How he'd been so kind. All of that was true. The fact that I wasn't happy now was no reflection on how things had been then.

'Where did he go to university?' she asked. Strange question, but I told her it was Manchester, just like us.

'Did you never meet him then?' she asked. I was beginning to be concerned about this. What was wrong with Sophie? She handed the photo back to me and leaned over to grab both of my hands, looking me in the eyes for the first time since she had seen the picture.

'Do you remember I told you how all the guys at university were in love with you?' She didn't wait for my response. 'There was one guy who I was really worried about. He turned up everywhere, just watching. Remember – I told you about him, but you used to laugh it off? I called him Creepy Guy.'

I had no idea where this conversation was going, so I just looked at Sophie and I'm sure she could see my confusion.

'You may never have clapped eyes on Robert before he bought your flat. But I can promise you that he'd seen you before – about a thousand times. He knew *exactly* who you were.'

'I swear to you, we'd never met. I would have remembered.'

'Liv, this guy used to follow you everywhere. You never believed me at the time, but wherever you were, there he was. I don't know how to tell you this. Robert… he's Creepy Guy.'

33

Robert Brookes lay on the faded peach candlewick bedspread and looked around him at the grubby room. He had never expected it to come to this, hiding out from the police in a dingy hotel in the back streets of Manchester. But he'd had no choice. He couldn't use his credit cards again, and he had to find somewhere that would let him pay cash.

He'd been round all the banks and withdrawn the maximum on each card. His gold card had let him take out £750 and, although he had been expecting more from his platinum account – the one Olivia knew nothing about – he was limited to the same amount. He'd got as much as he could on both debit cards too, so he had about £2500 to keep him going. He had also let himself into his office and signed out a pool car in somebody else's name. He just hoped nobody would notice for at least a couple of days.

With any luck his trick with the taxi would use up some police resources too. Did they really think he would be stupid enough to phone for a taxi from the house? Once he had placed the bogus call to one taxi firm, he had walked in entirely the opposite direction to the nearest supermarket and picked up the public telephone there to call a different taxi company.

Another thing he'd had to do was lose his mobile phone. His mind had been in such a muddle that he couldn't remember whether he could be tracked just by the SIM card, or by the phone itself. He'd read somewhere that in the US it was possible for the authorities to switch on the microphone on a mobile to listen in even when the phone was switched off. He couldn't risk being wrong about this. He'd extracted the SIM as he had walked to the supermarket and dropped it down a grid in the side of the road. Much as it had pained him, he had gone round the back of some local shops and stamped on his brand new iPhone until it was completely shattered. He had put the bits into a huge trash bin behind the butcher's where no doubt it would be mixed with all kinds of carcasses and offal.

Nobody was going to be looking in there.

The taxi had dropped him off outside the office and, as soon as he had purloined a car and grabbed an iPad that nobody knew was lurking in his desk drawer, he had started his search for Sophie Duncan. She and Olivia had been inseparable in their early days at university, until Jahander had come along to join the party. There had been other boyfriends before Danush, but nobody serious, and Robert had known he would just have to bide his time. He'd watched and waited. From the first moment he saw Olivia, laughing at some joke or other in the bar, he had decided that she had to be his. It was as if everybody else in the room had faded to a pale grey, with only Olivia glowing with colour and vitality in the centre. That was how he always saw her – at the centre of his vision – until that bitch Sophie made it impossible for him to be near.

He'd been racking his brains to remember everything he had ever known about Sophie. He had made it his business to find out about Olivia's friends, and Sophie had been top of the list. She'd been dealt with appropriately nine years ago – it hadn't taken much to drive her out of Olivia's life. She'd had to go: Olivia had to rely on *him* and not on random friends who wouldn't take care of her like he would. How had they managed to get back in touch? He must have got sloppy, but he couldn't think how.

One thing he did remember from all those years ago was where Sophie's mother lived, and he hadn't been able to believe his luck when the lovely Mrs Duncan – under some pressure, it had to be said – had revealed that her daughter was living there for the time being, and would be home soon.

That bitch Sophie had told him nothing, though. *Nothing.* And then he had pushed it just that little bit too far. He had dearly wanted to slap her around to wake her up, but before she'd passed out she had been screaming and he had no idea if the neighbours would have called the police. He'd had to get out of there.

From the moment he saw Sophie's photo on Mrs Evans' pinboard, he knew Olivia had out-manoeuvred him, and that wherever she had gone, she wouldn't be coming back. He wasn't ready to share that with the police, though. She had to be found. She had to be returned to where she belonged. *With him.*

He had made it absolutely clear to her exactly what would happen if she ever dared to leave him, and he had been sure she had understood his every word, every nuance. He had worked so damned hard to win her, but she was going to suffer for what she had done to him, and all he could think of was the pain he would inflict on her for the torment she had caused him.

34

The news from Jumbo the previous night had disrupted all of Tom's plans to interview Sophie. As he had ended the call and stepped back into the hospital cubicle, he could see a new greyness to Sophie's skin, and her eyes were bright with fever. For a moment, he wondered if she had heard Jumbo's booming voice even though he had moved away, but she would have needed extraordinary powers of hearing. He knew they would get nothing else from her until she'd had a chance to rest.

And of course, he'd had to tell Becky the news.

'It could mean nothing,' she'd said. 'He could have killed some other poor bugger too.'

But it had dinted her confidence, and he felt as if they were almost back at square one.

They were hoping that Sophie would be able to tell them more; give them some clue about what had happened to Olivia and the children, but when she'd opened the door to them this morning, Sophie looked as if she had barely slept, so Becky had volunteered to go and make some tea and toast while Tom started the questioning. He had watched Sophie as she walked towards one of the two sofas in the living room and lowered herself gingerly on to the cushions. It was clear that her leg was giving her hell.

'Why did Robert Brookes break into your house and hurt you, Sophie? What did he want?'

'Probably the same as you lot want. He wanted to know where Liv is, and why I was in Anglesey, not her. He wanted to know whose children I had with me – but they're irrelevant. There was no way I was telling him, because fuck knows what he would have done next. Probably gone after them – as if they'd know anything. They weren't Liv's children, and that's all he needed to know. She's scared to let those kids out of her sight, so she wouldn't even have trusted me with them in case he had something plotted.'

'What do you mean, "something plotted"?' Tom thought it was a very odd choice of phrase.

'You know bugger all about Robert Brookes, do you?' Sophie's nose flared and her top lip curled as she shook her head. 'He's the most manipulative, controlling, fucked-up person I've ever met. And always was, if you ask me. A real piece of work.'

The door from the hall was nudged open, and Becky came in bearing a tray.

'Let's get back to why you were pretending to be Olivia, shall we.' Tom had no doubt that Sophie had some strong words to say about Robert, but for now he wanted facts.

'She needed to get away. She wanted to be somewhere he knew nothing about. She was setting up her escape route, and I was only too happy to help her. Nobody was ever supposed to find out that it was me in Anglesey. I guess I've screwed that up big time.'

'What was she afraid of, Sophie? What did she think Robert was going to do to her?' Becky asked as she placed the tea and toast on a small table close to Sophie.

'What do you think? Look, guys, she wanted to leave him, but Robert is mental. There's no way he would ever let Liv go. Never, ever. So I was helping her. I will always help her, and I pray to God he never finds her.'

'So where is Olivia now?' Tom asked. 'Where is this hidey-hole she's found?'

Sophie shook her head. 'I told you last night. I honestly don't know. She would never tell me. Just in case Robert tried to get it out of me, I suppose. Not that I'd ever have told him. I've dealt with bigger bullies than him.'

Sophie sat back and folded her arms. Becky gave an exasperated sigh.

'You must know *something*, Sophie. For God's sake. We just want to find her – make sure that she and the children are safe.'

'I've told you; I don't *know* where she is. The arrangement in the past has always been that I cover for her during the holiday, and she's always back home at the end of the week. This time was different. This time, I knew she was never coming back. We usually have a handover meeting – when I give back the debit card I have to use so Robert can see some activity on it, the bill from the guest house, that sort of thing – but not this time. And she was adamant that I had to know as little as possible. She wouldn't let me help her unless I agreed to that.'

Tom looked at Becky. They were getting nowhere fast. Either she really didn't know, or she was a bloody good actress. Given her background, it could be either and he couldn't call it.

'And have you heard from her?' Tom asked.

'No, and I'm worried sick. If Robert got wind of what she planned, anything could have happened to her.'

Tom's thoughts exactly.

'Tell me about Dan. When did he get back in touch?'

Sophie shook her head slightly. 'I can't remember precisely. Some time last year, I think.'

'Why did he go in the first place? Do you know?' he asked.

Sophie shuffled around on the sofa, pulling a face tight with pain as she tried to make herself more comfortable. 'I know some of it. It was to do with his brother, Samir. I don't know all of it, but I know that much. Samir came over for a visit to try to persuade Dan to return to Iran. Dan refused and things seemed to settle down. Then Liv was pregnant, so he couldn't leave even if his feelings of family guilt had got the better of him. But something happened between Dan and Liv – she told him something about Samir. And the next day Dan was gone.'

'So where is he now?' Becky asked. 'We need to speak to him. I've tried the mobile number you gave me, but it seems to be switched off.'

'Your guess is as good as mine. He came to find me in Anglesey. I told him Liv was trying to work out what to do for the best, but she had to think of the children. Dan said he'd had enough of it all. He was going to have it out with Robert – tell him to let Liv go.'

'How did Dan plan to arrange this confrontation with Robert?' Tom didn't like the sound of this.

Sophie shut her eyes for a moment and dropped her head to her chest. 'That was my fault too. I knew where Robert was staying in Newcastle. Liv always told me where he was in case of an accident or something, particularly because she wasn't where she was supposed to be. I gave Dan the number of the hotel, and he called him. He said he was going to ask Robert to meet him at the house – I can't remember the details. One night last week, I guess.'

'Did he get through to him?'

Sophie nodded.

'What did Robert say?

Sophie gave a sigh of exasperation, rather exaggerated in Tom's view. Whether it was at their questions, or at Dan's insistence on meeting Robert, he couldn't quite be sure.

'I don't know. I thought Dan was being stupid. I wanted no part of it. He was going to tell me, but I was half asleep and I just put my head under the pillow and told him to fuck off.'

Sophie lifted her shoulders and held out her hands, palms uppermost. Her nonchalance and apparent lack of interest didn't ring true with Tom, but at least they could check with the hotel to see if Robert received any calls.

'Do you know what time he made the call, Sophie?'

'It was late, I know that. But he used my phone because his battery was flat, so you can check the recent calls if you like. I never delete anything. My phone's in my bag – have a look.'

Sophie pointed to where her bag was lying on the floor and Tom picked it up to pass it to her, but she just waved her arm around in a gesture which he took to mean 'just get the bloody thing out of my bag'. So he did.

He knew Dan was at the guest house a week last Tuesday, so with a nod from Sophie he started to scroll through her calls. The code for Newcastle was 0191 and he quickly found what he hoped was the correct number. He made a note of it and replaced the phone in Sophie's bag.

As he'd scrolled through, he had been hoping to see the name 'Liv' come up, but he was out of luck.

'Thanks for your help,' Tom said. 'If you think of anything else, just give me or Becky a call please.' Tom handed over his card as he stood up, then paused. 'Just one last question. You seem to have Robert Brookes' measure. What do you think he's going to do next?'

'He's going to try to find her, and I don't think he will ever give up until he does. Have you ever looked obsession in the face, Chief Inspector? Strip away the mask of normality, and it's a hideous, contorted serpent that lurks beneath the skin, writhing with frustration until the object of its desire is under its control.'

35

Robert couldn't remember the last time he had slept, but exhaustion had finally overtaken him, and he had drifted off for about thirty minutes. It was a restless sleep full of dreams and images from the past, which faded to dust the minute he opened his eyes. There had been something there, though; something he remembered that had seemed odd.

An image flashed into his mind. He'd gone back out to the car to get his suitcase on Friday evening and he'd heard a voice say, 'Robert.' For one moment when he turned and saw the shape of a woman backlit by a dying sun, he had imagined it was Olivia. But of course it wasn't. It was Edith Preston – possibly the last person he had wanted to see on this earth. She must have been watching through her window for his return. He had been too distraught to really listen to what she'd had to say, but suddenly it came back to him.

'I was getting a little concerned about Olivia because I haven't seen her or the children for days, and then when your car appeared in the early hours of Thursday morning, I was convinced something was wrong. But you'd gone again by the time I woke up. *Is* everything okay, Robert?' she had asked. At the time, he had been too busy trying to get rid of her to respond, or even to think about what she was saying, but he remembered it now.

He lay on his side and curled his legs up to his chest. She would have told the police this, he was certain. One more piece of evidence stacked up against him.

Where are you, Olivia? What are you playing at?

Robert straightened his legs and pulled a creased envelope from the back pocket of his jeans. He wanted to read what Mrs Stokes had said, just in case it gave him any clues to Olivia's thinking. Maybe she had let something slip when she'd said she was taking the children out of school. He didn't hold out much hope, though.

He shuffled up the bed a little so that his head was resting on the greasy padded headboard, put his thumb under the flap of the envelope to rip it open and withdrew four pages.

The first page was a letter from Nadine Stokes asking them to reconsider their decision regarding the children's schooling. She pointed out that their education was about more than learning – it included social development too, and in her view that meant mixing with other children.

Blah, blah, blah, thought Robert. She was probably right, but it didn't help him at all. She went on to talk about each of the children and their development. He couldn't really be bothered reading this. They all knew Freddie was still a bit of a baby – but, as Olivia said, he's only four and one of the youngest in his class – and Billy could be a bit of a show-off. He was sure Mrs Stokes was right and both would benefit from being with other children, but it was the least of his concerns right now.

He was about to screw the letter up and chuck it when he saw the first line of her report on Jasmine.

> Of late, we have started to feel that Jasmine is losing a little of her concentration. For a child who has always been so painstaking in her work, recently there has been a decline. One example that springs to mind is in regard to her work on the Second World War. When she returned from the Easter break she seemed delighted to be able to stand up in class and tell us all she had learned about evacuees. She said the island the family visits on holiday was fully evacuated during the war. Even the adults were forced to leave.

> Her teacher gently pointed out that children were evacuated *to* Anglesey not from it, and the island was overrun with evacuees from Manchester and Liverpool *arriving* on the island, not leaving it. Unfortunately, Jasmine became very upset. Her teacher said she went red, buried her head in her folded arms and started to cry. This behaviour is so unlike Jasmine, and we were quite worried. Not so much because her facts were inaccurate, but because she seemed so concerned about her mistake. We were keeping a careful eye on her to see if anything else was upsetting her, but there was nothing specific other than a slight reticence to speak of anything that happens in the home. Try as we might, we weren't able to draw her out about her holiday again.

Robert wasn't in the habit of analysing his children, but even he could see this was totally out of character for Jasmine. She was such a pernickety child. He put the letter down on the bed, and lifted his hands to rest them behind his head. *What could she have been thinking?*

Jasmine would not have got this wrong. He pulled his iPad towards him and switched it on. *Think, Robert, think.*

'Come on, come on,' he said out loud. Why did it have to take so long to boot up? And no Wi-Fi in this shitty hotel, of course. He would have to rely on 3G. Even bloody slower. Finally he managed to get Google up and running.

'Island evacuated during Second World War,' he typed.

The search results were displayed. The top result was Crete. Robert dismissed that. There was no way they had gone to Crete on holiday when they were supposed to be in Anglesey. They didn't have passports and anyway the boys would have talked about the flight.

Next down was 'Occupation of the Channel Islands' – a bit closer to home. Guernsey evacuated all children. But that couldn't be right. Jasmine had said adults too. He read on: 'The authorities in Alderney, having no direct communication with the UK, recommended that all islanders evacuate, and nearly all did so.'

Alderney. A tiny island in the Channel Islands, a speck in the sea between France and England. But why did it ring a bell?

Robert put the iPad down on the bed and closed his eyes, trying to catch a glimpse of an early evening a few weeks ago. There was something about Jasmine – some strange reaction one day when they were watching the television that he couldn't quite remember.

What was it?

Something Billy had said, he was fairly certain. They had been watching a wildlife programme on television. Robert had been reading the paper when Billy had suddenly said, 'Look, Jaz – it's our island.' Robert had looked up at the screen, but it clearly wasn't 'their' island at all. The sand was too white.

Robert shot upright. *That's what was wrong.* When he had looked at the beach in Anglesey, the sand was too dark. Nothing like the image that Olivia had shown him through the camera on her laptop at all.

He raised his knees and leaned forwards, wrapping his arms round his legs and resting his chin. What had that programme been about, and what was wrong with Jaz's reaction?

He closed his eyes. Jaz had been sitting on the sofa at right angles to him, and Olivia was to his left. As he had looked up at the screen when Billy mentioned 'our island', he had intercepted a glance between Jasmine and her mother. Jasmine's eyes had been wide open and her lips slightly apart. But Olivia had nudged him and he'd looked away from Jaz and towards his wife. He remembered she had whispered to him.

'Isn't he cute? He thinks every island with a beach is Anglesey. Perhaps we need to take him somewhere else soon, so he knows there are other beaches and other islands.' They had shared a fond smile, and the memory was forgotten. Until now.

What the hell was the programme about? Shit, why hadn't he been paying more attention? Still, it was only a few weeks ago.

He grabbed the iPad again and logged on to the BBC website. He was sure it was the BBC; they would have put the television on after the news. And it was definitely a weekday, because every weekend recently he had been working on laying the new terrace until it went dark.

He scoured the programmes.

'Got you,' he said, a grin spreading from ear to ear. He had found the right programme – now all he had to do was look back through the listings. Robert could feel his heart thumping in his chest. His fingers prodded hard at the screen in a futile attempt to speed it up.

'That was it – hedgehogs!' How could he have forgotten? Freddie had wanted them to build a hedgehog home in the garden; he vaguely remembered listening to him wittering on about it to Olivia.

But these were no ordinary hedgehogs. These were white hedgehogs and, according to the programme summary, there was only one place in the UK to find these in the wild. *Alderney.*

Robert pushed the iPad to one side and lay back with his hands behind his head. A huge weight had been lifted from his shoulders and he felt a rush of elation. He knew where she was.

Sleep tight tonight, my darling. Because tomorrow, I'm coming to get you.

36

When Sophie told me about Robert – who he was, and how he had always been there when we were at university – it was as if a light had been switched on in my head. Everything began to make sense and some terrible thoughts invaded my mind, ideas I couldn't allow to fester because I knew I wouldn't be able to hide my feelings.

I had honestly believed that the first time I'd met him was the day he came to view my flat. And he was so kind to me when my life turned upside down. But all that time he had known me – known who I was, what my life had been like with Danush. Why had I not listened to Sophie when she said there was a man stalking me? I thought she was exaggerating, and I never noticed him. I only had eyes for Dan.

Sophie was so much more observant than me. She watched people. It was her passion, and one she planned to turn to good use in her career. I would never have picked Robert out of the crowd at a party or in a club, but Sophie would home in on anybody whose eyes were only focused in one direction. I should have listened.

It's only now that I believe her – only now that I can look back on those days and realise the evidence that was in front of me, if only I had seen it. How could I forget the night that I walked home alone from the pub – a walk I had done many times since Dan and I had moved into our flat together? As I passed the park, a swing was gently swaying even though it was a still, cold night, and I was certain that I was being followed. I could feel hot eyes boring into the back of my neck; I had started to run, desperate to be home.

I was sure that my stalker was behind me, gaining on me with every second – and when a dark figure stepped out from behind a tree to catch me, I thought my heart would stop.

It was Dan. He had arrived home and found the flat empty, so he was on his way to meet me. When he saw how terrified I was, he wanted to go and check each of the drives along the road in case my pursuer was hiding. But I was too frightened and just wanted to get home. He hadn't seen anybody on the shadowed street behind me, and in the end we'd decided it was all my imagination. I never walked home alone again at night after that, though.

Could that have been Robert? Or maybe it was just some random pervert lurking in the bushes of the park. I would never know.

Was it a coincidence that Robert came to look at my flat the very day it went on the market? I can't believe that now. It was all part of his plan to get close to me.

I have lain next to this man for years. He knows every inch of my body, and yet all the time he has been hiding who he really is.

As Sophie told me everything she remembered and my memories came flooding back, the reality sank in. I felt a tightness in my gut and hoped to God I wasn't going to be sick – because I couldn't stop thinking of my beautiful baby boys. How could I wish that I had never met Robert, because then they wouldn't have been born?

I had to get away from him. Our whole life together had been a lie, and all I could think of were his threats. If I was going to have any chance at all of escape, I was going to have to plan carefully, and it wasn't going to be easy without money or freedom.

But we've done it. We're here, and we're safe. *Thank goodness.*

It's been a terrifying year and a half. There hasn't been a moment when I haven't been afraid. I never thought I could act, but for my children's sake, I had to learn. It was bad enough dealing with Robert on a day-to-day basis, eating meals together, sharing a bottle of wine – all the time behaving as if this man were my saviour – but the nights…

I don't know how I kept it together as he held me, touched me, and expected a response. Thank God I had insisted that I preferred the lights to be out when we made love – a stance I had taken since discovering the camera hidden in the bedroom. I explained it to Robert on the pretext of finding it more romantic, but the thought of him replaying our performance and perhaps analysing my expressions made me nauseous. I had no doubt that, if he had been able to, he would have studied my face and found something missing.

As it was, I was barely able to prevent myself from crying. Tears would frequently leak from my eyes, and if Robert felt them on my face, I had to pretend they were tears of pleasure. The feel of his naked body repulsed me; under my fingers, I imagined his skin as the flesh of a snake and I couldn't drive the image from my mind.

But Robert had to trust me and believe his little experiment with the children had taught me a lesson, because I was sure that if he caught the merest glimpse of what I was really thinking, he would take my children for the second time, and this time I might never see them again.

37

The only thing Robert could do was to trust his instincts. He had done his research, and from all that he had read it seemed the island Olivia had chosen was a peaceful, crime-free world that no doubt suited her perfectly.

He had to acknowledge that her flight had been far from an impulsive decision; she must have been planning it for some time. Sophie had been pretending to be Olivia at the guest house since the previous October, and somehow Olivia must have found a source of funds, because she couldn't have done all this without money. Perhaps he didn't know her as well as he thought. He had never considered her to be devious, but he had clearly underestimated her.

One thing was certain, though. She knew nothing of the person that Robert really was. She had only seen the bits of him that he wanted her to see. Perhaps now it was time she saw the rest.

She was his wife, and his whole life. Without her, there would be no point in living. And he'd told her exactly what he would do if she ever thought of leaving him, but still she'd done it. She had defied him, cheated, lied.

She had to be punished.

He could feel the blood rushing to his face, and his hands gripped the steering wheel tightly as he drove down the M6, heading towards the M40. Some idiot in a beat-up old BMW cut in front of him, and he took his aggression out on his horn, opening the window and gesticulating wildly at the driver. He wanted to put his foot down and coast past the smug bastard, but he couldn't. The last thing he needed was to be pulled over by the police for speeding.

The decision to drive to Poole and take a ferry to Guernsey had been difficult. It would have been so much better if he could have flown from Manchester to get to Olivia as quickly as possible, but the flight was more expensive and he was certain that the police would have alerted the airports to be on the lookout for him. After what he had done to Sophie, he was sure they would be trying to find him.

The muscles in his stomach clenched as he relived the pleasure of thrusting the knife into Sophie's leg. He would have dearly loved to kill the bitch for what she had done, but his goal was Olivia and if he became the subject of a full-scale manhunt it would put his plan at risk. They would be searching for him, but not with the same level of urgency that they would hunt down a murderer. At least, that was what he hoped.

Travelling by ferry seemed to be less dangerous to Robert. He was confident his passport wouldn't be scanned and would only be used to verify his name on the ticket. He'd checked and, as the Channel Islands are part of the UK, he only needed photo ID so he might just make it to Olivia without any warning flags being raised.

Each time he thought of what she had done, his jaw clenched at the injustice of it all. When her parents had been found dead, he'd been the one to take care of her, as he had done every day of his life since then. How dare she throw that all back in his face?

Of course he'd had to make sure Sophie was out of Olivia's life from the start. She was dangerous. He knew she had written when Olivia's parents died, because he had seen the British Forces stamp. He had destroyed that letter and all the ones that came later. Olivia was devastated that she hadn't heard from her friend, and she wrote to Sophie every week for months. In the early days of her grief Olivia rarely left the house, though, and she had asked Robert to post her letters. He smiled at the memory of her trust, and relived the pleasure of holding her while she sobbed at the lack of a response from her friend, claiming that the only person in her life she could trust was him.

Which was exactly the way he liked it.

So how had Olivia and Sophie revived their friendship? How had he missed it?

Sophie was a stroppy bitch, and he had hated her with a passion at university. Who did she think she was? She had seen him watching Olivia, but there was no law against looking at a beautiful girl, was there? And what was it she had called him? *Creepy Guy.* That was it. She had made it so difficult for him. If she was around he'd always had to back off, but he had just been biding his time, waiting until Olivia needed him, was ready for him.

There was one particular night at the university theatre when Robert had decided that Sophie was going to have to pay for her interference. She had caught him trying to take a photo of Olivia as they got ready for a stupid charity pantomime. Sophie had stormed up to him and grabbed the front of his shirt in both her hands, pulling his face close to hers.

'Fuck off, Creepy Guy. Take that camera out of here before I ram it up your pervy little arse. Leave my friend alone.'

Olivia had shouted out to Sophie. 'What's up, Soph? You need to get ready, honey – you're on in a few minutes.'

Robert had nearly killed her then. He could practically feel Sophie's neck in his hands; see her face turning mottled red as he choked the life out of her. But it wasn't the right time. Olivia would have turned to Dan for comfort, and that was more than Robert could bear.

So he'd done nothing. Sophie had shaken him one more time, pushing her angry face closer to his while muttering her final warning, and had gone back into the room, pulling a limp curtain across the doorway. He'd heard her say, 'It's that perv: your very own Creepy Guy. Come with me, Liv. Seriously, you need to know who this guy is.'

Olivia had laughed. 'Okay. Next time you see him, point him out to me. Let's sort it once and for all.'

'I can't believe you've not noticed him. Look, Liv, you really do need to be careful. There's something not right about him,' Sophie had responded.

Bitch.

From that moment on, he'd had to keep his distance. He'd still been able to watch her, though. He'd even followed her home one night, but then the wonder-boy Danush had stepped out from behind a tree just at the wrong moment, and Robert had had to slide silently into an open gateway to avoid being seen.

He was glad he had hurt Sophie. She deserved it for what she had done to him.

Now he pushed thoughts of Sophie from his mind. He needed to focus on Olivia; she was the only one who mattered.

Robert used the whole journey to Poole to devise his plan. Once the ferry arrived at Guernsey, he would have to find out how to get to Alderney. Even though a boat was going to add a further three hours to the journey, it seemed the safest option.

And then he would find her.

Olivia was going to get the surprise of her life. He smiled at the thought. She had been clever, but she had underestimated him.

Somebody must know where she was hiding. Taking the children out of the school system was a clever trick, but he would start wherever there were the most people – the town centre, if there was such a thing, or maybe he could ask in some of the bars. Somebody was bound to know.

You can't hide from me, Olivia.

And when he'd found her?

He'd told her two years ago exactly what he would do if she ever left him. And now he would prove to her that he had meant every word.

38

Sophie and I had devised my escape strategy in secret. I had uncovered each of the schemes Robert had devised to bind me to him, and I was aware of all the methods he was using to scrutinise my every move. I couldn't afford to overlook any part of his master plan. Sometimes I had to allow him to make me look stupid. I knew what he was trying to do, but I had to go along with it, or he would have stepped up his game.

His first trick was with the school, and it was so successful that he repeated it more than once. He promised to pick the children up, and then he didn't. He left them there, thinking their mummy had forgotten them. He diverted the home phone to his mobile so that when the school phoned to say the children were waiting, he could intercept the call and leave it unanswered. They would believe I had gone out and forgotten my children, or maybe I wasn't capable of answering the phone. So then they would have to call Robert and explain that I hadn't turned up.

After the first time I knew what he was doing, but what choice did I have? If I had gone to the school in spite of everything, he would know that I understood his game and he would have devised something worse. And the children were safe. I had no doubt he would finally collect them, acting the role of the caring father struggling to cope with a slightly demented wife.

I knew exactly how he would play it. He would race up to the school gates and apologise, stumbling over his words in his apparent anxiety, giving the clear impression I had forgotten my children – or perhaps that I had a problem: drink, drugs, or some sort of mental instability.

He told Nadine Stokes – the school's head teacher – that he was going to try to call me each day to check that I'd remembered to pick the children up, and he would do his best to make sure it didn't happen again. He tried to make me believe that I was the one at fault, and if it hadn't been for Sophie I might have started to think he was right. He would lull me into a false sense of security for a while, confusing me by telling me that I was doing well, making me question my own sanity. Then he'd do it again.

I know he had a word with one or two of the other mothers, asking them to keep an eye out in case I came for the children and then wandered off, or left with only two of them instead of all three. He put it down to me going through a rough patch. I wouldn't have known about this, but Robert chose badly. One of the women was a natural bitch – all women recognise them, but men rarely do. While most of the mothers he had spoken to treated me with sympathy if a little suspicion, the bitchy one couldn't wait to have a dig – to undermine me with the odd comment, thinly veiled with saccharine sweetness and a smile that failed to hide the glint of pleasure in her eyes at somebody else's apparent downfall.

Still I played along. Even when he suggested that dreadful schedule on the kitchen wall, I agreed it would be a good idea. Any fool could see that it wasn't there to remind me of what I should be doing. It was there to control me, so that if Robert came home unexpectedly, which he liked to do sometimes to 'surprise' me, he would know exactly where I was. When he dialled 1471 on the telephone to see who had last called, he needed to be sure I had logged every call. Otherwise, he would have been suspicious.

And then there were the cameras. He hid them well, but not quite well enough. I've always hated housework with a vengeance, but I did it. It was my job, after all, and I did it well. If I had to live in a cage, it might as well be a gilded cage in every sense. I was living in relative luxury with no freedom, so whenever I thought I was going to cry, I would get down on my hands and knees and scrub the kitchen floor. If I sat still and did nothing – because really, once the house was clean there was precious little that I had to do – a sense of dejection and hopelessness would descend on me. So I would immediately set to and polish the furniture. I knew every nook and cranny of that house, which meant that nothing within those four walls was a mystery to me. Not even his precious locked study. But once more I acted dumb and let him get on with his games, while all the time planning my escape with Sophie's help.

Getting out of the house was easier than I thought. There were no cameras in the hall or on the landing, or – thank God – in the children's bathroom. And there was no bath in our en suite. So I got into the habit of taking long baths every couple of days. I would go into the bedroom and play a game of pretending to grab a bathrobe, twist my hair up in a knot, select some toiletries from my dressing table and disappear off camera for an hour and a half. Then I would reappear in my bathrobe and lie on the bed reading a book. A perfectly relaxed day.

I had no idea how I was going to make my final escape, though, because I didn't have a pound to my name. I couldn't take any money from my household allowance, because Robert knew where every penny went. I had to earn some, and earn it quickly.

Sophie and I toyed with so many ideas, only drawing the line at prostitution. And yet, in many ways I'd been doing that for years – having sex with a man I didn't love who kept a roof over our heads. What's the difference, really?

Sophie offered to lend me the money – my escape fund – but how would I ever be able to repay her? Anyway, it wouldn't have been enough. I needed to have sufficient money to support us until we were safe. And I didn't know how long that might be.

Finally we came up with a plan that stood a small chance of success. It was risky, and there was every possibility that it wouldn't work, but I had to try something. So I borrowed just five thousand pounds from Sophie, and gambled it all by becoming an online trader. I had studied economics, for goodness sake; surely I could make some money this way? I bought the smallest laptop I could find and hid it in the blanket box in the spare room, under all the bedding we'd bought for when we had guests; all still in its packaging and unlikely to ever come out. I knew Robert wouldn't find it. Sophie had already used her unbelievably extensive contacts and had set up my false identity and bank account, and all transactions were online so it was remarkably easy to get going.

To start with, though, it was a disaster. I was basing my decisions on short-term information, and not really thinking and planning ahead. I realised I needed to look at the economic landscape as a whole, and by using my knowledge and working hard at it, the decisions became more educated. The first four thousand pounds disappeared in no time at all, but finally I got the hang of it. I started balancing my risk and things began to look up. The money had nearly gone though, and fear was making me too cautious. I was gaining, but too slowly. So Sophie lent me more – another ten thousand – money I might never have been able to repay if I'd failed in my task. I needed to make enough to escape, and gain the confidence to believe I could continue earning in the future, because Robert must never find us.

But now I've done it. I'm free and I feel as if the tight clamp that was holding my body and mind together has been released. It finally feels safe to sleep at night, and gradually I have stopped waking every two or three hours to check that my children are still here, still safe, still with me. It's been two weeks now, and we've hidden our tracks so well. The kids have been great. They've adapted brilliantly to island life, and even though I'm teaching them at home at the moment, hopefully they'll soon be able to mix with the other children – when they are used to their new names.

They thought it was such fun to start with when I asked them to pick a name from their favourite characters in books or on television. These were to be our holiday names. And they stuck with it. Billy is now Ben, Freddie is George – potentially the most difficult choice but as he's only four I don't think we need to worry so much – and Jaz is Ginny. She really wanted to be Hermione, but I told her to choose another name from Harry Potter, because Hermione was too memorable. Ginny is apparently Ron Weasley's sister, and so guaranteed to be cool in Jaz's eyes. I'm now Lynn. I would have chosen something more exotic, but Lynn's an easy name and enough like Liv that I'm comfortable with it.

There were a couple of dodgy moments when the children used their pretend names at home, but Robert never paid them that much attention so he probably put it down to the normal silliness of children. And there was the time when the Alderney hedgehogs came on the television. Jasmine's look of horror was such a giveaway, poor child. But I don't think Robert noticed.

I knew from the beginning that wherever I chose for our new home, we would have to visit it long before our final escape. A woman alone with three children, no matter what we had done to change our appearance, would stand out like a sore thumb if we had arrived out of the blue. So we've been here twice before, and made ourselves as visible as possible. When the police inevitably report that we're missing, they will have no photos and nobody here believes we are newcomers.

The children haven't asked many questions. Billy – no, I must call him Ben – asked me why I'd decorated my bedroom in our new house so that it exactly matches the bedroom at home in Manchester. I couldn't tell him the truth, and I hate lying to them. I said it made the house feel more like home. That time is over now, but for seven nights last week I had to lie on the bed pretending I was in Manchester while I spoke to Robert on FaceTime. I can't wait to rip the room to bits and change every single plum-coloured cushion from the colours of my nightmare. Tomorrow I'm going to get a big box and stuff every identifying feature out of sight.

I even had to kit out one room so that it looked bland enough to be a typical bed and breakfast room with the requisite pair of patterned cushions in a colour not too masculine and not too feminine – a nice mid blue – placed at an angle against the pillows and the matching throw over the bottom third of the bed piled high with neatly folded clean towels. I knew that when I spoke to Robert he would want to look around the room and see the view from the window, so thank goodness I was able to show him a strip of beach. There was nothing to make him think I was anywhere other than Anglesey. Not so much as an ice-cream van. Just a long stretch of bright, pale sand. He had to be reassured that everything was exactly as it should be, and I'd chosen my fake location well. Robert had never been to Cemaes Bay, so he wouldn't know the difference.

The children can't believe how lucky they are to be living this close to the beach every single day, and not just for holidays. It pushes everything else to the backs of their minds, and they will have had three or four months of this before the reality of winter takes the shine off. Perhaps by then I will be able to send them to school. But I don't know. While Robert is on this earth, I am not sure we will ever be safe, because he has made it very clear that he isn't prepared to live without me.

For now, though, I feel secure. There is nothing to guide him to us here, and gradually I am beginning to relax.

39

'Liv? Oh thank the Lord for that. I can't tell you how relieved I am to hear your voice.'

Sophie hadn't realised that she had been holding her breath.

'Are you okay, Soph?' Liv asked. 'I've been worried about you. You're usually so prompt. I nearly called you, but I didn't know for sure if it would be safe. Are you okay? Is your mum okay? I thought maybe she'd had another fall, or something.'

Liv was rambling, and Sophie knew she had to shut her up. But she didn't know how to tell her what had happened. Thank God she had left her special pay-as-you-go phone – or 'Liv phone' as she called it – in the car when she'd unpacked the shopping. At least Robert hadn't got his filthy hands on it.

'Listen – I don't want you to panic, but he was here. *Robert*. The arsehole was here. In my fucking house.'

Sophie could have kicked herself. She didn't mean to sound so angry. She had planned to be calm. But as soon as she mentioned his name her anger and hatred boiled over. She heard a gasp and realised how stupid she'd been. Liv had so much to worry about and she didn't need to add to her distress.

'Oh Sophie, no. Oh God, I'm so very sorry. What did he say?'

How could she tell her that it wasn't so much what he *said*?

'He's not going to give up, Liv. I'm sorry, but you've got to believe me. He was mental, incensed, practically foaming at the mouth. Look, I'd spare you this if I could, but he's going to move heaven and earth to find you. Are you sure you're safe?'

'Never mind me, what about you? Did he hurt you? Is your mum okay? Please tell me Robert didn't hurt her? I'm so sorry. I didn't mean you to suffer.'

Sophie heard a sob from the other end of the phone, and screwed her eyes tight. *Bugger.*

'Mum's fine. Don't worry. We're both fine – but Liv, are you sure you're safe?'

'I think so. I don't know how he could find us here. There was one little slip at home, but Robert wasn't paying much attention. We'll be fine. But it's you I'm worried about. How the hell did Robert find you? Why did he even come looking for you?'

'Listen, I need you to calm down because I've got quite a bit to tell you. So, first of all, where are the kids? Are they okay?' Sophie asked.

'They're fine. Actually, they're having a whale of a time.' There was a pause from the other end of the phone, and Sophie could practically see her friend trying to pull herself together. 'They're playing on the beach. I'm sitting on a bench nestled in the sand dunes, watching them. If it wasn't for everything else, I'd feel like I was in heaven. I just need to watch the waves for a moment and listen to them gently whooshing on to the shore, and I'm calm again. It's amazing how soporific it is.'

Sophie relaxed. Liv clearly felt she was in a safe place, and right now that was the priority.

'Well, don't fall asleep on me. I need to tell you what's been happening. First of all, Robert knows I'm the one who's been staying at Mrs Evans' place in Anglesey.' Sophie waited, expecting an explosion of sound from Liv.

'Oh,' was all she got. She waited to see if Liv would say more, but it seemed to take her a while to gather her thoughts. 'How did that happen? Do you know?' Liv said with remarkable calm. This wasn't supposed to have happened.

'I think I've worked it out. There was a dreadful couple staying at the place. The wife never had her stupid camera out of her pudgy little hands, and I'd been dodging around for a couple of days to avoid the silly cow. Anyway, I was coming out of the front door, and she got me. I turned back quickly, but apparently she'd managed to capture my profile. She sent the photo to Mrs Evans at the guest house. God, I'm a stupid idiot. I should have snatched the camera and thrown it in the sea. I'm so sorry, Liv.'

Sophie couldn't help thinking that she'd let Liv down.

'Sophie, darling, please don't apologise for anything. You've been amazing. You've done more than I could ever have asked of anybody. Just tell me what happened.'

'Your creep of a husband came a-calling.' Sophie told Liv the rest, leaving out anything to do with tying to chairs or knives in wounds. Liv listened without saying a word.

'Then finally, he asked me where you were.'

'And what did you say?' Liv responded quietly.

She couldn't tell Liv she had passed out at that moment so wouldn't have been able to answer even if she had known.

'Well, I don't bloody know where you are, do I, so I didn't tell him anything. You made the right call there. I wouldn't have told him, but it's better that I really don't have a clue.' Sophie paused. She was now going to have to explain about the police. But before she did, Liv started talking.

'But how did he know where you live, Sophie?'

Sophie sighed. Liv had still failed to completely grasp the depths of Robert's early obsession, in spite of all that had happened since.

'Liv – listen to me. Robert wasn't just some guy who had a crush on you all those years ago. He was as obsessed then as he is now. You came with me to see my mum lots of times, and Robert being who he is, there's more than an outside chance he was following you, *watching* you. It's what he does. So he would know *exactly* where my mum lives. He couldn't have known I'd be here, but he had a pretty good idea that she might actually know where I was – and I guess he just hit the jackpot.'

'Did he know about your visitor in Anglesey, though?'

'Yes – that bit worked as planned. Of course, because it was me and not you that was staying there, it didn't have quite the result we'd expected. I had to talk to the police too. They found me from the picture, but I think I handled that okay.'

'It's fine, Soph. We knew they would be looking for me and the kids. What did they say?'

Slowly Sophie went through her conversations with the police, making sure she didn't slip up and mention the hospital.

'So did they ask about your visitor?'

'Yes, of course they did.'

'And what did you tell them? I really need to know.'

'I told them it was Dan.'

40

The choice of Alderney as my hiding place came about by chance. I needed to find an island because I wanted the children – Billy and Freddie at least – to believe that they were still in Anglesey. Silly, really, because Anglesey is so big that I'm not sure they were ever aware that it *is* an island. But still, that was how my fevered brain was working. And there is something safe about an island. Particularly one with no car ferry service. Surrounded by water, it feels as if the sea is protecting us from harm. One minute the water shimmers calmly in warm sunlight, but the next it can be raging, boiling, as if to ward off invaders.

I knew I wouldn't be able to fool Jaz about where we were, but I came up with an explanation that I thought would satisfy her. I'd been talking to her a lot about her real father, ever since Robert took her and the boys from me two years ago. I wanted her to know about the other half of her life – the other culture that her father had loved so much. I had learned that Jaz was making up all kinds of stories about Danush, as if he were still a part of her life, as if any day now she was going to be with him. This worried me. Whatever actions I was prepared to take, I needed Jasmine to understand how things stood with her father. I had to teach her about him, make her understand who he was and why he couldn't be with us – without telling her everything, naturally. She was too young to grasp the harsh realities.

I had to explain Alderney to her in such a way that she would keep it a secret. I told her we were going to spend some holidays on a different island – one that I had been to with her father when we had been happy. But she wasn't to tell a soul. She understood she couldn't talk about her father if Robert was around. She'd tried once or twice, and Robert had gone berserk, shouting that *he* was her father. *He* was the one who was paying for her upbringing. *He* was the only father she had – and she'd better believe it.

After those incidents Jaz had never mentioned her father again in front of Robert. I told her we were coming here – to Alderney – so we could remember things about her father together, in a place where I had my best memories of him.

I'm ashamed to say that this was a lie. I hate the fact that I have lied to my beloved daughter, but Jasmine can read – she knows Alderney isn't Anglesey. Hopefully the two words are close enough for the boys. Billy is six, but his reading hasn't been going too well and the school were talking about testing him for dyslexia next year.

So yes – I've lied. But the lies are necessary not just for me, but for my children. *Especially* for my children.

The biggest problem I had to overcome was the travel. We couldn't fly, because the boys would have been so excited they would have been bound to tell Robert. So we had to drive as far as Poole, where we left the car and picked up the boat I had chartered. Of course Robert would check my mileometer, as he did every week, and Poole is considerably further than Anglesey, but I managed to make up stories to account for the extra miles. I even took the children to one of the ruined forts on Alderney and told them it was Caernarfon castle. I don't think Robert has ever been, so if their description on our return was a little wide of the mark it would have passed him by even if he were listening; but he would know that Caernarfon was at least an eighty-mile round trip from the guest house.

The children were conscious that the journey took longer, but Robert knew Cemaes Bay was further away than Moelfre, and when the boys said it took ages and ages, he put it down to the 'Are we nearly there?' syndrome and didn't take much notice.

The boat trip was harder to explain, but easier than an aeroplane. I researched some tourist boat trips around Anglesey, which made it less problematic than I'd first feared. I told Robert about the tours when we spoke on FaceTime, so that when we got home and the children mentioned their sea journey, it was old news and Robert just tuned out.

It was a huge risk, but we couldn't just turn up on Alderney on the very day that we escaped. We had to appear familiar to everybody. And for that, we needed to establish ourselves.

Thanks to Sophie, I have various pieces of documentation in my new name, Lynn Meadows, including a fake passport. Not so hard, it turns out – especially as it was never going to have to pass muster at border control.

By now I'm sure our *real* passports will have been found. I wonder if Robert will believe that I went to Iran? I hope so, but what he believes doesn't matter so much. It's what the police believe that counts.

It was hard to contain my excitement after our first trip here in October. I didn't want to leave. I just wanted to move everything along more quickly and establish our new lives, but I couldn't. There was too much to plan. Too much to organise. And it had to be perfect.

I found a house to rent that is sufficiently isolated. Nobody will notice our comings and goings. Not that anybody would think much about it anyway. It turns out that a lot of people come and go all the time. The house is right by the beach and, best of all, it has a ready-made escape route for the children. I am sure we won't need it, but it gives me an added sense of security.

During the October and Easter visits, I made sure we were as visible as possible. I had to avoid any children-only events, of course, until my three are confident in their new names. But we joined in some of the group activities such as the Great Shark Egg Hunt at Easter, although the children were more interested in finding the chocolate varieties than the real thing. And we made a point of regular visits to the main shopping street, stopping off for a drink at the busy café and choosing a prominent outdoor table, smiling and nodding a greeting to anybody who looked our way.

And now, here we are. We can relax. I may have left everything we owned behind us in Manchester, but one thing I am sure of is that there is nothing to connect us to Alderney.

41

'*Alderney*,' Tom said in amazement. 'Why the hell do you think that's where she is, Gil?'

'And where on earth is Alderney anyway?' Becky added.

'It's one of the smaller Channel Islands,' Tom answered. 'I think it's the closest one to France, if my memory serves me correctly. What's led you there?' he repeated.

Gil tutted in a most irritating way.

'Can we be clear that I am *not* saying she's there. Until last Wednesday, somebody using Olivia Brookes' email address responded to FaceTime messages from Robert Brookes. It doesn't necessarily follow that this person was Olivia, or that she's still there. However, you asked me to track down the IP address that she *appeared* to be using. You may remember I told you that most likely she'd purchased an IP address, and that it was a fake.'

Tom gritted his teeth. He knew he was being bad tempered, but he just wanted an answer, not a lecture.

'Yes, I remember.'

'Well, I managed to contact the company. Fortunately they're not one of the more difficult organisations that make you go through hoops to get any sense out of them. Their service is intended for people who want to hide their location from the general public, not for criminals.'

Tom wanted to tell him to get on with it, but he resisted.

'So, they've confirmed the real IP address, and the Internet service provider is a company in Guernsey. I contacted them to get the physical address of the user. However...' and once more Gil paused for effect, 'it turns out she was using the Wi-Fi signal from the airport on the island of Alderney.'

Tom was disappointed that they couldn't pinpoint her address, but at least now they knew where Olivia was. Or where she *had* been, which was not necessarily one and the same. Or, indeed, where *somebody* had been – as Gil had pointed out. What appeared to be great news and a real breakthrough could be yet another wild goose chase. If only he could shake off his grumpiness and feel more positive about their progress.

What progress? Tom felt the weight of their failure to find these children pressing down on him. Every apparently excellent lead seemed to be a dead end. And what did they really know?

They knew for sure that the blood on the study wall wasn't Olivia's, but they didn't know anything else, other than the fact that the blood was from a male. If somebody had been killed in that room, they couldn't just assume that Robert Brookes was the guilty party. But if he were and he had killed once…

There was no body, but according to Jumbo there was no doubt in his mind that there was one somewhere. There had been so much blood, and when Tom saw the photographs of the luminol he had been horrified by how far the blood had spread.

He had stood in that very room with Robert Brookes, not knowing that behind him, splattered across the wall, was some poor bugger's lifeblood. He felt he should have known, should have sensed something, but he knew he was being fanciful.

Given Jumbo's assertion that a body was either still on the premises or had been transported to an unknown location, the forensic team had taken both of the family cars to be tested. If a body had been taken from the scene, there was every chance that it was moved in one of the boots or even on the back seat, although either would be quite unlikely in the Beetle.

Becky was looking puzzled. Something was obviously not adding up in her mind, and Tom realised that he hadn't really been listening to Gil for several minutes. He had been thinking about the logistics of moving a dead body.

'That can't be right,' Becky said. 'She can't have been at the airport when she spoke to Robert on FaceTime. He would have known she wasn't at home. Surely he would have recognised an airport?'

'I can assure you, DI Robinson, that it *is* right. And I'm not sure he would recognise this particular airport – it's not exactly a cosmopolitan hive of activity,' Gil said. 'I've seen photos. But then it certainly doesn't look like somebody's bedroom either.'

Tom felt he had to interrupt.

'We can't trust a word that Robert Brookes said, and we know that

Olivia wasn't home last week. The only thing we *do* know is that according to his call logs, somebody responded to him on FaceTime up to Wednesday, and whoever it was – whether Olivia or not – was connected via this IP address, which bizarrely leads us to Alderney airport. But I do tend to agree with Becky that if it *was* Olivia, it would have been difficult for her to have these conversations from the airport itself.'

'Quite,' Gil responded. 'Which is *precisely* why I made some further enquiries. Apparently this particular Wi-Fi signal can be picked up in several places around the island – so people use it all the time. She could have been anywhere.'

'Terrific,' muttered Tom.

'Sir,' Nic was standing behind Becky waving a piece of paper in the air. 'I heard you mention Alderney, and I've been checking it out on Wikipedia. Less than two thousand people live on the island, so she's going to stick out like a sore thumb if she's just arrived with three children in tow. Somebody's going to know where she is.'

Tom felt some of his irrational testiness dissipate in the face of his team's enthusiasm and optimism.

'Okay. So let's get on to the local force in Alderney and ask for their help. Give them the background so they know it needs handling carefully. More to the point, we need to be worrying about where the hell Robert Brookes has gone. After what he did to Sophie Duncan and her mother, we have to find Olivia so we can keep her safe until he's under lock and key.'

Becky was making her way over to Ryan's desk to brief him, and Tom turned back to Gil with an apologetic smile.

'Thanks, Gil. And good work. I think this case is getting to all of us.' Gil raised his eyebrows in a look that clearly said, 'To some more than others,' which gave Tom a moment of guilt. He hadn't meant to be sharp, but how could they know so much and yet not know anything? And on top of that, there was all the stuff with his cottage, not to mention his frustration over Leo.

To cap it all, his mobile rang. Philippa Stanley.

'Bollocks,' he muttered to nobody in particular. He was tempted not to answer it, because right now there were more questions than answers, but at least the Alderney connection might just calm her down.

As he pressed the call button on his phone, he thought of something else they needed to do. While he couldn't for the life of him think how Robert could possibly have connected Olivia to Alderney unless there was something they didn't know – more than bloody likely in his opinion –

instead of just checking international flights out of the UK, they might want to consider making sure he wasn't on any flight to the Channel Islands. Just to be on the safe side.

Taking a deep breath, he spoke into his phone. 'Yes, Philippa.'

42

I often wonder whether I must have done something very wrong in a former life for all these terrible things to have happened to me. Until the age of twenty-two, I seemed to sail through life. My parents adored me, I did well at school, had loads of friends, and all the boys I fancied seemed to fancy me back. Even at university, life was sweet. I had to study hard, but I thrived on it, and I thrived on the fun times too. I wanted to be a part of everything – to capture and devour as many experiences as I could. Nothing frightened me, and nothing fazed me.

It's true that finding out I was pregnant with Jasmine wasn't part of the original plan, but Danush and I loved each other so very much. We couldn't bear to be apart in our last two years at university and when we decided to live together I thought the rest of my life was going to be perpetual bliss. How wrong could I have been?

I suppose things started to go wrong when Samir came over from Iran to talk to Danush about his family obligations. He had been sent by their parents to convince Dan that he should go back and marry his cousin, as had been planned for the whole of their lives. I was terrified. I couldn't lose Dan – he was everything to me. And yet I could see that he was wavering. Not because he didn't love me, but because he had such a sense of honour. I remember watching the pain on his face as he acknowledged that he was either going to lose me or lose his family. What a terrible choice.

Despite knowing how difficult this was for him, I did nothing to help. I ranted and raved about everything he would be giving up if he left me. He'd be giving up on love, giving up his life in the West as an engineer, so much of what he had always wanted, to go back to Iran – a place he also loved but that until now he had been prepared to sacrifice. For me.

I can't believe how I behaved. Dan was getting pressure from Samir, and I was applying an even greater pressure because I wanted him so much.

Samir had capitalised on my weakness. He had scoffed at my selfishness and made me feel like an ignorant kid. He was only a few years older than us but already qualified as a doctor. I *was* like a spoiled child, one who had never once failed to get something she'd wanted. And I was determined not to fail this time either. If that young version of me could see what I have become, what would she think?

I couldn't lose Dan, but I didn't know what to do to keep him. I tried to make him jealous – even with his own brother – to make him realise how much he loved me. Samir played along too. It was only later that he told me it wasn't because he found me attractive. He was hoping it would prove to his brother how shallow I was. My behaviour was, if anything, driving Dan away. I could see it, but I just couldn't stop.

I tried to excuse the way I acted by saying I was in love, which I thought was more important than anything in the world. But I recognise now that everything had always come so easily to me, and I had no experience of failure.

And then there was a miracle. I discovered I was pregnant.

It felt like a victory, but I really didn't plan it. Even the young, naive girl that I was could see that trying to persuade Dan to stay with me was one thing, but intentionally getting pregnant in order to keep him was another thing entirely.

But Dan did stay with me, as I knew he would. Samir had already returned to Iran to report back to his parents by the time the pregnancy was confirmed, but Dan gave him the news as soon as we were sure, and Samir was resigned to something he had no control over. I knew what he would be thinking – that I'd planned all this just to keep Dan with me. He would be disgusted with me. I didn't care, though. I'd won, or so I thought.

The day that Dan left I felt as if my life was over, and if it hadn't been for Jasmine, I don't know how I would have survived. Although Dan had stayed with me through the birth of my beautiful daughter and he still appeared to love me with the same passion and care, there were times when I knew he was thinking of his self-imposed exile from his family.

I can remember every minute of the day I lost him. It was November 6th, and I took my baby girl outside to take in the 'morning after bonfire night' special atmosphere that I remembered from my childhood. This one day of the year always seemed to dawn with a slight mist lingering from too many bonfires in back gardens, a thin pall of smoke hanging in the air from the smouldering heaps of old wood left to burn out overnight, their sooty scent mixing with a vague whiff of burned-out fireworks to give the day its unique perfume. And there were always surprises on the lawn – the empty shell of a rocket, or a blackened sparkler that somebody had discarded over the fence.

I was disappointed, though. Here on the outskirts of a city in the land of student flats, the morning dawned just like any other, the only new item on the lawn being an empty beer can that somebody must have tossed over the night before on their way home. And when I breathed in deeply, all I got were the usual morning smells of exhaust fumes and the occasional whiff of burned toast.

Although I didn't know it then, this day was never going to be like any other. It was the day my world shattered into tiny fragments, because that night, Danush never came home. He had gone from my life.

Now I know the truth. I know why he left, but it doesn't hurt any the less.

In the months after I lost him, it felt as if life could get no worse. My parents hadn't been Dan's greatest fans, and of course his disappearance only gave credence to their views. They were models of propriety, and when I screamed that they had never understood – Dan *loved* me – I saw the way my mum sucked in her lips, looking at my dad as if to say, 'We knew this would happen.'

It wasn't that they didn't like Dan, they just didn't approve of him as my 'live-in partner', as my mum called him. They didn't believe mixed marriages could work. It wasn't even the fact that he was Iranian. It was because he was a Muslim and, in their eyes at least, I was a Christian.

When he disappeared I thought his religion might have been the problem. Perhaps he had been mistaken for a terrorist and had been dragged off to a deserted warehouse to be beaten up. But the day after he went I had a text from him, saying no more than he was sorry. The police traced his phone to Heathrow, where he'd bought a ticket for Australia. A one-way ticket.

It seemed he didn't want me, and he didn't want his family either.

Despite their difficulty in acknowledging my love for Dan, my parents did everything they could to help. They knew how low I was, and they were concerned about their granddaughter. I had thought I was coping well with a new baby, and during those first two months we had seemed to be as happy as any young family could be. Yes, I was tired. Dan was too. But we didn't mind. It was the start of my dream. Once Dan had gone,

I struggled to focus on what Jaz needed and, although I was going through the motions of feeding her and changing her, sometimes I was so tired and weary I could barely drag myself to go to her in the night.

So I was out of options. I was going to have to sell the flat and move in with my parents, which was not in any way ideal, but what else could I do? Daily edicts to 'buck up' from my mum, or pronouncements such as 'worse things happen at sea' from my dad were going to drive me insane, and I knew it. I loved my parents dearly, but nothing bad had ever happened to them. They sailed through life on tranquil waters.

Once more my mistakes come back to haunt me. If I had been stronger then, the wheel of fortune which is my life would have spun again and stopped at a different place. But I was weak, and I took the easy option.

The flat sold the first day it went on the market.

The buyer was Robert Brookes.

43

It was getting towards the end of another day of sifting through information without reaching any conclusions, and Becky was becoming increasingly frustrated. There had been no sign of Robert Brookes, and she thought they had covered every base.

Given that he had left his car on the drive, he had to have had transport to somewhere. They should have known he was too smart to call a taxi on his home phone, but nevertheless they had tracked down the driver who had, of course, told them his passenger was a no-show.

Becky pressed her lips together and folded her arms. This man was beating them. She paced up and down in front of the evidence board, trying to find connections where there probably weren't any. They knew Robert had made withdrawals on all his cards, but the ATMs he had used had been in the centre of Manchester. If he was still there, it would be like trying to find a needle in a haystack.

She was worried about Sophie Duncan too. The young army officer had insisted on staying at home on her own, and said she wasn't in the least scared of Robert Brookes.

'If he turns up at Mum's, he'll wonder what the fuck's hit him by the time I've finished with him,' was all she would say on the subject. Becky liked her style and confidence, but given the state her leg was in, she just had to hope Sophie had seen the last of Robert. She had asked a patrol car to do a drive-by from time to time, but wasn't at all sure whether this would be any help or not. Last time Robert had paid a visit to the Duncan household, from the outside everything had seemed normal.

Ryan chose that moment to walk over to where Becky was pacing. She hoped he was going to brighten her day, but seriously doubted it.

'I've looked at all the ways I can find to get to Alderney,' he said, 'but it's not an exhaustive list because apparently boats turn up from all over the place all the time. It's got a harbour and it's well known for fishing – so what can you expect? If somebody chose to charter a boat...' Ryan lifted his shoulders, and curled his top lip.

'So what happens when people arrive on the island? Doesn't anybody check their passports?'

'You don't need a passport from the UK, ma'am. I looked up the regulations.' Ryan paused as if he expected praise from Becky for taking the initiative, and she could see the disappointment in his eyes when she failed to offer it. She had to try harder with this man.

'What did you find?'

'If you're arriving from outside the Bailiwick – whatever that is – of Guernsey, you are supposed to go through customs. But I've also read there are other places to anchor outside of the main harbour. Perhaps Robert could use that to his advantage?'

Becky suppressed a groan. That was all they needed, but if Sophie was right and Robert was looking for Olivia, this might be their one chance of catching him.

'Okay, Ryan. Contact all the advertised routes into Alderney from the UK and let them know who we're looking for. We've no idea if he's been able to track his wife down yet, but we can't assume that just because Sophie Duncan didn't tell him how to find Olivia, he's not found out by some other means. Spread the net as wide as you can, please.' Almost as an afterthought, she added, 'And well done, Ryan. Some useful information there.' From the way Ryan's mouth tilted up at one corner, Becky couldn't decide whether he was pleased, or saw straight through her attempts to mollify him. Oh well – what the hell.

An image of Peter Hunter flashed into her mind, and the day she had fallen under his spell. They had been working on a really tricky murder enquiry, and by scouring the evidence and picking up every tiny thread, she had uncovered a possible lead that had been missed. Peter had come across to where she was sitting and had spoken the exact words she had just used with Ryan. 'Well done, Becky. Some useful information there.' He had squeezed her shoulder as he'd walked away, but his thumb had lingered on the naked skin at the back of her neck, and she was sure he had stroked it gently. She had waited, then, for more small signs, flushing a little every time he entered a room, anxious to see if he would linger by her desk and maybe give her another sign.

Oh, he was good. She could see it now. He couldn't make a move until he was one hundred per cent certain of her, of course, so he had teased her with a touch here, a smile there, once even brushing the back of his hand against her breasts as he passed her a pile of folders.

Sleazeball.

With a small shudder and a sense of disbelief that she could think she was in love one minute and just a few short months later feel nothing more than revulsion, Becky pulled her mind back to the case.

She was waiting anxiously to hear back from the Alderney police. As an island almost free from crime, she could see why they had such a small team and hoped they had something for her. Like Tom, she had been relieved that the blood found in the house wasn't Olivia's, although it seemed some poor soul must have died there. And Becky wouldn't feel better until she knew the children were okay. She kept seeing that small, windowless room from Jasmine's picture in her mind, with three children huddled in a corner, and each time she felt a chill. But they had found nothing. No other properties, and no other suspects.

Becky looked again at all the evidence, and so much of it seemed to lead back to Danush Jahander – from when he first went missing to his proposed meeting with Robert. They had checked with the hotel in Newcastle, and the manager had confirmed that a call from Sophie's phone was put through to Robert's bedroom. It lasted about two minutes. Did that explain why Robert drove back to the house from Newcastle? Was it to meet Dan?

Hearing her desk phone ringing, Becky turned round despondently, walked across and sat down. Forcing herself to sit up straight and get with it, she picked the phone up.

'DI Robinson.'

'Good afternoon, Detective Inspector Robinson. I've just received a message that you wish to speak to me. I'm sorry, but I have been in Iran and I've only just returned. What can I do for you?'

'And you are...' she said, already anticipating the answer. She felt a flicker of excitement.

'Samir Jahander. How can I help you?' he asked, in a polite and almost accent-free voice.

'Dr Jahander, thank you for calling. We have a few questions about your brother, if you can spare the time?'

'Which brother would that be? I have four – and two sisters,' Samir answered. There was no inflection in his voice at all.

'Your brother Danush, Dr Jahander. We were wondering if you have had any contact with him recently. We spoke to your wife, and she said you hadn't heard from him in years. In fact, not since a year or so after he left the UK.'

Becky heard a whoosh of breath, as if Samir was blowing air between his teeth – the first sign of emotion.

'Danush is no longer part of my family, DI Robinson. I'm afraid he forfeited that right when he refused to fulfil his obligations to our family.'

'But I understood he left his English girlfriend and their baby. Did he not return to Iran?'

'Their baby,' Samir made the same sound with his breath. 'How very convenient that was. Danush saw sense, I do believe. He left. But he was so disappointed with life – the fact that he had been tricked into fatherhood, the fact that he'd been unable to finish his PhD, and the fact that our parents were unlikely to forgive him for the choices he made – that I'm afraid he took the coward's way out.'

For a moment, Becky thought he meant Danush had committed suicide.

'He went to Australia, DI Robinson. He stayed there for a couple of years, and then he finally returned to Iran, but not to my parents' town. He wanted to find his own way.'

'When did you last see your brother, Dr Jahander?' Becky asked.

'I hadn't seen him for almost nine years – not since before the baby was born. His girl was certainly not pregnant when I arrived. I stayed with them for a month, trying to persuade him to do the right thing.'

'So you've not seen him since, then?'

'No, Inspector. I said I "hadn't" seen him for nine years. And I didn't expect to see him again, but about a year ago he came to ask if I would lend him some money. I didn't tell my wife about this, because I was furious and I worried that she might mention it to my parents. Danush had ignored his family for all this time, and now he wanted *money*? But we had money that was rightfully his, so I gave it to him.'

'What do you mean?' Becky asked.

'When Liv sold the flat, half of the money legally belonged to Danush. She sent the money to me – to keep it safe for him. I never told him.' There was silence for a moment at the other end of the phone, and Becky said nothing. 'Perhaps that was wrong of me, but I didn't want him thinking Liv was a better person than I believed her to be, and telling him about the money might have sent him rushing back. But it was a long time since he'd left her, so I assumed it was safe to tell him.' There was a mirthless laugh from the other end of the phone. 'Which proves how little I knew my brother. He'd apparently never got over her, and he wanted to contact her. He wanted her to come to Iran – to meet my parents and to introduce them to Jasmine.'

'And did he contact Olivia?' Becky didn't really want to interrupt, but Samir had gone very quiet at the end of the last sentence, and Becky had a mental image of his anger building.

'My parents had been hurt enough, Inspector. Taking Jasmine to see them would have opened up old wounds that had started to heal. I told him he could do what he liked; he could return to Olivia if he must, and if he wanted to show Jasmine our country that was fine. But he was to take neither of them near my parents, and unless he agreed I wouldn't give him the money.'

'Was that the last time you saw him, Dr Jahander.'

'It was, but I've spoken to him since. He was very distressed to find Liv was married, but was confident the marriage was a sham. I told him he had no right to destroy somebody else's relationship, but he didn't seem to care. The last time I spoke to him, he told me Liv was scared of what Robert would do if she left him. She'd been scared for some time, apparently – and he said she'd gone away to think in peace.'

'And what was your brother planning to do about it, Dr Jahander?'

'He was going to have it out with her husband. He was going to tell him that he and Liv were meant to be together, and it was time for the husband to step aside.'

'And did it work?' Becky was holding her breath. She was sure she knew what the answer was going to be.

'I don't know, Inspector. I haven't heard from him since.'

Two hours with Philippa had done little to improve Tom's mood, and he felt like he was back where he'd started that morning – grumpy.

Becky was looking at him, and he guessed she was trying to gauge whether to ask him how it went with the boss. He decided to save her the trouble.

'Jumbo wants to bring in the ground radar to check over the terrace and the garden. That, amongst other things, is what we've been discussing, because Philippa agrees with him. I don't. I think we should wait to see if we can get a match on the blood first.'

'Why?' Becky asked. 'Surely we need to know if there are any bodies under there as soon as possible, especially given that the neighbours say that Robert Brookes has spent the entire spring building that terrace, and only finished it just before he buggered off to Newcastle.'

Tom scratched his head. 'Yes, of course. I know that, but I can't help thinking it might be a waste of time and money.'

'On what basis? Look, I'm sorry to disagree with you, Tom, but we have no idea who died there. We don't know if Olivia and the children are safe, and whoever *was* killed, we've no idea why.'

It seemed nobody agreed with him. The arguments that Philippa had put forward were perfectly valid. They shouldn't automatically assume it was Robert who had killed somebody in that room; Olivia could be the culprit – she could have murdered somebody and run away. But they were wrong, and Tom knew it. When did gut instinct cease to have any validity?

Becky leaned forwards and rested her forearms on the desk. Her cheeks finally had some colour in them and her eyes were sparkling. She was totally engrossed in the case, and it seemed to have driven out the demons she had been carrying with her.

'All we know is that somebody using Olivia's email address made contact with Robert from somewhere on Alderney last week,' she said, speaking quickly and quietly. 'But we only have Robert's word that it was Olivia on the other end of that call, and I don't set much store by that. Do you? Robert could equally well have a mistress or an accomplice who picked up his call. We've no evidence that Olivia is there at all. Or anywhere else, for that matter. He could have killed her two weeks ago. *And* the children. Just because the blood in his study isn't hers, it doesn't actually mean she's not already dead, does it?'

Tom held his hands up, palms outwards towards Becky.

'Whoa, whoa – I believe you.' Tom found himself smiling at her vehemence. 'Even though the blood isn't hers, her body could still be there somewhere – I know that – or the body of whichever poor bugger died there, for that matter. Robert could have killed her and possibly the children, and all this video footage and FaceTime nonsense could be part of his very elaborate cover-up. But if she's already dead and we don't have a bloody clue where Robert is, I just thought we could hang on until we've heard back from the Alderney police.'

'Ah,' Becky leaned back and screwed her face up in mock pain. 'Bit of a problem there, I'm sorry to say.'

Tom closed his eyes and shook his head. It was about time something went their way on this case. He looked at Becky and raised his eyebrows.

She squirmed a little, but she was going to have to tell him.

'Ryan spoke to a very helpful sergeant on the island, and asked him if he could identify any newcomers – people who had arrived there in the past two to three weeks. He forgot to mention that Olivia and the children could have been there at Easter, or possibly even last October. I had to call them back and explain. I have to say the sergeant wasn't too impressed when I told him that unfortunately we need to spread the net a little wider in terms of timescale and they're going to have to go through the process all over again. They were going to check the schools, but the trick with the home schooling has probably put the kibosh on that. We'll have to wait, I'm afraid.'

Somebody here is playing with us. The idea wouldn't let go, and Tom realised that this was the cause of his irritation. Taking the children out of school made perfect sense if Olivia wanted to disappear. But it was equally credible if Robert had decided to abduct them all and keep them prisoner, or kill them.

The double doors to the incident room burst open, just wide enough for the huge body of Jumbo to enter. Tom was surprised to see him, given that they usually got their reports by email or phone. He looked for Jumbo's wide, infectious grin – just what he needed to cheer him up – but it wasn't there.

Tom stood up and shook Jumbo's giant hand. 'To what do we owe this honour, Jumbo?'

Jumbo's mouth was set in a grim line, and there were deep furrows between his eyebrows.

'I like to be right, Tom. You know that. But sometimes, particularly when it involves a murder that until now we weren't sure about, it doesn't feel so good.'

'Sit, Jumbo. Tell us what you know.'

Jumbo grabbed Tom's chair, which creaked a little as he squashed himself into it. Becky was about to offer Tom hers, but he waved her away and perched on the desk, one foot on the floor and one leg swinging in a casual style that belied his true feelings. Jumbo leaned forwards and clasped his hands, turning his head from one to the other, as if to decide whether they were ready for this.

'Okay – first things first. I had the blood samples rushed through for DNA analysis, as you know. The tests showed the blood was from a male, but that's all. We checked against the two little boys – we picked up various items of theirs around the house to test against. I'm very relieved to say they came up negative. We also checked against Robert Brookes, in case he was the victim rather than the perp. Again, negative.'

'Pretty much as we expected,' Tom said, but he could see from Jumbo's face that there was more.

'Do you remember I told you we'd found an old sealed box in the attic? It was mainly papers covered in handwriting, but I couldn't make any sense out of it. Lots of complex calculations, printouts from a computer and so on. We've had somebody look at them. We don't believe they're relevant to our investigation, but we'll pass them over to you. However, the box was marked "Dan" and the name on the top of the documents is Danush Jahander. At the bottom of the box we found a few odds and ends belonging to him – some with his name on, some just oddments. It was as if somebody had grabbed everything of his in their arms,' Jumbo demonstrated by spreading his arms and then pulling them to his chest, 'and thrown it all in,' he said, flinging his arms wide.

Tom glanced at Becky. He knew what was coming, and from Becky's expression, so did she.

'In the box we found a large pair of men's leather gloves,' Jumbo continued, 'fairly battered and well worn, originating from a company in Iran. We managed to extract some DNA and we got a match. The DNA from the gloves is a match to the blood we found in the study. It looks like the person who died there was Danush Jahander.'

Even though he had been expecting Jumbo to say this once he had mentioned the box, Tom paused for a moment to think about this young man who had been so central to the enquiry, but whom Tom had never met. He had been concerned about Danush since they had found out he was back in touch with Olivia and had used Sophie's phone to set up a meeting with Robert. Now it was confirmed that the blood in the study belonged to him, it meant they had to open up a whole new channel of investigation.

'Thanks, Jumbo,' Tom said quietly. 'Are you certain there was enough blood spilled in that room for a person to have died?'

'It had been cleaned up, so I can't tell you for sure how thick the blood was lying. But it covered a wide area and I'm sure it was arterial blood. So yes. Somebody died in that room.' He looked down at his hands, clasped between his knees, and paused for a second as if in silent acknowledgement of a life lost. Taking a breath, he looked up and continued. 'There's more. We took both cars if you remember, and inside the boot of Robert's car we found traces of blood – and it matched the blood in the study.'

Becky frowned. 'If Jahander had bled that much, wouldn't there have been more than a trace?'

Jumbo shook his big head. 'Not necessarily. If Brookes had lined his car boot well with plastic – a waterproof cover for some garden furniture maybe or even good-quality bin liners – it would have been okay. My guess is that the body bled out in the study, based on the spatter pattern. We'll get some more feedback on that, but I'm still backing a slashed carotid. Your PC spotted that a sheet was missing from the bed, and there were cotton fibres found in the boot as well. They're a match with the other bed linen in the master bedroom.'

'Shit,' Tom muttered. If the body had been taken from the house, it could be absolutely anywhere now. But something else was bothering him.

'We know Brookes returned to his home on Wednesday night, or the early hours of Thursday morning to be precise. We can only assume he had agreed to meet Jahander there, expecting Olivia to be home too. Maybe he wanted a showdown between all three of them, and in theory she would have been back from holiday by then. Or maybe Jahander had said that he was going to see Olivia to persuade her to leave with him, and Brookes went to make sure that didn't happen.'

Tom could see from Becky's eyes that not only was she following him, she was probably ahead of him.

'So Robert came back to meet Danush and killed him,' she said.

'Danush Jahander died in that study,' Tom said. 'There's evidence that he was then transported in the boot of Robert's car, and we mustn't forget the missing knife, which I suspect we'll never find. Robert was back in Newcastle for the first morning conference session. The dog walker saw him leaving home at five fifteen that morning, so Robert didn't have enough time to faff about on back roads driving back to Newcastle.'

'I'll get a map and check out his likely route,' Becky said.

Tom shook his head.

'No need, Becky. I know it well. Given the approximate time he drove off from his house and the time his car was back in the garage in Newcastle, he would have had to go the most direct route. He'd have taken the M60 to the M62 to get him across the Pennines, and then up the A1.'

'Well, bugger me,' Jumbo mumbled. Tom waited expectantly for him to say more. 'What if I told you that our friend Robert had a bit of an obsession with Myra Hindley and Ian Brady?'

Tom's eyes met Jumbo's and no words were necessary. Becky was staring from one to the other with a quizzical expression.

'Come on, Becky, where's the obvious place just off the M62 that's totally deserted in the early hours of the morning – the perfect spot to dump a body?' Jumbo asked.

As a young southerner, it was clearly taking Becky a little longer than Tom and Jumbo to get it.

'Saddleworth Moor, Becky,' Tom said, putting her out of her misery. 'Back in the sixties, Brady and Hindley killed five kids, and four of them were buried on the moor, although one has never been found.'

'Of course. Sorry, I didn't make the connection,' Becky said, flushing a little. 'But would he have had time to dig?'

Tom shook his head. 'I doubt it,' he said. 'Unless you're going to say you found a tell-tale spade encrusted with peat while you were searching, Jumbo?'

Jumbo gave him a look.

'I didn't think so.' Tom pushed himself off the desk and stood up, thrusting his hands into his trouser pockets.

'You'd better take your pick of the reservoirs then,' he said, 'because we certainly can't drag them all.'

44

Sitting here on my beach watching my children play, I feel a small burst of happiness, and I realise it's the first time I have felt free to be happy since I lost Dan and two months later, my mum and dad.

Accepting my parents' death was one of the hardest things I've ever had to do. I can remember ranting and raving at the police inspector who came to the scene. The police tried to explain what had happened. They told me it would have been a very peaceful way to die.

But they were wrong about it all. They had to be.

They told me there was a carbon monoxide monitor in the house, but that unfortunately there were no batteries in it. Perhaps my father had taken them out to replace them, and just forgotten?

This didn't make any sense to me at all. My dad kept spares of every size of battery known to man. He was obsessive about stuff like that. I took the inspector and showed him the drawer where they were kept. Why would Dad not have replaced the bloody battery?

The police weren't listening.

I can remember that once the fumes were gone and the house was considered safe, a kind woman police officer had taken Jasmine into the spare bedroom and laid her on the new activity mat my parents had bought her as a 'welcome to your new home' present.

And then my phone had rung. I couldn't deal with it. I couldn't speak to anybody. I didn't know if I was capable of uttering the words: 'My parents are both dead.' I was sure every syllable would stick like glue to the roof of my mouth.

The inspector had taken the mobile from me and answered the call. I don't know what he said, but when he gave me the phone back I remember him saying, 'Robert Brookes says he's coming.' I had forgotten all about Robert. He was waiting for me at the flat. When my dad hadn't turned up with the van he'd hired, Robert had suggested that I drive to their house to see what was keeping him. I was supposed to call Robert to let him know when I'd be back.

I remember feeling a sense of relief that somebody other than the police knew what was going on. The news was now outside of those four walls, and it seemed somehow to make it more real. And I was glad Robert was aware of what had happened. I didn't know him well, but since he'd first arrived to look around the flat – the very day it went on the market – he had been kind to me. I immediately felt he was strong and capable. I couldn't wait for him to come and help relieve me of some of this burden.

It seemed to take forever for him to get there, but he has told me since then that he did the journey in record time. By the time he arrived, the crime scene team were crawling all over the place, but they weren't turning up anything surprising. There was no sign of forced entry and no indication, other than the rather paltry evidence of the missing batteries, of foul play.

A specialist gas engineer came to take a look at the boiler, and he was quick to point out one of the problems. He explained about the importance of an air vent to let cold fresh air in to replace the gases that would be rising up the chimney. For once, I'd snapped out of my zombie-like state, and was prepared to listen. I needed to understand this.

When he pointed out that the air vent coming into the house was blocked with an old towel, I nearly went ballistic.

'There's no way,' I shouted repeatedly. 'Why would he *do* that?'

The engineer simply pointed out that as far as he could see, every window in the house was triple-glazed and every door, including the internal doors, had draught excluders on them. He asked if my father was a bit obsessive about keeping bills low, and I had to admit that he was. The cold air vent would have been against everything my father was working towards in his draught-free environment. But would he be so stupid?

They had all looked at me sadly, and Robert had put his arm round my shoulders. I remember shaking him off with frustration; I didn't want comfort. I wanted somebody to believe me.

Only it wasn't just the air vent, apparently. There was a damaged joint on the flue of the, admittedly old, boiler. The toxic gases had been escaping from there. They made it sound like it was all my father's fault.

I remember my legs giving way as a black fog engulfed me. Somebody caught me and helped me to a sofa – I can't remember who – but I fought my way back from total collapse because somehow I had to convince the police they were wrong.

At the time, I thanked God for Robert, even though I didn't want hugs and comfort from him. It wasn't his fault the police were being so completely useless. Robert was the only person who kept me sane, and even in the midst of such chaos, he reminded me to feed Jasmine.

When I had run out of arguments, he was the one who apologised on my behalf to the police. I didn't want him to, but yelling at them wasn't achieving anything. I had to accept there was no evidence, and anyway I couldn't think of a single person who would want my parents dead.

The inspector knew something was wrong, I'm sure of it. I heard him talking to the crime scene technicians. I walked over to the door of the utility room where they were huddled, and heard him asking them to go over everything again, to make sure there was no way anybody had been in the house. I suppose there was just a chance that my dad could have blocked the cold air vent, but the batteries were the one thing that would never make sense to me. Not unless my father had had an abrupt change of personality or was suffering from early-onset Alzheimer's.

The thought of staying in their bungalow that night sent me into a panic. Could I sleep in a house where my parents had lain dead just hours before? I didn't think I could. I never wanted to come to this sad home ever again. But I didn't own the flat any more and my best friend was somewhere in the Middle East, so I just slid down the wall to the floor, wrapped my arms around my knees and cried and cried. I heard the policeman ask Robert if he knew of anybody who could help me, and he told the inspector not to worry. He'd take me back to the flat – his flat now – and he would look after me himself.

The policeman seemed surprised that Robert would do this for me, and I probably should have been too, if I'd been able to think straight. At the time, though, the only thing I cared about was curling up in bed and crying some more, trying to hold the pain inside me, because if I allowed it to escape it would shatter me into pieces. So I let Robert take over. He had already proved himself to be good with Jasmine, and he was so attentive. What else could I do?

First Dan, and then two months later my parents. It was no surprise that I was totally numb. I was grateful to Robert. So grateful that, after six months, when he asked me to marry him, I said yes. It was the easiest and most obvious thing to do.

What a fool I was. I walked straight into his trap, and the cage door slammed shut behind me.

45

At the end of the day, Tom was ready to go home. He needed quiet thinking time, and his home had an air of tranquillity that he had noticed the very first time he'd come for a viewing. His mother used to say that houses absorbed the personalities of the families that had lived in them, and he had teased her about it unmercifully. If she was right, though, this house must have seen some very happy, peaceful times and it was just what he needed now.

Of course he had the cottage in Cheshire, which was wonderful for the occasional free weekend, especially when his daughter Lucy could join him, but it was just that bit too far for a daily commute. Fifty miles with no traffic was okay, but the roads around Manchester were chock-a-block in the rush hour, and he needed to be able to get to HQ quickly if necessary.

It had taken him a bit of time to find this house, because he hadn't been prepared to settle for another cold shell of a home after the one he'd had in London, and he knew that as she got older Lucy was likely to want to spend more time in Manchester – the shops, the cinema, places to meet friends. The word 'clubs' jumped into his brain and he shuddered, thanking goodness that it would be a few years before he had to worry about that.

It was his intention to stay in Manchester for the foreseeable future, so he had decided that, since money was no object, he would buy a house. It was far too big just for him, but once he had seen it, he had fallen in love with it. Although it was a red-bricked semi in south Manchester, it had some unusual Edwardian features that grabbed him from the word go. The rooms were spacious with high ceilings, and in the sitting room there was an arched feature in front of the two bay windows, both of which still had their original stained glass. The hall was big enough to house his desk, and with its own small fireplace it made a cosy place to work. Two low bookcases crammed with every sort of novel known to man and stripped floorboards with colourful rugs created a welcoming entrance.

As he opened the front door and stepped inside, he felt his taut limbs begin to relax, and he put his briefcase and keys down on the desk, took his jacket off to fling over the back of a chair, and made his way to the kitchen. It was still light outside at the end of a glorious June day, so he grabbed a bottle of cold beer and took it into the garden.

Gardening wasn't really Tom's thing. Somewhere at the back of his mind he thought he might in the future get interested in growing fruit and vegetables, but only so that he could cook with them. For now, he paid a gardener to keep on top of things. Shameful, but necessary. If he hadn't taken the easy way out, he would have to spend every day off armed with a lawnmower and a weeding fork, and that wouldn't leave him much time for Lucy or Leo.

As he stood surveying his beautifully maintained flowerbeds, Tom's mind turned to the break-in at his Cheshire cottage, and to Jack. Without his brother, Tom would never have been able to afford this house or the one in Cheshire. He was still maintaining his ex-wife who seemed to feel under no obligation to work for a living. He sometimes wondered how he would have coped *without* Jack's money, although he would happily live in a bedsit if it would bring his brother back.

What he couldn't imagine, though, is why anybody would want Jack's papers. He had been dead for over four years now, and Tom had only just retrieved the papers himself from the solicitor's office. He had been determined to go through them when he was taking his sabbatical, but in the end that period was cut short by the unexpected offer of a chief inspector's job in Manchester, so he had run out of time. According to the solicitor, Jack's estate had all been in order, and these were just personal papers, so there had been no sense of urgency.

A memory sprang into his mind. When Jack had died, his girlfriend had tried to claim that she was the rightful heir to Jack's millions. His brother's will had been clear that the money had to go to Tom, but the girlfriend, Melissa, had contested it and lost. She'd only been with Jack for about six months, and she had been a very unlikely choice. Jack was a slightly mad genius, and he needed calmness and serenity around him. Melissa reminded Tom of a Burmese cat – slinky, beautiful, purring and rubbing up against you, desperate for attention. Until she was angry, and then the fangs showed. In fact, Tom remembered asking Jack what the hell he was playing at. Prior to meeting Melissa, Jack had been in a relationship for a few years with a woman called Emma. She was the polar opposite of

Melissa. She had a smile that would light up a room. Their relationship had seemed rock solid, and then suddenly it was as if he had lost his mind.

When the terms of the will were actually made known and Melissa had fought and lost her battle for Jack's money, she had said that even if she couldn't have the money she wanted something of Jack's and had applied to the solicitor for him to release Jack's papers to her. The solicitor had refused, and Tom had forgotten all about it. Until now.

Without really knowing why, Tom pulled his mobile from his trouser pocket.

'Steve? Tom Douglas here. Sorry to bother you, but I wonder if you could do me a favour?'

Tom asked Steve to go to the house and retrieve the spare key from its hiding place, then remove all the papers to somewhere safe. He didn't know why this felt like a good idea, but it did. And as soon as this case was over, he was going to give those papers the time they deserved.

Tom ended the call with a promise of a pint sometime soon, and pushed all thoughts of Jack's papers out of his mind. He needed to get back to work.

Something had been bugging him all day, something to do with the death of Olivia Brookes' parents.

He retrieved his briefcase from the hall and pulled out the file.

46

Sophie was relieved that her mum had been advised to stay in hospital for another day. She had so much to do, and she would have been really worried about leaving her at home on her own. The poor woman would probably be terrified from now on.

Sophie had arranged for an alarm company to come out to the house, and they had recommended a panic alarm next to her mother's bed. They were also going to change the Yale lock for a five-lever one, so she could ensure the doors were secure when she had to go out. At least if Robert Brookes decided to pay them another visit, there would be some resistance.

But Sophie didn't think he would come back. He was a man on a mission, and she hoped Liv had covered her tracks well enough. With any luck, she would stay hidden from Robert forever, because she couldn't go back to a life with no freedom, a life in which every minute of her day was closely observed and scrutinised by a man mad enough to plot and scheme to keep her by his side. He was also a man who seemed capable of great violence, although as far as she knew he had never laid a finger on Olivia. Yet.

In the meantime, there were a few things Sophie had to do, and one of them was to pay a couple of people for their services. She had already sorted out payment for the false papers in the name of Lynn Meadows. They were cash on delivery. But the video work was different. That had been edited and uploaded remotely.

Sophie couldn't think of any reason why she would be spotted or recognised, but she felt uncharacteristically nervous as she made her way down a narrow alley in Manchester's newly revived Northern Quarter, casting furtive glances over her shoulder every now and again. Somehow, this lane seemed to have been overlooked in the local regeneration, and it lacked the excitement and creative vibe of the surrounding area. She wasn't given to being fanciful, but she felt as if pale faces were lurking behind the black windows, watching and wondering what she was doing there. It was just starting to get dark, and it didn't feel like a good place to hang around – particularly when she wasn't exactly fighting fit. She was limping badly, and would seem like an easy target to anybody looking for one.

She approached a dark brown door, flaking with old paint. There was a buzzer on the wall. No name. She pressed and waited.

After what seemed to be a long thirty seconds, she heard a buzz and a click as the door opened. She hadn't been asked to announce herself, but she knew she was being observed. Stuart would never let anybody in unless he was sure they were safe.

She trudged up the two flights of dark concrete stairs, her bad leg sending stabbing pains that seemed to travel right up to her head with each and every step. *Bastard Robert Brookes. Fucking nut job.* When she reached the top, she paused to recover her breath. It wasn't the exercise that had exhausted her, it was the pain. Sweat dripped off her forehead, but she grabbed a tissue from her bag and, tutting with irritation at her own weakness, she scrubbed her face dry.

When she had recovered, she pushed open another door, and was met by the gloom of Stuart's studio. Although the stairwell had been dark, this was taking darkness to another level, and the only light came from the monitor that was partly obscured by Stuart's head. He didn't turn round.

'Got the money, then?' he asked, while still spinning the controller on his editing equipment.

'Why else would I be here?' she responded in a similar dismissive vein.

As she moved further into the room, she could see Stuart's face illuminated in the flickering screen. His huge, prominent eyes seemed about to pop out of his head, but they were the only large thing about him. He was as emaciated as a twig, and his head was shaped like an inverted triangle – wide at the top to accommodate the eyes, then narrowing to a pointy chin with a tight mouth. His greasy hair flopped down across his wide forehead, and was tucked behind his ears like a girl's. As he rotated his controller with one hand, he picked at an angry-looking zit on his chin with the other.

Stuart was the best, and Sophie had no doubt at all that he would never say a word to anybody about what she had asked him to do. His life outside of one of Her Majesty's prisons depended on it, because she had far more on him than he had on her. She could have forced him to do it for nothing, but there was always a chance he would have booby-trapped the work, and it seemed fair to pay him.

She leaned against the wall, taking the weight off her bad leg as she watched him weave his magic. Much as he was a totally unprepossessing git of a man, she was mesmerised by his skill. He could choose the exact spot for the perfect edit, and he was so quick it left her breathless.

'You did a great job, Stu. It was perfect.'

'Of course,' he answered, not taking his eyes from the screen.

'How long do you think it will take the police to spot it?'

'It all depends whether they've got any of the good guys working on it. Some of them are as sharp as needles, some are total tossers who wouldn't spot the obvious if it was shoved up their arses.'

'Well, I guess we'll just have to wait and see,' Sophie responded. It had to work, though.

'I must say, somebody is one very smart cookie,' Stuart said.

'How so?'

'Well, there was lots of subtle stuff in the shots. The vase of daffodils was an inspiration, really. It wasn't centre screen – nothing obvious – but there it was. A good guy who is concentrating will have spotted that. And the next day the flowers were gone, and the day after they were back again in the same position. Then there were the clothes – there was just a lot of stuff I would expect even an experienced continuity girl to get wrong, let alone somebody who's never done anything like this before.'

'Probably bought *Continuity for Dummies* or something,' Sophie said dismissively, pushing herself off the wall.

Stuart turned round and looked at her. 'Is there such a thing?' he asked, with a note of wonder.

'I don't sodding know. I made it up, you wanker.' Sophie grunted. 'Anyway, genius guy, here's your money. All there, and a bit of a bonus because you really pulled it off.'

Sophie placed an envelope on the desk, moving aside a cardboard box that looked to have at least day-old pizza in it. She was careful not to move any of the half-full coffee cups. She'd done that once and Stuart had yelled at her. If she'd spilled anything on his precious equipment, she was pretty sure she would be dead by now.

'You paid Mack yet?' Stuart asked, without turning his head. 'Cos when I pass on my contacts, I like to check they've been treated right.'

'Course I have.' Sophie looked at Stuart's strange, extra-terrestrial face with the flickering images from the monitor sending patterns of light across it. 'Is he really called Mack?' Sophie asked. 'Or is that just his moniker – you know, Mack the Mac Hacker?'

'Never asked. Don't much care either, but he's a bleeding magician. Was in and out of that guy's FaceTime logs without leaving a trace. Fucking brilliant,' he muttered. 'Make sure the door closes properly behind you.'

Stuart didn't glance her way again and, realising that this was her dismissal, she braced herself for the return journey down those bloody stairs.

47

Tuesday

By Tuesday morning, Becky was feeling as if the weight of the world was on her shoulders. They had heard back again from the Alderney police, who were continuing with their enquiries but, as yet, nothing had come to light. The sergeant confirmed they had spoken to the accommodation agencies, hotels and B&Bs. A few names had been put forward and they had investigated each of them, but as yet they hadn't tracked Olivia down – if indeed she was still there. They had to accept the fact that she may never have been there at all, or might well have moved on since she had spoken to Robert the previous week. Which meant she could be anywhere, including under the terrace.

Even though they were certain that Danush Jahander's body had been taken away from the house in Robert's car, Jumbo had got his way and a team was out in the back garden now, using the radar equipment to check the grounds. The rationale was that if Robert had killed once, they had to check for other bodies.

Tom had told Becky he was convinced they would find nothing, but this had become a murder enquiry and therefore they needed to explore every possibility. He was fairly certain that if Robert had killed Olivia and the children, he wouldn't have buried them there. But until they knew for sure that this family was safe, they couldn't take the risk.

Becky looked across at Tom. He had been quiet this morning too. He'd been puzzling over something in a file, but as yet he hadn't shared the details with her.

They also had the feedback on Robert's credit card activity from the previous week. Tom had reasoned that he must have stopped for petrol on his route from Newcastle to Manchester on the Wednesday night, but he hadn't used his credit card once. That was certainly outside his normal practice, and it suggested he wanted no evidence of his trip to be found. However, they did know he had bought some items from John Lewis in Newcastle on Thursday, and the shop had looked into the details. He had bought a knife – and it seemed it was the one in the knife block at the house.

The store had been incredibly helpful, and had managed to track down the member of staff who had served Robert. Becky had spoken to her on the telephone.

'Was he looking for a *specific* knife,' Becky had asked, 'or was it just a certain *type* of knife?'

The sales assistant had sounded slightly breathless, as if she had been running. But Becky knew that it was a kind of strange excitement at being asked questions by the police.

'Oh no. He was very precise,' she said. 'Even to the point of having the product code with him. I do remember him, because he kept looking at his watch, as if he needed to be somewhere. He said he was running some kind of event and had nipped out during the lunch break. I tried to get him interested in comparing two or three different knives – you know, just to show that I wasn't trying to push him into buying an own-brand item.'

'Wasn't he interested in the Sabatiers?' Becky asked, remembering that Jumbo had said the rest of the knives were all the same type.

'No. They do look very similar, but he said his wife would "flay him alive" if he came back with the wrong one. He laughed when he said it, though.'

'So was the product code written down then?'

'Yes, he had it on a piece of paper.'

Becky thought for a minute.

'Could you see if it was written, or was it typed in an email, or printed from the website – do you have any idea?' she asked.

'It was written in blue pen,' the assistant said. 'I know because he asked me to hold the paper while he checked out the knife. That wasn't the only item on the list, but it was the only one from our department. I'm afraid I did take a peek at what else was on there. Only to see if there was anything else I could help with, of course.'

'And…' Becky said.

'The only other item I can remember was in bedding, I think, but nothing else in the kitchen department.'

'So somebody had written a list for him then,' Becky said.

'I don't think so. I think he must have written the list himself, because he seemed concerned to check that he hadn't transposed any of the numbers. There was one number that he couldn't read, and he said he'd been trying to balance the paper on his knee as he wrote. I got the impression that somebody had dictated it to him.'

Becky wasn't sure at all where this got them, but she thanked the shop assistant and wrote up her notes.

Tom appeared to be waiting for her to finish.

'Becky,' he said, a frown of concentration adding years to his usual relaxed expression. 'Can I run something by you please?'

'Course. Anything that gets my mind moving because frankly it feels like it's sunk in the mire at the moment. Please – some light relief.'

'Hah. I'm not sure I can offer that, but there's something that's puzzling me, and I would really like your take on it. It's about the death of Olivia Brookes' parents – Mr and Mrs Hunt. It's nearly nine years ago, but at the time there was something about it that felt wrong. I couldn't get a handle on it, but I think I have now. I just don't know if I'm fantasising for all the wrong reasons.'

Becky leaned back in her chair and picked up the mug of cold tea that she had meant to drink half an hour ago. She took a sip and shuddered, but it was better than nothing. 'Go on, I'm all ears.'

'We were called to the Hunts' home at about two o'clock in the afternoon on the day of their death. I've told you how they died and how Olivia found them. But for some reason, I was never entirely convinced it was an accident. We couldn't find anything to prove otherwise, and I wasn't sufficiently confident back then to go with my gut, plus there was absolutely nothing to go on. Until I read through the transcripts last night.'

Tom closed the file and put it back on his desk. 'I've read through it so many times, but there are a few things I remember too. While I was talking – or trying to talk – to Olivia, who was practically hysterical, her phone rang. It was Robert Brookes. She was pretty much incapable of speaking, so I took the phone from her and explained what had happened. He said he'd be right there.'

'Wow. That's impressive for somebody who's just buying a house,' Becky said, slightly in awe of Robert's dependability in the face of adversity. 'Most people would just have said, "Let me know when it's sorted," I'd have thought.'

'Well, he turned up about half an hour later and I spoke to him. He seemed very concerned for Olivia. Even though it was still hot in the house, she was shivering, and he took off his jacket and put it round her.

When the policewoman who had been looking after Jasmine brought her back to hand her over to Olivia, she just ignored her baby so Robert took her. We were quite impressed. Anyway, I asked him if he had been in the house previously so we could rule out his fingerprints. He said he'd never been there before.'

'And?' Becky said, looking at Tom but not having a clue where this was going.

'I was the one who spoke to him on Olivia's phone, and I just gave him the bare facts about the parents. Nothing more.'

Becky waited. Tom's eyes were boring intently into hers. He was obviously expecting her to make some connection, but whatever he was thinking was eluding her. She waited.

'If he'd never been there before, how the hell did he know where they lived, Becky?'

Tom couldn't think how he'd missed this the first time round. It could have been the fact that Olivia was in such a terrible state, alternating between screaming that something wasn't right and collapsing, sobbing to the ground. Not that it was surprising. She was weak and bewildered by everything that had already happened to her, so this must have left her reeling.

It was no good berating himself now, though, and he was sure that if he'd asked, Robert would have had an answer. More than likely he would have said that Olivia had left some papers in the flat with her parents' address on, or that she'd mentioned in passing where they lived. There would have been an excuse – and one that would have been entirely plausible.

But why would Brookes harm the Hunts? How would he have got in, because the towel in the air inlet was definitely one from the house, and if somebody had removed those batteries it had to have been after the parents had gone to bed.

For a while, the investigation had centred on Olivia. First her boyfriend had gone missing, and then her parents had died. If she had done anything to hurt them, though, hers would have been an Oscar winning performance of monumental quality when she found their bodies.

Robert had been discounted. He was just the guy buying the house.

Why would they have even looked twice at him?
   The fact is that they didn't.
   But maybe they should have.

48

Finally, Robert thought as he stepped off the boat in Alderney harbour. *What a pig of a journey.* He had never intended to spend a night on Guernsey, but by the time he had arrived there was little choice. He wished he had just taken the risk and flown, but the police must be looking for him by now. This way he could slip on to the island relatively unnoticed.

Then all he had to do was to find Olivia. He smiled at the thought.

He didn't know if he would have to find somewhere to stay. It all depended on how quickly he could track her down. He tried to drag the picture of the beach she had shown him into his head, but as they had sailed into Alderney he had seen plenty of beautiful beaches, and it could have been any one of them.

Asking one of his fellow passengers on board the tiny ten-person ferry for an idea of where he might stay, he was pointed in the direction of the town. As he set off with the sea on his left, there was a smart-looking hotel, but his funds wouldn't run to that without using his credit card. He was sure there would be some cheap rooms somewhere on the island. He could start asking around about Olivia too. He couldn't risk leaving it too long, but on the other hand he had to have a plan of what to do when he found her.

Because he *was* going to find her.

During his journey south he had tried to think of all the reasons Olivia might have for choosing this island, but it wasn't until he arrived that he finally understood the biggest attraction. Lack of fast and easy access. A lack of escape. She had thought he would never find her, but just in case, she had chosen somewhere that would make it difficult for him to carry out his plan and get clean away. But that was okay. He was adaptable. He would find somewhere locally that would fit the bill just as well.

His plan had always been that if the time ever came when he had to hurt Olivia in the way he had promised, he would maximise the period of threat – the time when her pain came somewhere close to his own. And it would all lead to the final act, the denouement guaranteed to leave her in agony for the rest of her life as she realised she could have avoided it all. All she'd ever had to do was love him. That was all he had asked. He knew that he could never live without her and if he couldn't have her, he had to make sure that until the day she died she would regret not returning his love.

It would be more difficult to fulfil his plan here, but he would formulate a new one. He needed a route and a final place to stage the scene. He closed his eyes, and he imagined it in glorious Technicolor.

Maybe he should make it a little different. It would be so much better if Olivia were an unwilling witness to the whole event.

He laughed out loud. Arriving by sea had been a good idea, because one thing he had noticed was that this island didn't lack suitable locations for what he had in mind: a finale that would be imprinted on Olivia's mind for the rest of her life.

But first, he had to find her.

As he passed the hotel he saw just what he was looking for – a pub. It was time to get to know the locals.

He pushed the door open and stepped inside, eager to begin putting his plan into action.

49

It took me a long time to fully understand the depths of Robert's obsession with me. To begin with, it felt as if he was simply the most thoughtful, caring and considerate man, and although nothing about him thrilled me, I had convinced myself that safety and security were the two most important features in a relationship. And Robert offered those in spades.

He had done everything any man could do to take care of me. Losing Dan and then my parents had drained the lifeblood out of me. Robert married an empty husk and yet he tried to give me a life that would in some way compensate for my losses.

What he failed to offer was excitement and passion. I persuaded myself that what we had was normal. Perhaps if Dan had still been with me, we too would have settled into a rut of twice-monthly sex with nothing more intimate than a peck on the cheek on the other nights.

This wasn't Robert's preference, though. He wanted to touch me all the time. When he came home from work and drew me into a hug I would try to reciprocate, but I always found an excuse to pull away – the children needed something, the dinner was burning.

How could I be married and yet recoil from my husband?

At night, when I turned away from him in bed, Robert liked to stroke my back. I hated it, and I knew he could feel my body tighten as I silently urged him to stop. I used to hear a small sigh as he drew his hand away. For for the last two years, though – ever since the night he took my children and had stood silently in the doorway of Jasmine's bedroom, listening to me saying goodnight to my daughter – he no longer sighed. Instead he whispered softly against my neck, 'sleep tight, my darling'. Four harmless words of love that were a reminder; a threat.

And he watched me.

If he was in the room with me and I glanced up, he would be looking at me. Sometimes I would be working in the kitchen – cooking a meal or doing the ironing – and Robert would be outside in the garden, but still I would feel those eyes penetrating like cold darts. And if I quickly turned my head, his face would be at the window, just looking in. Watching. He would smile, give me a small wave, and turn away. As if it were normal.

I hated it.

I felt as if I was wrapped in a cocoon, or maybe a straightjacket – arms pinned to my sides, feeling sweat pour down my arms and my inner thighs. But the sweat was cold and clammy, and I knew if I tried to escape, the ties would be tightened inch by sticky inch.

I don't know what made me realise that I couldn't live like this, but I think it began when I was listening to some other mothers waiting to pick their children up from school. They laughed and joked, made rude remarks about their husbands being lazy sods or football mad or untidy pigs. But the love was shining in their eyes as they spoke. I couldn't join in. I couldn't think of a single thing to say, other than, 'He watches me,' and I knew how that would sound.

I decided I had to talk to Robert, to tell him that I was just a cold fish, and he deserved somebody better. He needed somebody to love and cherish him the way he loved and cherished me. I remember he asked me about the children. If I was devoid of feeling, did that mean I felt nothing for them?

This was a stupid question. My children are my life and I adore every single cell of their bodies. How could he ask that?

He pointed out that this meant I wasn't incapable of love, so was I saying that I was incapable of loving him? Was that the problem?

It was, and I knew it. But how could I tell him I wanted to leave him? I couldn't. We laughed it off in the end, deciding that I was premenstrual – the only excuse that men seem to accept without question, not having a clue what it really means.

Nothing else was said for a few days, but Robert started to talk about our next holiday. He said he would like to pay another visit to South Stack lighthouse on Anglesey, and he reminded me of the time we had been previously. I didn't understand what he meant, until from somewhere came a memory – a memory of standing at the edge of a cliff and Robert telling me that some man had jumped off to his death. He had called it 'a perfect place to die'. As I remembered that day, I felt a chill, as if a cold wind had whipped through the room.

We struggled on for a few weeks, but then Robert gave his virtuoso performance and took my children away. Those hours when I thought I had lost them were truly terrible, and somehow I felt it was all my fault.

As I should have expected, Robert told the police that I'd known he was taking them away and must have forgotten, but this was merely the start of his campaign to undermine my sanity. The school, the other mothers, the need for a regularly updated schedule to let him know exactly what I had been doing – which he didn't hesitate to mention to people like my doctor, the teachers, the children's health visitor, the social worker. I began to realise that if I filed for divorce, there was a chance that he would be able to keep my children from me due to my apparent unpredictability and instability. He was amassing evidence, and he was so clever. He was painting me into a corner, and ensuring that I would never be allowed to keep my children if I left him.

I was trapped. I felt totally impotent. All my inheritance had been invested in our home, and I had no access to money – no means of escape. I was frozen, paralysed. Inertia set in, and for weeks I felt the weight of lethargy dragging me down.

And if I had thought he was watching me before, I now felt like an amoeba under a microscope. The weird thing about being watched is that you don't always know it's happening.

But somehow, you can feel it.

50

Tom's phone was ringing as he walked into the incident room carrying two cups of coffee. Becky was hunched over her desk, her dark hair swinging down to cover her face, but Tom could tell from the tension in her body that something had happened. She was on the phone, and it was only as he juggled with the cups and pulled his mobile out of his pocket that he realised he was the person she was trying to reach.

'Becky – I'm here,' he said, without bothering to answer the call.

Her head jerked up, and her eyes were dark with concern.

'What's up?' he asked, grabbing a seat and facing her across the desk, pushing one of the coffee cups towards her. 'You look like you've seen a ghost.'

'I've just had a call from a man who runs a boat company in Guernsey. They operate a ferry service around the Channel Islands, including runs to Alderney. He called me because he saw an extract on the news about Olivia and the children, with the added news that the husband is also missing.'

Tom felt an unusual sense of impending disaster.

Becky nodded her head at what she undoubtedly recognised as Tom's immediate grasp of the implication.

'He dropped Robert Brookes in Alderney Harbour this morning.'

Tom was instantly on his feet. *Fuck, he's found her*, he thought. Gulping down a hasty mouthful of coffee, he signalled Becky to follow him as he snatched keys and phone from his desk and spun on his heel towards the door.

'Grab your things, Becky. Make sure you've got photo ID. We'll sort everything out on the way.'

He knew Becky wouldn't waste time asking questions, and she picked up her briefcase from the floor by the side of her desk, opened it and shovelled in a few files and her mobile, at the same time shouting over her shoulder.

'Nic, sort out two flights for us from Manchester to Alderney. Fastest way possible. Call me.'

Having no idea of flight times, they started to run. It would be beyond frustrating if they missed a flight by minutes.

As they jogged towards Tom's car – the closer of the two in the car park – he asked if the team had heard anything from the Alderney police.

'Yes and no. They haven't managed to track Olivia down, but if Robert's on Alderney we can be pretty sure she's there. If she's renting somewhere it must be a private rental. Nobody appears to recognise the description or the names; but she's a smart cookie – she'll have changed them.'

Tom knew this was right. If he'd been Olivia, he would have made a point of being seen around the place in April when nobody was looking for her, and now be keeping a relatively low profile. Doing nothing to stand out, and making sure the children didn't resemble any description. Of course, photos would have made all the difference – a fact she had clearly grasped when she destroyed every single one of them before she left.

The Alderney police would do their best, but they didn't know Robert Brookes like Tom was beginning to, and he was certain Olivia was in danger.

Tom clicked his remote twice at the car to open both sides, and they leaped in, attaching seat belts as they raced out of the car park.

'Becky, get on the phone to Sophie Duncan. Tell her that now is not the time for being loyal to her friend. We need to find Olivia, because she's potentially in danger. If she doesn't know where Olivia is, you can bet your life she knows how to contact her. Get Sophie to speak to her. We're not pissing about now. This is bloody serious and she needs to understand that.'

Becky ran her finger down the page of contacts from her file, and dialled a number. Tom could only hear one side of the conversation as Becky spoke to Sophie. She explained that they believed Olivia could be on Alderney, and they wanted to know where.

'Come on, Sophie. This isn't a game. If you know where she is, tell us. We want to help her, and you more than anybody should recognise that Robert Brookes is dangerous.'

There was a pause as Becky listened. Tom didn't have to look at Becky to feel every muscle in her body tighten.

'*What?*' she yelled into the phone. 'Are you sure about this?'

She listened some more and hung up.

'Shit,' she said. 'Shit, shit, *shit*.'

Tom glanced at her white face, her eyes looking like black holes.

'What?'

'Sophie. She doesn't know where Olivia is, but she can and will contact her. She's going to text Olivia's number to us as well.'

Tom waited.

'She says Robert won't hurt Olivia. It's not Olivia he's going for. It's the children.'

51

Becky had known for some time that her level of fitness had dropped considerably since she'd started her disastrous affair with Peter Hunter. She'd stopped going to the gym just so she could be sure of being at home on the off-chance that he might try to call. *Pathetic.* But now it was catching up with her as they charged through terminal one of Manchester airport to catch their flight. It would have to be bloody terminal one.

Following as closely behind Tom as she could, Becky wove her way through the shoppers in duty free, nearly sending a woman holding a bottle of Chanel perfume flying. If they missed this flight, there was nothing for hours, and they still hadn't worked out the timings at the other end to get from Guernsey to Alderney. But one thing at a time.

Since speaking to Sophie, Becky hadn't really had time to think. All she was focused on was trying to get hold of Olivia. But the phone just kept going to voicemail. What if Robert had found her?

She had talked to the Alderney police again, and they were doing everything possible, including trying to contact Olivia on the number that Sophie had provided. None of their investigations had revealed whether Olivia was living on the island or not, but the sergeant did say he had a plan and he would explain what he was doing when they arrived.

As they reached the gate, Becky bent over to try to get her breath back. The monitor had said 'Final Call', and she was stunned to see that there were at least twenty people still waiting to board the plane. They could easily have walked and now she wouldn't be feeling so sick. Even Tom was puffing and panting a bit. He grinned at her pain.

'Made it,' he gasped, leaning one hand on the back of a row of plastic chairs as if he needed holding upright.

As they made their way on to the plane, they both got their breathing under control, and the moment's euphoria at having made the flight collapsed under the reality of what was about to happen.

Tom and Becky spent the flight going through every little detail they knew about Olivia's home in Alderney, from the conversations with Robert about the view from the window to Sophie's comments about the location. They were few and far between, but she had mentioned a bench nestled in a sand dune, with the house in the background. Surely that would help?

The flight took ninety minutes, and there was nothing they could do but discuss the case – or, in Becky's mind, go round and round in circles and always end up back at the same conclusion.

After the first half hour had passed, Becky was desperate to find out from the cabin crew whether there would be a flight they could catch to Alderney. *God, planes were frustrating places to be when you needed to be in contact with earth!*

The flight attendant came back up the aisle and crouched down by Becky's side.

'The next flight to Alderney takes off fifteen minutes after we arrive. We'll get you straight to the plane.'

The ground crew were as good as their word when they arrived in Guernsey, and Tom and Becky were invited to disembark first and then jump in an airport car which whisked them to the waiting plane.

Under any other circumstances, Becky would have enjoyed the flight. Flying over the sea at such low altitude was wonderful – especially when they saw Alderney in the distance with its white beaches and turquoise seas. But the closer they got, the more agitated Becky began to feel.

'Come on, come on,' she muttered, as the little plane made what seemed to be remarkably slow progress towards the short landing strip.

Once again, they were first off the plane and they rushed into the tiny arrivals hall where they were met by the local police.

'Have you found her?' Tom asked as he shook the sergeant's hand.

'Sorry, sir. Nothing yet. Have you any more idea of where she might be?'

'We've been thinking about this on the plane,' Becky said, 'and the only thing we know for certain is that she's near a beach.'

The sergeant gave her a look that said, 'You have to be kidding me,' but it wasn't until they were in the car and speeding away from the airport that Becky understood why. Every corner they turned, there in front of them was the sea.

The sergeant relented slightly by commenting, 'At least we can rule out the town,' but it was obvious that it wasn't much help.

Tom was sitting in the front passenger seat, and Becky leaned forwards to listen to the conversation.

'How do you propose we go about it, Sergeant?' Tom asked.

'I've resorted to bush telegraph,' the sergeant said. 'My wife and my constable's wife have been on the phone for the last two hours, talking to everybody they know – asking if anybody knows anything or has any idea where we should be looking. Trust me, this is our best plan. In the meantime, we'll take the coast road. As far as I can find out, your man hasn't hired a car. He could have hired a bike, but without using a credit card a car would be difficult. There's always a chance he's nicked one. Nobody locks their cars around here, and they all leave the keys in. That might help us, or it may be that the owner won't realise it's missing for a couple of days if your man's been smart about it.'

Great, thought Becky. *Bloody excellent.*

52

Today has been another perfect day. The sun has been shining, and yet we were the only people on this bit of beach. We spent hours this morning exploring the crystal-clear rock pools, and we've just finished building Billy's 'best-ever sandcastle'.

I'm taking a moment to be lazy, and I lie back in the soft sand, gazing up at the blue sky overhead, listening to the children squabbling amicably about how to construct a drawbridge.

I only half hear them, though, because my thoughts turn to Sophie. It's hard for me to accept that Robert has been to see her, and I'm certain that she didn't tell me everything. Robert wouldn't have calmly asked her where I was, and then politely left when she refused to tell him. I feel so guilty that I dragged her into this, although to be fair she was the one who persuaded me that I had to get out of this marriage, as she slowly but surely pulled me out of the pit of despair in which I was mired.

'Listen, Liv,' she had said on the third or fourth time that we met. 'You might think the children are safe as long as you stay with Robert, but he's clearly unhinged. What if he moves the goalposts and you're not prepared? What if he becomes so obsessed with knowing your every move that he keeps you locked in the house? A total prisoner? You've got to get out.'

We had already explored the legal route to escape, but it appeared there was none. I had no proof of Robert's threats, but on the other hand he had plenty of proof that I wasn't quite stable. I was told that I could be classified as a hostile partner, and at the very least Robert was sure to be awarded contact time with the children – which is all he would need to carry out his plan.

In spite of all my anxiety, I feel seduced by the peace of this island. It seems that nothing bad can happen to me here and I think it's the simplicity of the place that gives me that sensation of safety. People smile all the time, and go out of their way to be helpful. The roads are calm with little traffic and not even a roundabout to be found. But it's the sea that brings the serenity to me. It's rarely out of sight, and whether it's calm and turquoise blue or dark grey with white breakers thrashing against the churning water, I can't take my eyes off it.

Even though the Dan situation isn't completely resolved yet, I know it will be. And then, finally, I will be able to move forwards with my life. At the moment it feels like I'm living in a bubble, floating safely amidst turbulent air. I can almost picture myself and the children within this bubble. The air around us looks dark and grim, with black clouds and grey, stormy seas. But inside our bubble it is a day like today – sunny, bright and filled with laughter. I have to stop the darkness from seeping in and destroying our happiness.

I turn my head to watch my beautiful children playing in the sand, Jaz – no, Ginny – in her favourite ice-blue T-shirt and the boys with their chubby little legs covered in white sand as they stand in the shallow sea and shovel water into orange plastic buckets to try to fill the moat of their sandcastle. How long will it be before they realise what a fruitless task that is? But they need to discover this for themselves.

I sit up and look behind me at the house we rented. It couldn't be more perfect. It's secluded, but yet doesn't feel lonely. At night I can sleep with my window open and hear the waves lapping gently on to the shore. I can't wait for the first big storm, which should be spectacular here.

The house is painted a pale cream colour, and has a small lawn leading down to a gate through to the beach. I didn't choose it specifically for its seclusion, even though it is a bonus. I chose it because along the back of the house is a veranda with doors from all the bedrooms, and from that veranda there's a spiral staircase down to the terrace behind the kitchen and living room. I couldn't believe my luck at finding such a perfect spot, because as I visualise my bubble, I am reminded of one thing. The outer casing of a bubble is fragile and can pop at any moment.

That's why we have a plan, and it's time we had another practice.

I've made it into a game for the children. It's our war game. The children are evacuees who have missed the last boat. When the enemy soldiers arrive, the children have to hide. I want them to take the 'game' seriously, but I don't want them to have nightmares, so I've tried to make it fun.

The first thing we did when we came at Easter was to find a convenient bunker. This island is not short of them, that's for sure. Not the closest bunker to the house, though, but one that they could safely get inside, and hide. So we had a great couple of days exploring those that wouldn't be too far for a four-year-old's little legs. We cleared out the rubbish that had accumulated in there, and then I bought a plastic cool box and filled it with biscuits and the children's favourite drinks, plus a couple of battery-operated lights and a fully charged mobile phone. The plastic box, I reasoned, would protect the food from any four-legged predators. We covered it with a few dark grey blankets so that if anybody glanced in they wouldn't see the bright red plastic. We check it every couple of days – I have spares of everything in case somebody finds the cool box and takes it.

There is one thing about this island, though. I don't think anybody would ever dream of taking anything that wasn't theirs. The lady who rented me the house was surprised that I wanted a key, saying she hadn't locked her door for twenty years. Nobody seems to steal what doesn't belong to them, and there's nowhere for a burglar to run anyway. Or a kidnapper for that matter.

But I will be keeping all my doors permanently locked. I may think I'm safe here, but I have to be careful for the sake of the children. I can't become complacent.

Once we had established our hiding place for the enemy invasion, we practised the escape from the house – out through the bedroom doors, on to the veranda, and down the spiral staircase. Across the grass, through the gate and along the coastal path. Past the first two bunkers, slide down the hill, and into the little bunker that's hidden in the side of the cliff. It's a bit of a drop from the door, but I piled some stones up so the little ones can clamber in and out easily.

I want to practise over and over again but the children would get bored, and I'm worried that if the time comes, they might refuse to go. Freddie cried the first time, but he seems okay about it now. Let's hope we never have to try it out for real.

I push myself to my feet and wander up to the bench where I've left the beach bag. I want to take a picture of the children so I grab my phone from where it's hiding under a pile of towels and I can see that I have missed several calls – starting two hours ago. Most are from Sophie, but there are a couple of numbers I don't recognise too. The phone starts to vibrate with a new call. It's Sophie, but it's not a scheduled time, and that's not like her.

For a moment, I feel a tremor of nerves, but dismiss them. I must learn to be more confident. I touch the screen to answer.

'Hi, Soph. This is a nice surprise on a beautiful day,' I say. 'Have you been trying to call me?' But my smile fades in a second. She tells me the last thing I want to hear.

'Liv, it's Robert. He knows where you are. He's found you.'

My body freezes. I can't speak.

He's come to get my children, just as he said he would.

I hadn't always understood what he was threatening me with, but when he took my children two years ago he waited until the police had gone and we were alone. Then he put his threat into words, each one spoken clearly and slowly so I could be in no doubt of what he was telling me. I tried not to listen, as if not hearing it would somehow make it not real. I tried not to look at him, as if not seeing him would make him disappear. He put his face close to mine, though, and breathed into my ear, so I could hear every word.

'Olivia – you are my life. Nothing else matters, only you. If you leave me there will be no point in me breathing. Do you understand? I think about you every second of every day. I cling to the belief that one day, you will feel the same about me.' He took a deep breath. 'But that's not going to happen, Olivia, is it?'

I couldn't speak.

'You're mine, Olivia. Even if you can't love me the way I love you, you're mine. And I can settle for that, as long as I can see your face every day, touch your body when I want – yes, Olivia, when *I* want – and know that you will always be here each evening when I get home. But if you leave me, one day I will take your children – just like I did tonight – and nobody will ever find me.'

He moved in even closer, so that his lips touched my ear.

'If you leave me, you will never see any of us again. You will be left with nothing.'

53

Marjorie Beresford was feeling guilty. She was supposed to be looking after her father, but this morning she had been into town and instead of coming straight back from the butcher and fishmonger as she had promised, she had decided to stop off for a cappuccino. It was a lovely day, and the tables at the brasserie were set outside.

And after all it was only a cup of coffee – just an extra ten minutes.

The problem was that ten minutes had expanded to half an hour as she had chatted to people she hadn't seen for weeks. She didn't get out much because her father needed almost constant nursing now. But he wasn't prepared to go into a home, and so what else could she do? It was good to talk, though, and she couldn't help it if she got a little carried away and forgot the time. Just this once.

It was as she was paying the bill that the nice young man had come in, saying he was looking for his sister. She'd come to the island a while ago with her three children, and he thought she had said she was renting somewhere. He'd promised to visit, but he'd stupidly lost the address. He was asking Joe, the owner, but Marjorie couldn't help overhearing. All the man knew was that his sister's place was near a beach. Was it okay for him to ask around – to see if anybody knew where it might be?

Marjorie was certain it must be Lynn that he was talking about. And she had three children.

She wasn't sure whether to say anything or not, but by the time she had paid and spoken to a few other acquaintances on her way out, she saw that the man was sitting disconsolately at one of the outdoor tables, and she felt sorry for him.

'Excuse me,' she'd said. 'I didn't quite catch your name?'

'Jonathan,' he replied, with a friendly smile that held more than a hint of sadness in her view.

'I'm Marjorie. What's your sister's name?' She was surprised when he gave a small laugh.

'I don't know.'

'Excuse me?' she said.

'I'm sorry,' he said. 'It's a long and complicated story. My sister got herself into a bit of trouble in England. She owed some people money. The usual thing – she'd over-stretched herself when her husband walked out, and she took out what seemed like a sensible loan. Only the interest was about a thousand per cent, and she just got in deeper and deeper. I gave her some cash to pay them off, but she used it instead to run away. She came here. I want to find her to tell her I've settled all her debts. She's totally in the clear and can come home whenever she wants. My parents are missing her and the children – but I don't know what name she has dreamed up for herself. Her real name is Olivia, and when she was younger she was called Liv by a lot of people. But I don't know what name she will have adopted – or what she'll be calling the children either.'

Marjorie looked at the sad face of the man opposite. What a good brother to have, she couldn't help thinking. She had a brother herself, and he did absolutely sweet Fanny Adams to help with their father.

'Your sister's very lucky to have you,' she said frankly. 'Look, I don't know if it helps or not, but I take care of a property for some people who used to live on the island but have gone to America for a few years. They let it privately, and there's a lady living there at the moment with three children. They took it at the end of last October, though, so I don't know if it's the same woman. Her name's Lynn. I can't remember the children's names, but there's a girl and two little boys. Could that be them, do you think?'

The man called Jonathan beamed at her.

'That's wonderful, thank you. It sounds just like them. Can you tell me where the house is?'

And so she had. And because of that she ended up being forty-five minutes late in getting home. Her father was now in a mood, and when he deigned to respond to any of her questions, he was monosyllabic at best. She needed to make amends for her thoughtlessness.

As she left his bedroom, having received his order for a sandwich, the phone in the hall started to ring. She wanted to answer it, because she so enjoyed chatting to other people – people other than her father, that would be – but she couldn't. First things first, she needed to at least make him a cup of tea.

She stood in the kitchen waiting for the kettle to boil, but she could still hear the message being recorded on the machine. She recognised Pam's voice – somebody else she hadn't seen for weeks. Pam no doubt wanted to know if they could get together for coffee one morning. Chance would be a fine thing. But as she added the water to the teapot, she thought she heard Pam say something about the police.

Abandoning her tea-making, she went into the hall.

Her face flushed with distress as she listened to the full message.

Oh goodness. What have I done? she thought.

54

I'm too stunned to move. How is it possible? How has Robert found us? I know I didn't leave a single scrap of evidence in the house, and even though he now knew we had not been to Anglesey, I can't think of anything that would have led him here. I'm almost dazed.

A shout from the children jolts me out of my contemplation. Jaz is pointing towards the road behind me and shouting.

Oh, God – no. Please don't let it be Robert.

I never gave the children any hint that they should be scared of their father. I didn't want them to live in terror, and I didn't think he would harm them as long as I was the dutiful wife. But when I understood the depths of his obsession and acknowledged the full extent of everything he had done, I finally started to believe that we could never be safe with him.

As I turn to see what Jasmine is pointing at, I'm relieved to see that it's nothing more than a couple of horses going by. She loves horses, and I'd always thought we could arrange riding lessons when things have settled down.

I have to force myself into action.

I need to get the children to safety and call the police. I can't call them now; it would take too long to explain.

As I stand up, my phone starts to ring, but I ignore it. Nothing matters except getting my children away from danger. I've been inactive for less than thirty seconds but it feels as if I may just have risked their lives through my inability to move.

'Jaz!' I yell. 'Come here quickly.'

I run down the beach as fast as I can and grab Freddie, swinging his sturdy little body into my arms. I shout to Billy who is at the edge of the sea, filling his bucket with water.

'Leave your bucket. Leave it – don't argue. Just run as fast as you can back to the path.'

I can see that I am scaring them, and Freddie starts to cry.

'Sorry, darlings,' I say in a slightly calmer voice, although kids pick up so easily on emotion. 'It's a practice for the invasion. I need you all to go to the bunker. You need to hide from the enemy.'

I try my best to smile.

The kids trudge up the beach – not as fast as I would like, but the sand is soft, and it's not that easy to run.

We stumble across the dunes at a half-run, and past the bench. I pick up my bag and hear my phone still ringing. I don't have time for that.

As we reach the path that runs along the back of the house, I hear the worst sound in the world echoing through the empty house and out through the open dining-room window. It's the sound of a ringing doorbell.

The children look at me. But for a second I am glued to the spot. Billy tugs on my hand.

'What's the matter, Mummy?' he asks, confused by my sudden tension.

I crouch down and pull Jasmine towards me.

'Okay – enemy soldier alert. You're in charge for this practice, Jaz. You know where to go. Take the boys and run. Stay there until I come for you – okay?'

Jaz looks at me in horror.

'Aren't you coming with us?' she asks in a shaky little voice.

'I'm going to follow. Let's see how well you've learned the drill. Go on, darling – you're a brave girl, let's see what you can do.'

I turn her round and give her a small shove. The boys are looking a bit confused, but my smile tells them everything is okay.

I can't go with them – he will be round the back of the house in seconds, so they need to go, and I need to head him off.

Jaz glances over her shoulder at me once, and I try to paint a fun, happy face for her, but I don't think she's fooled. She knows the enemy is real.

I can't help wondering if I will ever see my children again.

I turn back to the house. He has stopped ringing the bell, and I hope and pray he's looking through the front windows and isn't on his way around the back. I need to delay him. If he comes round here now, he will see the children who are not moving nearly quickly enough.

I run at full pelt towards the back door, fingers sticky and struggling with the lock. Finally it's open, and I race through the kitchen to the hall where I see the outline shape of a man through the frosted glass of the front door as he rears up from where he was trying to peer through the letterbox. I would recognise the shape of that head anywhere.

'Just a moment,' I shout, trying to sound chirpy and relaxed.

Anything to give my children time to get away.

I grab a tea towel, as if I've been drying my hands, and pull the kitchen door closed behind me. I want him to think the children are here – playing in the garden or on the beach. My heart feels as if it's going to punch through my chest, but I can't phone the police. He would be on to me in a second, and his patience will be running out. I'm sure the only reason he rang the bell is because he can't be one hundred per cent certain that I'm here. If somebody has given him this address, it can only be a 'maybe' in his mind so, if he doesn't want to be reported to the police himself, he will have to pretend to be civilised. At least until he knows for sure.

Finally, I take the key from where it hides on top of a cupboard – too high for little fingers to grab and unlock when I'm not looking. I take a deep breath as I turn the key, draw back the bolts and pull the door towards me.

There he is: his face a white mask, his arms hanging by his side, hands clasped into hard fists.

'Hello, Robert,' I say as calmly as I'm able.

But Robert isn't calm at all. He pushes me with both hands and I slam backwards into the newel post at the bottom of the stairs, trying to suppress a scream. Because if I scream, he will expect the children to come running. And he mustn't know they're not here.

He steps into the hall and kicks the door shut with such force that it springs open again and crashes into the hall cupboard.

Still he doesn't say a word. He just stares at me, and I stare back. His mouth is pinched into a hard line and his eyes are burning.

We stand like that for almost a minute – a precious minute. I'm not prepared to break the silence – the longer it goes on the safer my children will be. And then he utters a single word.

'Why?'

He says it with such anguish that if somebody didn't know the truth about Robert, didn't know what he really was, they would feel sorry for him.

I say nothing. *Delay, delay, delay.* That's all I can think of.

He walks towards me and reaches out his arms. I think he is going to try to hug me, and I feel sick. I feel sick because of all the times I let him hug me after I knew what he was and what he'd done – all so that I could get my children safely away.

But he's not going to hug me. He's going to strangle me.

His hands go round my neck and he shakes me. I am coughing, spluttering, and I think I'm going to die. As soon as he's started, he stops. His hands drop to his side, and he seems almost defeated for a moment. I hope so.

'No, Olivia. I'm not going to kill you. You know I can't do that. But I don't know how you could do this to me – leave me, without a note, without telling me where you were. Do you know the police think I've already killed you? They're probably digging up the terrace this very minute. They will have had crime scene guys crawling all over the place – all because you didn't tell me you were leaving.'

I can't help the feeling of satisfaction. Cruel, but nothing compared to Robert's cruelty.

'Are you coming back to me?' he asks.

I put my hands up to rub my neck, and don't reply for a moment. There are no words I can use that would describe my utter loathing for this man, and I think that maybe by now the children have had long enough to get away.

'I'll *never* come back to you.'

I want to tell him that I've seen beyond his mask now. I know what he's done, and I know who he is. I want to tell him he'll never see any of us again, but I've said enough.

His moment of weakness has passed, and he's laughing at me now. He thinks it's funny. Then his face settles into an expression that I know has been there all along, but I've never seen it myself. His chin drops towards his chest, his eyes turn into hard pebbles and his mouth opens slightly to display clenched teeth. It's the face of evil. He pushes me again, but this time to get past me. He's looking for my children.

I can't stop him. I don't have the strength. If I'd thought about it, I would have left weapons around the house – something to hit him over the head with, or stab him in his gut. But I never thought he would find me. The war games exercise with the children was the ultimate precaution, but I didn't believe we would need it.

I want to run, but I can't run towards my children and I can't run away from them either. The magical isolation of this house has one drawback – I can't run to a neighbour for help. I wouldn't get more than a hundred metres before Robert would catch me and, anyway, I mustn't take my eyes off him. I need to follow his every move, because I can't let him find my children.

I want my phone, but it's in the kitchen.

It doesn't take more than seconds for Robert to search the downstairs rooms, and he pushes past me and takes the stairs two at a time to check the bedrooms. I hear wardrobes opening, and a bang as he sinks to his knees to look under the beds. I race to the kitchen while he is upstairs, but my phone has gone. Robert has taken it.

I know he's in my bedroom when I hear a bark of brittle laughter. He has discovered the decor, which I haven't had time to change yet.

'Very clever, Olivia. I underestimated you,' he shouts, as I hear him dash into the next room.

There's a crash of a door being flung open, as he discovers the balcony, and I have a terrible thought. I never checked the viewing distance from up there. Will he be able to see the children running away?

I've got to interrupt him, so I race upstairs and shout to him. 'Robert!' He can't miss the urgency in my voice. 'They're not here. I swear to you, they're not *here*.'

He spins round and stares at me. Time stands still for just a second, then he starts to walk towards me, speaking slowly.

'Where are they, Olivia? I'm going to find them, you know, even if I have to torture the truth out of you.'

I stand up tall, my back ramrod straight.

'Do you think for one minute you could do anything to me that would make me tell you where my children are?' I spit the words out at him. 'That I would sacrifice their lives to save myself some physical pain?'

I goad him. I need to get him out of this room, away from that window. I turn round and start to walk down the stairs. He follows, grasping my long, dyed-brown hair, winding it round his hand and twisting it to get a firm grip. He yanks it backwards so that I nearly fall over.

As we reach the hallway, he wraps my hair more tightly and pulls me through the kitchen into the dining room. I try to reach for him and grab at his arm, but each time I do he pulls harder at my hair. He's dragging it downwards so I have to walk bent over double, and I can't reach him to defend myself. He is unbuckling the belt of his jeans as he strides towards the dining room, and in that horrifying moment, I know he's going to rape me.

Still tugging my hair down low so that I am practically crawling, he kicks my legs from under me, and I crash to the floor. I brace myself for what seems to be inevitable. While I am still struggling to get off the floor, he plants one foot heavily on my stomach to pin me down and hauls my hands over my head. He wraps his belt tightly round my wrists, and fastens it to a radiator pipe. I am helpless.

He grabs a chair and turns it around so the back is facing my head, with the four legs on either side of my knees so I can't kick him. He straddles the chair and leans towards me, his crazy eyes staring at me.

'Where are they, Olivia?' His face is hovering over me, and I notice his lips are swelling and spittle is collecting in the corners of his mouth. I pray that when he rapes me, he doesn't try to kiss me. I feel myself shudder. He leers at me. 'I wouldn't have believed it possible, but at this moment, my darling wife, I want you more than ever. You have never really *submitted* to me, have you? I should have tried this before.'

I want to be brave and shout obscenities at him, but I don't want anything to accelerate the inevitable. The longer it takes, the more chance that my children will be safe.

'I *will* fuck you one last time, Olivia. And it will be like never before – something you will remember for the rest of your life. But first, you're going to tell me where the children are.'

I close my eyes. I can't bear to look into his demonic expression.

'Let's see how brave you are, shall we?' he says. He takes his Swiss army knife – a present I bought for him last Christmas – from his pocket, and opens it to a serrated blade. He pushes the chair out of the way, and jumps on me – one knee on each side of my thighs to keep my legs under control – and leans forwards.

He runs the blade of the knife down the exposed skin of my inner arm, from my elbow to my armpit. Bubbles of blood burst through, and I feel a sharp stinging pain.

'A taste of the agony to come. I don't want to do this to you, Olivia. But because of you we can never go home, so unless you get the children and come away with me right now, I'm going to fulfil my promise. The one I made to you two years ago. I *told* you what would happen if you left me. So where *are* they?'

I will never tell him. *Never.*

But then I hear the worst noise in the world. The door from the kitchen into the dining room is slowly opening, and I hear a tearful voice. It's Freddie.

'Where are you, Mummy? We don't like escaping the enemy soldiers without you. Where are you?'

I don't make a sound, but over Robert's shoulder I see my three children framed in the doorway, watching.

55

Becky was becoming increasingly anxious. She had called Sophie, who said she had finally managed to make contact with Olivia to warn her. She had tried to get an address too, but as soon as she had mentioned that Robert was on the island, Olivia had ended the call. That was about twenty minutes ago, while Becky and Tom were still en route. But nobody had managed to get through to her since. That didn't feel right.

The sergeant was doing an excellent job of giving them a tour of Alderney. They were working their way around any properties that might fit the few details they had.

'The problem is,' he said, 'a lot of these properties are owned by people who only come to the island a few times a year. If they're rented privately, we might not know about it. So it's going to be difficult. We can knock, but if we get no answer does it mean that he's holding her hostage, or does it just mean the house is empty?'

They pulled into the drive of a lovely stone house, and Becky could see immediately that the back garden stretched almost to the sea. How wonderful to live somewhere like this. They knocked, but there was no answer. Tom disappeared around the back of the house and was back in seconds.

'I don't think it's this one. The beach isn't sandy, and I'm sure Mrs Evans said Robert was muttering about the colour of the sand,' he said. 'Olivia may have shown him the view from her window, but it certainly wasn't a view of Cemaes Bay.'

'You're right, Tom. I should have remembered that.' Becky could have kicked herself. They may not have known the significance of the colour of the sand, but it was definitely the sand that Robert was interested in. Mention of the bench hadn't proved to be as helpful as they had hoped. There were benches dedicated in loving memory of husbands and wives all over the island.

They climbed back in the car, and set off for the next property – this time focusing only on those close to sandy beaches.

'As a matter of interest,' the sergeant said as he overtook two cyclists, 'what do you see happening if we find Mr Brookes?'

'We'll arrest him on suspicion of murder,' Becky answered.

'Sorry, Inspector,' the sergeant said with a slightly pained expression. 'You have no jurisdiction here. You can't arrest him, and I can't arrest him on your say-so.'

'Shit,' Becky muttered quietly. Did that mean if they found him, he could just walk away?

'It's okay, Becky,' Tom said, turning round in his seat and giving her a reassuring smile. 'I knew about this. When you were chasing everybody to get things done as we boarded the plane, I made a call and asked for a warrant to be issued. Somebody's on it. They're going to have to deliver the original here. What happens then?'

Tom looked at the sergeant.

'We have to present it to the Chairman of the Court of Alderney. When do you think your warrant will arrive, Chief Inspector?'

'Tomorrow at the earliest – and call me Tom, please. This is Becky.'

'Ray,' he responded. 'So, we're going to have to work out what to do with your Mr Brookes if we find him. Any ideas?'

The brief silence that followed was interrupted as Ray's phone started to ring. Before he had time even to announce himself, Becky could hear a squawking down the line.

'Calm down, Marjorie. I can't tell what you're saying. Take a deep breath and try again.'

There was a pause while Ray listened.

'Okay. Thanks, Marjorie. You've done really well. And you did nothing wrong at all. Don't worry about it – just look after your dad. I'll pop round later and let you know how we've got on.'

Ray hung up, and put his foot down.

'I think we've found him,' was all he said.

56

Robert is hugging the children, but the sight of him even touching them is enough to make me want to scream. Why did they come back? I must have got it wrong. Maybe it was too much of a game. Maybe I should have warned them that there was *real* danger. But maybe Jaz knew. Maybe she came back for me – to make sure I was okay.

The boys seem pleased to see their father, but Jaz is just looking at me. Her eyes are as round as saucers as she takes in the fact that I'm tied to a radiator pipe. I want to tell her to run – but what about my boys?

'What have you done to Mummy?' Jasmine asks, her voice revealing her bewilderment at the fact that I'm lying on the floor with blood running down my arm and on to the carpet. My poor baby girl.

Robert ignores her. He has no answer that would make sense to a child as smart as Jaz.

Her eyes flash towards me, then to my arm, then back to Robert. He's kneeling on the floor now with his arms round both of the boys. I'm watching them, willing them to be safe, trying to think. There must be something I can do.

'I've missed you, Billy. And you too, Freddie. Have you been having a good holiday?' Robert asks in a soft voice. But I can see the madness in his eyes, and I think Jaz can too.

'I'm not Billy any more. I'm Ben.' Billy says with pride. 'Do you like my new hair?'

Robert turns to look at me and shakes his head very slightly. I gaze back at him, pleading with my eyes. But it makes him smile.

'Robert,' I begin. But he ignores me.

'Listen kids, why don't you show me around outside? I'd love to see the beach. I've only ever seen it on video when I was talking to Mummy.' He gives me what I can only describe as a look of pure malice.

'What about Mummy?' Billy asks.

'Mummy can stay here for now. She's had you all to herself for weeks. It's my turn now. Come on – let's go.'

Jasmine's eyes are still darting round the room. 'I'm staying with Mummy,' she says with a note of defiance in her voice.

'No, you're not. You're coming with me,' Robert answers through a mouth that has tightened. He reaches out for Jasmine, but she bats his arm away.

'I'm staying,' she says, my lovely little warrior.

Robert stands up and grabs Jaz by her arm. 'Come on, guys – take me outside.'

Jasmine still doesn't move until he tugs hard on her arm and she nearly falls over. She shrieks in pain.

I have to escape. I have to find a way of saving them. I pull on the belt, but it won't move and my shoulders are so sore and lacking in strength. I feel as if I am watching some awful movie, and the four sides of the image have turned black, leaving the centre where my husband and children are standing sharply in focus.

The boys have realised that something is wrong. They look at Jaz then back at me.

'Stay here, kids. Don't go with him – he can't make you all go. Come here, Freddie.' I want my youngest to be out of his father's grasp, but I'm too late. Robert grabs him round his middle and hangs on.

Only Billy is free, and he seems stunned into inactivity. *Do something, Billy.*

'Jasmine, carry your little brother,' Robert demands as he tries to pass Freddie to her. I'm not sure that Jaz can carry Freddie very far. He's a solid little boy, and she's so slight. When she does nothing, Robert yanks on her arm again. I can see tears spilling down her cheeks, and she looks up at Robert. How can he resist these beautiful faces?

'Leave my children *alone*, Robert. If you hurt one hair on their heads, I *will* kill you.' I know my screaming won't help. It will just amuse him, and fuel the fire. But if I can just make the children realise the danger...

Robert laughs, as I knew he would. The hysteria in his laughter is more pronounced than ever.

'If I can't have you, Olivia, then you must pay the price. I'm only doing what many men before me have done; men like me who have been betrayed, deceived, abandoned.' All traces of laughter in his voice die with the final three words as his anger bubbles over, spilling its malignancy into every corner of the room. The children have started to cry, and there's not a thing I can do.

'Say goodbye to Mummy, children. It's time to go.'

He puts Freddie down and lets go of Jasmine, pushing the children towards the door.

Robert kneels down at my side and puts both hands around my neck. I cast a last, longing look at my children as he pulls me towards him and then smashes me back against the radiator. My head explodes with pain, but through the fast encroaching blackness I feel his breath against my skin and hear him whisper four words:

'Sleep tight, my darling.'

57

My head feels like somebody has taken a machete and cleaved it in two. I try to reach it with my hands in an effort to push back the pain, but I can't move them. My shoulders ache, and I can feel a stinging wetness on the inside of my arm. What's happening?

Somebody is speaking, trying to make me listen.

'Olivia. Come on, Olivia – wake up.' A gentle hand is stroking my face – not the hand of the person speaking though. It's a man's voice, and this hand is too gentle. I hear a woman speak.

'I think she's coming round, Tom.' I hear a grunt.

'That's her hands free,' says the gruff voice. Another voice is talking in the background, firing urgent staccato instructions. I hear 'ambulance', 'more bodies', 'children' and suddenly I am awake. What does he mean, *more bodies*? And where are my children?

I try to sit up, and a strong arm goes round my shoulders.

'Olivia, can you speak?' I try to nod my head, but it hurts so much. In an instant, it all comes hurtling back at me at such great speed it nearly knocks me over with its force.

'Robert's got my babies,' I murmur almost to myself, trying to remember if it's real, or I just imagined it. But I know it's real and my voice gains strength.

'He's taken them – he's taken my children.' The last word comes out as a sob.

'We know, we're going to find them.'

'Somebody said "more bodies" – what did he mean?' I hear a gasp of shock and my eyes focus on a pretty young woman with dark hair and tired eyes.

'No, no – we haven't found more bodies. I think the sergeant was trying to get some reinforcements – people to come out and look for your children.'

Thank God. But how long have I been unconscious?

As if reading my thoughts, the other man – the one with the strong arm – starts to talk.

'Do you know what time it was when Robert arrived here? We need to get an idea of how far he may have gone so we can organise the search properly.'

I don't know. I can't think – but I know I've got to.

'Check my phone. Sophie called me, and I got the children up from the beach. Then he was here. It all happened quickly – fifteen minutes, twenty at the most.'

The young woman was already on to the task.

'Shit. We missed him by about three minutes, Tom – worst case, eight.'

I recognise the policeman in uniform. He's the island sergeant, but I don't know who the other two are. I know they're here to help me, though, and there's no time for introductions.

'I know where he'll have taken them.' My voice cracks with emotion, but I have to keep it together. 'He'll have taken them to a cliff – somewhere high above the sea.' The sergeant is listening, waiting to issue his instructions.

'Why, Olivia? Why would he take them to a cliff?' the man called Tom asks.

I can barely speak. The images flashing before my eyes are too horrific. But I can remember that day at South Stack. And the last words he said to my children: 'Say goodbye to Mummy.'

'He's going to jump off – and he's going to take my babies with him.'

'Becky, you need to stay here with Olivia. Olivia, Becky is a detective inspector, and if your husband returns, she'll look after you, okay?'

No, it is certainly not okay.

'I'm coming with you,' I say. I can see that the man is going to argue. There's something about him that I think I vaguely recognise, but I can't place it. 'I don't know who you are, but I *do* know that those are my children. I'm coming with you.'

I struggle to my feet and nearly keel over when the pain in my head hits a crescendo. My skull feels as if it needs physically holding together or it will shatter into pieces, but I can't let them see that.

'You'll slow us down, Olivia. Stay here.'

'No. If Robert sees you and he's anywhere near the cliff, he'll jump. I'm the best chance you have of talking him out of it.'

I'm sure I hear him mutter some expletive, but I don't care. What are we hanging about for?

Tom Douglas looks at the local sergeant. 'What's the plan, Ray?' he asks.

'The good news is that there are no steep cliffs nearby, and his speed will be hampered by three children. I've got the local fire brigade boys rallied – they'll go out in civvies so they won't spook him. And the lifeboat's on its way out to sea. They'll head out and circuit the island. They'll call if they spot him. Do we still want the ambulance here?'

I try to shake my head, but it's not a good idea. 'No,' I say. 'I'm not going in any ambulance. I'm coming with you.'

The police officers all look at each other, and the local sergeant shrugs. 'No time to argue. In my view if Brookes left here through the back gate, he would have turned right on the path. Turning left would just take him to the beach, with no cliffs for a couple of miles. My constable has just let me know he's joined the cliff path about 250 metres along. There's no sign of Brookes yet.' Ray was edging towards the door. 'I'm going to follow him now, make sure he hasn't stopped anywhere in between. I've got your number.' And he's gone – out of the door and running.

'What are we waiting for, then,' I cry, frustrated by the apparent lack of action.

The young woman puts her arm round me. 'We need to be near a car so when they find your children we can get there as quickly as possible. Ray's left us the police car and it's a four-wheel drive so we'll be able to take it over the rough paths.' She takes my arm and guides me to a chair 'Let me look at your head,' she says kindly. But strangely I don't mind the pain. It's just a reminder of what I have to do.

I stay seated for about thirty seconds and then leap up, a corresponding pounding in my head reminding me to go steady or I might pass out again.

'Can we just go – head off in the right direction? *Please*. I can't sit here and do nothing.'

I intercept a look passing between the police officers, and sense that they feel the same frustration.

Tom gives a slight nod. 'He's been gone about fifteen to twenty minutes now. Average walking speed is roughly five kilometres an hour, but with the children?'

I know Robert would have carried Freddie and Jasmine could keep up with him. Only Billy would slow him down, and probably not for at least the first kilometre. I tell them, and Tom seems to agree.

'Becky, you drive and I'll navigate,' he says, earning him a surprised look from Becky that I don't understand. 'Where's that map you had?'

'In the car,' she answers, picking up her bag. 'Are you going to tell Ray?'

But Tom already has the phone to his ear, walking towards the front door.

'Ray, we're going to head for a point about one and a quarter kilometres along the cliff path from the house. Yes, we've got a map. We'll catch you there.'

58

Becky didn't know what to say to Olivia. It was two hours since Robert had taken the children, and nobody had seen them. Olivia was sitting in the back of the car, her head resting against the window, tears running down her cheeks. But she wasn't making a sound.

'Olivia, I can't imagine how you feel, but at least we can be fairly sure that nothing has happened to the kids. We would know if that was the case. The cliffs were crawling with people looking for them within minutes of Robert taking them. We're going to find your children.'

Becky glanced at Tom, knowing that he hated people giving promises that they didn't know they could keep. But he simply nodded to her, his top lip clenched between his teeth.

Just ahead, Becky caught signs of movement, and sat up straighter in her seat. They were parked on the grass, as close to the cliffs as they could safely get. Olivia must have sensed something, because her head came off the window and she leaned over Becky's shoulder.

'What's up?' she asked, her voice ringing with hope.

'I thought I saw something, but it was probably a rabbit,' Becky said. But it wasn't. She could just glimpse the top of a head as somebody wove up the cliff path from below.

Olivia jerked backwards and went for the door handle.

'Whoa,' said Tom. 'Stop, Olivia. If this is Robert, we have to take it calmly. Don't make him jump or react quickly. He's much closer to the edge than we are.'

The path that was winding up towards them from a lower level had bumps and turns, and all they saw was a tantalising glimpse of the top of a head every few seconds.

A groan from the back of the car and sounds of held breath being finally exhaled signalled their recognition of Ray, heading towards them at a half-jog. Not fast enough for it to be good news, not slow enough for it to be bad.

As Ray approached the car, flushed from his exertion, Tom and Becky opened their doors and got out, turning to let Olivia – who was hemmed in by the safety lock – out too. Becky was glad of the fresh air and the opportunity to stretch her legs. A blustery wind was blowing clean sea air into her lungs and she took a deep breath.

'Any news?' Tom asked. An anxious Olivia peered up at Ray through eyes swollen with weeping and, Becky suspected, from the continued pain in her head.

'He's nowhere on the cliff paths. We're as certain as we can be. We can only think he's gone into hiding somewhere.'

Becky looked around her. All she could see was open countryside.

Ray interpreted her look correctly. 'It's not quite as simple as it seems. The place is riddled with bunkers from the war, and then there are the old forts. The first bit of Brookes' escape was past a few houses that are probably empty at this time of year, so he could have broken in. They might not even be locked. We're starting a systematic search of the obvious places, but I'm sorry; we're just going to have to be patient. Can you tell me what the children are wearing, Mrs Brookes? Knowing what colours we're looking out for might help.'

While Olivia was describing Jasmine's blue T-shirt and matching stripy shorts, Becky turned back towards the sea. What would Robert's next move be? How could they flush him out? It wouldn't be dark for hours, so what was he hoping would happen?

There was a crackle from Ray's radio behind her, and he grabbed it.

'*What?*' Ray shouted, and Becky spun round to look at him. Worry lines were creasing his brows. 'How the *fuck* did he get there?' Ray was already jogging towards the car, and they all followed. 'Call Ed and tell him to redirect his men – but be subtle. No charging in. Got it?'

Ray headed towards the driver's side, and Becky jumped in the back with Olivia. Nobody spoke, scared to distract Ray from his manoeuvre of the car so close to the edge of the cliff. Becky felt Olivia reach out towards her, her hand like a block of ice, and she squeezed the bones of Becky's fingers until they felt they were going to break. Ray swung the car on to the track and switched his siren on.

'Don't worry – I'll turn this off once we get close. We were wrong. It seems he turned the other way out of the garden, not knowing the island I suppose. It's pretty flat for a mile or so – mainly beaches. We sent a couple of people out that way, but he must have hidden for a bit because nobody saw them. The lifeboat has just spotted him over beyond Fort Clonque.'

Olivia seemed to breathe out. 'I know the fort. It's in the sea, isn't it? Just a causeway to it, so it's at sea level.'

Becky suddenly understood Olivia's thinking. If it was at sea level, it was safe.

'The fort's at sea level, but that's not where they were. They were up above it. On the cliffs.'

59

I'm holding on to Becky's hand for dear life, but when Ray explains where my children are, the blood rushes to my head and the pounding intensifies. I think I'm going to pass out again, and I will myself to hold it together. The children must be exhausted. They've been walking for hours. Freddie will be crying, and Billy will be dragging his feet and complaining. And Jaz? She will be saying nothing, trying to understand what's going on, and worrying about me. The last image she has of me is one of her father smashing my head against a radiator.

I'm relieved when Ray turns off the siren. If Robert hears it, he'll know we've found him. I need to get to him first.

Ray races the car up a steep hill, past another huge old ruined fort, lights flashing and drawing looks of surprise from the few people and cars that we pass. He pulls over at the side of the road where there is a narrow footpath.

'Becky,' he says, 'why don't you stay in the car with Olivia. Tom and I have got this.'

Not a chance.

'I'm coming,' I say, praying they won't keep me locked in the back.

Tom turns round to look at me, his face sympathetic but serious.

'Olivia, your children are going to need you, so you can come. But it's essential that you stay down and out of sight. If he sees you, it may all be over. Do you understand?'

I agree, not knowing if I will be able to keep my promise when I see my babies.

Ray has already set off across the field at a run.

'What's Ray doing?' I whisper urgently, afraid that Robert will hear me.

'He'll have gone to check if he can see Robert. Don't worry. He won't approach him if the situation is dangerous.'

We hurry along the path, trying to keep our eyes on Ray ahead of us.

The ground is uneven, with bright yellow gorse and pale lilac crane's bill trying to encroach on the narrow trail. I have to keep looking down to avoid stumbling, but I don't want to take my eyes off Ray. Suddenly he crouches down and turns towards us to hold up a hand in warning. I can't see Robert, but I know Ray can. He signals us to get down low, especially Tom who is taller than the rest of us. We bend at the waist and the knees and quietly make our way forwards.

I have this mad notion that I can communicate with Jaz. I've always believed that telepathy is a skill or a sense waiting to be discovered, and now I am going to give it my best shot.

Jaz, darling, can you hear me? I repeat in my head. *Get on the ground, Jaz. Get the boys on the ground and wrap yourselves together in knots, arms and legs, so he can't separate you. It will make it harder. Do it, Jaz. Just do it, sweetheart.*

We reach Ray and finally I can see Robert and the children just below us. I swallow a sob of relief that they are still alive. Robert is standing, but Jaz is already on the ground, probably exhausted from the walk, and she is leaning forwards with her head down. Freddie is beside her, trying to snuggle closer to her, and without looking up she reaches out an arm to wrap around him. Billy is on his feet, staring at his dad but I'm too far away to read the expression on his face. I imagine he is totally bewildered.

Everywhere is quiet, and I try to separate out the sounds, so that I might hear the children's voices. The intermittent crashing of waves on to the rocks at the base of the cliff and the shrill, piping call of an oystercatcher mask the sounds I am listening for. But faintly I think I can hear the gulping noise Billy makes when he is trying not to cry, and his big sister saying, 'Shh, shh.' Or perhaps I'm imagining it.

Then I hear the low growl of Robert's voice, more distinct, because he is facing us. The wind is whipping some of his words away, but I know what he's saying.

'Stand up, Jasmine, and pick Freddie up.' I can see from his hand movements what he wants her to do. He wants her to hold Freddie because he can't hold them all at once. But Jasmine isn't moving. She's pulled Freddie close to her, not quite doing what I implored her to do in my thoughts, but she's making it difficult for Robert.

Tom and Ray are whispering, trying to decide what to do. Robert is too far away, and if they rush him now, he still has time to grab my babies – or at least two of them – and jump. I can't hear what the police are saying, but I edge closer to the front so I am level with Ray.

Suddenly, Robert reaches down and snatches a handful of Jasmine's hair to drag her to her feet. She cries out in pain. A knife pierces my heart, and I lose all sense of reason. He is hurting my baby, so I stand up and run. A hand reaches out to grasp my ankle and pull me back before I'm seen, but I kick it away and I'm free.

'Jaz!' I scream. 'Lie on the ground, lie on top of Freddie. Billy, Billy – lie down.'

Jasmine's head whips round and her silky hair slides out of Robert's hand. She pauses, but just for a second, then flings herself to the ground, knocking a screaming Freddie over, covering his little body with hers. But Billy stands still, staring at me. Robert reaches out for him, but Jaz is too quick and Billy's hand is nearer to hers than it is to Robert's. She grabs him and yanks him off his feet. He tumbles to the ground with a shout of surprise.

I pray that the policemen will stay down. If Robert sees them before I get to him, he will snatch one of my children, and take them with him into the hell of churning water below. I daren't take my eyes off Robert's now, but I can see in my peripheral vision a bright orange boat, bobbing just off the shoreline. The lifeboat. But it will be useless if Robert takes one of them over the edge with him. The rocks will get them before the sea.

'*Robert!*' I yell, with all the accumulated pain and anguish spilling out in those two syllables. He is crouching down, trying to disentangle the children, but also watching me as he does it. He can't get a hold though. As I run, I can see that as soon as he grabs one child's arm, the other is wrapped round a leg, and he can't tear them apart. At least, not before I get to him.

Or that's what I'm thinking. But I'm wrong.

In his fear of everything that's happening, and because he has heard my voice, Freddie has managed to crawl out from under Jasmine, who is so intent on saving Billy that she hasn't noticed, and Robert plucks Freddie up and holds him in his arms.

He backs towards the edge of the cliff as Jasmine cries out, feeling that she has failed to protect her brother. I am desperate to comfort her – but not yet. I stop dead.

'Robert,' I say, trying to keep my voice level, 'stop this. *Please*. Put Freddie down.'

Jasmine and Billy are crawling away from Robert towards me, and with one hand I signal them to get behind me. Jaz understands, and pulls Billy with her. But I never take my eyes off my husband.

'You never understood, did you Olivia,' he says. 'Do you know what I had to do to win you, to make you mine? Do you know how much love it takes to do all the things I had to do?'

I do know. I've worked it all out for myself, but there was never anybody to tell, and no proof of anything but a life of love and devotion. What can I say to make this right?

'I understand, Robert. I know how much you love me and I know how good you've been to me. I'm so sorry I hurt you.' I start to walk towards him slowly. Perhaps I can still convince him that what he feels is a love that is pure, and not tainted by his acts of evil. Can I convince him there is still a chance for us?

I try to make my expression one of sorrow as I take another step.

'I don't want you to die,' I lie. 'Can't we talk? Please, Robert?'

For a moment I think I'm getting through, and then Robert glances behind me, and his eyes change. He's seen somebody. He knows it's not just him and me. He pulls Freddie tighter to him and starts to back up towards the edge of the cliff. I can't let him get close but he only has about eight metres to go.

I can hear Jasmine and Billy crying behind me, and I take one look at Freddie's terrified little face. I don't stop to think or to plan. Robert has my baby. I lean forwards and rush at him. Two steps and I leap to try to knock him to the floor. He's not a big man, but he's bigger and heavier than me, and he absorbs the shock without falling. He has loosened his hold on Freddie, though, and Freddie has wriggled free.

Robert grabs me round the neck and pulls me to him, squeezing hard, muttering insanely under his breath about his perfect love. I want to break free, but I hear Jaz screaming, and over Robert's shoulder I see Freddie is backing away from us, not realising that in just a few tiny steps his foot will come down and meet thin air as he tumbles down the cliff face.

I can't breathe. I'm fighting not for my life but for Freddie's and I can't shout out. I try, but the pressure on my throat forces nothing more than a squeak from my larynx.

I can't turn my head, but from nowhere I see a dark shape swoop towards Freddie and pluck him right from the edge.

Thank God. My children are safe.

I can die now.

60

From where I am sitting on the sofa, I can see the chief inspector – Tom, as he told me to call him during our interminable two-hour wait at the cliff top – at the dining-room table, nursing his hand in a packet of frozen peas wrapped in a tea towel; an injury sustained as he dived to the ground to grab Freddie back from the brink. According to the doctor it's just a sprain, but I will never be able to thank him enough for what he did.

Robert has been arrested for crimes committed on Alderney soil, and has been taken to the cells. A UK warrant will be delivered tomorrow, and then apparently they have to decide if Robert should be returned to Manchester to be charged with offences committed there, or remain here to be charged for his attack on the children and me. I asked Ray what offences in Manchester, but he told me it is something I need to discuss with Tom.

I am hemmed in on all sides by children. Jaz is on one side and Billy on the other, both crushed up against me so that rather wonderfully I am almost unable to breathe as they squeeze themselves as tightly as possible against my ribcage. Freddie is on my knee, curled up in a tight ball, his head pressing against the bruises on my neck. The pain just reminds me of what I almost lost.

The children are shocked, and I don't know how I am going to be able to get them past this. I'm hoping that the peace and calm of this island will soothe them. Jasmine is going to take the longest to recover, though. Her serious little face settles from time to time into a frown as if she is trying to puzzle something out in her own head.

Tom is looking at me, and I know he wants to talk to me about something – something serious. He stands up and walks over, speaking in a quiet even tone to avoid any hint of tension creeping into the calmness of the room.

'Olivia, do you think we could have a word, please? I know you don't want to leave the children, but Becky will stay with them. We can just sit over there in the dining area so you can still see them, but it's probably best if we're not overheard.'

I have a quiet word with Jaz, just to make sure she's okay, and suggest she chooses a DVD that they might all enjoy. Perhaps a harmless, happy cartoon would be best.

I follow Tom, but make sure I am never out of their sight, and Tom sits with his back to my children, as if he doesn't want them to hear what he's saying.

'Tom, how can I ever thank you for what you did today?'

He smiles at me kindly. 'You risked your life, and we nearly lost you. I don't think I would have forgiven myself if that had happened.'

They have told me how Tom scooped Freddie into his arms and passed him to Jasmine while Ray tackled Robert to the ground; how Becky guided my distraught children to safety while the two men secured Robert with handcuffs. But I was already unconscious, and once again they had to resuscitate me.

The first thing I saw when I came round was the incredible sight of my three children, hovering over me, their dirty, tear-streaked faces looking more beautiful than I have ever seen them. I drag myself back to the present as Tom reaches over and gives my hand a gentle squeeze.

'We knew Robert was coming for the children. Sophie told us. It must have been impossible for you to believe what he planned to do.'

'It was, but sadly he wouldn't have been the first father to do that, would he? And he wanted me to suffer for not loving him.'

Who would have believed me if I'd told them what I suspected – that my children's lives were in danger? Thank God Sophie understood, incredible as my story sounded. But then she had witnessed Robert's obsession all those years ago, and knew that he was capable of anything. It wasn't long after that we worked out the rest of it.

What would I have done without Sophie? I had asked Becky to phone her as soon as we were safe. Even though I want to speak to her myself, the children have to be my priority. I'll call her later, when they are tucked up in bed.

Tom leans forwards and lowers his voice still further.

'I'm sorry to add to the horrors of today, but I need to ask you about Danush Jahander. What can you tell me about him?'

I knew this was coming, of course, and I should have been prepared. But hearing his name on somebody else's lips still makes me ache for him.

I try to keep my voice steady.

'You know about him leaving all those years ago – I remember you now from that dreadful night. It seems so long ago, but you were kind to me then and you were so supportive about my parents.' I nearly lose it at that point. Whichever way I look at it, it seems it is my fault they died. But Tom wants to talk about Dan, so I drag my mind back.

'I'm sure you know that I got a text from Dan when he left to say he was sorry, and then I heard nothing more from him until about a year ago. He'd tracked me down; he wanted us to get back together. I couldn't do it. I love Dan so much, and I always will, but I knew what Robert would do.'

I can't look at Tom as I tell him this. I trace shapes on the table with my finger, and focus my attention there.

'So what happened?'

'I saw Dan a few times, and he begged me to leave. He even wanted me to take Jaz to Iran to meet his family. I nearly did, too. But I couldn't make him understand that I needed time, and the risk to both Dan and my children was far too great.'

'Did you know that Danush contacted your husband two weeks ago? Apparently he wanted to set up a meeting.'

I concentrate fiercely on the shapes on the tablecloth that are becoming increasingly intricate. My voice drops to little more than a whisper.

'Sophie told me. Dan's still a bit hot-headed and he didn't want to wait for me. But Robert was in Newcastle, so I guess it wasn't possible for them to meet. I haven't heard from Dan in two weeks, and he's not answering his phone. So I assume he's still mad at me for running away. Maybe now... I don't know. It's all so long ago.'

I still can't look at Tom. My head is swamped with an image of Dan, laughing at something I'd said, reaching out an arm and pulling me close to him and burying his lips in my hair. Tom is speaking again, but I keep the image in my head. I like to look at it.

'We think your husband arranged to meet Danush at your house last Wednesday. We know Robert came home that night.' I feel a tight band squeeze my chest. I know what Tom is going to say. 'I'm sorry, Olivia. You've had a huge amount to deal with today, and I hate having to add to your burden, but we believe your husband killed Danush Jahander.'

I let my head drop down on to folded arms, resting on the table. The grief wells up in me, as at last I feel free to mourn my lovely, beautiful Dan. In my mind I can still see him. I pull back from his imagined embrace, look into his chocolate brown eyes and smile while Tom continues with the details. Dan smiles back. I think he's proud of me.

'We found blood in your husband's study. We matched it to DNA from a pair of gloves we found in a box in the attic belonging to Danush. But we do need to be certain that it was Dan's blood, so we'd like to take a DNA sample from Jasmine, if it's okay with you.'

I lift my tear-stained face and look at Tom. I hate myself for what I'm about to say, but I have no choice.

'Take one by all means, Chief Inspector, but I'm not sure it will help you. Unfortunately Jasmine isn't Dan's daughter. She's Samir's.'

61

Wednesday

Tom was surprisingly quiet on the flight back. But Becky was jubilant. At last this family could live in peace. It was tragic that Dan couldn't be part of it, but to live without fear must be such a relief for Olivia.

'Are you okay, Tom?' she asked. 'Is your hand hurting?'

'Yes, but I'll live,' he replied.

Becky waited, but there was no more to come.

'Is everything okay?' she asked. She was puzzled by his expression. He was deep in thought and kept chewing his bottom lip in a most un-Tom-like way.

'Fine, thanks.'

Bloody hell, this was like pulling teeth. At least Sophie Duncan had sounded elated when Becky had phoned to say that Olivia and the children were safe. She hadn't mentioned Danush – she would leave it to Olivia to explain.

'What do you make of the whole Dan and Samir thing, then?' she asked, in a last ditch attempt at starting a conversation.

'Not a lot. She said she told Dan that Jasmine might be Samir's all those years ago, and that's why he left.'

'But why, though? Why did she have an affair with Danush's brother if she loved him so much?'

Tom shook his head.

'Ours not to reason why, Becky. People do all sorts of daft things for no reason that anybody else can understand.'

Becky hoped this wasn't a barbed remark about her and Peter Hunter, but it was so unlike Tom that she discounted the idea.

'I think it was all tied up with her trying to make Dan jealous and simultaneously trying to charm Samir,' Tom said, 'and it all got a bit out of hand. Something like that. Anyway, despite Jasmine's blood parentage, Olivia has always thought of her as Danush's child, and that's what she's brought her up to believe. We'll test Jasmine's blood, but I'm fairly sure that we will find a match to her paternal uncle – which is what Danush is.'

'So what's eating you?' Becky persisted.

'I don't know. There's something wrong. I know it, I can feel it. But I don't know what it is.'

They were silent for a few moments, each lost in their own thoughts. Tom picked up some notes he was studying, and immediately put them down again.

'There's something else I've been meaning to tell you, although I'm not sure if it's the right thing to do. I don't want to lose you from the team now that I've got you.'

Becky turned her head sharply towards him. 'What? I'm not in the shit for something, am I?'

'No, of course not. When we were waiting for the plane at Guernsey airport I had a call asking if I would be interested in filling a temporary post back in the Met.'

'You're not going to take it, are you?' Becky said, unable to disguise the horror in her voice.

'No, but I thought I should tell you it's Peter Hunter's job. I don't know how this will affect your thinking, but it seems his wife has finally given up on him and she's left. He's taken a leave of absence – he's been signed off with stress.'

Becky was silent. She really didn't know what to say, and Tom being the man that he was, he didn't press her for a comment.

She stared out of the window at the white clouds below. So Peter was free now, was he? Just a few months ago, that would have filled her with joy and hope for the future.

She tried to dig around in her own emotions. *What do I feel? Do I want him back?* But all she came up with was emptiness and she realised that finally, she felt nothing – neither satisfaction that he had got his comeuppance nor joy that he was free.

Becky leaned back against the headrest and turned slightly towards Tom with a grin.

'You're not getting rid of me that easily, Tom.'

'Good decision,' he muttered with a trace of a smile, turning his attention back to his notes.

62

Thursday

Tom had spent the night thinking about everything he knew and everything he suspected. He hadn't seen Leo; he had just sat in his kitchen with a bottle of wine, a plate of pasta and a pen and paper. Nothing got written down, though.

He needed to see Philippa.

As he walked into her room, Philippa stood up with a beaming smile, reaching across the desk to shake his hand.

'Well done, Tom. That was a particularly excellent piece of police work, and I'll make a point of seeking out DI Robinson to tell her. But please pass on my congratulations to the team.'

'Thanks, Philippa. But before we get over-excited, have you got a minute?'

'Of course, take a seat. Why so glum, Tom? You should be ecstatic.'

Tom wasn't quite sure where to start.

'You know Robert Brookes is claiming he's innocent of Jahander's death, don't you? He swears he never left the hotel that night, and that somebody else must have taken his car and driven it back to Manchester to frame him. And of course there isn't a body as yet.'

Philippa shrugged. 'Nor likely to be, if it's at the bottom of a reservoir, as you suspect. And of course he's going to proclaim his innocence. We wouldn't have expected anything less, would we? Who else could have wanted Jahander dead?'

Tom shook his head. He had a feeling it wasn't that simple.

'Robert asked us to check if the spare keys to his Jag were in the drawer at home. They weren't – but we've only got his word they were ever there.'

'Tom, we have an open-and-shut case here. We know that Jahander called Robert Brookes in Newcastle. We know that they arranged to meet and Brookes came home. He was seen by not one, but two people. We found the blood in the house and in his car, which was back in Newcastle by the morning – a knife was missing, and it was subsequently replaced. By Robert. And Jahander is missing. Nobody has seen or heard of him since last Wednesday.'

'I know, Philippa, but there's something not quite right about the whole thing. Robert bought a replacement knife but we have no idea what happened to the original, and it's odd that although he had the precise product code written down, it was the *wrong* product code. Yes, somebody did call Robert from Sophie Duncan's phone. But they could have said anything. We have no evidence other than Sophie's word that it was Danush setting up a meeting. But that's only one of the things that seems off. I tried to write it all down, but it didn't make any more sense than just picking random threads out of my head.'

'Well, whatever's bothering you, fire away with those random thoughts and I'll jot them down. See if we can sort it all out that way.'

'I think Olivia Brookes has played a very clever game,' Tom said. 'She managed to convince her husband that she was somewhere she wasn't on at least three occasions that we know of. With Sophie Duncan's help, of course.'

'Who can blame her? From everything we've learned, it seems that Robert's obsession was getting more and more out of hand. Olivia is a clever and resourceful woman, and thank goodness for that.' Philippa nodded her head, as if with respect.

'She is. But I'm fairly certain that Olivia must have been the one to tamper with the videos on Robert's computer.'

Philippa gave Tom a puzzled frown.

'Why would she do that? Was it to fool Robert into thinking she'd been there all along?'

'It could have been. But she wasn't coming back – so what did it matter what Robert thought? I think we were supposed to work out that they were fake, but assume *Robert* had tampered with them. Which, of course, is exactly what we did.'

Philippa was tapping her pen on the desk.

'I'm struggling to see quite why this matters, Tom.'

'Okay, why did we search the house?' Tom didn't wait for an answer. 'Because we thought that Robert had lied to us repeatedly. If he hadn't done a runner, the next thing we were going to do was check his computer. We would have found the videos, analysed them and discovered that they were all faked, as was the schedule on the kitchen wall. Once we knew that, we would have been certain that Robert had been lying to us about Olivia's whereabouts and when she'd last been in that house, and I would have had to call in the crime scene boys. I think this trail of evidence was all left for us so we would eventually bring in the forensic team, search the house and find the blood.

Tom wasn't making any headway, and he could understand why not. He hadn't been able to work it all out himself, but he was sure that he was pretty close.

'And there are little things, like the security light suddenly being knocked out of position so that it shines in the neighbour's house and wakes her up. Too many coincidences.'

Philippa was leafing through the papers on her desk.

'Tell me about the folder you found in Robert Brookes' possession.'

Tom sighed. This made it all so much worse.

'We think this is what he was hiding behind the bookcase. It had a false back with a space that appeared to have been accessed recently. The folder's a good fit, but we'll never know for sure. Anyway, inside the folder there were hundreds of photographs of Olivia, and a key.'

'And what do you surmise from that.'

'The photographs of Olivia were from when she was a student at university. They were obviously taken without her knowledge – they're a bit grainy as if a not-very-good telephoto lens was used. Olivia at parties, Olivia doing a charity pole dance, laughing, dancing, studying in the library – just hundreds of them – all taken before she claims to have met Robert Brookes. My guess is that he was obsessed with her for a long time, and perhaps thought he was in with a chance until she had the baby.'

Philippa nodded, as if this sort of obsession were normal. But of course, it just made his ramblings seem even less compelling.

'And the key?' she asked.

'I would never be able to prove this, I don't suppose. But I suspect it's a key to Olivia's parents' home. If he's as smart as I think he is, Robert would have had the locks changed when he was put in charge of selling the house. As a precaution. This is his memento.'

Philippa leaned back in her chair.

'Wow. You think he killed her *parents*?'

'I'm sure of it, but I've no evidence. At some point when he was checking out the flat – I don't know, measuring space for his TV or something – he must have nicked her keys and had one cut. Knowing what we know about him now, he probably had the whole lot copied, just in case they ever came in handy. He would have known that without her parents, Olivia was all alone and she would only have him to rely on. It was the perfect way to make her utterly dependent on him at the worst time of her life.'

'You seem to be saying that you believe Olivia has framed Robert Brookes. So let me get this straight. You think he killed the parents, but you *don't* think he killed Danush Jahander.'

Tom shook his head. 'No, not at all. I'm absolutely certain he killed Jahander.'

Philippa lifted her arms and let them fall by her sides in total bewilderment.

'But it wasn't last week. I think he killed Danush Jahander nine years ago.'

63

Tom had stayed with Philippa for the best part of an hour, going over everything he believed to be true, and in the end she had told him to go home. She wanted him to think very carefully about this and about his next steps. So he had called Leo. She was at home today with no lectures, and she sounded unusually welcoming.

'You sound depressed, Tom. Come here to my apartment. I'll make you my version of a late lunch, and we can talk or just listen to music, or you can sleep if you like.'

That sounded like bliss to Tom. Leo was the most soothing company he could imagine, and within half an hour he was ringing her doorbell.

To begin with, he said nothing about the case, other than to tell Leo what a magical place he thought Alderney was. He found himself saying they would have to go there some time, and Leo agreed. He couldn't think about what that might mean just now.

They ate lunch, which meant Leo had been to the deli on the corner and bought some delicious cheese, crusty bread and red onion marmalade. It seemed perfect with a glass of wine, and Tom felt himself begin to unwind.

'Have you thought any more about the cottage?' Leo asked. He knew she meant the break-in, but this was a gentler way of reminding him.

'Steve's taken all the files into storage for me so the papers are safe. But you know what? I'm going to look through them all when I next get a few days off. I'm going to find out what on earth is so interesting about my brother's documents. Because there's something, I'm sure of that.'

'If you need any help, you only have to ask.' Leo said, standing up from the kitchen stool and heading towards the coffee machine. She pointed to it and raised her eyebrows.

'Yes please, that would be perfect.'

'Well, you go and relax, and I'll bring you some coffee as soon as it's ready,' she said, making shooing gestures with her hands.

Tom sat on the sofa and leaned against the soft cushions, his head back, gazing blindly at the ceiling. He felt, rather than saw, Leo place a mug of coffee on the small table next to him, and she knelt between his legs resting her hands on his knees.

'Tell me,' was all she said.

And so he did. Without taking his eyes off the same point on the ceiling where a thick beam was supporting the roof, he told her everything he knew, and everything he suspected.

'So if you're right, who was the man that visited Sophie Duncan?'

'We've shown Mrs Evans a photo of Dan, but it's nine years old. She wasn't able to confirm or deny it. We were obviously supposed to believe it was him, though – we had to have as much evidence as possible that he was alive and kicking ten days or so ago.'

'Can you prove any of this?' she asked. At that he shifted his gaze to look at Leo and after a brief pause shook his head.

'I don't think so. If I'm right about how they did this, we would need enough of the blood found at the scene to test for citrates.'

'What would that prove?'

'If, as I suspect, nobody really did die in that room, the blood must have come from a living person. To take so much blood and not kill somebody it would have to be done a pint or two at a time over a period of days or even weeks – and the blood would have to be stored ready for being sprayed on the wall. They'd need to add a chemical to stop the blood from coagulating. Some form of citrate. I looked it up last night to be sure, but it's not part of a routine forensic test.'

'So what's the problem?'

'Jumbo told me they found microscopic amounts of blood. Enough for DNA, but not enough to test for citrates.'

'And what does Philippa say?'

'She said emphatically that she doesn't want any further investigation. We have what appears to be a cast-iron case against Robert, and I have absolutely no evidence at all that he's been set up. If I can prove it, she'll look again but gut instinct alone isn't enough. And of course, if I'm convinced Robert Brookes killed three people nine years ago but I can't prove it, we should go with what we've got. I can't prove a thing about either then *or* now. What I do know is that he swore he didn't know Olivia at university, but he was lying. And when we told him that the person visiting his wife in Anglesey – when we still believed it *was* his wife – was

Jahander, he actually thought it was funny, which you might expect if he knew the guy was dead.'

'So Philippa wants you to leave it, and you don't agree.' It was a statement, not a question.

Tom closed his eyes. He didn't want to say this, but he had to.

'Do you remember last year I told you there was one secret that I would keep from you – and from anybody – for the rest of my life?'

He knew she wouldn't have forgotten, and he had always wondered if this was the last remaining hurdle that they couldn't overcome. He didn't need to wait for her answer.

'The truth is, I let a murderer go free. I acted as judge and jury, and my conscience has plagued me ever since. I still think I was right. But it's not my job to make those decisions. It's why we have a justice system – and a bloody good one at that. Sometimes, occasionally, you know that the outcome of playing it by the book won't be morally right. That's Philippa's view in this case. But I'm not sure I can do it again and live with it.'

Leo grabbed his hands, and pulled one towards her cheek. She kissed the palm gently.

'Then let Philippa be the one to make the decision. If this man goes free, will he kill those children?'

Tom leaned back again, and he felt his eyes sting.

'Probably.'

'So you're locking him up for life for a crime he did commit, only not in the way your evidence suggests. That *can't* be wrong, Tom. But let this one be on Philippa's conscience. Not on yours.'

He said nothing and stared back up at the beam.

They were both silent for a moment. Tom felt her move closer, her soft breast brushing against the inside of his leg. He almost groaned. He could hear her breathing, shallow and fast, and he could smell the subtle spice of her perfume. So close.

'I think what I love most about you, Tom,' she said, her voice low and hesitant, 'is how honest you are. You never let anybody down. You're the first man I've ever felt I could truly trust.'

Tom held his breath. *If only she meant it.* Despite all his efforts to control his feelings, he knew without a doubt he was in love with this woman. He lowered his head, and looked at her beautiful, wary eyes. She met his gaze and he felt as if nothing else existed in the world.

He felt Leo's hands move. They slid up his thighs and she leaned towards his chest.

'Stay with me tonight,' she said softly.

Tom reached out a hand and stroked her hair. 'And tomorrow?'

She turned her face and kissed his hand where it lay against her hair.

'And tomorrow,' she smiled, 'and maybe even the day after.'

64

November

The car is bumping along the narrow track, and I'm trying my best to avoid the largest of the boulders and the holes in the road. At last I've got a decent car instead of that stupid Beetle that Robert bought me. Pretty as it was, it had to be the most impractical car possible for a woman with three young children. I can still remember my horror when Robert turned up with it. Fortunately, he translated my open mouth as awe and delight.

'Fuck, Liv, can you just be a bit more careful. You'll have me back in bloody hospital if you jerk me around much more.'

I laugh out loud. It is so wonderful to be with my friend. Unfortunately Sophie has been forced to have another round of operations on her leg as Robert's attack did more damage than the doctors had originally thought. But she said she wouldn't miss today for anything. She knows how much I need her.

We have reached the end of the track, and it's time to get out and face the early November weather. A thin drizzle hangs in the air, as if suspended. I shiver, but there is something magnificent about the bleakness of Saddleworth Moor. Standing here, it's hard to believe we are so close to Manchester. The only signs of life are the sheep and a scattering of stone farmhouses in the distance, nestling in their protective hollows. The hills are treeless at this height, but the ground is covered with a blanket of grass interspersed with patches of bare peat, forming a carpet of green and brown mixed with the faded purple of spent heather.

'How far do we have to walk?' Sophie asks me, grabbing her walking stick from the back seat.

'Not far,' I reply, hoping I have remembered correctly. I don't want any more damage to Sophie on my conscience.

'Are you sure it's the right place?' she asks.

To be honest, I'm not. But it will be close enough.

We start walking away from the track and on to the moorland, clambering over a wooden stile.

'Do you think he'll come?' I ask Sophie. I'm nervous about seeing him, but it's right to have him here.

'He said he would, and he's never let you down before, has he?' Sophie plonks herself down on the spongy surface, clearly oblivious to the damp that must be penetrating her jeans. 'Do you want me to leave you on your own for a bit?' she asks.

But I don't want to be alone. I just want to wait to see if he comes.

We're quiet while we wait, perhaps both listening to the silence. Finally we hear the distant sound of tyres crunching over stones on the rough track. A pheasant is noisily disturbed from the undergrowth and its loud raspy cackle makes me jump.

The car pulls up behind mine, and a man gets out, slamming the car door behind him. I gasp. He has grown his hair to just below his collar, where it curls in the damp air. Just for a moment, I believe the impossible.

Sophie is struggling to her feet. 'You found us then,' she calls.

He nods, but it's me he's looking at, examining my face, checking if I seem okay.

'How've you been, Liv? It's months since I've seen you. Come here.' He opens his arms, and I don't need asking twice. My throat is tight, and I can barely speak.

'Thanks for coming, Samir.' My voice breaks on the name. I so nearly called him Dan. But I owe this man so much – almost as much as I owe Sophie.

'I don't know what to say to you both, how to thank you for everything you've done.'

'He was my brother, Liv. What else did you expect?' Samir says. The pain is still raw for him, of course, even after all these years.

'And you're my best friend,' Sophie chips in. 'We couldn't have let you do it on your own. I nearly blew it when I let that stupid woman take my photograph, though.'

'But you didn't. And in a way, Robert's reaction to that photo made it all so much more plausible. It was very dangerous for both of you,' I say, knowing this to be true. 'What if…'

'Shh,' Samir says, raising his finger to my lips. 'It's been five months since Robert was arrested. He's been convicted of murder, and nobody's come chasing me for a DNA sample. They're not going to now, so stop worrying.'

I pull slightly away from Samir and nod. I don't know if it will ever be safe, but my children have to be protected for life.

'Shall we go?' I say. 'I don't think it's much further.'

We start to walk, eager to get there, but at the same time this final acknowledgement of death is hard to bear.

'Why do you think this is where he buried him?' Samir asks.

That's hard for me to explain, but I try my best.

'Robert didn't have much of an imagination, and he was always fascinated by the Moors Murders, particularly the fact that the body of the last victim – Keith Bennett – has never been found. He brought me here about seven years ago when I was pregnant with Billy. He said a walk would do us good. We stopped just a bit further on from here – and I sat on a stone because I was tired. Robert started to talk about the Moors murders.'

I don't know if I can go on with this story, knowing what I know now. But Samir needs to understand what happened to his brother, and I can't shy away from the truth.

'I can remember one sentence, word for word: "I wonder how many other bodies are buried up here – you could be standing on top of one right this minute." It seemed a gruesome thing to say, but he was smiling.'

I look from Samir to Sophie, knowing that they have begun to understand Robert's warped mind.

Without a word, I hold out both my hands. Samir takes one, Sophie the other. Each in turn gives my hand a small squeeze of encouragement.

'When did you realise that he'd killed Dan and your parents?' Samir asks. 'When did you figure it out?'

I look at Sophie and give her a hint of a smile. It had all started to come together when I met her again – nearly two years ago now. As soon as she told me that Robert was Creepy Guy, everything had fallen into place.

'When Sophie said she'd met you, and you had never heard one word from Dan after he left me, I knew he had to be dead. He loved you so much, Samir. He would never have cut you out of his life, or the rest of your family. And never for a moment did I believe my parents' death was an accident.'

For a moment, I can't speak so Sophie continues the story for me.

'I made Liv go through everything – from the day she met Robert. When she told me that he had been knocking on her door within hours of the flat going on the market, and bought it without a single quibble, I knew there was no way this was a coincidence. Then he rode in on his sodding chariot when Liv's parents died, but at no time could she remember telling him where they lived. So we started to question everything from the moment he so charmingly introduced himself, until the night he threatened to kill the children.'

'And Dan?' Samir asked again, looking at me with his gentle brown eyes, so like his brother's.

'The first real evidence I had that Robert knew more about Dan's death than he should have was when I heard him telling Jaz that her father had run away to Australia. I never told Robert that. I never told anybody, because I was so ashamed that he had left me with our baby. The police knew, but until this started and I told you two, I hadn't told anybody else. Robert must have killed Dan and then taken the train himself, with Dan's phone and credit card. Poor Jaz. He had no right to tell her that.'

'And how *is* my daughter?' Samir asks with a straight face. I close my eyes for a second. I am ashamed of this lie, but I'd had no choice. I say a silent prayer of apology to Danush before turning to his brother.

'Oh God, I'm so sorry, Samir. I was hoping it wouldn't come to that.'

Samir laughs. 'I'm joking, Liv. I'd be proud if she was really my daughter. I've told my wife everything. She did a great job with the police and she's fully behind us.'

I glance at him with a worried frown. I had always trusted Samir to know what was safe, but he had run the biggest risk of all. He had slowly but surely extracted his own blood, pint by careful pint over a period of days, ready to set the scene of the murder. We had hoped that Samir's old gloves pushed into a box of Dan's stuff would be enough DNA evidence for the police, but there was always the chance that they would check Jasmine's DNA too. They would know the blood came from a paternal uncle, so the lie was a necessity. And I know Dan would forgive me for that.

Every step we had taken had been dangerous with so many potential pitfalls. What if Mrs Preston had recognised that the person getting out of the car in the middle of the night was too tall to be Robert? We had hoped that the security light would blind her as Samir made his way up the path, but there had been too many factors that relied on the skill of the police and the nosiness of neighbours.

I breathe out a long, slow breath. It seems it's all over, and finally we can sleep safely in our beds at night.

I let go of Samir's hand and grab his arm, pulling him closer to my side so I can rest my head against his shoulder. If I close my eyes I can imagine, just for a second, that he is Dan.

'I think we're here – or as near as I can possibly guess. This is more or less where Robert made me stand and think about what might lie beneath my feet, so knowing his warped mind, we can't be far away.'

I look at each of them in turn. Sophie gives me a sad smile, and Samir nods his head just once.

I open my bag and pull out a single white rose. I bring it to my lips and give it the briefest kiss before dropping to my knees. I lay the rose gently on the sodden earth, and feel the warmth of Samir's hand on my shoulder.

'For you, my darling Dan. For everything you were, everything you meant to me, and for our beautiful daughter. I'm sorry I ever doubted you.'

About the Author

Rachel Abbott was born and raised in Manchester, England, and trained as a systems analyst before launching her own interactive media company in the early 1980s. She sold her company in 2000 and in 2005 moved to the Le Marche region of Italy.

She recently moved to Alderney, one of the Channel Islands, where she now writes full time.

Rachel Abbott's first book – *Only the Innocent* – became an international bestseller, reaching the number one position in the Amazon charts (both UK and US).

Her second novel – *The Back Road* – reached the number 2 position in the UK, and was in the top ten for four weeks.

The next book from Rachel Abbott

If you are wondering about the break-in at Tom's cottage in Cheshire, all will become clear in Rachel's next book as Tom uncovers the mystery surrounding the death of his brother, Jack.

To keep up to date with Rachel Abbott's new releases, please complete a **contact form** on the Rachel Abbott website or blog.

Connect with Rachel Abbott online:

Twitter: **https://twitter.com/_RachelAbbott**
Facebook: **http://www.facebook.com/RachelAbbott1Writer**
Website: **http://www.rachel-abbott.com**
Blog: **http://rachelabbottwriter.wordpress.com**

If you would like to find out more about the wonderful island of Alderney, take a look at the **http://www.visitalderney.com**.

Acknowledgements

Once again I owe a debt of gratitude to many people for their help in writing this book, and I sincerely appreciate the advice so willingly given by so many people.

There are a few people who I must mention specifically, and as always I would like to thank John Wrintmore for his insights into the workings of the police, and for answering every question – no matter how trivial. For this novel, I also had to seek advice from Colin Solway of the Alderney Police, who was immensely helpful and gave his time freely. Any mistakes are entirely mine, and are made in the interests of the story.

For this book, I also needed help with some of the forensic details, and I would like to thank Mike Silverman, whose book *Written in Blood* is released on 13ᵗʰ February 2014.

There were many people who offered nuggets of information – some of which didn't quite make it into the book – but to all the people on this surprisingly long list, thanks for taking the time to inform me about everything from swapping IP addresses to forensic archaeology. To name but a few, my thanks go to Kate Britton, Steve Rodgers, Lindsey Thomas, Tim Dickinson, Brenda Duncan, Becky Scrivener, John Raffle, Diego Benito plus the staff at Aurigny, Eyetek, Tor Project and iPrivacy.

My early readers have been fantastic, providing excellent feedback and suggestions, and there is a small group of people that have helped in so many ways over the past year. Thank you Kath, Judith, Charlotte, Ceri, Ann, John, Kathryn, Rick, and Andria. A special thanks the wonderful people of Alderney, who have been so welcoming. I apologise for taking a few liberties with the geography of your beautiful island.

Alan Carpenter, my long-suffering designer, has produced a wonderful cover, yet again, despite my indecisiveness and constant changes of direction.

My particular gratitude, as always, goes to my agent, Lizzy Kremer – the best there is. She has been a wonderful source of support and guidance, as have the rest of the team at David Higham Associates – especially Laura and Harriet. I don't know how many times Lizzy and Harriet read this manuscript, but their help and direction, together with input from two terrific editors, Clare Bowron and Lizzie Dipple, have made this a far better book than it might otherwise have been. I can't thank you all enough.

Look out for other novels by Rachel Abbott

Only the Innocent

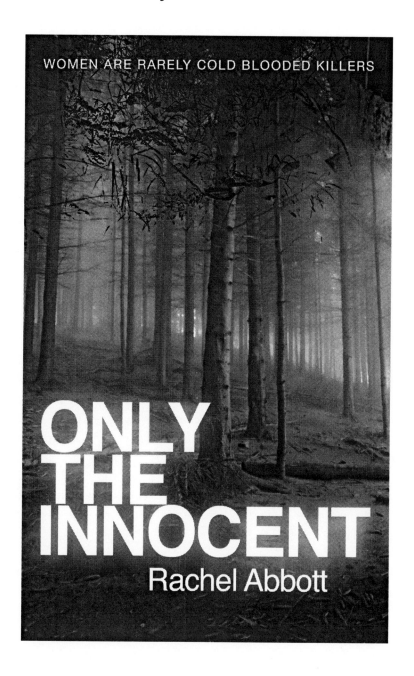

WOMEN ARE RARELY COLD BLOODED KILLERS

ONLY
THE
INNOCENT

Rachel Abbott

Only the Innocent: by Rachel Abbott

When Laura Fletcher approaches her home in Oxfordshire to find hordes of photographers crowding the gates, she knows there is something terribly wrong. She is faced with the shocking news that her husband is dead - brutally murdered - and according to Chief Inspector Tom Douglas, there is little doubt that the murderer is a woman.

In a marriage that has taken her from the glamorous five star luxury of London, Venice and Positano to a bleak and draughty manor house in rural Oxfordshire, Laura has learned to guard her secrets well. She is not alone. It would appear that *all* the women in her husband's life have something to hide.

But there is one secret that she has never shared, and when the investigation reaches its dramatic and horrific climax, she realises that she has no choice. She has to give Tom Douglas the final piece of the puzzle. And this changes everything, leaving Douglas with a terrible dilemma: whether to punish the guilty, or protect the innocent.

ONLY THE INNOCENT is a spellbinding psychological thriller that will leave you breathless!

Praise for Only the Innocent

"Rachel Abbott's *Only the Innocent* is not your average whodunit murder mystery. The question that drives this thriller is not *who* did it, but *why*. Abbott carefully constructed a world of mystery, depravity, sex, violence, manipulation and intrigue on so many different levels that I can honestly say you truly have to read until the last page to understand and appreciate the complexity of the story."

"It's a long time since I read a book that occupies my mind constantly and is all consuming. When I was reading this one, or when I was not, I could think of little else."

"I could not put this book down – it was a completely addictive page-turner – so much so that I read until 3 am finishing it."

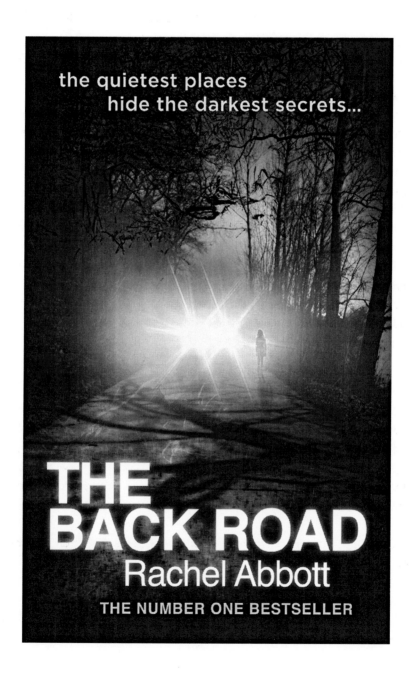

the quietest places
hide the darkest secrets...

THE
BACK ROAD
Rachel Abbott
THE NUMBER ONE BESTSELLER

The Back Road: by Rachel Abbott

A girl lies close to death in a dark, deserted lane.
A driver drags her body to the side of the road.
A shadowy figure hides in the trees, watching and waiting.

The small community of Little Melham is in shock.

For Ellie Saunders, last night's hit and run on the back road could destroy everything she has. She was out that night, but if she reveals where she was and why, her family will be torn apart. She is living on a knife-edge, knowing that her every move is being observed.

Ellie's new neighbour, former Detective Chief Inspector Tom Douglas has moved to the village for some well-deserved peace and quiet, but as he is drawn into the web of deceit his every instinct tells him that what happened that night was more than a tragic accident.

As past and present collide, best-kept secrets are revealed and lives are devastated. Only one person knows the whole story. And that person will protect the truth no matter what the cost.

The Back Road is an electrifying thriller that will keep you guessing to the very end.

Praise for The Back Road

"It is one of those books that holds you hostage and is hard to put down until the end" *Confessions of a Reader*

"An absorbing mystery of love, deceit, secrets, and murder...truly a spellbinding novel of suspense." *Mysterious Reviews*

"One of Best Mystery Suspense Novels Read This Year!" *Amazon Vine Voice*

"Pure Genius: A Masterclass in the Perfect Thriller!!" *Love Books*

"There are red herrings galore in this well scripted plot and even when you think you have the story sussed, Abbott throws a spanner into the works." *Crime Fiction Lover blog*

Lightning Source UK Ltd.
Milton Keynes UK
UKOW03f0958090514

231390UK00002B/41/P